Joby's War

by Ken Dykes

The characters and situations in this book are entirely fictional. Any resemblance to actual persons living or dead is purely coincidental.

© 2014 **Ken Dykes** all rights reserved.

To my wife Wendy.

ACKNOWLEDGEMENTS

Grateful thanks are extended to my long-suffering wife who has bullied, cajoled, threatened and, at times, even encouraged me to 'get on and finish it'.
To my friend Alan Nobbs who solved the mysteries of formatting when my brain was completely formatted out.
Also to my good friend Rose-May Law-we for her invaluable assistance with some of the intricacies of the, at times, somewhat complex French conversation.
Thanks also to John Amy for the cover design.

FOREWORD

Jonathan Bernard Fulbright was born in the year 1893 in a village in rural southern England. At infant school he was known to friends and teachers alike as Jo. That is, until a new boy, Jonathan Thomas Wilkins, another Jo, moved into the area. To avoid confusion in the classroom the former was soon referred to as 'Jo B' and the latter as 'Jo T.'

Jo B stuck and for the rest of his life he would be known as Joby. We first hear of Joby as an unattached 21-year-old joining up with a group of his mates soon after the outbreak of the First World War in August, 1914, all anxious to become involved in this great new adventure 'before all the fun is over.'

The prediction that 'It'll all be over by Christmas,' just five months away, was a long way short on accuracy—and it turned out to be not very much fun either.

Two years later, in yet another massive, and pointless, Allied offensive he was badly wounded and became part of the horrifying statistics that numbered the hundreds of thousands of young men killed, injured or missing in that terrible four-year conflict.

In the horrific confusion of total war he was, for reasons unknown, taken to a French-run forward dressing station and then on to a French military hospital.

It was here, while slowly recovering from his injuries, he met the woman who was to become the one and only true love of his life, a young French nurse named Delphine. And although they were to know each other only for a few short weeks before parting forever, his love, down the next four and a half decades, remained constant.

Fast forward to the early 1960s and we find Joby, still unattached and now approaching seventy with no surviving relatives, in a cottage at

Longdown Farm, near the village of Binfield, employed as a general farm worker by the Trenchard family.

During his lonely life apart from his one great love, Joby has become a very well-known and popular character in the district, mainly on account of his permanent, and usually successful, feud with Fred Appleton, gamekeeper on the neighbouring estate. After all, in the 1960s nobody loved a gamekeeper.

Joby has developed into a very worldly-wise (call it crafty if you will) character, highly skilled and knowledgeable in all rural activities. His many humorous scrapes with Fred Appleton form the basis of our story but the lives and loves of the other villagers, particularly the Trenchards, add colour, depth, variety and more humour to this tale of English country life in the mid-twentieth century.

Joby becomes closely involved in the personal lives of the family who have 'adopted' him and is instrumental in the outcome of many of the situations they encounter.

An early tragedy in which the parent Trenchards meet an untimely and farcical demise leaves the plot open to develop around their two grown-up sons—and their love lives.

Then one day Joby gets a mysterious visit from two total strangers when echoes of the past, his past, are revived, the results of which bring our story to a bitter/sweet conclusion.

Chapter one

THE old man slowly peeled back the bedclothes, gingerly lowered his bare and bony feet onto the small square of threadbare carpet, the only floor covering, and pulled himself upright to sit on the edge of the bed.

An early morning summer sun was already brightening the bedroom, frustrating the efforts of the thin and shabby curtains to keep the light at bay and from where he sat he could see his own reflection gazing at him from the age-spotted mirror on the Edwardian style dressing table which stood against the opposite, once-white, distempered wall.

Joby Fulbright stared back, rubbed a chin that sported a week's growth of grizzled stubble and smoothed down a few straggling strands of grey hair. A prominent nose formed a narrow ridge down the centre of a thin and lined face. Pale and watery blue eyes squinted out wearily from among the creases below bushy grey eyebrows.

He was approaching three score years and ten, although, it has to be said, he had not weathered that well and could easily have passed for at least five years older, which, even by today's mid-twentieth century standards was not considered all that ancient.

Sitting and staring at the mirror his thoughts went back to the time when that reflected face had been a young man's face, with bright eyes and sand-coloured hair. But much had happened since then.

Joby was just 21 when he, and so many of his boyhood friends, had marched excitedly away to war in 1914. Going off to fight the Germans.

'It will all be over by Christmas,' they had said. 'Let's get in quick before we miss all the fun.'

But it wasn't over by Christmas and it certainly wasn't much fun.

He was aware of no other soul from that little band of chums, striding out on the biggest adventure of their young lives, who had survived to celebrate the Armistice in 1918.

Neither was he aware that the same scenario was being played out in cities, towns and villages the length and breadth of the British Isles.

In fact throughout Europe hundreds of thousands of young men from Britain, France, Belgium and, yes, Germany too, were marching off for the 'great adventure' to the stirring sound of bands, the waving of flags and with the cheers of their families and friends ringing in their ears.

So very many of them were destined never to return.

And it was only two years later, in 1916, that Joby himself was to become another part of the war's horrifying statistics, just one of the 60,000 Allied soldiers listed as dead, wounded or missing on the horrendous battlefield of the Somme.

So many times since, he had relived the horror of the trenches, the deafening gunfire, the screech and thunder of shell bursts, the smoke, the mud, the shouts, the cries for help, the screams of pain, the startling numbness of being hit, of falling, of losing consciousness.

Not he, nor anyone else, would ever know how, amid that terrible confusion and bloodshed, he came to be in a forward dressing station run by foreigners, how he finished up in a French military hospital. Nor the circumstances of how he was eventually rediscovered and returned to his own unit.

Neither would he ever know how he survived the next two years of carnage. But survive he did.

All these recollections had spilled through his mind on an almost daily basis over the past four and a half decades. But there was another, quite different, picture from those brutal times, even more clear, that entered his mind just as frequently.

The memory of a small round face, soft dark hair, smiling hazel eyes, pleasant, soothing, French-accented voice.

Delphine.

Remembered, too, were those three short weeks of recovery. The crowded, airless ward where Delphine was nurse to more than two dozen wounded troops, all but he, French. The first limping, stumbling walks along the corridor on his favourite nurse's arm. The longer walks outside with his new love at his side.

And the one, all-too-short, evening hour of passion which had sealed that love. Just hours later a two-man English speaking deputation arrived to whisk him back to rejoin those who remained of his British comrades in the front line.

The two young lovers were fated never to meet again.

Joby had found real love for the first time in his young life and although, when the horrors of war had ended, he had no way of tracing Delphine, he carried the intensity of the feelings in his mind, along with the vivid images of those sacred and magical last moments.

Never buried deeply, they were to surface, in quiet moments, summer and winter, rain or shine, by sun and candlelight, for the next forty-four years.

Joby and Delphine became just two more innocent casualties of that terrible conflict and the political and civil turmoil that followed throughout Europe after the fighting had ended.

And, in spite of their love for each other, with lives to be lived, it was almost inevitable that they had each drifted into a life apart from all that they longed for and hoped for.

Joby shook his head, as if to chase the daydreams away, looked once again into the mirror and stroked the stubbled face with his fingers.

'Sunday,' he muttered to himself. 'Better get shaved.'

Joby always shaved on Sunday morning for no other reason than that it was Sunday morning.

And, in the absence of his employer's two grown-up sons, he had agreed to help out at the farm which had been his workplace for longer now than he cared to remember.

Because the two boys would be away on some jolly or another for the whole day, their father would need some assistance with the milking, morning and evening, so Joby wouldn't be going to church today.

He never went to church anyway.

The mid-morning sun of that same June Sunday blazed down from a sky as blue as a starling's egg. Farmer Joe Trenchard stepped out through the kitchen door of the farmhouse, the only door he ever used, and stood for a long moment looking around the yard, his hand shading his eyes against the glare.

He turned and called back through the open door.

'You're right love. Can't see her nowhere.'

Peggy Trenchard was worried about her favourite bantam hen, a little brown and red nothing of a bird which normally spent its time wandering in and out of the kitchen.

'That's strange Joe,' she said, her forehead creasing into a frown. 'I haven't seen her for two or three days now. Hope to God a fox hasn't got her.'

'Not much chance of that love,' he reassured her with a laugh. 'She's too wily a bird for old Charlie to catch up with.'

Silly, really, that Peggy should think so much of that little bantam when there were dozens of other assorted hens, ducks, cats and two dogs about the place. Not to mention a herd of dairy Holsteins with their assorted followers and calves.

Still, she had nursed, tended and raised the bird from the time Joe had found it as a wet and bedraggled day-old chick, peeping itself hoarse in a corner of the cartshed with never a sign of a mother.

He'd carried it in his hat, still peeping loudly, into the kitchen. For Peggy it was love at first sight.

The chick became her own special pet and, as it grew, they seemed to develop a relationship that was out of the ordinary for farmer's wife and bantam hen.

Joe knew he had to do his best to find it.

He took his old 'porkpie' hat from the nail behind the door and stuck it over the brown, shiny dome of his head which stood up out of an atoll of greying hair.

'I'll take a look around,' he called as he started slowly across the yard, pausing only briefly to savour the cool shade of the huge oak tree which stood in the middle of a patch of poultry-cropped grass that passed as a front lawn. Morning milking was done, breakfast was over and Joby had returned to his cottage.

Then he stepped over the low, unpainted railing fence, erected only to keep the larger stock out of the farmhouse, and headed for the hay barn.

He already had an idea.

The first cut hay was all in now, baled and stacked in the big Dutch barn. Good hay, too, Joe reckoned.

It was early June, 1962 but in these modern times, with new '60s ideas and farming theories, he was still far from convinced about all the proclaimed advantages of making silage—and haylage hadn't even been thought about.

The barn, which had open sides, was filled almost to the top at one end with the big, sweet-smelling, tightly-packed blocks of hay that would provide winter fodder for his cattle when the grass stopped growing.

A series of bales had been left layered, like a giant stairway, up one side of the stack and Joe, still agile despite his 58 years, climbed them steadily until he was standing, or rather, stooping, in the four feet high space between the top of the bales and the barn roof.

In one corner a few extra bales had been piled on up to roof level. Joe moved over to have a closer look—and found Peggy's bantam tucked up cosily in a sheltered hollow between two of the bales where she had made her nest.

'Setting,' murmured Joe. 'Just as I thought.'

He stooped his way over to the edge of the stack nearest the farmhouse and let out a yell.

'Peggy!...Peggy!... Come and take a look at this.'
.
 His wife appeared at the kitchen door wearing a flower-patterned apron and holding a tea-towel in her hands.

'What is it?' she called.

'Come and see!' shouted Joe.

Peggy brushed away from her face the few strands of straying hair that had plagued her all morning.

Her hair had once been a shiny blue-black, now it was lightened by many a streak of grey.

'I've only got my slippers on.'

'Don't matter. Everything's dry.'

As she came across the yard beneath him, Joe, looking down, couldn't help but admire the woman who had shared well over thirty years of his life and borne him two fine sons.

In his eyes her beauty hadn't changed since the day they first met. Peggy was only a year or two younger than her husband but she, too, made nothing of climbing the bales to the top of the stack.

'What is it? I'm busy you know.'

'Your silly bird,' replied Joe quietly. 'Look. Over there at the end. Setting a clutch of eggs she is.'

Peggy went and looked.

'Oh, so she is. What a clever little thing you are, Clara.'

She spoke to the bantam hen as if it were a child. The bird gazed back with hardly a blink of its beady yellow eye and no sign of fear at all.

Kindred spirits, thought Joe as he took a handkerchief from his waistcoat pocket to mop the sweat from the back of his neck.

'What made you look up here, Joe?' asked Peggy, making her way over to join him where he sat, legs dangling over the edge of the stack, gazing at the oak tree.

'Just a hunch,' he said.

Then he added: 'Take a look at that day. Smell that air. Makes you feel young again. Don't you think so?'

'You've just never grown old,' she smiled, and leaned over to give him a peck on the cheek.

Joe made a grab for her but she was too quick for him, giggling like a schoolgirl and backing away across the top of the bale stack.

But she didn't go far.

There wasn't far she could go, just supposing she had wanted to. Soon the pair of them were laughing and wrestling, and then embracing, on the sweetest smelling bed a farmer and his wife could wish for—new hay.

'Joe!' cried Peggy, the excitement flushing her already rosy cheeks.

'Not here! Not now! I'm in the middle of getting…'

But she, like her husband, couldn't resist the effect of the warm sun, the soft hay and her own emotions.

Within a short time they were both entering that state of absolute pleasure that they had found so often together in the past. A mutual enjoyment of each other and for each other that had kept them both young at heart all these years.

They rolled over and over in the hay, close to the far edge, out of sight, as their passion mounted.

At the very instant that their senses reached a simultaneous peak of ecstasy the bale on the edge tipped up and they fell, still locked in an urgent embrace, to disappear with a prodigious splash into the slurry pit.

The Reverend Simon Pindle, vicar of Binfield, scurried down the churchyard path with his head bent low against the weather and huddled himself, as well as a six-feet beanpole of a man can, into the lych-gate of St Swithin's Church.

He shivered, clutched his Prayer Book a little more tightly beneath his arm, and hunched his thin shoulders, trying to get some extra protection from the elements out of his ageing and ill-fitting vestments.

It wasn't so much the cold. After all, it was almost midsummer-- and he was wearing a pair of his favourite old corduroy trousers as well as a thick woollen jumper beneath the official robes.

No, it was the soft, persistent June rain, a kind of fine drizzle that filled the still air, drenching his clothing and penetrating in misty swirls the ancient tiled shelter beneath which he now stood.

In spite of all his efforts a few drops managed somehow to seep down the back of his clerical collar.

Still, he thought, with the entire congregation now seated in silence inside he shouldn't have more than a few minutes to wait.

Mr Pindle had a lot on his mind.

He gazed forlornly back up the wide pathway leading to the church's south door. Weeds were spreading ever-widening clumps in the gravel.

The churchyard grass was nearly thigh-high among the old and teetering gravestones. It was long overdue for cutting but at the moment the massed stems were drooping in a delicate display of glistening arches, each decorated with shiny beads of water deposited by the moisture laden atmosphere. And he had run out of 'volunteers' whom he could ask to cut it.

The flagpole on the square tower had snapped off in last winter's storms and really should have been replaced by now. The trouble was that it could only be reached by way of a rickety wooden staircase which itself had long since been declared as unsafe by the local builder.

On the inside wall of the nave was a damp patch in the white plaster, ringed by a growth of grey-green mould. It was getting bigger. And this wet spell, he mused mournfully, wouldn't help in the slightest.

His mind wandered back to a time when things were not so bleak. Back to a sunny April day in 1927.

Was it really thirty-five years ago that he had arrived in Binfield as the new and keen young parish priest?

Even now the village was only moderate in size but then it had seemed much smaller.

Different too. Much cosier somehow. Much closer—and the congregations were larger by far.

He had been here a long time now, longer than was usual in modern Church policy. Still, his incumbency had included the dark days of the Second World War—and the war had changed many things.

The new generation of clergy was chopped and changed about from parish to parish like pawns on a chessboard and seemed more concerned with flashy fund-raising schemes, meetings and paperwork, than with the more traditional duties of priesthood.

Mr Pindle was content that his own life had been more settled, orderly, predictable.

He quite enjoyed opening the vicarage fete and making an appearance at the annual whist drive organised by the parochial church council in aid of the repair fund.

Bingo calling, sponsored pea-pushing and other such modern fund-raising schemes were just not his scene.
It was the faint low sound of an approaching vehicle that brought his brain jolting back to the immediate business of the day.

They had arrived.

He began to feel a rising excitement. A peculiar sensation almost of elation, mounted within him as he anticipated the imminent proceedings.

Nearly twenty years earlier, during the war, he had officiated at a double wedding when two sisters from the village had married a couple of airmen from the nearby base. Not a day too soon for one of them, he seemed to recall.

Then there were the twin babies, christened in a double showpiece ceremony one Sunday afternoon. He tried to recall the names but couldn't. Well, none of that party had been back to church since.

Now today, to top it all, he was to experience his first double funeral. What an occasion.

Tragic that poor Joseph and Peggy Trenchard had died so mysteriously together up at Longdown Farm.

There would be an inquest, of course, but for the moment the funeral was more important. Most of the farming families of the district were represented inside, their Land Rovers, cars and station wagons lining the verges outside for fifty yards in each direction and all but blocking the narrow village street.

There was no doubting the fact that Joe and Peggy had been one of the most popular couples in Binfield's not inconsiderable agricultural community.

Mr Pindle supposed that their eldest son, Benjamin, would take over Longdown now.

At length the slow moving cortege of funeral cars appeared, weaving between the rows of parked vehicles and headed by two flower-decked hearses.
One of the hearses had to be hired by village undertaker George Moone from a rival company in the nearby town of Witherstoke. Never in his wildest dreams did George imagine he might ever need two hearses on the same day.

As well as the hearses there were three other cars in the procession.

In the first were the two Trenchard boys, Benjamin and Robert, sitting stiffly upright on the edge of the seat, unmoving, like tailors' dummies in a shop window. With them travelled Grace Cope, a friend of Peggy since their schooldays, herself a widow and usually referred to by the brothers as "Auntie Grace".

Filling the other two was an assortment of cousins, second cousins and cousins several times removed. Most had never even met Joe or Peggy but as blood relatives warranted a place in the official parade. Joby Fulbright had a seat in the first of these.

As the line of vehicles drew to a halt outside the church George Moone stepped smartly, yet with dignified solemnity, from the leading hearse, the one carrying the coffin of Joe Trenchard.

Dressed in a long tail coat and with his black top hat bound round with a wide band of black silk, he organised with quiet efficiency the unloading of the polished elmwood box with shiny brass handles that contained the mortal remains of the late and genuinely lamented Joe Trenchard.

The actual removal of the coffin was accomplished by four sombrely dressed men who had disembarked from somewhere inside the vehicle.

They slid it out backwards and carried it reverently into the lych gate where the vicar, with a few whispered words, had it set down upon one of the two long wooden benches inside.

Then the first hearse was driven slowly off a discreet distance to allow the second to inch forward to a position opposite the lych gate. The process was then repeated with the coffin carrying the body of Peggy Trenchard.

The mourners' cars were driven up and an attendant opened the rear door of the first to allow the newly bereaved brothers to alight.

Tiny rivulets of water ran their meandering traces down the rounded, highly waxed roof of the gleaming black limousine as Benjamin Trenchard stepped out into the wetness of that June day, the drizzle soon settling in a fine spray on his almost black hair.

He was tallish, perhaps five feet eleven, and slim without looking undernourished. His deep brown eyes, set in a pale face, making him attractive in a rather gaunt sort of way. He wore a formal dark suit and black tie but no top coat.

Benjamin was twenty-eight, quiet and serious. When he smiled, which was not very frequently, his whole face seemed to light up. He should have smiled more often.

But Benjamin Trenchard had nothing very much to smile about today as he stood aside to allow his younger brother Robert to get out of the car.

Standing together outside the lych gate the two made a striking contrast. True, there was a physical likeness about the straightness of the nose and shape of the mouth but there the similarity ended.

Robert, at twenty-three, was two inches shorter than his brother, broader too. His mop of light brown hair topped a wide face that shone with a healthy glow. His deep blue eyes transformed a good looking face into a handsome one.

And while Benjamin was always considered the shy and studious one—after all, he had attended the Springshott Agricultural College—Robert was the extrovert, a popular local sportsman with quite a reputation among the district's eligible females and, it was acknowledged with a wink in The Drovers Arms, some of the ineligible ones as well.

They stood there in silence for a moment. Then, at the beckoned signal of the vicar, moved into the shelter of the lych gate and slowly on up the churchyard path behind the two coffins which had once again been lifted shoulder high and were now being carried into the church.

Inside, the stone flagged aisle was just wide enough for the two to be laid side by side on pairs of wooden trestles.

The service was short and simple and it seemed only minutes before the whole company was following the pall bearers back down the path to the waiting hearses.

As in most villages, the churchyard itself had received its full complement of occupants long ago and burials were now made in the cemetery, a hundred yards away up a little side lane.

The assembled families stood in respectful silence as the coffins were reloaded.

The pair of hearses moved slowly away at a sedate pace towards the cemetery gates while the congregation followed on foot. Only a few whispered polite exchanges between friends who had not seen each other in several weeks disturbed the silence.

Then, with the hearses unloaded once more, the procession wound its way along neat gravel footways between the stone crosses and marble headstones that marked the last resting places of recent generations of Binfield residents.

It was Sid Mears, in semi-retirement the man responsible for the upkeep of the cemetery, who knocked the sombre edge off the proceedings.

Shouting and waving, he came at a half run down through the rows of grassy-mounded graves to meet them.

In the middle distance behind him two workmates appeared to be in heated discussion close to the newly dug grave, the piles of soil from which were held back by retaining boards.

'Reverend,' gasped poor old Sid as he came panting up. 'Reverend. Hang on a minute. I've got to talk to you.'

Mr Pindle stopped sharply in astonishment. The procession came to a ragged halt behind him.

He paused for a second to regain his composure, then he continued his dignified march.

'Not now, Mears.' He almost hissed the words out of the side of his mouth. 'Can't you see I'm in the middle of a funeral? A very important funeral.'

'But it's urgent,' persisted the heated Sid.

As the vicar resumed his funereal pace along the path, Sid went shuffling crabwise beside him, his progress impeded at regular intervals by the round, grass-covered mounds which he side-stepped over without seeming to notice.

Mr Pindle looked down at him without stopping and without moving his head.

'I don't care how urgent it is,' he returned in an angry stage whisper. 'It will have to wait. Come and see me afterwards.'

And that, as far as he was concerned, was the end of the conversation.

'A'right. Have it your own way,' said Sid.

He shrugged his shoulders, stood aside, and held up his hands in a gesture of apology as the Trenchard brothers and the other mourners walked slowly by, their faces registering a variety of expressions ranging from puzzlement to anger.

At the graveside the coffins were set down, one each side of the gaping hole. It was the signal for old Albert Ramson, lifelong farmer friend of the Trenchards, to say the few words he had prepared.

Albert gave a little cough to clear his throat.

'We all know how Joe and Peggy loved the land and how they loved each other,' he began.

'They lived together, side by side. They worked together side by side. Now they will rest in peace together side by side.'

He paused, almost overcome by emotion.

'Just as they would have wanted,' he managed to croak. The vicar took over again, his droning voice making the sad, final graveside procedure even more gloomy.

'Man who is born of a woman hath but a short time to live and is full of misery…cut down like a flower…in the midst of life we are in death…earth to earth, ashes to ashes, dust to dust…'

Four men used two straps of woven nylon to lower Peggy's coffin into the grave as Mr Pindle scattered a handful of chalky soil onto the lid.

Then they started to lower poor Joe.

It wasn't until that very moment it suddenly became obvious to Mr Pindle, and the watching mourners close enough to see, that there wasn't room for the two coffins to lie side by side.

Mr Pindle looked down aghast as Joe's coffin swung gently to and fro against the side of the grave.

The four men, bent over their task, stopped their lowering and looked up expectantly, as though awaiting some instruction.

'I tried to tell you,' said Sid, who by now had pushed his way through the throng to watch the abortive proceedings.

'You wouldn't listen, would you? It'll take us another hour or more to take out that extra six inches. It wasn't our fault you know,' he added, looking defiantly around at a sea of scornful faces. 'We was given the wrong measurements.'

The vicar was speechless for a very long twenty seconds.

Pulling himself together he took Benjamin Trenchard by the arm and led him a short distance from the rest of the assembly for a hurried and whispered consultation.

A few seconds later they were joined by Robert and, soon after, by Sid Mears and George Moone.

The question was, whether or not to delay the burial long enough for the grave to be enlarged.

And technically, as Mr Pindle pointed out, Peggy Trenchard had already been laid to rest and he was unsure of the legality of removing her coffin again while the work was done.

Then there was the weather.

All five men looked up into the grey overcast which showed no sign of easing its relentless drizzle.

At last, further delay was decided against and that was how Joe and Peggy Trenchard came to be buried one on top of the other in a position they had so recently assumed in life.

'Just as they would have wanted.' As some unidentifiable voice at the back of the gathering was heard to pronounce.

Chapter two

THE inquest was held two weeks later in the courthouse at Witherstoke under the supervision of Mr Julius Rumbold who, as well as being the borough's foremost solicitor, was also the district coroner.

He sat in a high-backed carved wooden chair behind a wide, polished oak bench where the magistrates usually sat when a court was in session.
It was several feet above the level of the rest of the courtroom.

He leaned forward, his hands clasped together on the bench, and bent his head forward to gaze down on the other occupants of the room over a pair of half glasses.
Mr Rumbold was a big man, not over tall but very heavily built. In fact he could best be described as enormous.

His black hair was swept straight back and the receding hairline revealed a wide expanse of pink forehead which contrasted oddly with the darkness of the hair and beetling brows which overhung almost coal black eyes.

He had a wide nose, thick lips which he constantly moistened with the tip of a pink tongue, and an undefinable number of chins that marched down into the white collar of the largest shirt size available in Witherstoke.

He was dressed in a charcoal grey suit of similarly large proportions and the pink fingers of his clasped hands resembled a heap of pork sausages lying on the table before him.

There was a jury of eight townspeople, who sat in two rows of four, to one side of the dreary, dark panelled room.

The court clerk, a small and dapper silver-haired gentleman in a dark pinstripe suit, sat at a desk immediately below the coroner's bench.

Opposite the jury was the witness box and beside that two tables against the wall.
Behind the first sat two police officers, an inspector and a sergeant, while representatives of the local Press occupied the other.

The seedy looking character wearing the worn tweed suit, liberally spotted with cigarette ash, was from the *Evening Clarion*. The two rival weekly papers, the *Witherstoke News* and the *Witherstoke Gazette,* were represented respectively by a scruffy youth with spots, which he was trying to hide behind a wispy beard, and a fresh-faced young woman.

The main body of the courtroom was taken up with members of the public and the witnesses who were to be called, including, in the front row of seats, the Trenchard brothers and, immediately behind them, their aged farm worker Joby Fulbright, two police officers and a pathologist.

There was a variety of spectators, among whom were several friends of the family, villagers from Binfield, other farmers, and just plain curious onlookers. The room was virtually full.

The murmuring of whispered conversation ceased abruptly as Mr Rumbold called the hearing to order.

First to give evidence was Benjamin Trenchard, whose duty it had been to identify the couple in a formal little ceremony at the hospital mortuary where the bodies had been taken on the day they died.

'You are Benjamin Trenchard of Longdown Farm, Binfield, near Witherstoke, eldest son of the late Joseph and Margaret, also known as, er, Peggy Trenchard?' The tone of the coroner's voice made it more of a statement of fact than a question.
'Yes sir,' replied Benjamin quietly.

'And on the evening of Saturday the seventh of June this year you were present at Witherstoke Hospital where you were shown the

bodies of two people whom you identified as the aforementioned Joseph and Peggy Trenchard?'
'That is so, sir.'

'On that day, at the time your parents are thought to have met their deaths, neither you nor your brother, er,' the coroner looked down at the papers before him. 'Er, Robert, were at Longdown Farm. Is that correct?'

'That is correct sir,' replied Benjamin. 'My brother and I left the farm earlier that day, while father and Joby were doing the milking, to visit the Saliston Agricultural and Game Fair about 65 miles away. We left about eight o'clock and didn't get home until just after eight in the evening. It wasn't until then that we learned of what had…what had happened.'

'And when you left the farm that morning, did you notice anything at all unusual about the behaviour or the mood of either of your parents? Any signs of depression or anger? Anything that gave you any cause for concern?'

He tilted his head to peer at Benjamin over his reading glasses.

'I'm sorry to have to ask these questions, Mr Trenchard, but as you are probably aware, we have to have the fullest possible information. We have to explore every possible avenue.'

'It's quite all right sir. I understand. No, there was nothing at all unusual.'
The young man's eyes moistened at the memory of that morning.

'In fact, both my parents were in good humour,' he continued. 'The hay was all in. When the morning milking was finished they were looking forward to a day on their own together. That is, until it was time for the afternoon milking when Joby…' Benjamin turned and indicated the grizzled farm worker behind him… 'Mr Fulbright, was coming in to give father a hand. Joby doesn't usually work weekends.'

'Thank you Mr Trenchard. I don't think you can help us any more,' said the coroner. 'And I see no reason to call your brother to give evidence. You may step down.'

Next to come to the stand was Joby Fulbright, the Trenchards' only employee at Longdown Farm.

Joby was more of a family retainer than an employee. He had first worked for Benjamin's great-grandfather. He fiercely disputed any suggestion that he was nearing retiring age but it was pretty accurately calculated among older villagers that he was, in reality, nearer seventy than sixty.

He lived alone in the somewhat tumbledown farm cottage at the end of Longdown Farm Lane. For years Joby had stoutly resisted all efforts by the family to make any alterations or improvements to the property or its equally ancient services.

He refused all offers of help, laughed at the suggestion that the plumbing be renewed to provide a proper bathroom, scorned the idea of a plan to put in central heating ('I likes me ol' log fire too much,' he had said).

And he had insisted that he didn't need—and wouldn't use—an inside lavatory, preferring to trudge down to the ivy-covered wooden privy at the far end of the garden ('where a lav ought ter be,' he had declared).

Rather than cause ill feeling by threatening him with health inspectors, the Trenchards, after years of trying to improve his lot, decided it was better to leave Joby to his own devices.

In stark contrast, Joby's cottage garden was one of the neatest in the village and he was reckoned to be one of the finest vegetable growers in the district, often walking off with many of the major trophies at the annual parish autumn Flower Show. He was also a dab hand with flowers and occasionally earned himself a few bob at weekends doing oddjob gardening around the village.

Joby was a character. As well as being virtually a full time employee at the farm he was also acknowledged to be the part time local poacher.

He didn't see it that way, of course.

'Natural losses,' he would say, when hearing of a mysterious decline in the number of reared pheasants suffered by the Squire's gamekeeper, Fred Appleton.

'You're bound to get natural losses.'

Joby was a permanent thorn in Fred's flesh who would have given anything to get him up before the magistrates.

Not above five feet six, Joby was as thin as a rake handle. A slight curvature of the spine gave him a slight stoop which made him look smaller still. His thin, leathery face, bony nose and watery blue eyes was the reason why his adversaries, principally Fred Appleton, referred to him as "Weasel".

On the other hand, his 'customers' in The Drovers Arms liked to call him "Whippet" on account of the fact he was always too quick to be caught.

Joby had lived alone for many years and as far as anyone in the village could tell, had no living relatives. At least, no-one had ever seen any, neither had he himself ever mentioned any family.

In fact, although a regular in the village inn, and happy to chat to most of his fellow drinkers on just about any countryside topic, Joby never revealed any details about his own past and simply clammed up when faced with questions about it.

All anyone knew about him was that he had served in the Great War, was thought to have been wounded and had appeared in Binfield in the early 'Twenties looking for farm work when he was taken on at Longdown by old Mathew Trenchard, the new young owner's great-grandfather.

Today Joby was wearing his usual attire, the only clothes he seemed to possess. A decidedly greasy tweed jacket with leather elbow patches, shiny black trousers and a pair of not so shiny brown leather boots. Around his neck, above a collarless shirt, he wore a grubby red kerchief. On his head he sported his only concession to the importance of the occasion, his Sunday cap, while on his chin he sported several days growth of grey stubble.

'Kindly remove your hat in the courtroom Mr Fulbright,' came the haughty voice of the clerk.

Joby reluctantly slid the cap forward off his head, revealing the few long and straggling strands of grey which were normally kept covered.

The coroner began his cross-examination.

'You are, er, Jonathan Bernard Fulbright of Longdown Farm Cottage, Binfield?'

A wave of whispered surprise rippled around the courtroom as this piece of hitherto unknown information was taken in by the scores of locals attending the hearing.

The coroner banged his gavel for silence.

'People usually calls me Joby'
.
The coroner looked at the papers on his desk.

'But you are Jonathan Bernard....er...Joby Fulbright of the aforementioned address?'

'Yes my Lord.'

'Just Sir will do,' interjected the clerk.

'And can you tell us what happened on the day in question? The day you went to help Mr Trenchard with the afternoon milking?'

'Well, Your Honour…' began Joby, accentuating the silent H.

'Just Sir will do,' interrupted the clerk, impatiently.

'As I was about to say,' continued Joby, giving the clerk a withering look, the mornin' milkin' wus finished 'bout 'alf pas' eight. And I went 'ome for a snooze an' a bit o' lunch.'

'Yes,' interjected the coroner. 'Let's get on to the relevant part of the day shall we. The afternoon.'

It was the coroner's turn to be treated to Joby's look of disapproval.

'Well.' He began again. 'I wus to be at the farm 'bout 'alf past three. An' I was on time. When I got there I left me ol' bike leanin' against the kitchen wall an' went to look for Mr Trenchard.'

He paused, looking around as though expecting some kind of applause or acknowledgement for this staggering feat of public speaking.

'And then what happened?' asked the coroner.

'Nuthin.' I couldn't find 'im could I? Nor Mrs Trenchard neither.'

'Carry on. What did you do then?' asked Mr Rumbold, a note of mild encouragement in his voice.

'Well, the kitchen door wus wide open so I just went in an' called out. But there wusn't nobody there. Just some saucepans an' things on the stove with vegetables an' spuds an' suchlike in. Like they wus ready for cookin' for dinner. But it wus middle o' the afternoon.'

Joby looked around again and then continued.

'I looked all over the place. In the milkin' parlour. In the calf pens. In the cartshed. Everything seemed a'right 'ceptin' there just wusn't nobody there.'

Joby paused for effect.

'It wus a bit spooky I can tell you. Like that ghost ship the Maria Celestial.'

He stopped for breath, quite exhausted by his efforts.

'Mary Celeste,' came the voice of the clerk.

All eyes turned towards him.

'Mary Celeste,' he repeated a little louder. 'That was the name of the ghost ship.'

'AS I wus sayin,'' went on Joby, treating the clerk to another glare. 'There wusn't nobody there.'

'So what did you do then?' asked the coroner.

'Well, I got on with the milkin' didn't I? They cows 'ad to be milked. And I wusn't to know what 'ad 'appened, wus I?' demanded Joby defensively.

'No, of course you wusn't, er, weren't,' Joby was reassured by the coroner. 'At the time you probably did the right thing Mr Fulbright. What happened next?'

'Well,' Joby began again.

'Well, with nobody to 'elp me, the milkin' took some time. I wus expectin' Mr Trenchard to turn up any minute. But of course 'e didn't.

"'Bout five o'clock, after I'd turned the cows back out to grass, I went back to the farmhouse and called out again. But there still wusn't nobody there.

'I started gettin' a bit worried 'cause Mr Trenchard's a'ways bin a bit of a stickler fer time keepin'. I thought they might 'ave 'ad an accident somewhere on the farm so I went inside and 'phoned for Constable Wheeler.'

Joby paused again.

'When the constable arrived I told 'im about not bein' able to find Mr and Mrs Trenchard an' he said we should 'ave to make a thorough search.'

'Yes,' interrupted the coroner. 'We shall be hearing from Pc Wheeler in due course. I believe you have given us all the help you can, Mr Fulbright. You may step down now.'

'But…but. I wus goin' to tell you about 'ow we found 'em an' all,' protested Joby. He was enjoying his moment of fame as the centre of attention and was just getting into his stride.

'I'm sure you were,' returned Mr Rumbold. 'But I'm also sure the constable can give us all the necessary information in that direction. Thank you, Mr Fulbright. That will be all.'

It was a somewhat disgruntled Joby who stepped down from the witness box with a sigh and took his seat again in the row behind the Trenchard brothers.

Percy Wheeler, Binfield's village bobby for nearly fifteen years, was next to be called.

He gave his evidence in the business-like manner which years of adherence to police procedures had taught him, with many a reference to his notebook. And that evidence was delivered in the standard police monotone.

'At approximately five pm on the afternoon of Saturday, June the seventh, I was at the police house when I received a telephone call. At first I was unable to ascertain the identity of the caller who, in an agitated voice, kept repeating "they've gone, they've gone, you better get up 'ere quick".

'I told the informant to calm down and was then able to discover that the caller was Mr Joby Fulbright…'

Here the coroner interrupted with an impatient, 'Yes, yes, constable. Let's get to the important evidence shall we?'

Pc Wheeler gave the coroner an aloof, sidelong glance and then continued.

'As a result of the information received I went to Longdown Farm, Binfield, arriving at five ten pm, and, in company with Mr Fulbright, began a systematic search of the farmhouse and buildings,' he paused for effect.

'We could find no trace of Mr and Mrs Trenchard.'

Pc Wheeler looked around the courtroom again.

'I then walked a short distance up to a gate from which many of the farm fields are visible but could see nothing unusual. There were no vehicles or farm equipment that I could see out in the fields.'

The policeman took a handkerchief out of his trouser pocket, wiped his brow, replaced it in his pocket and took another look at his notebook.

'At approximately six-thirty pm, while walking back across the yard, I noticed the corner of a piece of light coloured material hanging over the edge of a large stack of hay bales in the Dutch barn. The material was sort of flapping in the breeze and it was that movement that caught my eye. The barn is really just a big roof supported on steel girders and has no sides.'

The constable looked round for effect once again before proceeding.

'I decided to investigate and climbed up on to the top of the bales, a height of approximately fifteen feet. The object I had seen from below was a tea towel.'

'A tea towel, constable?' asked the coroner, one eyebrow raised and a bemused look on his face.

'Yes sir, the sort you use for drying the washing up.'

'Yes, I do know what a tea towel is, constable,' returned the coroner with a hint of irritation. 'Get on with it man.'

'On further investigation on top of the hay bales I found several articles of clothing,' went on Pc Wheeler.

'Men's clothing or women's clothing?' the coroner wanted to know.

'Both sir,' replied the constable.

He glanced uneasily towards the public seats and went on.

'There was a pair of boots, a pair of men's corduroy trousers and a pair of white underpants. Oh, and a man's white handkerchief,' he added with another reference to his notebook.

'You said there were articles of women's clothing as well,' prompted Mr Rumbold.

'Yes sir. A pair of slippers and…uh…a pair of knickers.'

'Knickers, constable?'

'Yes, knickers, sir.'

'And what did you deduce from all this?'

'I deduced that both Mr and Mrs Trenchard had been in the barn together, on top of the hay bales sir.'

'Very good constable. What did you do then?'

'As a result of what I found I climbed back down to the ground and went round the back of the barn. There I saw what I took to be Mr Trenchard's tweed hat, floating on the surface of the slurry pit,' reported Pc Wheeler.

'What,' asked the coroner, 'is a slurry pit?'

At last the constable had one up on the coroner and he relished his next piece of information.

'Well sir, it seems that as well as giving several gallons of milk a day, every dairy cow also produces several gallons of waste products, mainly in liquid or semi-liquid form. This effluent, known as slurry, is usually channelled away from the milking parlour or cowshed to a suitably unobtrusive part of the farmyard where it is stored in a pond, or pit, to await redistribution over the land as fertiliser.'

He paused for breath.

'At Longdown Farm the slurry pit is adjacent to the rear of the hay barn.'

The constable stopped and smiled a polite but self-satisfied smile at Mr Rumbold.

'I see,' was all the coroner had to say.

He made a few notes on the papers before him and then turned again to the witness.

'Then what did you do?'

'My immediate concern was that Mr and Mrs Trenchard had met with an accident and may have fallen into the pit,' went on the policeman. 'I instructed Mr Fulbright to find some rope and a heavy piece of iron to use as a drag. Meanwhile, I went into the farmhouse and telephoned for assistance from Witherstoke police station. I also called for an ambulance.'

The constable took another look at his notebook.

'While we waited for help to arrive, Mr Fulbright and myself decided to start dragging the pit. It was only a few feet deep and within a few minutes we had located some heavy obstacle.'

He paused once more.

'I waded into the pit and managed to get a rope wound round the obstruction. Mr Fulbright and myself then pulled on the rope. With his assistance I was able to drag what turned out to be the bodies of Mr and Mrs Trenchard to the side and out on to firm ground. Soon after this a police car with four officers arrived, followed shortly afterwards by the ambulance.'

The whole courtroom seemed frozen into silence and another long pause in the constable's evidence, brought about by genuine emotion at recounting the story, gave the proceedings an unreal, almost eerie, atmosphere.

'At this point Inspector Lewin took control of the situation and the bodies were removed to the hospital mortuary,' added Pc Wheeler.

Benjamin Trenchard, sitting in the front row of seats, gazed blankly in front of him, as though in a trance.

He had, naturally, been informed of most of the circumstances surrounding the tragedy before the inquest began but hearing it retold in public had a stunning effect on him. His brother Robert sat with his head bent forward, face buried in his hands.

The coroner continued his cross-examination.

'Before they were removed, did you notice any signs of injury or violence on the bodies?'

'None sir,' replied the constable. 'Mr and Mrs Trenchard seemed to be locked together in a sort of embrace.'

'Apart from that you saw nothing at all unusual about the bodies?'

'No sir. Except, that is, their faces.'

'Their faces? What about their faces?'

'It was the expression on their faces that I noticed sir,'

'Expression? What sort of expression? Fear? Anger? What?'

'Well sir.' Pc Wheeler glanced again towards the public seats. 'They were both…uh…smiling.'

The pathologist gave evidence next. He told the coroner that both Mr and Mrs Trenchard had been in apparently excellent health prior to their deaths. They had both died from the same cause, asphyxia due to drowning.

But, he added, he also found indications that sexual activity had occurred immediately before death and his opinion was that, in their resultant euphoric state, they would probably not have been aware of what was happening. They would certainly not have suffered any pain.

'It would be,' he declared, 'just like dying in one's sleep.'

Mr Rumbold, in his summing up, told the jury that their duty was not to enquire into the reasons why the couple should have been doing whatever it was they were doing in the hay barn but simply to decide in what manner they came by their deaths.

'You must ask yourselves whether there is any possibility of foul play involving a third party, which I venture to suggest there clearly is not.

'Then you must ask yourselves whether there is any reason to suppose that Mr and Mrs Trenchard intended to take their own lives, a supposition for which we have certainly not heard any supporting evidence.'

The coroner paused and looked at the jury.

'If you have any serious doubts about the circumstances of these deaths, your proper decision should be an Open Verdict.'

He looked around the room.

'My personal view is that, for some reason, and we may never know what that reason was, Mr and Mrs Trenchard went up into the hay barn together.'

Mr Rumbold looked around the room once more, peering over his half-glasses, his huge hands still clasped together on the desk top in front of him.

'And it is also my view that during, or just after, some…er…sexual activity, they fell, unintentionally, from the pile of bales and were drowned in the slurry pit.'

The jury took only a few whispered moments, without retiring, to consider the decision. Then their verdict was announced by the jury foreman.

"Death by Misadventure".

And up in the hay barn Clara continued to brood her clutch of eggs undisturbed.

Chapter three

THE smell of breakfast bacon was still in the air as Benjamin Trenchard, new master of Longdown Farm, emerged from the kitchen door and paused to savour the view across the yard.

In the past few weeks the soft yellowy-green of the young leaves on the oak tree had taken on their high summer gloss of dark green, the delicate hanging fronds of tiny pale golden flowers had disappeared and already a few small acorns were visible among the foliage on the lower branches.

Family tradition had it that the tree was planted by one John Trenchard, a West Countryman who appeared mysteriously in the village with the look of a fugitive in his eye and a tidy pile of gold coins in his purse. By popular rumour he was on the run from the Revenue men who fancied he might help their investigations into a series of daring smuggling escapades.

No confirmation of this story ever arrived—and neither did the Revenue men.

John Trenchard settled down, bought Longdown House with nearly 100 acres of good farming land and a piece of ancient woodland, married a local girl, planted his oak tree and lived happily ever after.

That was five generations ago and the Trenchards had been here ever since.

In more recent times the farm had been extended to nearly 400 acres by further purchases and a long lease from one of the national insurance companies, many of whom were moving into land purchase for long-term investment potential.

Benjamin's gaze slowly traversed the scene before him, the hay barn away to his left, partly hidden by the great oak tree, the old cartshed which now housed the tractors, the milking parlour, calf pens and the big implement shed at the far end on the right. He felt a tingle of pride, a sense of belonging.

'Mornin' Mr Trenchard.' The greeting came from Joby who, with Robert, had been engaged in the morning milking while the senior brother was attending to some of the seemingly endless paperwork in the small downstairs room next to the kitchen which served as a farm office.

Until two months ago Joby had always addressed Benjamin as "Master Ben" and to the younger brother as "Master Bob". Robert was still "Master Bob" but Benjamin now warranted the more respectful title of "Mr Trenchard" as befitted the new head of the family business.

'Morning Joby. Milking all done?'

'Yessir. Wusn't expectin' to see you s'mornin' though. Master Bob said as how you wus busy with they accounts or summat. Wouldn't be out 'til s'afternoon 'e said.'

'That's right, Joby, I was busy with the accounts. Still should be. But it seemed criminal to be inside on a day like this.'

Benjamin looked up at the clear blue sky. 'Anyway, it's wrong that a farmer should spend more time filling in forms than working on the land. I wanted to get the combiner ready for that last bit of barley at Cowdown.' He looked up at the sky again.

'At this rate it'll be dry enough to start in an hour. Once that's in all we've got to worry about is the thirty acres of wheat in Home Meadow.'

He paused, then added: 'Seems almost as if everything's coming in too easy this year.'

'Things *never* comes in *too* easy Mr Trenchard,' replied Joby philosophically.

The rich country tones of a woman's voice, calling from the kitchen, interrupted their little exchange.

'Would you like that cup of coffee now Mister Benjamin?'

The question was immediately followed by the appearance in the kitchen doorway of the Trenchard brothers' newly acquired cook and housekeeper.

'No, thank you Ivy. I'll leave it for the time being,' replied the young farmer. 'We've got some machinery moving to see to. We'll be in at lunchtime.'

The two men started across the yard to look for Robert. As they went Ivy could hear Benjamin talking about the pick-up baler and how they would need some barley straw brought in for the stock this winter.

Ivy smiled as they disappeared, still deep in conversation, round the end of the milking parlour. Then she turned back into the kitchen to busy herself with the final clearing of the breakfast things and with the preparations for lunch.
She hummed a tune to herself as she bent over the big stone sink.

Ivy Green was happy. Happier than she had been in nearly two years, since that terrible Monday morning when Pc Wheeler had called at her cottage to break the news that she was a widow, that her Jim had died in a road accident.

Jim had worked on the Home Farm at Ashley Estate, which covered a very large slice of the countryside around Binfield, since he left school, even lived in an estate cottage since his marriage to Ivy.

But after more than twenty years of working on the land he quite suddenly, at the age of forty-three, made the biggest decision of his life—that he could do better for himself, his wife and their teenage daughter by leaving the farm and going to work at a factory in Witherstoke.

Ivy had been doubtful but agreed to go along with her husband's scheme.

'Look, we'll get a new council house, soon as I qualify as a tenant in Witherstoke,' Jim had assured her. 'Posh new place with central heating an' all. An' I'll be bringing home nearly five quid a week more. We'll be in clover. I seen Mr Baughurst, the agent for the estate, an' he's as good as said they won't push for possession of the cottage 'til we're settled in the new council house.'

But it wasn't to work out quite as Jim had planned. He had boarded the bus for town that first Monday morning with his sandwich box under his arm and his thermos in his coat pocket, all ready to begin a new career.

Opposite the factory gates he had got off the bus and, eager to make a start, had marched smartly across the road towards the works entrance—straight in the path of an articulated lorry delivering a load of steel rods.

Not only was Ivy unexpectedly a widow, she was also a young mother with some very serious problems to face up to.

Jim had never been much of a one for future planning and the small insurance policy he left behind didn't do much more than settle the funeral bill.

But Ivy's precarious financial situation wasn't her main worry.

She soon found a few moderately paid but regular part-time cleaning jobs around Binfield and her daughter Sandra left school to take up the career she'd always wanted.

Mad about horses and ready to help out at any stable in return for the chance of a little riding, Sandra, a natural horsewoman, was offered the job as trainee assistant instructor of the riding school in the next village.

Neighbours and friends were as helpful as they could be but Ivy's biggest problem was the cottage.

Mr Baughurst at the estate office was very understanding but pointed out, quite gently it's true, that in leaving his job on the farm, Jim had forfeited his tenancy rights.

'Naturally,' said the letter which arrived a discreet three months after poor Jim's demise, 'We would not wish to force the issue but it must be pointed out that the cottage will be required eventually to house the replacement farm worker.

'We regret…' etc, etc. 'Yours sincerely…' etc.

Next day Ivy had visited the office of the housing manager of Witherstoke District Council. After all, they had promised to provide the family with a council house as soon as Jim started work at the factory.

She was ushered in to a small and stuffy office and seated in front of a desk behind which sat a small and stuffy man.

'You see, Mrs Green,' whined the deputy housing manager, who had a beak-like nose and close-set eyes, 'We just can't give you a house. We have every sympathy, of course.'

And he put on a sickly sympathetic smile which made him look rather like a budgerigar with stomach ache.

'The fact is, Mrs Green, that your husband never actually started work in Witherstoke. Consequently he could not qualify for a council house. If only he had managed to actually clock-in at the factory we might have been able to do something but as it is…'

He drew in a deep breath and shook his head.

Ivy hardly heard the rest.

'…very sorry…tragic case…wish we could help but…'

Ivy's hopes of finding a new home that she and Sandra could afford, or of staying in the old one, had gradually faded as the months went by. The estate sent more letters, each one polite enough but each a little firmer than the last, asking when they could expect vacant possession.

In mid-June of the following year, just about the time that the Trenchard brothers were burying their parents following that family's tragedy, she had received notification that the estate intended to apply for a court order.

And it was just a week or so later that another letter arrived.

This one was from Benjamin Trenchard, who informed her that he and his brother were looking for someone local to live in at Longdown Farm as cook and housekeeper. She had been recommended. Would she be interested?

Would she be interested! To Ivy the job seemed heaven-sent—and so it might have been.

She went up to the farm to look things over and discuss the situation.

And she jumped at the chance when the position was formally offered.

The brothers, too, welcomed the prospect of someone they at least knew by sight taking the job and by the middle of July, Ivy and Sandra moved into their own rooms in the rambling Georgian house that was the hub of all activity at Longdown Farm. Almost immediately it was obvious to all involved that the arrangement would be a great success.

As Ivy had said: 'It's an ill wind that blows nobody any good.'

That was why, today, Ivy was happy. She was the kind of woman who blossoms when content—and she was content now, safe in the knowledge that she and Sandra had a secure and comfortable home once again.

At forty-three she was still a handsome woman, with thick, wavy chestnut hair, which she normally wore caught up in a kind of pleat, almost green eyes, a small, slightly up-turned nose and a full wide mouth. She would have been the first to admit, probably with a lilting, head-thrown-back laugh, that she was a little on the plump side but her generous figure became her well and there were several men in the village, Pc Wheeler not least among them, who as eligible suitors admired her not altogether from afar.

For more than a year, since her husband's death, worries over home and family had cut across all her natural womanly instincts. Now, at last, she had time to start thinking of life again.

Why, only yesterday Pc Wheeler, visiting the farm on some pretext while the brothers were not around, had asked her once again to go to the cinema in Witherstoke with him. Sandra, herself now an 18-year-old, had last night urged her mother to take up the offer and Ivy was thinking that, this time, she might just accept the invitation.

Hence the happy humming.

Benjamin and Joby, attracted to the implement shed by a whistle that was both loud and tuneful, found Robert already at work preparing to move the combine harvester. In fact he was filling up the fuel tank from a four gallon gerry can when the other two arrived.

'Looks like you had the same idea as me, Bob,' said the elder brother. 'Nearly ready to start?'

'Just about, Benny boy,' returned the younger man cheerfully.

Benjamin winced at the over-familiarisation of his forename while Robert's already wide smile broadened into a huge grin at his brother's obvious discomfort. He enjoyed his bit of teasing.

Benjamin took a deep breath to help calm his rising annoyance at Robert's deliberate baiting.

'How long will you be on the barley?' he asked. 'Finish today?'

'Christ yes. Barring accidents I'll have the combinder back up to Home Meadow this evening, ready to start the wheat in the morning. If this weather holds it'll all be in by…what's today? Tuesday…by Thursday night at the outside. Another day baling and carting the barley straw that we need. Joby can burn off the rest. We can have a lazy weekend with luck.'

Benjamin was well pleased. Robert obviously had matters perfectly under control and seemed to be enjoying his extra duties as top hand.

'Fine,' he said. 'I'll finish off the rest of the paperwork, get changed and come down in an hour or so with the grain trailer.'

He walked over to the wide doorway of the big shed and looked up at the clear blue August sky.

'Don't believe we'll need to use the drier at all. It can go straight into the silo.'

He turned and made his way back up the yard towards the house, leaving Robert and Joby working on the harvester.

'Right then Joby,' he heard Robert say. 'Let's get the bugger started.' And, more faintly, Joby's response. 'Rather you than me on that gurt big thing!'

The day went as planned. The barley harvest was completed and the grain piled into the huge improvised silo that took up the whole of one end of the implement shed. The combine harvester was moved up to Home Meadow ready for the last field of wheat.

After their evening meal Benjamin and Robert were relaxing in the expansive farmhouse sitting room. The furniture was old and big and comfortable. The decor, a kind of creamy brown, was just as old.

The two brothers slumped opposite each other in two great armchairs, the sort that sit squarely down on the floor, not the modern types that seem to perch up on spindly legs.

There was also an enormous matching sofa that looked as though it would seat about six, a dark polished sideboard and an occasional table, with lace doilies scattered on its top, resting against one wall between the two windows. There were three or four smaller leather bound chairs, more upright than the armchairs, positioned around the room.

In one corner was a full-length, glass fronted china cabinet which seemed to be overflowing with oddments of porcelain and delicate crockery, collected by successive Trenchard wives over the generations.

Because of the season there was no fire in the magnificent brick fireplace. The mantle shelf above it was crowded with more bric-a-brac, the centre-piece being a large ornate clock with gilt decoration round the face and standing sentinel at each end stood, or rather sat, a pair of Victorian china dogs, complete with gold painted chains.

On the chimney breast wall above the clock some long-dead champion bull of indeterminate breed gazed balefully from a dark and faded gilt framed oil painting.

On the opposite wall were two fox masks mounted on dark stained wooden shields while on the fourth wall, opposite the windows, was a row of small prints of hunting scenes.

'Any plans for the weekend Ben?' asked the younger of the pair.

'No. Not yet. Hadn't really thought about it,' came the reply.

'Only, I just thought,' Robert paused. 'You might be able to do me a favour.'

Benjamin looked up from the newspaper that he had been only half reading. His brow furrowed slightly, a hint of suspicion written in his dark eyes.

'What sort of a favour?'

'Well…it's difficult to explain…'

'I bet it is,' returned Benjamin with some sarcasm. 'Your favours usually are.'

'No, the thing is…I'm in a bit of a spot…'

'That's nothing new either.'

'No, listen. The fact is that I've been out once or twice with Steve, you know, Stephanie Morris, lives up by the school.'

Benjamin did know her. By sight at least.

Stephanie Morris was what Robert liked to describe as "a little cracker". And with her curly brown hair, attractive nut-brown eyes and trim—though not too skinny—figure, Benjamin had to admit to himself that Robert was right.

'And?' he prompted.

'Well,' went on the younger man. 'Steve's older sister Margaret, you know, married that Mike Storey guy that works in the transport office of Kent's Haulage, she's having a party on Saturday night. Sort of a housewarming. They moved into one of those new houses on the estate just off Church Lane last year. Only just got round to celebrating.'

'So?'

'It's a bit awkward.' It was Robert's turn to frown. 'You see, she's invited me to the party, to make up the numbers and partner Steve. Trouble is. Well, trouble is I can't go. I've got this appointment in Witherstoke the same night. Can't be put off.'

'Appointment?'

'Well, all right. I've got another date. It's with a bird I've been working on for months. Can't break it.'

'Where does the favour come in?'

Robert looked at Benjamin and gave him a big, blank, helpless grin.

'To be honest, Steve's sister was so disappointed when I said I couldn't go that I told her…well you…I said you'd go in my place.'

'You what?' Benjamin exploded, half rising from his chair.

Robert stood up and stepped back, hands held up in a mock gesture of defence.

'Hold on. Calm down. Look, I'm sorry. I know I shouldn't have but I was in a fix. It just sort of came out. And anyway, it's not such a bad thing is it? Free party. Steve's not bad company you know. Do you good to get out on a Saturday night. Don't know what you find to do, stuck in all evening. In fact I'm doing YOU a favour. And you so ungrateful.'

He was a past master at the art of fast talking and it usually worked. It didn't fail this time.

'All right,' said Benjamin. 'I'm not promising anything but maybe I'll look in for an hour.'

While Robert was doing his fast talking act, Benjamin had had time to think about it, if only briefly, and had decided that an evening with Stephanie Morris wasn't such a daunting prospect after all.

'I knew you'd come up for me,' said Robert, a decidedly relieved smile on his face.

'The party starts about nine o'clock, though I don't suppose it'll really get going much before eleven when the pub turns out. You know the road? It's number eight, on the right, the one with the coloured glass door panels.'

The rest of the week went quickly by with only a slight hitch holding up the last of the wheat harvest. A couple of hours spent replacing a minor part on the combinder and then work continued smoothly.

The harvest was finished by Thursday afternoon. By midday Friday the baling and stacking of the required barley straw was completed and Joby managed to burn off the remaining unwanted straw without setting fire to any of the hedgerows—a major success for him.

While Benjamin and Joby did Friday afternoon's milking, Robert got the machinery cleaned and greased and stored away in the big shed.

On Saturday there was just the milking. Robert and Benjamin shared this work between them as Joby didn't like working weekends.

By the time the pair were cleaning up the milking parlour after the afternoon session, Benjamin was beginning to feel a distinct sensation of excitement, albeit suppressed lest his brother should notice his air of anticipation.

Perhaps, thought Benjamin, perhaps tonight could be the night—or at least the start of something.

But along with the excitement was a certain inexplicable tension, a nervousness that Benjamin had experienced on earlier, similar occasions when a direct encounter with a member of the opposite sex was imminent.

He made a brave attempt at shrugging off this feeling as he small-talked over tea with Robert and Ivy. It wasn't too difficult. After all, the brothers had had one of the smoothest and most successful harvests they had ever known so there was plenty to occupy the conversation.

At length Robert rose from his seat at the dark oak table in the little dining room that was crammed between kitchen and living room.

'Thanks Ivy. I'm going up for a bath. Have to go to Witherstoke tonight.' He looked at his watch. 'Crikey, I'd better get a move on too, or I'll be late.'

He gave Benjamin a broad wink, pushed his chair back into place at the table, turned and went out through the living room towards the stairs.

'Don't use all the hot water!' Benjamin shouted after his retreating figure and a muffled 'OK' echoed back through as Robert's footsteps sounded on the wide central staircase which he climbed two at a time.

'Are you going out tonight Benjamin?' Ivy asked.

'Yes. Just going for a few drinks with some…er…some friends,' he replied.

'Oh, that's good.' Ivy was genuinely delighted. Benjamin rarely went out and seldom seemed to enjoy himself.

'You deserve a bit of relaxation and it'll do you good I'm sure.'

'Yes, I'm sure it will,' said Benjamin.

Later, clad in a towelling dressing gown, Benjamin was in his room deciding what he should wear to the party.

He had already spent over an hour making his preparations.

First a shave. A careful shave. He always used an ordinary safety razor with soap and hot water. Electric razors tended to bring him out in a rash and, with his dark colouring, "five o'clock shadow" became evident much earlier in the day.

He completed the shave without a single nick, in spite of the newness of the blade, rinsed his face in hot water and finally splashed his newly smooth chin with water straight from the cold tap.

Benjamin fixed the two rubber nozzles of the hair shower set onto the bath taps, dampened his dark hair with tepid water and worked the shampoo into a thick lather. With the suds thoroughly rinsed out he rubbed in a dab of conditioner that smelt like over-ripe apples, then washed that out too.

He towelled and combed his hair and by the time he had finished a long session in a deep bath—to which he added a foaming bath oil—it was practically dry.

He spent more time cleaning his teeth, using two applications of mint flavoured fluoride toothpaste, and dallied even longer with splash-on cologne, talc, deodorant spray and, finally, Old Spice aftershave which stung his freshly scraped face.

Now it was a question of what to wear.

By just after eight-thirty he had made his decision, dressed, and was ready for the party.

Benjamin came down the stairs followed by a waft of aftershave, cologne and talc.

He was wearing light brown cord trousers, casual and cut slim, dark suede shoes and a white open necked shirt under a dark blue V-necked sweater.

He felt pleased with himself—and with good reason.

Ivy was sitting in one of the armchairs, her lap full of knitting. As he came into the room she glanced up and a look of scarcely-disguised admiration lit up her face.

'My, you look smart. And don't you smell nice? You sure you're not meeting some young lady?'

Benjamin was afraid that the embarrassment would show as he made a pretence at a cough.

'No. Nothing like that. Just a party.'

He looked at his watch. 'I must be going now, Ivy, or I'll be late. I shan't be out too long.'

'You go out and enjoy yourself Mr Benjamin. You've earned it.' And Ivy gave him an encouraging smile.

As the young farmer started across the yard towards the parked Volvo, the figure of a boy appeared round the corner of the farmhouse, cruising on a bike towards the kitchen door.

What at first appeared to be a boy turned out to be Sandra, Ivy's eighteen-year-old daughter whose work at the riding stables seemed to keep her away from the farm for most of the daylight hours.

In fact Benjamin often went several days at a time without catching sight of her at all.

'Hello Sandy.' Benjamin paused in his walk to the car as the girl dismounted and parked her bike, a gents' racer, against the farmhouse wall. 'Another long day?'

'Oh. Hi Benjamin.'

She sounded tired as she turned from the bike to face him. In sharp contrast to his smart appearance she was wearing a thick, shapeless sweater, grubby jodhpurs and well-worn riding boots.

Her blonde hair was scraped back, as usual, and pushed up under a flat tweed cap.

'Yes,' she continued. 'We're pretty busy right now. Every kid from miles around must be learning to ride at the moment. Must be the weather. Bet their enthusiasm dies down a bit when it starts getting cold and dark and wet.'

'And I bet you're right!' returned Benjamin. ''Bye now.'

'G'bye.'

He was getting into the car as she let herself in through the kitchen door. Sandra paused just inside the door, listened to the sound of the car starting up and driving off, then she walked through into the living room.

She took off her cap and tossed it onto the nearest chair, pulled at the rubber band that held her hair in a long pony tail and threw back her head, shaking it vigorously to allow her loose hair to cascade down her back. Then she ran the tips of her fingers of both hands firmly through her scalp.

'Supper dear?' asked her mother.

'No thanks, mum. I had something at the stable. I'd love a cup of tea though.'

'I'll get us both one. Did you see Benjamin?'

'Yes. I'll say I did. All done up like a dog's dinner. What's he up to tonight?'

'Says he's going to meet some friends for a party,' returned Ivy. 'But I think there's more to it than that. About time too!' she added with a laugh.

Meanwhile Benjamin was well on his way to the village.

Chapter four

At The Drovers Arms he pulled into the little car park at the side, locked the car and walked towards the middle one of the inn's three doors.

It bore the legend "Bottle and Jug". He had to take a bottle to the party and with plenty of time in hand he intended to bolster his courage with a nip or two before he went.

The Drovers Arms was one of those rare establishments, an unspoilt village pub.

It had been run for as long as Benjamin could remember by Alf and Grace Blissett, though nowadays their daughter Mary (Molly to her friends) helped out with barwork in the evenings.

They didn't cater for meals, not even chicken in a basket.

A packet of crisps or peanuts, perhaps a cheese sandwich when the darts team was playing at home, was all you would get at The Drovers.

'A village pub,' Alf had declared upon occasions too numerous to count, 'is for village people, local people, to meet and have a drink in. When they want something to eat it's time they went home.'

And he took pride in serving a really first class pint of ale.

With no bright lights, juke boxes, fruit machines, skittle alley or scampi to attract them, outsiders rarely visited the place. Which was the way Alf wanted it.

In the big, board-floored public bar the regulars congregated each evening to play darts, dominoes or cribbage. It was the domain of the mild-and-bitter man. Women were seldom seen in the "Public" bar.

.

At the other end of the building, furthest from the car park, was the "Saloon" bar with a few small tables and upholstered chairs where the snootier elements could meet in relative comfort to chat over their gins and camparis.

Sandwiched between the two main bars was the "Bottle and Jug". It was a small, square room with a fixed bench seat round two sides. A third wall was almost completely taken up by a large brick open fireplace. The bar itself filled the fourth side of the room.

Dark wood panels from floor to ceiling made the room appear even smaller than it was and a large, square walnut veneer table in the centre took up most of the floor space.

The Bottle and Jug was used by the village as a kind of off-licence, where people popped in for the odd bottle of brown ale or Guinness to take home.

A few of the older residents also gathered there to enjoy their drinks away from the noisy bustle of the public and the hubbub of chatter in the saloon. But often as not, as on this evening, it was empty.

As Benjamin came through the door Alf Blissett poked his head round from behind the counter of the public bar where he invariably sat on a high stool.

He was quite surprised to see the young farmer who, on the rare occasions he visited The Drovers, always used the saloon.

Alf, who was small and bald and walked with a limp, got down from the stool and hobbled into position behind the bar of the Bottle and Jug.

'Evening Mr Trenchard. What brings you in here?'

'Just on my way to a…to friends for the evening,' said Benjamin. 'Thought I should take a bottle of something with me. How about whisky? Could you sell me a bottle of Bell's?'

'Of course, Sir,' returned Alf, slipping easily into the extra courteous approach he reserved for the better cash customers who were obviously going to buy more than half a shandy and a packet of crisps.

'But I'm afraid it's a bit on the pricey side. The brewery you know. We have to sell spirits by the measure. None of your supermarket prices here I'm afraid.'

Benjamin winced as Alf told him the price of a bottle of whisky.

'I see what you mean,' he said with a wry smile. 'Still, I'd better take it. Oh, by the way, better pour me a double Scotch, to be going on with.'

Alf reached up for one of the short stemmed glasses hanging upside down in a long row above the bar, turned and pushed the rim against the Bell's optic on the back wall. He waited until the pale amber liquid had emptied from the glass bulb, released the pressure, paused for the optic to refill then repeated the procedure.

'Anything with it, Sir?'

'No thanks Alf. Just a little water if you don't mind.'

Alf placed the glass with the double whisky on the bar in front of Benjamin. He took a small water jug from a towelling mat at one side of the bar and stood it beside the glass.

'It's not only the brewery's fault,' said Alf, half apologetically. 'What with the revenue going up as it does with every budget I'm surprised anyone can afford to drink at all.'

He hobbled off through the doorway in the back to what was apparently some sort of store room.

Benjamin lifted the water jug and added hardly more than a dash to the whisky in the glass. Setting down the jug he lifted the glass and took a good stiff pull.

The liquid glowed its way down his throat and seemed to extend its soothing influence almost immediately to his whole body.

If there was one thing Benjamin enjoyed it was a good drink, whisky for preference, although, as with most things, he indulged in fairly strict moderation.

Another good swallow and the drink was almost gone but the young man found the tension and apprehension about the coming party easing considerably.

Alf reappeared with an unopened whisky bottle in his hand.

'There you are Sir, Bell's. I'll just wrap it for you.'

He disappeared again and Benjamin drained the glass.

When Alf returned he had a small sheet of plain brown paper which he laid on the bar.

Placing the whisky bottle diagonally across it he rolled it up, tucking in the bottom edge as he did so. A final twist at the top and the discreetly covered bottle was stood on the bar beside the empty glass.

'There you are, Sir.'

Benjamin reached into his hip pocket for his wallet. 'Better give me another large one,' he said.

Ten minutes later he came out of The Drovers and made for his car. In one hand he carried the paper-wrapped bottle. Inside he carried the glow of two hastily-downed doubles.

At ten minutes past nine Benjamin pulled up outside the Storeys' house and although it was still early by party standards there were already half a dozen cars parked in the short driveway and on the road outside.

Lights blazed, seemingly, from every window and the muffled sounds of loud dance music, punctuated every few seconds by a high-pitched shriek of laughter, echoed oddly down to the road.

Benjamin locked the car and, with paper-wrapped bottle in one hand, stood looking at the brightly lit house.

He took a deep breath, strode purposefully up the path and pushed the illuminated button beside the front door. From inside came a two-tone "dang-dong" chime.

Almost at once an indistinct shape appeared the other side of the red, blue and green-panelled glass door. It swung open and a woman Benjamin didn't know stood on the threshold.

In one hand she held a half-empty glass, in the other was a half smoked cigarette.

'Come on in.' She waved both arms in an exaggerated gesture of welcome without spilling the drink or dislodging the ash of the cigarette. Then she turned and called back into the house. 'Here's another one Maggie. My, they're all turning up early tonight.'

Margaret Storey appeared. She was short and on the plump side. She wore a long, loose floral-patterned dress and her mousey hair was piled up on top in a too-formal style. Already a couple of stray ends had worked loose and were drooping over one ear.

Benjamin couldn't help thinking of the contrast between this plain woman and her younger sister.

'Oh, it's Robert's brother Benjamin isn't it?'

She didn't wait for confirmation.

'Robert said you might be coming. Don't know what we should have done without you. Too many girls.' And she emitted what was virtually a scream of laughter which the newcomer immediately identified as the one heard from the roadway a minute earlier.

'Let me introduce you,' said the hostess and she took his arm, pulled him, a little unceremoniously, inside and closed the door with the side of her foot.

Benjamin's nerves came rushing back.

'I thought you might like a bottle of something,' he blurted, holding out the brown paper package.

'You shouldn't have,' replied Margaret Storey, taking the package and unwrapping the bottle. 'Ooh. Whisky. Lovely!'

She led him up the hallway to the lounge, pushed open the door and the solid thump-thump of an over-amplified rock number blasted out.

Inside four couples were dancing, or rather, gyrating, to the music. They looked over, without pausing in the dance, as Margaret shouted to make herself heard above the noise.

'Hey, everyone. This is Benjamin.'

Then she pointed to each couple in turn.

'That's Ray and Jean.' Benjamin nodded and got a wave in reply.

'That's Martin and Sheila.' Again the waves.

'That's Joan and Les.' More waves.

And that's Harry with my sister Steve.'

Benjamin gave a shy smile and held up a hand in greeting to the girl he was supposed to partner for the evening.

Harry, a man in his mid-thirties, wore a huge grin all over his face and gave Benjamin the thumbs up sign.

Steve smiled and waved both arms enthusiastically without faltering in her dancing.

She looked terrific. Her soft brown hair fell bouncing around her face as she moved in time to the music. She wore tight-fitting, dark green velvet trousers tucked into high heeled knee length brown boots. Her loose white silk shirt had wide sleeves and was hanging open to about the fourth button down.

From the jiggling movement inside the smooth material as she danced, Benjamin assumed that she wore nothing underneath.

'Come and meet the others.' Margaret's voice interrupted his concentration and he was bundled back out of the door and across the hall to the dining room.

Inside, the table was covered with plates and dishes containing sandwiches, crisps, peanuts, those little cocktail sausages on sticks, vol au vents and an impressive array of other edible bric-a-brac. At one end was a large crusty loaf on a board, a bread knife lying beside it, a butter dish and another board on which reposed half a dozen good sized wedges of various cheeses.

A couple who were bending over the table, plates in hand, looked up as Margaret and Benjamin came through the door.

'This is Benjamin,' announced the hostess. 'And this is Bill and Angela. Trust them to get to the food first!' And there was another piercing shriek of laughter. 'Come into the bar,' she added.

The bar was in the kitchen. In fact the bar was the kitchen. It was the brightest lit and most crowded of the rooms that Benjamin had yet seen.

One complete worktop surface area was covered with bottles of wine, mainly the supermarket non-vintage varieties, English sherry, a dozen bottles or more of mixers, lemonade and squash and, Benjamin noticed, a half bottle each of whisky, gin and vodka. Most of the whisky and vodka had already disappeared.

Next to the drinks were twenty or so upturned glasses of various shapes and sizes and, at the end of the worktop, four half-gallon cans of bitter, one of which was opened with little spurts of foam peering from the two small holes in the top.

There were six people in the kitchen, talking, laughing and drinking. Margaret went through her introduction routine once more.

'This is my hubby, Mike. This is Roger and Mandy. And John and Pat. And this is Erica, Harry's wife. You know, you saw him dancing with Steve, in there. Look Mike, Ben's brought a bottle of whisky.' She handed it over for inspection.

'You shouldn't have bothered you know,' said Mike with an appreciative smile. 'But it's very good of you.' He added the bottle to the small stock of spirits.

'Now,' said Margaret. 'You know where the food is. You know where the drink is. And you know where the dancing is. The "little room" is at the top of the stairs on the left.' She followed this piece of information with yet another shriek of laughter.

'What will you drink?' asked Mike.

'Whisky please. With, er, just a little water.' Benjamin watched as the host took a glass and poured a good measure from the opened half bottle, the label of which declared the contents to be "Tartan Brae—a blend of fine old whiskies".

Benjamin took the drink.

'Water's in the tap,' laughed Mike.

Benjamin leaned over to reach the cold tap at the kitchen sink and Erica, who was propped against it, glass in hand, swayed into him. 'Er, sorry,' Benjamin managed to stutter.

'Don't be. I'm not,' Erica replied in a husky voice and there was another shriek of laughter from the hostess.

'That's right Benny,' she called across the kitchen. 'Make yourself at home.'

Benjamin sploshed a little water into his glass and stepped back quickly, then took up a position, his back against the worktop, a good two yards from Erica who was still propped against the sink and eyeing him in a seductive way from beneath over-long false lashes.

He took a stiff pull at the drink and began to feel better again as the amber liquid warmed its way down inside him. As the idle chat around him continued he casually picked up the opened whisky bottle and inspected the label more closely.

Nowhere did the label say that the contents actually came from Scotland and Benjamin supposed it to be a good imitation from Japan or Taiwan.

He was suddenly roused from his contemplation by the husky voice of Erica who had, without him noticing, sidled along towards him and at the same time entwined her arm round his before he had chance to move.

'I can see you're not much of a talker,' she whispered, fluttering her lashes at him. 'Let's go in for a dance.'

'But…but…I'm not much good at dancing…' faltered Benjamin.

'You don't need to be,' returned Erica. 'Just follow me.'

She put her almost empty glass down on the window sill behind the taps then firmly took Benjamin's whisky glass from his fingers and placed it beside her own.

'But…'

It was no use. Erica wasn't taking no for an answer and she ushered him out of the kitchen, across the hall and into the lounge where the four couples were still writhing and swaying to the music.

Erica pulled him bodily into the centre of the floor and immediately began to dance.

 At least she started wiggling her not inconsiderable hips and throwing her body about roughly in time to a tune that Benjamin had never heard before.

'Come on, Benny,' she called. 'Let's move it.'

Benjamin winced and began to move his feet. He was self conscious, in spite of the alcohol he had consumed, and didn't know what to do with his hands. His body seemed to have no desire whatever to manoeuvre in the way expected of it.
His own taste in music, although wide, was somewhat quieter.

He glanced over at his gyrating partner.

Erica, like her husband, was in her mid thirties, although the thought occurred to Benjamin that she hadn't looked after herself particularly well for a good few of those years.

 She was dark-haired, her hair piled up and held with slides from which a thin strand had come adrift and was hanging forlornly down one cheek. Her face was flushed, not so much with the effort of the dance as with the effects of several too-hasty gins. She had thick dark eyebrows above brown, close set eyes which in turn sat astride a prominent nose. A moustache of shadowy brown covered her top lip.

She was quite tall for a woman, perhaps five feet eight or nine, well built, with wide shoulders, large breasts, thickish waist and rounded hips.

She wore a red dress, with a plunging front that showed too much cleavage, held up by narrow shoulder straps that allowed glimpses of small tufts of black hair under each armpit. The dress was almost floor length and Benjamin was thankful to be spared the sight of her legs which he guessed, quite rightly as it happened, to be hairy.

After a couple of minutes the record track ended.

Immediately Erica went over to the unit and took the record off amid a chorus of "oohs…" from the other dancers.

'We want something a bit more romantic,' she announced, selected another disc, placed it on the turntable and set the stereo in motion once again.

This time the music was very different. It was Andy Williams, or someone who sounded remarkably like him, crooning a slow ballad.

'And while we're at it we'll turn off a few of these bright lights,' declared Erica, though as far as Benjamin could see there was only a single standard lamp shining dimly in the corner.

As the light clicked off the room seemed to be plunged into complete darkness but after a few seconds Benjamin's eyes became accustomed to a much more subdued light, created by the reflected glow from the hallway filtering through a small glass panel above the lounge door. Even so, the other people in the room were no more than indistinct shadows.

'There. That's better isn't it?' said Erica.

It came out as more of a statement than a question and no-one considered that it needed a reply.

She was suddenly back at Benjamin's side and, taking the tops of his arms in a firm grip, drew him into a close embrace.

'Much more friendly, don't you think?' she said. 'Now you can loosen up a bit. You're so tense.'

Benjamin tried to speak but all that came out was a peculiar sound in his throat that could have meant anything.

'Are you alone? I mean, did you bring anyone with you tonight?' asked Erica in a hoarse whisper.

'No…I…well…'

'Oh good. We won't be disturbed then, shall we,' cooed Erica, with what was intended to be a wicked little chuckle. To Benjamin it sounded more like the triumphant cackle of a vampire alighting on its victim.

'As a matter of fact I'm supposed to be partnering Stephanie tonight,' Benjamin managed to croak.

Erica pulled him into an even closer embrace, her face coming close to his.

'She's with Harry, over there.' She nodded towards a vague blurred shape on the other side of the room. 'Looks like they've settled down for the rest of the evening, doesn't it?'

The music and the crooner grooved on while Erica pressed herself ever more intimately to her reluctant partner.

The other couples in the room could be seen dimly, scarcely moving, swaying gently. A soothing, rustling sound, as of hands on silk, formed a gentle background to the music.

Benjamin felt something warm and wet against his face as Erica reached up and tried, unsuccessfully, to thrust her tongue into his left ear.

By turning his head hard to the right he was just able to keep her mouth at bay.

She eased away from him very slightly and Benjamin relaxed at the thought that she had finally got the message. But, quite unexpectedly, she took his right hand and, before he could resist, placed it firmly and squarely on her left breast.

Benjamin's hand recoiled as though he had touched a red hot poker.

'There now. We're not shy are we?' whispered Erica.

'I…I…,' he began to stammer in a cold panic.

Suddenly the music stopped as the record track ended and Benjamin took the opportunity to disentangle himself from the passionate half-nelson of his partner.

He stepped back.

'Er…thank you,' he managed to gasp. 'I think I'll just go and pay a visit upstairs.'

And leaving Erica in the middle of the floor he turned and fled through the door, up the stairs and bolted himself in the toilet.

Benjamin swung the flap down onto the lavatory seat and sat down to assess the situation.

He had come to the party in the full anticipation of an enjoyable evening with the delicious Stephanie. That was one thing. But a night of wrestling the insatiable man-eating Erica was quite another.

He sat, chin on hands, elbows on knees, pondering the options. Should he resign himself to the dreadful Erica?

Or politely but firmly rebuff any further advances?

Or should he simply slip quietly away?

He stood up and pressed the flush lever. He had already decided on the middle course and took a deep breath as he unbolted the door and stepped out.

Erica was outside, leaning, or rather draped, against the opposite wall.

'You've been a long time. I thought you must have fallen down the loo,' she giggled.

Benjamin stood transfixed to the spot. His mouth opened but no sound came out.
Once again the initiative was with the awful Erica.

She came towards him, took him by the hand and said in a low voice: 'I've got something to show you.'

As though in a dream, Benjamin allowed himself to be led along the passage to a half open bedroom door. From downstairs came the mixed and muffled sounds of music, voices and laughter.

Erica pushed the door wide, led him in, then elbowed the door shut behind them.

The room was in a kind of twilight, lit only by the light from the passage coming in through the gap down the side of the door which had remained slightly ajar.

The double bed was scattered with sweaters and light jackets, the outdoor clothes of the party guests, and Benjamin's brain was still numb as Erica suddenly pushed him back across the bed and flung herself on top of him.

Benjamin felt her wet, gin-flavoured kisses round his mouth and neck and ears and a wild tension seized him as he realised that there were fingers groping at his trouser zip.

With a heave and a roll he dislodged his female assailant and leapt to his feet. His full senses had returned with a surging shock of adrenalin.

'Don't be so SHY, Benny,' came the hoarse stage whisper from the shape on the bed.

But by then Benjamin was half-way out of the door. Two seconds later he was down the stairs and past a surprised couple, glasses in hand, standing in the hallway.

The front door slammed behind him and the garden gate was left swinging open as Benjamin continued his headlong flight from the frightful Erica.

In less than ten minutes he was sitting on the edge of the bed in his own bedroom at the farm, his feelings a tangled mixture of anger and humiliation.

Before he went to bed Benjamin poured and drank two stiff measures from the bottle of whisky he kept in his bedside cabinet but rarely touched.

Later he fell into an uneasy and fitful sleep and dreamed of being chased around the yard by an oddly ferocious cow while Ivy and Sandra Green stood watching and laughing.

Reggie Broadman drained his whisky glass and planted it purposefully on the bar, a faint, self-satisfied smile on his face. It had been another successful day.

'Same again. Make it a double.'

It was an order rather than a request and the barman winced at the blunt manner of this apparently affluent young man who had the looks but not the manners of a gentleman.

Reggie never noticed the glare to which he was treated as he swung round on the bar stool to survey the interior of the saloon bar of the Red Lion in Witherstoke. Apart from himself there were only two or three other drinkers, not surprising so early in the evening.

Reginald Broadman was twenty-eight, a six-footer, with straight dark hair cut and Brylcreemed immaculately, his upper lip was adorned with a similarly flawless "Clark Gable" moustache. He wore a smart dark grey single breasted suit with matching waistcoat, faintly striped pale shirt and navy blue tie. His black shoes were highly polished.

He looked successful.

The younger son of a Kent farmer, his education, at a not-very-fashionable private school in West Sussex, had ill-prepared him for the cut and thrust of commerce, mainly due to his own total lack of interest in lessons and disregard for any kind of regulations.

A residential two-year general course at the Springshott Agricultural College, which he had treated as more or less an extended holiday, did little more to add to his overall education.

But he did have a few things going for him.

Years of practice at getting out of scrapes with minor authority had endued him with a razor sharp brain capable of coming up with the most plausible explanations for the many, sometimes delicate, situations in which he was apt to find himself. Once invented, they invariably became, in his own mind, matters of fact.

Coupled with a ready wit and an almost endless repertoire of jokes and shaggy dog stories, he could be a total charmer in just about any company.

As a salesman he was brilliant. And in his own field, as sales representative of a large agricultural machinery and equipment suppliers, he was virtually unsurpassed.

Today he had been to a farm just outside Witherstoke where he tied up a deal on a new tractor which had netted him £25 in cash for his own back pocket.

As far as he was concerned a deal was not a deal unless there was a reasonable kickback involved.

He didn't normally operate this far west but "a friend of a friend" had tipped him off about a sale that was just waiting to be made.

It had seemed a shame not to make it and it turned out to be well worth the trip.

It was while he was musing over his afternoon's work that his eye was taken by the young woman who had come into the bar. She was blonde, passably attractive in an ordinary sort of way, and was smartly dressed in a two piece suit and high heeled shoes which showed off shapely ankles.

And she was the only unaccompanied female in sight.

Chapter five

THREE weeks had passed since the party, the memories of which Benjamin still found hurtful and embarrassing.

He hadn't said very much to Robert in the meantime, certainly nothing about his entanglement with Erica, and the younger brother knew Benjamin well enough to leave the subject alone.

In any case there was something else to absorb their interest. The annual Squire's XI versus Village XI cricket match.

Robert was, popularly, captain and opening bat for the Village and Benjamin was duty bound to take part, albeit rather lower down the batting order.

Sir Oliver Pumphrey-Haig Bt, owner of Ashley Hall and its estates, Squire of Binfield, could trace his ancestry back over 600 years. And the remarkable thing about the family was that in all that time they had been noticeably unremarkable.

Not a single military hero had appeared on the family tree, no sign of a distinguished statesman or scholar, not a trace of a great churchman—not even a black sheep.

In fact there were those who reckoned that George III must have been going through one of his mad phases and honoured the wrong man with a minor peerage when he put his seal to the document a hundred and fifty years earlier.

However, over the generations, the Squires of Binfield had always treated their workers and tenants well and were long time benefactors of the village in general.

They it was who had donated and developed the village cricket ground, later adding a modest pavilion which they had since repaired, renovated and modernised on a fairly regular basis and which doubled as a village hall.

The annual match was one of the highlights of village sporting life, with lunch and an evening buffet provided for players and officials, again financed by Sir Oliver.

His own team, mainly composed of estate workers, would be led by his daughter's fiancee, the Hon Tristram Bradley.

By way of a change the Saturday of the annual match dawned bright and clear, promising a fine late summer treat for what was generally regarded as the season's last proper fixture for the village side on the third weekend of September.

In a community where agriculture had been traditionally the main occupation of many of the residents for generations, this event had taken on something of a "harvest home" celebration with wives, partners, friends and relatives later joining the cricketers for a social evening get-together.

Over breakfast Robert made his first tentative approach.

'Molly Blissett will be helping out with the catering at the pavilion today,' he announced, as though imparting to his brother some vital piece of tactical information for the match.

Benjamin waited for him to continue but that appeared to be the end of the matter.

'Well?'

'She's taken quite a shine to you, apparently.'

'What do you mean?'

'Nothing. It's just that she fancies you.'

'Look, what are you getting at? If you've been arranging things again behind my back…'

'No, no. Nothing like that. It's just that I saw her in the pub this week and she was asking after you. Said she would be at the match today and, well, mentioned that she hoped she might see you.'

Molly, real name Mary but known to almost everyone, heaven knows why, as Molly, daughter of The Drovers Arms landlord Alf Blissett, was 24, attractive, in a rounded, country sort of way, and currently unattached.

Robert had indeed seen her in the pub earlier in the week but it was he who had raised the subject of his brother Benjamin's poor track record in the romance stakes. And Molly, great sport that she was, had promised she would try to 'help get him started.'

'If you think…' Benjamin began.

'I don't think anything, Benny boy,' broke in Robert. 'Just trying to be helpful in passing on a message. Nothing to do with me. No skin off my nose.'

And with that he rose from the table and sauntered out of the room.

Benjamin thought for a minute.

Here was a turn up for the books. He had, of course, exchanged casual 'hellos' with her a few times but had not detected any indication that these were anything more than polite courtesies.

Molly certainly was a nice looker and with a generous figure. Not exactly his cup of tea perhaps, but this could be an opportunity not to be sniffed at.

Benjamin thought about it on and off for the rest of the morning, or at least until the match got under way. The more he thought about it the more attractive the situation became.

By the time the captains were on the pitch and the coin tossed for choice of innings he had made up his mind to make a move.

Conditions for the match were perfect.

Joby, as usual over the past few years, was one of the umpires. His official white coat so long that one could scarcely see his feet beneath its hem, so that he appeared to be gliding slowly over the ground. His opposite number was one of the older farm workers from the estate.

The sun was warm and beamed down from the blue of a sky broken only by a few of the smallest of fluffy white clouds.

A classical English late summer day.

Squire's XI won the toss and decided to bat, which meant that Benjamin, Robert and the rest of the Village side would spend the first part of the day in the field. No chance then, for the time being, of the older Trenchard making that intended move.

As the lunch break approached, Benjamin, who had spent all his time in the outfield, saw Molly several times coming in and out of the pavilion. On one occasion, when he was fielding long on and not far from the building she smiled and waved at him.

So there could be something in what Robert had said.

At 1.00pm precisely, Joby, after consulting the pavilion clock gave a glance and a nod at his white-coated colleague who returned the signal. They removed the bails and the teams came in for lunch.

By now Squire's XI were 104 for five, not a great score but reasonable for this particular match. And Tristram Bradley, captain and opening bat, was still there on 37 not out.

The smattering of spectators, including Sir Oliver, his wife, Lady Evelyn, and their daughter Verity, along with the rest of the batting side and a few other bystanders, applauded enthusiastically as the batsmen, followed by the fielders, came in.

Lunch, a cold meat and salad affair, was laid out on one long trestle table down the middle of the pavilion and the teams arranged themselves along each side, the two captains at either end.

Several women helpers, including Molly Blissett, served up cups of tea or glasses of fruit squash. She came up behind Benjamin and laid a hand on his shoulder.

'Hullo Benjamin, how are you these days? Haven't seen much of you lately. Tea or squash?' she added, not waiting for his reply.

Benjamin looked round. Her hand was still on his shoulder. In the other hand she carried a big jug of orange drink.

'Oh, fine. Squash please.'

She leaned forward and proceeded to pour the drink into an empty glass on the table in front of him. Her well-formed left breast was about two inches from his right cheek and separated from it only by the thin material of her floral dress. Her rather modest perfume, smelling faintly of apple blossom, wafted invitingly into his nostrils.

She looked down, gave him a delicious smile, then straightened up and began to move on to the next player.

'Give a wave if you need anything else,' she called above the babble of chatter and laughter going on around them over the meal table.

The lunch break was a fairly short interlude and there was no further opportunity for conversation. The village side were soon on their way back into the field, the two batsmen following.

Runs came slowly so that by 2.45pm Squire's XI had added only 45 runs for the loss of three more wickets. At this rate they could be batting all afternoon—and Tristram Bradley was still at the crease, playing a captain's innings, with just one run needed for his half century.

Robert was bowling to him now.

He turned at the end of his run-up, flicking the ball from one hand to the other.

Joby, bent over the wicket so that his white coat trailed the turf, watched intently as the ball hurtled down the pitch, beat the bat of the Squire's captain and thudded into his left pad.

Robert, part way down the pitch in his follow-through run, turned on his heels, glared into Joby's eyes and let out a yell that might have been heard in Witherstoke.

'HOWZATT!!!'

Half the Village side echoed his confident appeal for a 'leg before wicket' dismissal.

A hush descended as all eyes turned to focus on Joby.

Somewhere in a distant tree a wood pigeon broke the silence as it cooed its 'my toe hurts, Betty' call.

At last the verdict came.

'Not out,' declared Joby with a shake of the head.

Robert's face contorted into a picture of disbelief and heavy sighs of disappointment were heard around the ground. Village was desperate to remove the stubborn Tristram before too many more runs were added to the steadily mounting total.

The ball was lobbed back to the bowler and he caught it, or rather snatched it from the air, in a clear show of exasperation.

As he passed close beside the umpire on his way back to bowl again he paused to rub the ball against his thigh.

'That was out,' he hissed under his breath.

'Twus outside off stump,' Joby stage-whispered back. 'An' I'M the bloody umpire!'

Robert started his run-up to bowl again, approaching the bowling crease at a rapidly accelerating run. His arm arched over. Not a bouncer but a quicker, short delivery.

Tristram, whose eye was well and truly in by this time, saw it a mile off, leaned back and connected in the middle of the bat. The ball sailed up and away towards the square leg boundary.

A six, or at least a four, was a certainty.

Benjamin, again fielding deep on the on side, also saw it a mile off and set off like an express train, his long legs covering the ground with surprising speed.

Just as it seemed the ball must cross the boundary above and in front of him he made an enormous leap, flung up one arm and somehow got his fingers to it.

He fell headlong and rolled over several times before the ball, which had been deflected upwards, dropped back into his now outstretched hands.

An even louder 'HOWZAT' appeal echoed from eleven Village throats, augmented by a dozen or more from spectators.

Joby thrust the forefinger of his right hand skywards.'OUT!' he yelled, just as enthusiastically.

Benjamin stood up, just a foot inside the boundary, the ball safely cupped in his two palms.

He'd just dismissed the opposing captain with the catch of the day. So sure were the batsmen that it would be a boundary that they hadn't even bothered to run.

Tristram was out for 49.

There was a ripple of well-deserved applause and Benjamin was gratified to note that Molly, the lunch things now all cleared, was sitting watching the match, not twenty yards away. And she was applauding more than most, a large, admiring smile on her face. The last wicket fell soon after, and Squire's XI finished on 153 all out.

After just a ten minute break the match was restarted.

Now, of course, Squire's XI were in the field and the Village opening batsmen, one being Robert, were at the crease.

They opened well enough with 22 runs going on the board before Robert's partner fell, caught in the slips.

Benjamin was down at number ten and not likely to be needed to bat for an hour or more so he took the opportunity to go outside the pavilion and sit next to Molly.

'That was a wonderful catch you made,' said Molly.

'Oh, lucky really,' returned Benjamin, the colour coming to his face at the praise from this attractive young woman.

'Lucky be blowed,' said Molly with a laugh. 'It was brilliant.'

Benjamin couldn't help noticing what good teeth she had, or the tiny dimples each side of her full mouth.

'Er…Molly,' he began.

'Yes?'

'Are you staying on for the social after the match tonight?

'Yes, of course.'

'Do you have a partner for the evening?' He was amazed at his own forwardness.

'Well, no, not exactly,' returned Molly. 'I thought I'd just come along and enjoy myself.'

'Would you save a dance or two for me?' asked Benjamin, a slight redness returning to his cheeks.

'I should be jolly annoyed if you didn't ask me,' laughed Molly, with a delicious toss of her head which sent her thick brown hair bouncing.

'That's great,' said Benjamin.

Now, having accomplished what he had been planning all day, he felt totally drained but mightily relieved.

'Look… I'd better think about going inside…to get ready…to bat I mean,' he stammered, and with a nod rose and walked towards the pavilion.

Molly watched him go with a smile. Doing Benjamin Trenchard a favour was not going to be the slightest bit difficult, she mused.

The Village innings laboured slowly on. At tea they stood at 121 for six. Robert was still there on 41 not out and, with four wickets still to fall, the match seemed to be swinging in their favour.

Benjamin got no further chance to converse with Molly during the tea interval but he was treated to another of her delightful smiles. A smile that seemed, if anything, a little warmer than ever.

Soon after the evening session began the Village was dealt a double blow.

Robert was caught at long on, doing exactly what his opposite number had done and making the same mistake, attempting to hit the ball out of the parish for his half-century. The younger Trenchard was dismissed for 47.

His replacement, a hairy giant of a man who was tractor driver on a neighbouring farm, lasted only a few deliveries.

Brian 'Badger' Brock was not noted for his batting style. His normal game was to try to hit everything, not out of the parish, but out of the county. Sometimes it worked and sometimes it didn't. After all, he had been known to knock up 50 or more in less than half an hour.

This time he went for just 4. A boundary it had to be admitted.

Village were on 135 for eight and it was Benjamin's turn to take up the bat. They were very much down to the tail-enders. The tide had turned and with only two wickets left in hand they still needed 19 runs to win.

Squire's XI could smell the scent of a famous victory. Their bowling tightened up, their fielders became more alert.

Benjamin strode to the crease.

Cricket was not his game but he was determined to put on a good show.

It might have been the expectations of the coming evening that sharpened his attention. Or possibly the fact that Molly was still sitting watching the game and was willing him on.

Whatever, Benjamin and the surviving number eight batsman, the owner of the village grocery store who was in his fifties, managed a cautious dozen runs before the grocer was stumped, trying to reach for an out-of-reach off break.

Seven runs to win and the last batsman was approaching the crease.

It was George.

George Goodall, local garage proprietor, was also well into his fifties and was chosen to play for Village mainly for his slow spin bowling. He had in fact taken three of the Squire's XI wickets but was not noted for his batting prowess, hence his lowly last-man position.

Benjamin walked to meet him and they had a brief exchange as they approached the wicket.

Away in the distance came the sound of a lawn mower. From closer at hand could be heard the voices and laughter of young children playing on the swings in a corner of the sports field, totally oblivious of the drama being played out on the cricket square.

'We only need seven more,' whispered Benjamin. 'Don't try anything dramatic, just concentrate on trying to keep the ball out of your stumps.'

The first ball which George received, the last of that over, was meant to intimidate. The bowler strained to put some extra venom into the delivery, tried too hard and an intended bouncer ended up as a wide.

Village were one run nearer the target but George now had to face an extra ball. It hissed down somewhere near the line of his off stump. The bat flashed. There was the thud of ball on pad and a collective 'Owzat!' echoed round the ground.

The estate umpire at the bowler's end leaned forward and studied the line for a long moment, then shook his head. 'Not out.'

Village supporters heaved a sigh of relief.

The field changed over as Benjamin prepared to face again. He took a look around.

Molly was still watching from her seat in front of the pavilion way over on his left side.

The bowler came in on a longish run and he, too, tried a bouncer.

Benjamin was tingling, he didn't quite know why.

Was it Molly and the possibilities of the evening ahead?

Was it the anger and resentment he still harboured deep inside over his farcical encounter with the dreadful Erica at the recent party?

The ball was a bouncer of sorts. Not too fast, it pitched short and popped up invitingly towards Benjamin's chest.

Normally he would have ducked or side-stepped out of the way but this time all the pent-up emotion seemed to explode within him as he leaned back, swung a mighty blow at the ball and heard the smack as his bat connected. Right in the meat of the blade.

There was a roar—or at least it sounded like a roar, bearing in mind there were only a few dozen spectators, some of whom supported Squire's XI—as the red leather sailed away into the blue.

There was an even bigger cheer as it arched over the boundary line and thudded into the grass just feet from Molly's chair.

'SIX!' came the yell.

Joby, a huge grin on his face, raised both arms in the customary signal to the scorer, although there was really no need.

Benjamin had scored a six. And Village had won the annual match against Squire's at the last gasp.

The field trooped off, standing aside to allow Benjamin and George to receive the applause as they walked towards the pavilion.

Benjamin was the hero of the Village side. He smiled one of the broadest smiles he'd ever smiled. Molly applauded louder than anyone.

Life was good again, thought Benjamin. He had played an exemplary game, he had a date with an attractive young woman and the sun, though now low in the sky, was still shining.

Once the various players had discarded their equipment, both teams reassembled in front of the pavilion where Sir Oliver was to make the presentation.

Village, of course, got the trophy.

In a brief congratulatory speech, both Robert and Tristram received mention from Sir Oliver for their sterling batting efforts.

But it was Benjamin who gained most praise. Had there been a Man of the Match award he doubtless would have claimed it.

However, warned Sir Oliver, Village had better keep on their toes. Next year would be a very different kettle of fish, he added darkly, though with a broad smile on his face.

Robert was no less enthusiastic about his brother's performance.

As they drove home together, to get ready for the evening's entertainment, he was lavish with his praise.

'I didn't know you had it in you, Benny boy,' he gushed.

Benjamin just smiled. For once he didn't mind the familiarity.

'Well, it just shows you don't know everything,' he replied.

'And what about tonight,' added Robert. 'I saw you chatting with Molly at one stage.'

Benjamin smiled again.

'We'll see, shall we?'

The two were soon showered and changed and ready to return to the pavilion for the social evening.

Robert, as captain of the village side, had decided that a white shirt and pale flannels would be in keeping with his status. In any case, he had a heavy date planned for that night and wanted to be as comfortable as possible.

Benjamin was dressed more sombrely, as was his custom, in dark grey slacks, pale blue shirt and darker blue, striped tie.

They would, of course, be travelling separately.

They paused at the kitchen door to call a dual goodbye to Ivy who was sitting sewing in the living room. Of Sandra there was, as usual, no sign. She would still be busy at the stables.

As they strolled to their respective vehicles Robert came to a halt.

'Look, what do you have in mind? I mean, for later tonight?' he asked.

'How do you mean?' replied Benjamin, a hint of suspicion in his voice.

'Well. Look. Did you have anything planned? Uh, where to go or anything? You know!'

'No, I don't know.'

Robert decided to come straight to the point. 'Castle Lane's a nice quiet little spot to park a car.'

'Castle Lane? Castle Lane's supposed to be haunted isn't it?'

'Exactly. That's why it's so quiet,' returned Robert with a knowing wink.

'Look, do you mind!'

'Sorry, just trying to be helpful,' said the younger brother.

Naturally Benjamin knew Castle Lane. Anyone born and bred in the village knew every little lane and byway.

It was an unmade track which led up to the village's allotment gardens, which portion was well used. Beyond the allotments it became more and more overgrown on its way to where the ruins of an ancient castle were now barely discernible amid the undergrowth of a small wood.

It ended some 50 yards short of the ruins where two footpaths led off, one going on to the wood, the other an ancient byway heading across farmland towards the neighbouring village of Maplewell.

At this same point it widened into a grassy space which gave access to fields on either side via two wooden five barred gates.

Benjamin was silent.

Yes. It was quiet up there. And it was relatively close. He would bear it in mind.

Within minutes the two brothers' cars were following each other into the pavilion car park and they were sauntering side by side towards the brightly-lit building which was already alive with the sound of conversation, laughter and some muted music.
The bar facilities were already in full swing.

Down one side of the hall was a long table laden with pork pies, scotch eggs, cooked chicken drumsticks, plates of ham, dishes of crisps and salads and several large platters holding cubes of pineapple and cheese skewered on cocktail sticks.

Some of the more enthusiastic eaters were already forming a queue, paper plates in hands, led by Joby who had refused to remove his white coat of authority.

As the two brothers entered there came combined shouts of welcome and applause from the members of the Village side, who seemed to have taken up a monopoly of the bar.

'Good old Robby'…'Well done Benjy'…'Here come the heroes'…'What are you having?'

After five minutes of back-slapping and praise at the bar Benjamin managed to slip away, whisky in hand, and made his way over to one side of the hall where Molly was seated at one of the small tables surrounding the dance area. As he pushed through the crowd, he received many another pat on the back.

He arrived at her side and she turned to face him as he approached.

'Mind if I sit here?'

'Not at all. By the way. I've got a bone to pick with you.'

Benjamin was a little taken aback.

'Why…what's the problem?' he stuttered.

'Nothing really,' returned Molly, that delicious smile still lighting her face. 'Except that you damned nearly killed me. I know you were keen to win. But that six. Three feet nearer and I should have been a goner.'

'Oh…yes. I had meant to apologise about that. It was a bit too close for comfort wasn't it? I didn't get round to saying sorry. Events just…sort of took over…'

'Only kidding. It was a wonderful way to end the match. Look, for heaven's sake sit down. You're making the place look untidy.'

Benjamin took a seat and began to smile again. He had been smiling a good deal more than normal today and felt more at ease than he had for a long time.

Molly was easy to chat with. Her experience behind the bar of The Drovers had seen to that.

She too had changed and was wearing a white silky blouse, buttoned down the front and a dark green ankle length circular skirt, white ankle socks and flat pumps.

Her thick, dark brown hair was worn shorter than was fashionable for young women, with curls and waves just touching the nape of her neck. It positively shone with health and vitality.

The pair spent a very pleasant couple of hours, chatting and dancing together. Later in the evening the music turned to a more romantic level and the lights were dimmed.

Benjamin and Molly were now dancing closer than ever, she with her head against his chest, her arms around his back. His chin rested just above her forehead and he had the pleasant scent of her hair in his nostrils.

Both had had a little to drink, not too much by any means, and were relaxed and comfortable.

'I should think about getting home soon,' whispered Molly.

'I'll drive you,' replied Benjamin.

'No need, it's hardly more than a five minute walk.'

'I wouldn't dream of letting you go home alone. Anyway, it's dark and cold.'

'If you insist.'

'I do.'

Ten minutes later they were in Benjamin's car and heading up the road towards The Drovers Arms, less than half a mile away as the crow flies.

But even crows don't fly that straight and within a minute or two Benjamin had slowed and turned into Castle Lane, 50 yards short of the village inn.

'Are you sure you know the way to The Drovers?' asked Molly with a giggle.

'Well. I just thought you might like the scenic route. And it's not that late really, is it?' Benjamin was amazed at himself.

'Isn't Castle Lane haunted?'

'So they say. But I don't believe in ghosts, do you?'

'Not until I see one.'

And there was another giggle.

They bumped slowly on up past the deserted allotments, the headlights illuminating the trees and bushes which lined the track. Twice the lights picked up a rabbit, eyes shining pink in the darkness. They hopped almost nonchalantly into the enveloping gloom beside the path.

At the point where the track widened, by the field gates, Benjamin executed a three or four point turn to face the car back down the lane.

Then he switched off the lights and loosened his tie.

Molly immediately snuggled across and rested her head on his left shoulder.

Benjamin was just a little surprised at her forwardness.

'You've done this sort of thing before, haven't you?' he laughed.

'Well, I didn't think you'd taken the trouble to drive up Castle Lane *just* for the scenery,' Molly replied with a smile. 'Especially at this time of night!' And she huddled even tighter so that the top of her head was resting under his chin.

Benjamin was once more aware of her faint scent, this time mingled with the shampoo-clean smell of her glossy hair.

His left arm was round her shoulder. She had taken his right hand in both her own.

He nestled his face into her hair and lightly kissed the top of her head.
The response was immediate.

Molly turned her face up towards him and they kissed.

At first just a light brush of the lips. Then a firmer contact. Then a full blooded, open mouth, passionate kiss that set Benjamin's pulse racing.

Molly's hands guided his right hand, gently but firmly, to her left breast.

It was his turn to respond.

As they kissed he felt the increasing firmness of the nipple under his palm as he caressed the silky mound.

And Molly gave a gentle moan.

Once more Benjamin astonished himself as, slowly and deliberately, he began to undo the buttons on the front of her blouse.

No fumbling. No rush.

Each button slipped from its buttonhole easily and smoothly as though guided by the most expert of fingers.

They broke momentarily for breath from their kiss and their embrace and to take up a new, more comfortable position.

Molly took the opportunity to reach round with both hands under the back of her blouse to unfasten the strap of her bra.

Now, as they embraced once more, Benjamin's right hand was inside the front of her blouse and underneath the bra, cupping her left breast.

Her skin was warm and soft, as silky as the material of her blouse. His forefinger and thumb closed gently around the erect nipple and there was another soft murmur from Molly.

As their lips met again, Molly's left hand began gently to stroke the top inside of Benjamin's left leg.

Their mouths parted and he began to kiss her neck, her throat, the lobe of her ear.

His pulse was really pounding now and Molly was emitting tiny whimpering sounds.

The increasing spiral of their combined passion was abruptly shattered as, without warning, her whole body suddenly stiffened as though turned to steel and she let out a strangled half-cry, followed by a series of gasps and an ear-splitting shriek.

Benjamin leapt away from her, or as much as one can leap in the confines of a car.

Not only was he startled. He was downright scared. And mystified. What had he done to provoke this reaction?

Looking at Molly he could just make out that she was staring through the side window behind him and pointing, a look of horror on her white face.

He turned.

In the near darkness of this late summer night, in "haunted" Castle Lane, through the misted-up glass, he saw a pale and ghostly figure, not ten feet from the car, near one of the field gates.

Molly gave another scream, fumbled for the catch, pushed open the door and jumped out of the car.

Clutching her gaping blouse with both hands she raced off down the dark lane towards the village, leaving the passenger door swinging wide.

In just a few seconds she was gone.

Benjamin turned back to where the figure had been.

It was still there.

Except that now it began to glide towards him.

The fire of his so-recent passion disappeared in an instant and his legs turned to jelly as the apparition approached.

Then came disbelief, rapidly followed by anger as the ghostly figure spoke.

'Wosson? Woss all the screamin' an' 'shoutin' about?'

It was Joby. And he was still clad in his too-large umpire's white coat.

'What the hell are you up to? You bloody stupid imbecile!' Benjamin was beside himself with fury and frustration.

'ME? I'm jus' takin' me usual short-cut 'ome. It's what YOU're up to is what I wants to know!'

Benjamin reached over and pulled the passenger door shut. He started the engine, slammed it into gear and screeched off down the narrow lane.

Of Molly there was no sign.

She must have covered the few hundred yards down to the village and along to The Drovers in record time.

Benjamin was furious.

What should he do? Go to The Drovers and try to see Molly to explain? Phone her?

The whole situation was too farcical for words. He was embarrassed beyond belief.

He decided to cut his losses and return home.

It was a still very angry Benjamin who slammed the car door, slammed the farm kitchen door and slammed his bedroom door.

Ivy heard the commotion and turned over in bed. Best left alone, she thought.

In his room Benjamin resorted to the whisky bottle once again. He drank two large measures altogether too quickly, threw off his clothes and climbed between the sheets.

His head was spinning and his stomach was churning.

Half an hour later he had to stumble out to the bathroom.

He threw up in the toilet pan, flushed it clean, splashed his face with cold water and felt much better.

Eventually he slept. Not a refreshing, dreamless sleep.

He was playing cricket once again, the hero of the side. All the spectators were attractive young women cheering his every move when suddenly he was given out, caught behind, although his bat was nowhere near the ball. A ridiculous decision. The fans abandoned him, the crowds of young women cheered the umpire. It was Joby.

And Robert? He, of course, was desperate to know how his brother had fared in Castle Lane. But it was abundantly obvious that things had not gone to plan so once again he decided not to raise the subject.

Molly said not a word to anyone. Whom could she tell about the ghost of Castle Lane? And what was she doing up Castle Lane anyway?

And Joby, still a little baffled by his own inadvertent involvement in the drama, indeed, not even realising there had been a drama, was still fearful of his boss's mood. That is, until Monday morning when Benjamin, now recovered, came up to him quietly and placing a hand on the old man's shoulder, had simply said: 'Sorry about Saturday night Joby. Lost my rag a bit. Shouldn't have done.'

And Joby , still mystified, had replied: 'Tha's a'right boss.'

Meanwhile late summer was slipping quietly into autumn.

Reggie Broadman was back in the Witherstoke area and up to his old tricks. Well, his previous visit had been quite successful, why not try again?

The young woman in the Red Lion, who, it transpired, had been into town for a new job interview and was waiting for a bus back home, had been taken in completely by his line about owning his own business and had readily accepted a lift, after a couple of stiff drinks.

OK, so even in her semi-inebriated state she had drawn the line at "going the whole way" but some heavy petting in the car had been an interesting diversion before the hour-long drive back to his wife and baby daughter.

This time he was into something different, acting as unofficial go-between for the sale of some livestock between two farmers, against company regulations of course, but putting at least £15 in backhanders into his own pocket.

Now, in the early evening, his car parked in the railway station yard, he was leaning against the wall just outside the ticket office, as though waiting for someone.

More and more people were streaming towards the station entrance to catch trains for home as the working day ended. And it wasn't long before he spotted a likely pick-up.

She was young, shapely and auburn-haired, by no means a great looker but with a super figure which her clothes showed off to perfection. What her face lacked her body made up for.

As she was about to pass him to enter the station foyer he stepped away from the wall and effectively blocked her path. In his hand he held an unlighted cigarette.

'Excuse me. I'm sorry. Look, do you have a light?'

She pulled up, startled.

'No. I don't smoke…'

Before she could say any more or continue into the station he laid a hand very lightly on her arm.

'Hey. Don't I know you? Wait a minute. Where was it?'

She eyed him, appreciative of the attention from this personable, and very dishy man.

'I don't think so. I don't believe we've met.'

'Yes. It must have been…you're not on the stage are you? Or was it some big charity bash? Look, I know I'm not mistaken. I could never forget someone like you. You may not remember me but I assure you I've seen and admired you before.'

She was intrigued. She thought for a moment.

'I was at the Round Table charity ball in Witherstoke, back in the spring.'

'Yes, of course. I knew I was right. You looked terrific that night, couldn't take my eyes off you. But you were with…?'

It was a probing question, intended to extract information. And it didn't fail, producing a lot more than Reggie could have hoped for.

'Yes. My boyfriend.' She looked a little sheepish. 'Ex-boyfriend I should say. We've broken up now.'

'But there must be someone else?'

Another probe.

'Not at the moment. I'm enjoying my freedom too much.'

The truth was that there had been no recent opportunity.

'I know the feeling,' returned Reggie, warming to his theme. 'I recently broke up with a long time girlfriend. She didn't seem ready to make a permanent commitment..'

He threw his arms in the air and exclaimed: 'Look, I do apologise. I'm forgetting my manners. My name's Clive. Clive Banham. My car's in the car park. Can I give you a lift home?'

Chapter six

THE first frost came early.

An unseasonal and severe cold snap lasted throughout the last two weeks of October and into November, bringing a distinctly winter feel to the countryside.

There was ice on the ponds and the grass stayed white and frozen all day in the shelter of wood and hedgerow.

And it was the early frost which, indirectly, brought Joby Fulbright into confrontation with the law.

Late autumn and winter were Joby's favourite times of the year.

The shooting season gave him the chance to garner his own little share of the fruits of the land.

The odd brace of pheasants would invariably come his way.

Well, the odd few dozen brace, for he had a select circle of acquaintances who not only willingly paid him half the going rate for a plump gamebird but could also be relied on to keep their mouths shut.

Then there was the other great love of his life.

Ferreting.

In recent years Joby's ferreting activities had come to a complete halt due to the absence of rabbits. This was caused by the highly contentious introduction into the English countryside ten years earlier of the deadly viral disease, myxomatosis, which in two seasons had wiped out around ninety-five percent of the country's rabbit population.

An action designed to rid farms and estates of a major agricultural pest had been all too successful, depriving many a countryman of a favourite winter pastime.

'Bloody 'myxi,' had been Joby's reaction. 'Them as brought it in orter be strung up by the balls!'

Happily for Joby, and his thousands of fellow ferreters, the rabbits were recovering, gradually developing immunity to the deadly plague. They would never again be seen in such numbers as before but at least there were enough to make a rabbiting expedition worthwhile.

Ever since he was a lad Joby had kept ferrets and catching rabbits not only supplemented his own diet but, at 1/6d a time to his favoured clients, boosted his beer money, an income sadly missed during the bleak 'myxi' days.

In a mild winter rabbits would live in thick undergrowth above ground. It was only in the coldest of weather that they moved full time into their subterranean tunnels.

And they needed to be underground before the ferret could be used to flush them out into the purse nets set over the holes.

So it was that Joby was out ferreting that Saturday afternoon a full month earlier than usual.

Naturally he had permission from the Trenchards to catch rabbits on the land they owned and it was in Hazelly Row, the overgrown boundary hedge between Longdown Farm and Ashley Estate, that he made his start.

Joby was working with a new ferret he had acquired that year, a young jill polecat called Jo. His old hob was kept in reserve in an ancient wooden carrying box lined with straw.

He netted up a seven-hole "bury" along his side of the hedge, slipped in the ferret and was surprised when she flushed a rabbit into a net within a couple of minutes.

'Blimey! She's a fast worker,' Joby muttered to himself as he dispatched the rabbit, slung it into the big inside pocket of his old black overcoat and reset the net.

But that turned out to be a flash in the pan.

Joby knew there would be other rabbits in the warren. All the signs were there. Fresh droppings nearby. Fresh earth scraped out of the holes. That faint musty smell that meant rabbits.

But he waited and waited.

Nothing.

His breath came like clouds of smoke in the cold afternoon air as he blew on his hands. His feet were getting chilly but he dare not stamp them for warmth. Any noise, and especially vibration, would make the rabbits harder to bolt. And they were already proving difficult enough.

Of Jo there was no sign. His ferret appeared to have gone to sleep.

'Bugger,' muttered Joby.

After nearly twenty minutes a slight movement of white and brown caught the corner of his eye and there, on the far side of the hedge ten yards away, was his ferret wandering along the edge of the field.

She had found an unnetted bolt hole and decided to explore on her own.

'You daft bloody animal.' Joby called out aloud. 'Wha d'y think yer up to?'

The ferret ignored him and shuffled on along the far side of the hedge, getting further and further away.

Joby knew he shouldn't go onto Squire's land but he was about to lose a new ferret. It would only take a minute.

He pushed his way through the hazels, climbed the fence into the next field and scurried after the ferret.

As he stooped to pick it up a bony hand descended on his shoulder.

'Gotcha!'

It was Fred Appleton, the Squire's gamekeeper.

Fred was tall and thin, his lean frame clothed in traditional keepers' attire of heavy green tweed jacket and knee-length breeks. Thick woollen socks went from knee to ankle, disappearing into sturdy brown waterproof boots.

His face was narrow, lined and leathery. By contrast his nose was big and fleshy, a purpley-red colour, lined by blue veins. Clearly the result of many years spent outdoors in all weathers, although Joby had always maintained it was caused by 'too much of the drink' and often referred to him as 'old grog blossom.'

Fred had been standing in silence, watching Joby, for nearly half an hour from behind a big oak tree on his own side of the boundary.

'What's in your pocket?'

Without waiting for a reply he dived an arm into Joby's overcoat and gave a shout of triumph as he pulled out the dead rabbit.

Joby seemed shocked into total silence.

Another probe revealed a dozen or more folded purse nets in another pocket.

Fred was beside himself with glee. He had caught Joby red-handed on Squire's land with a ferret, nets and a dead rabbit.

'This'll be a case for the magistrates,' he chortled in delight.

There was no need to ask for the intruder's name and address. For more than a dozen years Fred had been trying to catch Joby poaching on Squire's land.

He could hardly believe his luck when fate delivered his arch enemy so easily into his hands.

Finding a dead pheasant on Joby would have pleased him more but a rabbit is a rabbit –and poaching is poaching.

Joby was silent still.

Stunned and frustrated., he could scarcely believe his own carelessness.

'You'll be hearing from the Court,' Fred informed him cheerfully as he led him down the side of the field to a gate into the lane.

'That'll mean a nice hefty fine and a warning to stay off Squire's land in future.'

Fred was all smiles as he closed the gate behind the dejected Joby.

'I'll have the rabbit and the nets--and you can say goodbye to yer ferret. I'll find it on the way back home.'

Joby trudged back to his cottage in a daze.

Perhaps it was the early cold weather that had been to blame, causing him to work the new ferret too soon. Whatever, he had been caught out by the hateful Fred Appleton who would now relish the thought of seeing Joby in court.

Perhaps the Squire wouldn't prosecute.

But that was a forlorn hope and Joby knew it.

Fred Appleton would never allow this longed-for moment to be missed.

Confirmation of Joby's fears arrived through his letterbox two weeks later in the form of an official looking buff envelope containing a court summons.

Joby needed time off work to attend court but couldn't bring himself to ask Benjamin.

He approached Robert that afternoon and it was an astonished Robert who broke the news to his even more astonished brother that evening.

'What was he doing on Squire's land?' Benjamin wanted to know. 'He's got four hundred acres on Longdown to catch rabbits.'

'Says he went over the fence to fetch his ferret,' returned Robert. 'Fred Appleton was waiting for him behind a tree.'

'The fool! Well, we'd better get a solicitor to represent him in court. That young Stephen Bunting, you know, old Archie's nephew, he's supposed to be pretty much on the ball. I'll find out if he's available.'

But Joby was having none of it.

'I don't want none o' them lawyer blokes pokin' their nose into my business,' he declared when confronted by Benjamin. 'I'll just tell the Beak what 'appened. I'll tell 'im the truth.'

Benjamin finally gave up with a shrug.

'I'll come along and give you a character reference anyway,' he sighed.

By the time the day of the hearing arrived most of the village had somehow heard about Joby's fall from grace, thanks mainly to Fred's tongue-wagging, and there was a good attendance of spectators at Witherstoke Courthouse to watch the proceedings.

A couple of traffic offences were dealt with, then it was Joby's turn.

Joby had been sitting in the courtroom next to Benjamin. The set-up was much the same as for the earlier inquest except that instead of the Coroner there were three local magistrates seated on the raised dais.

Chairman of the Bench was a retired army Colonel. On his right was a thin-faced lady in tweeds, the wife of a very successful local businessman who was "something in the city". Third member was the town Mayor, an ex-officio magistrate who, as a former trade union official, led the minority Labour contingent on the town council.

'Call Jonathan Bernard Fulbright!'

There was once again that murmur of comment as the unfamiliar and unused names were announced.

Joby, dressed in his usual old tweed jacket and black trousers, stepped forward and was led to the dock.

The court clerk, papers in hand, faced him.

'You are Jonathan Bernard Fulbright of Longdown Farm Cottage, Binfield?'

'Yes but they calls me Joby and I can explain everythin'…' began Joby.

'Not now,' returned the clerk. 'You will have an opportunity to put your case in a little while.'

'Yes, but...'

'Not yet Mr Fulbright. Please be patient. Do you have legal representation?'

'What?'

'Do you have a solicitor to speak for you?'

'I can speak fer meself.' I ain't dumb.'

'Quite,' returned the clerk.

'Now. The allegation before the court is that you did, on Saturday the ninth of November this year at Binfield, trespass in search or pursuit of game or conies upon land owned by the Ashley Hall Estate, contrary to section thirty of the Game Act 1831. How do you plead? Guilty or not guilty?'

'It wusn't like that at all. I wus jest after me ferret...'

'Mr Fulbright,' snapped the clerk. 'You will get the chance to tell the court your side of the story later. For the moment we need to know do you plead guilty or not guilty?'

'Well I can't be guilty fer trying to rescue me ferret, can I?'

The clerk turned to look up at the magistrates, exasperation on his face.

'I believe that is a plea of "not guilty" your Worships.'

Joby was told to sit down.

There then followed the evidence of the prosecution, mainly that of Fred Appleton who could hardly conceal his delight at recounting to the court, indeed to the world at large through the three members of the local Press, how he had apprehended his old enemy.

'Caught him red-handed, I did. On Squire's land with a ferret, nets and a rabbit in his pocket. Poaching. Open and shut case....'

The lady magistrate broke in.

'Thank you, Mr Appleton, the evidence is all we need. Your comments are not necessary.'

Fred started to leave the witness box but was called back by the clerk.

The clerk turned to Joby.

'Have you any questions you would like to put to the witness Mr Fulbright?'

'I'll say I 'ave.'

Joby stood up.

'Now then, Appleton...'

The clerk interrupted.

'Mr Fulbright, I think you should address the witness as Mr Appleton.'

'Huh! Well now **MR** Appleton. 'Ow long wus you wotchin' me from be'ind that tree?'

'Very nearly half an hour,' replied Fred with a broad smile, keen that everyone should know how completely he had outsmarted the elusive Joby.
'So you seen me come along t'other side o' the 'edge?'

'Of course.'

'An you seen me set me nets?'

'I did.'

'Did I set any nets on Squire's side 'o the fence?'

'No.'

'Were there any rabbit 'oles on Squire's side of the fence?'

'Not that I could see.'

'Did you see the ferret?'

'Yes. It ran right past me. Not much of a rabbiter is it?'

A ripple of muffled laughter ran round the court and the Chairman banged his gavel for silence.

'So then you seen me climb over the fence?'

'That's right.'

'Then what?'

'Well, you were so busy chasing the ferret you didn't see me. I apprehended you. Red-handed. On Squire's land with a dead rabbit and…'

The clerk intervened once more. 'Thank you Mr Appleton, just answer the question.'

'Did you see me put the rabbit in me pocket?'

'No.'

'Ah! Then the rabbit must 'ave already bin IN me pocket when I got over the fence?'

'I…it…the rabbit was in your pocket when you were apprehended on Squire's land…'

Joby broke in. 'But whose rabbit wus it? Squire's or Mr Trenchard's?'

'It…I…all I know is the rabbit was in your pocket and you were on Squire's land.'

'And the ferret. Did I 'ave that in me 'and?'

'You were just about to pick it up when you were apprehended.'

'So I didn't hachully 'ave a ferret hon me when I wus happretended?' exclaimed Joby, warming to his theme.

'Well, you…'

'And where's my ferret now **MR** Appleton?'

'It's in a hutch at my cottage, waiting for the court to decide on its future. As are the nets. The rabbit's been eaten.'

'So what you're sayin' is that you've pinched me ferret, you've pinched me nets and you've pinched me rabbit jest becus I got over the fence to stop me ferret from breakin' the law on Squire's land?'

'I…you…'

It was Fred Appleton's turn to be speechless.

'No more questions yer Honour!' exclaimed Joby triumphantly.

Fred Appleton was told to resume his seat in the courtroom. He gave Joby a sullen scowl as he passed.

The local police inspector stood up.

'That concludes the evidence for the prosecution your Worships,' he announced.

The clerk turned to Joby once more and directed him from the dock to the witness box.

'Now Mr Fulbright, you can tell the magistrates your recollection of events.'

'Well, they've 'eard it all ain't they? I wus out ferretin' on Mr Trenchard's land, mindin' me own business.

'I caught a rabbit, then me ferret went walkies through the 'edge into Squire's field. She's a jill polecat, a young 'un, ain't got much savvy. I went over the fence to fetch 'er back No 'arm in that is there? You can't be dun fer trying ter stop yer ferret breakin' the law, can yer? Then this MR Appleton grabs me an' sez I'm poachin. But I never did have a ferret in me 'and. And the rabbit I 'ad wus already dead, caught on our side of the fence.'

The magistrates went into a huddle.

The clerk stood up and turned to join the whispered discussion.

They resumed their places then the Chairman asked: 'Can anyone tell us if Mr Fulbright DID have permission to catch rabbits on the Longdown side of the fence?'

Benjamin stood up.

'Your Worships, I, with my brother, am the owner of Longdown. Mr Fulbright has worked for our family for many years and it has always been fully understood that he may catch rabbits anywhere on the farm whenever he wishes.'

There was a hasty whisper between Chairman and clerk.

'Thank you Mr Trenchard,' said the Colonel.

With a brief nod of approval to each of his fellow magistrates, the Chairman sounded his gavel.

'Case dismissed,' he announced. 'You may step down Mr Fulbright. Next case please.'

''Ang on a bit.'

It was Joby.

Everyone turned to look. He was still standing in the witness box.

'Mr Fulbright…?' asked the clerk, a puzzled look on his face.

'Wot about me hexpenses? I want me hexpenses.'

'What expenses?' the clerk wanted to know.

'Well, fer a kick-off there's me nets.'

Hurried whispered consultation between Bench and clerk.

The chairman sounded his gavel.

'Mr Appleton to return Mr Fulbright's…er…rabbiting nets forthwith.'

'An' wot about me rabbit? Ee went an' et me rabbit!'

Another whispered consultation which went on somewhat longer with several glances at both Joby and Fred Appleton.

Another gavel.
'Mr Appleton to pay Mr Fulbright the sum of one shilling and six pence compensation for the rabbit he confiscated without proper authority.'

'While we're at it, Mr Fulbright, I suppose you will ask for the return of your ferret?'

'No thanks! He can keep 'er. She ain't no good. 'Bout as much use as a one-legged man in an ass-kickin' competition she is!'

There was a rousing round of applause as Joby and Benjamin left the courtroom.

Fred Appleton, who had already hurried out, was red-faced with fury. Not only had Joby escaped again but had turned the tables completely. He had to pay for the rabbit, return the nets and was left with a useless ferret.

The Chairman was still gavelling for order as most of the court spectators trooped out.

In The Red Lion across the road there were congratulations all round and not a few drinks.

Benjamin, standing at the end of the bar, was 'in the chair' and liberally dispensing liquid cheer to Joby and his supporters. The hero was standing, back to the counter, his friends around him, reliving his famous victory.

'Mr Trenchard.'

Benjamin turned at the sound of the rather small high voice. Right behind him was the young woman he recognised as one of the reporters in the courtroom.

'Yes?'

She held out her hand. 'Hullo, I'm Kate Downey from "the Gazette". I was in court just now and thought it might be a good idea to get some background stuff for the story we'll be running.'

Kate Downey was small, not exactly petite, but slim with a good figure and legs. She was about 25 but looked a good deal younger. In fact she had the kind of face that makes even a mature woman look like a schoolgirl. The most striking thing about her was her long, thick, reddish brown hair that hung halfway down her back.

It was very attractive hair. Kate knew it and occasionally tossed her head just a little to show it off. She did so now.

'Well...' Benjamin began, his eyes running appreciatively over the young woman before him.

'Well, the one you want to speak to is Joby there. He's the man of the moment.'

Kate looked straight into Benjamin's face.

'I'd rather speak to you,' she said, with what looked decidedly like a twinkle in her eye.

'I've got a notebook full of quotes from Mr Fulbright. From the court case. Wonderful stuff. He's quite a character isn't he? No, I really wanted to get to know a bit more about local farming. The countryside in general perhaps. What on earth is a jill polecat for instance?'

'Well, it's simple really...'

'Look,' she interrupted. 'It's a bit crowded in here. Is there any chance you could maybe meet me later on where we can talk a little easier?'

'Well...I need to run Joby back to the farm this afternoon, then I'm...'

'Brilliant,' cut in Kate. 'I will be through at the office by about five. I could come out to the farm, or, better still, if you could meet me at my place about half past five we can have a cup of tea and a chat in peace.'

She handed him a card.

'My address is on there. Shall we say half past five then?'

Without waiting for his reply she was gone, leaving Benjamin gazing after her, mouth half open as if to speak.

He looked down at the card, tapped it a couple of times on the palm of his other hand and with a thoughtful look slipped it into his jacket pocket.

The lunch break in the pub was a long one. After Joby's village pals had dispersed Benjamin treated the old fellow to a bar meal. Steak and kidney pudding with all the trimmings followed by apple pie and custard, washed down with several pints of mild.

Benjamin had a more modest ham salad with a half of light ale.

He had other things on his mind. Kate Downey being among the foremost.

Later that afternoon he dropped Joby off at his cottage.

By now Joby was decidedly unsteady on his feet, and a little drowsy. He would sleep for several hours, dreaming of his big day in court and the way in which he'd scuppered the enemy's gunboat.

Soon after, following a quick shower and a change of clothes, Benjamin was back in his car, heading for Witherstoke.

He roughly knew the area of the address on the card and it took only a few minutes to find the road. The house was one of a terrace of fairly substantial Edwardian buildings, many of which had been converted into flats.

Kate's flat was on the ground floor. Her car was already parked outside.

He pulled up behind her Mini, closed and locked the door, and walked up to the front door.

The bell seemed unusually loud, the response almost immediate. A shadowy figure showed up behind the patterned coloured glass and the door swung open. It was Kate.

'Mr Trenchard. You're right on time. Come on in.'

Benjamin stepped inside.

On his right stairs led up, presumably to one or more flats on the upper storeys.

On the left was the doorway to the flat Kate had rented for the past year or so since coming to join the editorial staff of the "Witherstoke Gazette", the town's oldest traditional weekly.

She led him into a sizeable sitting room with an archway leading into a small kitchen/diner. There was a French window to the rear. Benjamin correctly assumed that the only other door led to the bedroom and bathroom.

'Sit down Mr Trenchard, take your jacket off if you like.'

Benjamin complied with both invitations. He was already feeling warm, the heating, he thought, was a little high. He sat on the sofa, laying his jacket over the back.

Benjamin looked around. 'These houses are deceptively roomy, aren't they?' It was a conversational observation.

'Surprising just how much room we've…I've…got,' agreed Kate. 'I'll show you the rest of the flat later on.'

She settled down in an armchair almost facing him, kicking her shoes off in the process. Her close fitting, rather short and formal pinstripe skirt rode up a little to reveal an inch or two more of a pair of very attractive legs. The top two buttons of her cream blouse were undone. Her hair, she tossed her head ever so slightly just to accentuate it, looked fabulous.

On her lap she had a reporter's notebook and a pencil.

'Look, I do apologise.'

She jumped up again.

'Can I get you a cup of tea or coffee? A drink maybe?'

'Well. I know it's a bit early. I don't suppose you have a whisky do you?' Benjamin needed a drink to bolster his confidence.

'I'm sure I can find you one somewhere.'

Kate went into the kitchen/diner and, after clinking around for several minutes in a sideboard, returned with a tumbler half full of whisky in one hand and a glass of red wine in the other.

'Hey, that's on the big side isn't it?' laughed Benjamin, taking the whisky glass. 'You're not trying to get me tipsy are you?'

'I'll do my best,' returned Kate, with a laugh of her own and another slight toss of the head.

'Hope you didn't mind me joining you,' she added, indicating her glass of wine.

She resumed her position in the armchair opposite.

'Now then, before we do anything else I want to know about ferrets.'

'It's easy really,' said Benjamin, relaxing into his theme. 'There are two types of ferrets. Pure white ones--well they're more of a yellow colour really—and they always have pink eyes.

'Then there are polecat ferrets, which have a lot of brownish markings, especially round the face, and they have brown eyes.

'Mind you, they can interbreed and the young ones of a crossed mating can turn out either white or polecat. They're always either one or the other, even though you'd expect them to be halfway between the two.'

Kate scribbled in her notebook.

'I see, so Joby's ferret was a polecat. But what's a jill?'

'Just country language for male and female ferrets. A jill is a female, the male's called a hob. He's usually half as big again as she is.'

'Right.'

More notebook scribbling.

'And what about you, Benjamin. You don't mind me calling you Benjamin do you? Are you married? Engaged?'

'I...well...'

He was startled by this sudden new line of questioning.

'Regular girlfriend?'

'Well...I...'

'I get it. You like to play the field a little.'

'I wouldn't say that exactly...I...'

'Oh I don't blame you. Life's for living, I say. And these days it's foolish to tie yourself up when you're young. Every one should sow a few wild oats, don't you think?'

Kate had consumed only about half her glass of red wine but Benjamin noticed her cheeks had a distinctly pinkish tinge.

He took a deep breath.

'You have a very modern outlook Miss…'

'Kate. Please call me Kate. Well I suppose that's down to being a journalist. I don't shock you, do I?'

'No, no of course not,' Benjamin was trying to convince himself. 'I find it rather refreshing.'

'Is there anything else about me you find refreshing?'

Kate gave another imperceptible shake of her head which set her hair dancing once again.

She reached up and undid another button on the front of her blouse. It was now almost half open, showing a small but beautifully firm cleavage.

Benjamin realised almost with a start that she was not wearing a bra.

'I find everything about you refreshing.' The whisky was beginning to kick in now. 'You're a very attractive young woman.'

Kate stood up, placed her now nearly empty wine glass on a small table, came across to the sofa and curled up neatly beside him, her feet tucked up underneath.

'What about our interview?' he asked softly as he slid his arm round behind her head.

'There's plenty of time to talk later,' Kate replied, leaning slightly forward to free her hair which she flicked back with both hands so that it now tumbled over his arm and cascaded across the back of the sofa.

Her face was turned up towards his. He looked down. Her cheeks were a little pinker than before. Her lips were full and were now slightly parted. Her eyes were grey with just a hint of green. They looked steadily into his own.

He bent towards her and her face came up to meet his own. They kissed very tenderly.

Their lips parted but their faces remained only a few inches apart.

'I've wanted to do that since the moment I saw you in court,' Kate confided.

'You don't believe in wasting any time do you?' returned Benjamin quietly.

'I told you before. Life's too short. Why wait around for something to happen when you can *make* it happen?'

'And what do you want to happen?'

'I want to get you into bed.'

Kate said it in such a matter of fact way that, for Benjamin, complying seemed the natural next step.

Kate swung her legs off the sofa and stood up.

She reached down and took both of Benjamin's hands in her own, pulling him upright, then taking him by one hand and leading him across the room to the bedroom door.

She turned the handle, pushed the door open and stepped through, still holding Benjamin by the hand.

This room was also deceptively large. There was a wardrobe, dressing table and chair and a square wicker linen basket.

The double bed, against one wall, had a small bedside cabinet on each side. On one stood a dimly lighted table lamp. The bedclothes were turned down.

Kate turned Benjamin round and sat him on the edge of the bed.

Then she stood before him and undid the waistband of her skirt. It slid to the floor and was promptly kicked away. Her legs were bare.

She undid the few remaining buttons of her blouse, including the cuffs, and edged it off her shoulders, letting it drop to the floor.

Kate stood before him, wearing nothing but the briefest of panties. Her small firm breasts pointed invitingly, it seemed, straight at his face, her auburn hair fell deliciously over her shoulders.

She came slowly towards him.

His outstretched hands reached out for hers. Just as their fingers were about to touch there came a loud ringing at the front doorbell.

In an instant the mood was shattered. They both jumped.

'Who…?'

Kate started out of the bedroom, crossed the sitting room and peered out through the door into the hall. A blurred figure was visible through the glass panels.

'Kate?' It was a man's voice.

Kate quietly closed the door to the hallway and ran back through into the bedroom.

'Hurry,' she gasped in a hoarse whisper. 'It's Dave.'

'Who's Dave…?' Benjamin began.

'He's my boyfriend.' She fumbled into her blouse and groped for her skirt. 'He's supposed to be in Belgium until Saturday. You've got to get out.'

'But…'

'No buts. He'll kill me. Get your jacket.'

Kate was nearly fully dressed again.

Benjamin was in the sitting room jacket in hand.

Kate opened the French door and virtually pushed him bodily outside.

'Go down the garden. There's a gate at the bottom. Follow the pathway to the end of the terrace and back to the road.'

The door was slammed shut and curtains hastily drawn.

Benjamin was left standing in the cold and dark of a late November evening. He pulled on his jacket and cautiously made his way down the garden path, went through the gate and stumbled along the little path that ran behind the gardens of the terrace. He had the strangest feeling that he was not the first to make such an exit from the premises.

As instructed, he found the alleyway leading back to the road and within minutes was seated back in his car in front of the house.

Of Kate and Dave there was no sign. All seemed blissfully quiet.

He started the car and drove slowly away.

To describe him as confused and frustrated would be an understatement.

He needed a drink. Badly.

Fifteen minutes later he pulled up outside The Drovers. Through a lighted window he could see Molly Blissett serving up drinks.

Now was not the time to enter into any kind of conversation with Molly.

He backed out and drove on to the farm.

It was ten minutes or more before he had composed himself enough to get out of the car, lock the door and walk round to the back door.

Sandra and Ivy were sitting at the kitchen table with cups of tea. Sandra, as usual, was wearing soiled jodhs and a scruffy sweater to which clung strands of straw.

Benjamin managed a gruff 'Hi' as he walked through and on up the stairs to his room.

Mother and daughter returned 'Hello' and 'Hi,' and exchanged inquiring glances with raised eyebrows as he disappeared but didn't make any further comment.

Something had obviously soured Benjamin's evening. Better not to ask.

In his room Benjamin reached for the whisky bottle once more.

He toyed with the glass for a while and after a few swigs of the amber liquid put it down on the bedside table.

He went back in his mind over the events of the day.
Kate was certainly a very modern and liberated woman.
Perhaps a bit too modern and too liberated.

Benjamin at last climbed into bed and fell into a deep sleep. Later that night he dreamed he was driving the old Fordson Major tractor down towards the river.

He drove into the river at a place where the cows had worn a wide track down through the bank in order to drink. The tractor got half way across when the engine spluttered and stopped, leaving Benjamin stranded in mid-stream.

He awoke with a start and it was already early morning.

It had been nearly two months since Reggie Broadman had been in the Witherstoke area.

Now he was back again and looking for another profitable little "business transaction", as well as the possibility of further amorous diversions.

He was beginning to enjoy Witherstoke which had so much to offer a man of his tastes and talents.

Christmas was on the horizon and the thought had struck him that there was ready cash to be made out of the trade in turkeys.

Many local farmers reared varying numbers of the birds in disused barns or outhouses as an extra cash-crop, without the actual figures or resultant profits being recorded in any bookwork, or indeed, appearing in the records of Mr Inland Revenue.

Problem was, the more you reared the more difficult it became to dispose of them quickly and quietly.

A skilled "negotiator" who could be guaranteed to keep his mouth shut, while creaming off a percentage of course, was invaluable. If there were plenty of farmers and smallholders anxious to offload their excess birds, there were just as many butchers and village shops who could cope with extra orders.

It was just a matter of getting the two sides of the marketing equation together. And at that, Reggie was a past master.

After two days probing the countryside he had "signed up" four sellers and seven buyers, involving over a hundred turkeys, with a net profit to himself of around £25.

Not a bad couple of days, considering he was still drawing his salary from the company.

It hadn't been difficult. He simply telephoned head office to say he was engaged on a long and delicate discussion over the sale of some expensive equipment. He said he needed a number of extended visits for a deal which, in reality, he had securely tied up two weeks before.

Of course he had to stay over, which meant two evenings free, and brief calls home about his latest "business arrangements" came as no surprise at all to his long-suffering wife.

His success rate took a bit of a tumble when, after meeting a young woman in the bar of the Red Lion, where he was staying, and plying her with a fair amount of alcohol during the evening, he failed to persuade her to visit his room. She also finally refused the offer of a lift home, which left him several pounds out of pocket and considerable sadder but no wiser.

Tonight was different. He reverted to his railway station ambush ploy and at the second attempt successfully tempted a rather plain looking little mousey woman of around thirty who nevertheless had the best pair of knockers he'd seen all day.

Once in his car the conversation took a fairly predictable line.

'Haven't I seen you before? I mean. On television or in a magazine or something?'

'What makes you say that?'

'It's... it's just that you seem familiar. Have you been in films? Or TV advertisements?'

'No. But I wouldn't mind the chance.'

And she laughed.

'Really? Well, there's just a possibility I could help you there. You see, I have a cousin who is a television director. They're preparing some short documentary pieces about the cultures and customs of the British countryside. He's looking for a number of attractive young women. Just small parts or course. But it's a start. Tell me, what do you do at the moment?'

'I'm assistant manageress of a family seed merchants, on the retail side..."

'There you are then!' Reggie exclaimed. 'You're obviously just the sort he's looking for.'

As he had discovered early in his womanising career, flattery gets you everywhere.

Chapter seven

SEVERAL weeks passed and Benjamin had heard nothing from Kate. Nor was he inclined to make any inquiries himself.

In any case the third Wednesday in December was, by tradition, the day of the annual shoot at Longdown. That day was fast approaching and he had plenty to occupy his mind.

Although the family had never been heavily into game shooting, they held the sporting rights on the farm "in hand". That is to say that the shooting was not let out to any third party or syndicate.

Consequently, apart from the occasional walk around with a gun by one or other of the brothers, the woodlands and hedges of Longdown provided something of a sanctuary for the pheasants reared on neighbouring shoots, particularly those of keeper Fred Appleton on the Ashley Estate.

And Joby Fulbright was adept at attracting even more onto Longdown than normally might have been the case.

It was just a question of liberally scattering a few large pockets full of grain around a few likely "gamey" areas two or three times a week once the shooting season got under way.

The Trenchards had always acknowledged the fact that pheasants reared by other shoots would regularly be found on their land so by way of being good neighbours they held an annual shoot of their own to which they invited representatives of some of the adjacent shoots, as well as a few family friends.

The Longdown shoot this year was to follow the usual pattern. Three drives covering the various hedgerows, clumps and rough ground followed by lunch. The afternoon would see just two rather more serious drives taking in the two main areas of woodland on the farm.

Guests this year would be Sir Oliver, as usual, his son-in-law to be, Tristram Bradley, along with James Long, Eric Robinson and John Marks, three farmers whose land also bordered Longdown, and, just by way of courtesy, the Reverend Simon Pindle.

The other two places, to make eight guns in all, would be filled by Benjamin and Robert, who would endeavour to put their guests into the most productive spots and who would only really take shots if none of their guests was in a position to shoot at a particular bird.

The morning, more of a shooting "ramble" than an organised driven day, was not expected to produce very many pheasants, perhaps a dozen or so, but was always enjoyable as a social event.

After lunch the guns might expect to encounter rather more in the way of testing shots. There was some good shooting ground on Longdown where pheasants could be expected to fly high and fast. A good team might shoot ten brace or more in each of the two drives.

The day dawned bright and clear. Just a hint of frost. By breakfast time a high cloud was beginning to build up and a moderate breeze was blowing.

A perfect shooting day.

Under careful instructions from Benjamin, Ivy was busy in the kitchen.

Longdown Farm shoot lunch had a good reputation and the Trenchard brothers were anxious that the tradition should be maintained.

They knew that Ivy wouldn't let them down.

By nine o'clock Joby, who would be in charge of the half dozen or so beaters, had arrived and was busy in one of the implement sheds, arranging bales of straw where the beaters and pickers-up would sit to eat their sandwiches.

At half past nine the beaters began to arrive, several on bikes, others in a battered pick-up truck which would also double as a game cart.

And Joby would, in theory at least, be in charge of the beaters and, in his own mind, the one-day-a-year counterpart of his deadly rival, Fred Appleton.

Just before ten the guest guns appeared in a variety of up-market vehicles. Both the Squire and Tristram drove up in Land Rovers and, as agreed, would help ferry the guns around the farm. The Trenchards' old four track would also be pressed into use. Benjamin met the guns at the back farmhouse door as they came in from the yard.

'Morning Benjamin,' called the Squire as he strode up the back path. 'My word, you've picked a cracking day again.'

'Certainly have, Sir Oliver,' returned Benjamin. 'Hope we can show you some quality birds to match. Come in for a glass of hot toddy.'

The other guests were welcomed in like manner until soon the farmhouse kitchen seemed packed with tweed-suited, green wellie or leather brogue shod countrymen, laughing and joking and calling their "hullos" to each other over their steaming glasses.

Only Mr Pindle, the vicar, seemed ill at ease. He stood to one side, nodding silently to all and sundry, his long dark overcoat and black wellies looking decidedly out of place.

Ivy had vanished temporarily into the dining room where she was busy with the table.
At last Benjamin called the gathering to order.

Then, as his father had done for many years, he made the traditional formal shoot captain's announcement.

'Firstly may I welcome you all to Longdown for our annual "maraud" and thank you for rearing so many good birds this year. I've no doubt most of you will recognise some as your own!'

There were guffaws of laughter all round.

'Now the serious bit, safety, for which I make no apologies. Each drive will start when you hear two short blasts on the whistle. Please wait for that signal before loading your guns. The drive will end with a single long blast on the whistle, at which point all guns should be unloaded.'

He paused and looked around. They were all used to a safety talk and were all taking it in.

'No ground game, please. We have a few dogs in the beating line and anyway, Joby will never forgive me if one of the guests shoots a rabbit!'

More guffaws all round.

'Please ensure that your gun is unloaded and broken at all times between drives, preferably in a gun slip. Be particularly careful negotiating fences. Any questions?'

Eric Robinson had a query. 'What about foxes, Benjamin? Where do we stand on them? I know my keeper has been complaining at the number this year.'

'That's a matter for your own conscience,' returned Benjamin. 'All I will say is that you must have a good clear shot and be close enough to kill it cleanly. And don't do it in view of the Squire. As joint master of the local hunt he might not appreciate it!'

A few more chuckles.

'Right then gentlemen. Shall we get started?' And Benjamin led the way out of the farmhouse.

The first drive comprised Hazelly Row, that wide strip of hazel and bramble separating Longdown from the Squire's land—and the scene of Joby's recent clash with Fred Appleton—together with a small stand of trees and undergrowth, known as Pumphouse Clump, the overgrown site of some long-redundant machine shed used for pumping water from the river to the house.

Four of the guns would be positioned around this thicket. Two more would walk parallel with the beaters coming along Hazelly Row. Benjamin and Robert would walk fifty yards behind the beaters to account for birds which might decide to turn back.

Naturally there was agreement from Sir Oliver for guns to be sited his side of the fence for this drive.

The whistle to start the day began.

The beaters moved slowly with a good deal of bush-bashing with their sticks accompanied by a variety of peculiar vocal sounds intended to drive the birds from their hiding places.

There proved to be eight or ten pheasants "in residence".

Six flew straight on over the clump, as expected, to cries of "forward" from the beaters. Of these, four were accounted for by the guns.

Two more broke out sideways and flew across the adjacent fields. One was shot, the other escaped without being fired upon, judged, rightly, by John Marks to be too low.

One more which flew back along the hedgerow was downed by Robert.

The long blast came on the whistle. End of the first drive and six pheasants in the bag. Most of the guns had had a shot. A satisfactory start.

The guests stood in a loose huddle and chatted with their hosts as the beaters made off to prepare for the next drive.

It would be a relatively complicated affair which involved "blanking in" several thick hedgerows towards an overgrown dell, the remains of an ancient chalk pit, of which there were many in the area.

Blanking consisted of beaters quietly walking the hedgerows, tapping gently, to "persuade" any hiding pheasants to run for shelter in the dell, from which they would later be flushed over the guns.

Meanwhile the guests continued their chatter, passing round hip flasks of Whisky Mac to keep out the still-chilly breeze.

At one point James Long took Benjamin to one side for a whispered conversation.

'It's about the vicar, Benjamin. He doesn't seem too sure of himself. He twice fired at birds that were obviously going over one or other of his neighbours. He doesn't seem to have grasped the etiquette. Could you have a word?'

Benjamin nodded.

'Will do. Sorry about that. We invited him as a matter of courtesy. When I asked him he said he had shot before. I'll speak to him after we've got into position for the next drive.'

It was time for the guns to make a move towards the old dell, a few hundred yards away. They set off in single file along the side of the field, with Benjamin in the lead. Robert was near the back of the line, Mr Pindle bringing up the rear.

They had progressed no more than a hundred paces when a shot rang out.

As one they stopped and turned to gaze at Mr Pindle.

Benjamin ran back to where the vicar stood sheepishly holding a smoking shotgun.

'What were you shooting at, Mr Pindle? I said all guns must be unloaded between drives. What happened?'

Mr Pindle's thin face was contorted with a mixture of confusion and embarrassment.

'I was…well, I…I was just trying to put the safety catch on.'

Benjamin gently took the gun from him, broke it open and pulled out the spent cartridge. Another live one was in the other chamber. Benjamin removed it.

'Mr Pindle, if you unload your gun when the second whistle sounds for the end of the drive, and leave the gun open, it won't need the safety catch on, will it?' Benjamin was quiet but firm.

'Do you have a gun slip?'

'No…I…no.'

'Then take mine.'

He slid his own gun from its canvas and leather carrying slip, broke it open and laid it across his left arm. He placed Mr Pindle's gun into the slip, then he physically placed the strap over the vicar's shoulder.

'We don't want a nasty accident, do we?'

He turned and it was then he saw Robert's face. It was a ghastly white.

Robert had been walking no more than ten yards in front of Mr Pindle when the gun went off. He was now pointing to a spot a few feet behind him where there was a four inch wide hole in the damp earth, steam still rising from it, where the mass of tightly packed cartridge pellets had struck.

Both brothers knew just how close Robert had come to losing a leg—or worse.

Mr Pindle looked too, and squirmed a little more.

The party continued their walk and with whispered instructions, Benjamin placed the guns in position around one end of the dell.

He had already made up his mind about Mr Pindle. He was clearly a menace. A dangerous menace.

Benjamin walked with him for eighty yards or more, away from the dell, down the side of another hedgerow. At a safe distance from the others he whispered to him that this would be his position.

'You may be lucky enough to get a woodcock come along this side of the hedge,' he confided in a stage whisper.

The whistle sounded. The drive was begun and soon there were pheasants flying out of the dell, more than a dozen. Five were added to the bag.

Even Mr Pindle managed to get a shot in.

The whistle sounded again and Benjamin walked down to retrieve the errant vicar.

'Did you do any good?' Benjamin wanted to know.

Mr Pindle was smiling. 'I think I may have done. There was a woodcock. I'm sure it was a woodcock. Came down the hedgerow as you said. I believe I got it.'

Benjamin was surprised. Normally the sight of one would have resulted in at least two or three cries of "Woodcock! Woodcock!"

'Where is it now?'

'Just in the bottom of the hedge. Over there.'

Benjamin went to look and soon returned with the pitifully mangled remains of a small brown bird.

'Not a woodcock, I'm afraid, Mr Pindle. It's a hen blackbird. Look, are you sure you're up to this?'

Mr Pindle was obviously upset.

'I think I'd better give the rest of the day a miss. I don't seem to have done very well. If it's all right with you, and won't cause too many problems, I think I'll pop off home now. I won't stop for lunch. It's only a short walk back to the farm from here. Give my apologies to the others, won't you?'

This time he checked that his gun was, indeed, unloaded, handed back Benjamin's gunslip and walked slowly off towards the farmhouse.

Mr Pindle felt wretched. He would let his newly-arrived curate, what was his name? Michael Stott, take matins on Sunday. Mr Pindle was going to have a long weekend off.

Benjamin watched him for a few seconds and wondered whether to call him back. Then decided not to and went to join the others. No-one was surprised that the vicar had left. Neither were they sorry.

Forty minutes later, after another short drive which added four more pheasants to the bag, the party was gathered in the dining room of Longdown Farm.

The now-depleted seven guns had been joined, as was the custom, by some of their womenfolk.

Lady Evelyn had arrived, accompanied by her daughter, Verity. With them was Verity's close friend and former college chum, Deborah Brandon, who was staying at the Hall. Mary Robinson and Sheila Marks were also in attendance.

Beers and gins and tonic were dispensed and the hubbub of conversation began to rise in scale.

Then Benjamin banged on the top of the oak sideboard to bring the gathering to order—and to the table. The diners brought their drinks with them to their allotted seats.

Ivy came in with a huge tureen.

No fuss with starters for this shoot lunch. Straight into a most delicious beef casserole accompanied by huge dishes of mashed swede and potato and bowls of steaming brussels sprouts. There were two big plates of fresh crusty bread and a couple of pots of butter on hand.

Benjamin, at the head of the table, found himself fairly busy replenishing drinks, although the old hands were helping themselves from several bottles of good red wine. He also found himself seated next to Deborah Brandon.

Deborah was tall and slim, her blonde hair was cut in a style that might have been considered unfashionably short for this part of rural England. It gave an impish look to her face. And it was a very pretty face.

Deborah was "down for the week" with Verity from her job in London. She was well-educated, sophisticated and came from a fairly well-to-do family.

She was also looking to improve her social status into the landed gentry while on this trip into the country. A visit to a local shoot seemed a good way of starting her campaign.

Benjamin found her conversation and attention during lunch quite stimulating.

Although obviously a "townie" she seemed genuinely interested in farming, wanting to know the acreage of Longdown, numbers in the family, and the difference between leasehold and freehold farming land.

Meanwhile, in the open-fronted implement shed outside, the beaters and pickers-up were lounging about on the straw bales Joby had placed there earlier.

The midday meal for them was sandwiches, accompanied by hot soup, ladled into cups from a huge metal saucepan brought out by Ivy from the kitchen, and bottles of beer provided by Benjamin.

Many a joke and jibe punctuated their eating and the dogs were ever-attentive, waiting for the expected scraps of discarded sandwich.

Inside the farmhouse the lunch continued with a wondrously short-crust-pastried apple pie with thick, sweet custard. There followed a cheese board, simply a huge wedge of well matured Cheddar with a variety of water biscuits, and a bowl of fresh fruit. Glasses of port followed.

Several of the men lit up cigars and the chat continued for another fifteen minutes.

At last Benjamin rose.

'Well, gentlemen…ladies and gentlemen, that is,' he corrected himself. 'Time, I'm afraid, to venture forth once again. Just two drives this afternoon but I think we can show you some pretty testing birds.'

The shooting party, augmented now by the ladies, trooped out of the farmhouse with many a word of praise for the repast.

'Splendid lunch.' 'Very good.' 'Excellent apple pie.'

Lady Evelyn took Benjamin's arm as they walked towards the vehicles. 'I shall have to have a word with Ivy. See if I can persuade her to come up to the Hall.' And as Benjamin half turned in alarm added with a wink: 'Just joking Benjamin. Although if…at any time… she is looking for a position…'

They both smiled.

Lady Evelyn let go of Benjamin's arm to join Sir Oliver and Verity.

The arm was immediately claimed again by Deborah.

'Look, Lady Evelyn's going to stand with Sir Oliver, Verity's with Tristram and I thought it might be a bit crowded tagging along with either of them. Do you mind if I join you?'

Benjamin was taken aback a little though not displeased with the idea. 'But…I shall be doing a fair bit of walking, rather than standing.'

'Fine. That suits me. I need a walk after that lunch. That's settled then.' And it was.

Meanwhile Joby had rousted his team of beaters with a 'Come on you lazy buggers. Time to get yer arses movin' again!'

The first drive after lunch once again saw Benjamin and Robert as "back guns", walking behind the line of moving beaters, while the other five were standing forward.

It was a very successful drive with more than the usual number of birds being flushed, presenting the forward guns with some fine shooting. And Benjamin was particularly pleased with himself that two cock birds which came screaming back over the treetops on the freshening breeze were each downed cleanly with a single barrel.

Deborah, who had been walking, quite correctly, slightly behind him to his left, praised him for both. A townie she might be but she knew a good shot when she saw one.

Tally for the drive was twenty-four pheasants and a woodcock, which the Squire was delighted to claim.

Final drive of the day took a while to prepare as the limited number of beaters had to blank in a couple more hedgerows before the wood itself could be driven.

Once again the guests stood in a huddle and chatted for fifteen minutes until Benjamin got them moving again to their shooting pegs.

The pattern followed that of the previous drive with Robert and Benjamin, once again accompanied by Deborah, acting as walking guns while their guests stood forward.

The line of beaters advanced slowly through the trees and undergrowth, the sound of tapping sticks punctuated with cries of "Forward!" or "Back left!".

Occasionally Joby's shouted instructions could be heard above the rest.

'Keep a straight line on y' right!'

'Bide back bit on th' left!'

'Fer Chrisakes, keep up George!'

Another good drive accounted for twenty-six pheasants and a wood pigeon.

Sixty-five pheasants from a modest farm shoot was pretty good going considering no birds were raised or released on the land.

And that didn't include the "various"—one woodcock, one pigeon and a very unlucky hen blackbird.

The party returned to the farm, where the birds were being laid out in a row by the back door, and went inside for a cup of tea and biscuits.

A number of the better, plumper birds were already tied up in pairs, one cock and one hen, and after seeing to the paying off of the beaters Joby was on hand as the guests came back out of the kitchen door.

As the guns came through he offered a brace of birds to each one with a well-timed: ''Ope you henjoyed your day, Sir.'

He was not disappointed.

As each congratulated him on the day's shooting, came the traditional handshake, leaving a crisp banknote in Joby's hand.

Five guests. Twenty-five quid. That sorted out his beer money for a few weeks to come!

The rest of the bag would be sold to a local game dealer—though not before Joby had "liberated" half a dozen for his own customers.

During tea Deborah had remained attentive to the older Trenchard brother.

Now as the guests were preparing to depart she singled Benjamin out once again.

'I've had the most exhilarating day, Benjamin. Didn't want it to end. Thank you so much for looking after me so well.'

'The pleasure was all mine. I'm sorry I couldn't give you more attention…Perhaps….'

'Yes?'

Benjamin found his confidence rising as they walked together towards the vehicles.

'Perhaps we could meet again. When we have a little more time?'

'Well I'm staying at the Hall until Saturday.'

'What about a drink one evening?' He paused for a second. 'Or dinner?' he added.

'That sounds perfect,' returned Deborah with a smile.

'Friday? I can pick you up at the Hall around, shall we say, quarter to seven?'

'Until Friday then,' replied Deborah as she climbed into the Land Rover with Tristram and Verity.

Benjamin watched and waved to them all as they departed. Then he made his way slowly back to the house.

As they drove away, Deborah settled into the rear seat of the Land Rover and Verity immediately turned to her.

'Deborah. What are you up to?' she demanded with mock severity in her voice.

'What do you mean?'

'You've been clinging to Benjamin Trenchard like a leaf all afternoon. You know what I mean.'

'He's a very attractive man. And anyway, he's asked me out to dinner on Friday evening. That is, if it's all right with you?'

'Of course it is. But Benjamin Trenchard is hardly in your league, dear. Handsome though he might be.'

'Well that's obvious. I'm looking for rather more than a few hundred acres of farmland but I thought it might be amusing. And, of course, Benjamin Trenchard does know all the other farming families, large and small, in the neighbourhood. Might be a reasonable starting point.'

Benjamin paused to turn for a final glance at the departing vehicles, then walked through the farmhouse door. Robert and Ivy were seated at the kitchen table, each with a cup of tea.

'I'll join you I think,' said Benjamin. 'Didn't get time earlier on.'

'We noticed,' said Robert. 'How did you get on with Deborah?'

'Well…I…'

'Take no notice of him,' said Ivy, rising. 'He's teasing again. You sit down while I get you a cuppa.'

'Matter of fact I'm taking her out for a meal on Friday,' announced Benjamin, a note of triumph in his voice.

'By the way, Ivy, we have to congratulate you on a terrific shoot lunch. It was very well received.' He thought for a moment and then added quietly: 'Mum and dad would have been proud.'

Ivy nodded knowingly. 'I'm glad it all came up to expectations.'

All three of them were still sitting at the kitchen table, discussing the events of the day, when Sandra came in.

As usual she was wearing old jodhpurs and a shapeless sweater. There was a streak of mud, or something even more unsavoury, down one side of her face, which she seemed not to notice.

'How was the shoot?' she asked.

'Brilliant,' returned Robert. 'And thanks to your mother all the guests departed happy and well-fed!.'

Sandra smiled as she washed her hands at the kitchen sink. Then she kicked off her riding boots by the back door. 'I must go and get cleaned up,' she said. And she disappeared upstairs.

Friday evening couldn't come quickly enough for Benjamin. The chores on the farm, mostly paperwork, dragged on. But come it did and six-thirty saw him driving towards Ashley Hall.

He had paid particular attention to his personal preparations that evening and, after his usual careful ablutions, had decided to wear a smart, dark blue suit.

He had already booked a table for two at The Grosvenor in nearby Stockbury, one of the smartest hotels in the area and one which had an especially high reputation for its restaurant.

And he had requested a quiet corner table.

This was to be a no-expenses-spared occasion.

At the Hall his ring on the front door bell was answered by Sir Oliver's butler who, appraised of his expected call, showed him into the library to wait for Deborah.

He didn't have long to wait.

In less than five minutes she appeared in the doorway.

'Hope I didn't keep you long.'

As she entered Benjamin rose from the chair he had occupied and gazed with admiration at his date for the evening.

'Not at all.'

Deborah was appealing enough in country tweeds. With the added advantages of carefully-applied make-up, well coiffured hair and a very simple black dress with a hemline just above the knee, she was a head-turner.

Over one arm she carried a short fur jacket, in the other hand a small, black evening bag. She wore black open court shoes with a slim, fairly high heel—the higher stiletto was now considered "old hat" in the London fashion circles. The shoes showed off to their best advantage a pair of very slender ankles and shapely legs.

Benjamin and Deborah came out of the library and through the front door, which was held open by the butler who had been hovering nearby. On the gravelled forecourt he opened the passenger door for Deborah, carefully closed it, walked round to the offside door and settled himself in the driver's seat.

Benjamin drove in silence down the driveway towards the road. The dark shapes of rhododendron bushes glided by as he racked his brain for a topic to open the conversation.

It was Deborah who spoke first.

'I must say I thoroughly enjoyed the shoot on Wednesday. You're something of a crack shot on the quiet, aren't you?'

Benjamin sighed with relief that the silence had been broken and was more than a little pleased with the compliment.

'The shoot isn't desperately difficult to organise. After all, it's only one day a year.'

After that the conversation flowed more easily and they soon arrived at The Grosvenor Hotel.

They found a parking space and walked together through the portico entrance into the hotel reception room.

Off to the left was the wide entrance to the restaurant, an imposing wood-panelled room. The head waiter stood at the doorway and several waitresses, clad formally in black and white, were visible beyond, moving between the pale squares that were the dining tables.

The figure at the door, in immaculate evening dress, approached them, a clipboard in one hand, a pen in the other.

'Good evening Sir,' and with a nod to Deborah, 'Madam.' He turned back to Benjamin. 'Have you booked?'

'Trenchard. Mr Trenchard. A table for two.'

The head waiter consulted his list.

'Ah yes, Mr Trenchard. We have the table you requested. Will you go straight in, or would you prefer a drink in the cocktail lounge?'

Benjamin glanced at Deborah who gave an almost imperceptible shake of her head.

'No. Thank you. We'll have a drink at the table.'

'Right Sir. Please come this way.'

He led them through the other tables to a spot near the far side. The room was barely half full but more people would be arriving over the next hour or so to fill the spaces. This was Friday night at the area's most popular—and expensive—restaurant.

On the way several diners turned to look and to admire the handsome young couple. Benjamin twice nodded in silent recognition of familiar faces, to neither of which could he immediately put a name.

They arrived at a corner table.

'Could I take Madam's fur?'

Deborah slipped the jacket from her shoulders and handed it over. The waiter took the fur over one arm while holding the chair for her to sit.

While Benjamin was seating himself their attendant beckoned the wine waiter who was to bring their drinks.

Deborah wanted a glass of dry white wine. Benjamin surprised himself by asking for a Campari and soda.

A waitress then arrived with two large, ornate menus, placing one in front of each of them and then departing.

Deborah opened hers and almost immediately gave a tiny squeal of delight at seeing the section headed "Our French Collection".

'I'm really in the mood to go Continental tonight. It seems ages since we were last in France. Though it was only last summer.'

Benjamin glanced at the prices down the right hand side and winced inwardly. Deborah's menu, of course, showed no prices at all, although it would have made small difference if it had.

Eventually she chose the *foie gras* followed by *magret de canard* with *pommes sautees*. The *Roquefort* and *tarte aux poires* would come later.
Benjamin settled for a *pate maison*, poached salmon with new potatoes and green beans and would later have a fruit *sorbet* followed by English Stilton.

The wines proved more difficult and Benjamin found himself ordering not only a good claret to complement Deborah's duck but a not-too-cheap Chablis to go with his salmon.

Although both would finish their meal with a good cognac, more than half the wine he had ordered would be left on the table.

All this was put to the back of his mind as Benjamin bent to the somewhat daunting task of keeping his companion amused.

His apprehensions, however, proved unfounded. To some extent the drink took its effect and both he, and especially Deborah, found conversation easy and relaxed.

Once more she was attentive, wanting to know even more about his family, his friends, his hobbies, his likes, his dislikes. And about other farmers in the area. Especially farmers who were also major land owners.

By the end of the meal Benjamin was beginning to believe that he had not only made a big impression on Deborah but that this evening could be the start of something bigger.

His reverie suffered something of a jolt when, finally, he was presented with the bill.

He had expected a fairly hefty punch in the wallet. He hadn't reckoned on a severe kick in the bank balance. Then he noticed the "fifteen per cent service charge", which did not appear to be optional, added at the bottom.

Benjamin had come out with about twice as much cash as he had expected to need, having given particular regard for the reputation of the place.

This bill would virtually clear him out of cash.

The head waiter came to collect the settlement.

'I trust everything was to your satisfaction Sir?'

'Perfect. Could we have the lady's coat?'

'Of course Sir.'

A waitress had already fetched the fur and as they stood at the entrance to the restaurant the head waiter helped Deborah put it round her shoulders. He gave a sickly smile and Benjamin felt bound to hand him his last remaining pound note.

Then a sudden dread flowed over him. What if Deborah suggested "going on" somewhere?

Well, he reasoned, a pound wouldn't have got them very far anyway.

He was mightily relieved when, as soon as they were in the car, she announced: 'I'm really tired, Benjamin. I hope you weren't planning to make a night of it?'

'No. No, of course not. I'll take you straight back to the Hall.'

So that was it.

She would invite him in for a drink and they could continue their little tryst.

All sorts of possibilities ran through Benjamin's mind as he drove up the gravel drive to the Hall.

He pulled up on the forecourt and they both got out of the car.

Side by side they strolled towards the front door. Under the lighted portico Deborah rummaged in her bag for the key, turned it in the lock and swung the door open.

She turned to Benjamin who all but collided with her as she stopped, halfway through the door.

'Thank you Benjamin. It's been a terrific evening. We must do it again next time I'm down. I'm afraid it won't be this side of Easter though.'

She held out her hand. 'Well, goodnight.'

He took her hand and lamely shook it.

'I…well…goodnight….'

Then she was gone and the massive studded door closed solidly behind her.

Benjamin stood for a long moment on the doorstep.

Then he turned and walked slowly back to his car. It didn't happen like this in the books.

A strangely pensive and confused Benjamin drove back to the farm.

He went through the kitchen where Ivy and Sandra, as was their custom, were chatting over a cup of tea with no more than a passing "good night" and went up to his bedroom and shut the door.

Mother and daughter once more threw each other questioning glances but said nothing.

It was barely ten o'clock but Benjamin was already exhausted and ready for sleep. Depressed and thoughtful, he sat on the edge of the bed.

He couldn't understand why, when a number of women had recently all but thrown themselves at him, tonight's encounter had ended with the door being, in effect, slammed in his face.

A sadder, wiser, and decidedly poorer, Benjamin finally dropped off to sleep.

The last two weeks of December were virtually dead as far as the sale of agricultural machinery was concerned so Reggie Broadman concentrated on delivering festive bottles of cheer to some of his most regular clients—and to the ones on whom he could rely, in a trade-in deal, for co-operation and discretion in the finance direction.

This activity led him, inevitably, into the Witherstoke area once more.

The pre-Christmas scams in which he was involved were finished or well sewn up by this time so he was also free to search for some light entertainment on the side.

It came, quite unexpectedly, at the home of one of his more shady acquaintances.

Having called at the farm, unannounced, it had been his intention to hand over a bottle of good brandy, with a nod and a wink, and the hint of further rewards in the future on completion of satisfactory purchase arrangements.

But both the farmer and his wife, it transpired, were out for the entire day.

The bonus was that Hazel, their twenty year-old daughter, was on her own in that rambling farm house with nothing more on her mind than how to find a man for the coming party season.

Hazel was not a beauty, which probably accounted for the fact that she had had a number of boy friends, mainly attracted temporarily by promises of a sexual nature, at first veiled, later more explicit.

On each occasion, after several such promises had been fulfilled, the suitor involved had decided there was not much else to keep him. And had left.

In any event, her promiscuity had resulted in Hazel acquiring something of a "local bicycle" reputation among the neighbouring male population.

Hence her difficulty in finding a steady partner.

Hazel had opened the door to Reggie's knocking and stood on the threshold, a look of surprise and delight creeping onto her face at the sight of this handsome young male.

'Yes?' she asked.

'I was looking for…is Mr Granger in?'

'No. Mum and dad are both out at the moment. Will be for some time,' added Hazel, giving Reggie a knowing sort of look.

Reggie glanced at his wrist watch. It was just after ten o'clock.

'Any idea when they'll be back? I have something for your dad.'

'They said they wouldn't be in 'til after tea. Gone to do some Christmas shopping.'

She looked at Reggie again. She recalled having seen him at the farm a couple of times earlier in the year. Meanwhile it had been weeks since she'd last had any close contact with a man and gentle stirrings were reminding her of the fact.

'Would you like to come in for a drink? I'm sure dad wouldn't mind. Not if you're a friend.'

Reggie was an expert at reading the signs.

'More of a business colleague than a friend. But thank you. That would be very acceptable.

And in he went.

Over the next hour and a half, up in Hazel's bedroom, the action was intense.

She had never had the luxury of a "home" game before, and for Reggie a comfortable bedroom, as well as a broad daylight matinee performance, proved a great turn-on—and infinitely preferable to the back seat of his car.

Hazel, it seemed, was almost insatiable and they both indulged themselves to the full.

By the time Reggie left he was weak at the knees and she was looking decidedly dealt-with.

Half an hour later, in the quiet of a country pub, Reggie was recovering over a "pint and a ploughman's".

It had been an exhausting morning. There had, of course, been the usual promises, to make contact again soon, but he was doubtful that he would want a similar session for some time to come. And anyway, Hazel gave the impression she was on the look-out for a long term relationship.

That was certainly not part of Reggie's game plan. Which was why he had decided to use the old "Clive Banham" alias. It would certainly put her off the track for a while.

Chapter eight

CHRISTMAS came and went.

For the brothers at Longdown Farm it was a busy time socially. They were invited to the homes of various neighbours for evening drinks which gave them the chance to catch up on local farming gossip.

Throughout all the festivities and socialising Benjamin kept as low a profile as he could.

He realised that there were those who may have heard how he had wined and dined the attractive young guest from the Hall and who would be eager to hear about any new developments.

But he quietly smiled away any suggested romance and simply explained the episode as a courtesy exercise.

Christmas Day itself was something of a quiet affair.

The two brothers sat down with Ivy in the spacious dining room to an excellent festive board. Roast turkey with all the trimmings, home made Christmas pudding, mince pies.

Guest for the day, as in many previous years, was "Auntie Grace" whom Robert had collected from her house in the village.

In the six years since Grace's husband had died, Peggy Trenchard had always invited her old school friend to spend Christmas day at the farm, although she had a married daughter whom she frequently visited.

Following the deaths of Peggy and Joe, the brothers had naturally decided to continue the tradition.

And of course, Joby, who had no known family of his own, was also invited.

Of Sandra there was, as yet, no sign. She had left early, as usual, for the stables and, Christmas Day or not, there were all the essential daily duties of a busy yard to be completed.

She arrived back at the farm as the pudding plates were being cleared and closed the kitchen door behind her.

'Smells good! Hope you've left some for me!'

She pulled off her riding boots by the back door and went to the dark brown eartenware sink.

'Do I have to change for dinner?' she called as she washed her hands under the running tap.

There was a chorus of response from the dining room. 'No!' 'Come and get it while it's warm.' 'Stay as you are.'

Sandra came through wearing her familiar shapeless sweater, well-worn jodhs and with thick socks on her feet. Her hair was scraped back and banded up at the back.

It is doubtful if either of the brothers had ever seen her in any other outfit.

Ivy fetched her plate and the group chatted as she tackled her Christmas dinner.

This was something of a novelty. Rarely were all four members of the household at home at mealtimes and Ivy and Sandra would normally eat separately from the brothers. With the addition of Auntie Grace and Joby it was quite a gathering.

After the meal they went through to the comfortable chairs in the big sitting room for coffee and a glass of port.

Although Benjamin and Robert half-heartedly insisted on helping with the washing up, Ivy and Auntie Grace banished them from the kitchen and got on with the job themselves.

The brothers and Sandra chatted easily until the two older women rejoined them, while Joby, feeling the effects of several glasses of unaccustomed port, half dozed in one of the generous armchairs. Then, under Grace's influence, the conversation turned to reminiscences of Christmases past.

At one point she turned to Benjamin and declared: 'It's time you found yourself a wife, my boy!'

Recalling his recent forays into the romance stakes Benjamin shuddered. Robert stifled a laugh. Ivy gave a polite smile. Sandra suppressed any reaction by biting her lip and turning away.

Getting little response from Benjamin, Grace turned her attention to Joby.

'How about you, Joby? By the way how did you get a name like that?'

The old man stirred himself, then sat upright. The snooze and the port had moved him to become a little more animated than usual.

'T'wus at school,' he at last announced.

'At school?' queried Grace.

'Me proper name's Jonathan, Jo for short. Then another lad called Jonathan, Jo for short, came to the school. We cudn't tell t'other from which when people wus talkin' to us. My mates started calling me Jo B, "B" for Bernard, me second name, and Jo B just stuck.'

Aunt Grace persisted with the interrogation.

'And didn't you ever marry?'

Both Trenchard brothers looked quickly in his direction. Grace had touched on a subject over which Joby was notoriously reluctant to speak.

The old man rubbed his chin thoughtfully. His eyes seemed to glaze over and his mind went into far-away land as a distant vision of his beloved Delpine came into his brain. When his answer came, his voice was a half whisper.

'There wus someone, once.'

All faces turned to his at this previously unknown piece of personal information.

With a slight shake of the head, Joby seemed suddenly to return to the here and now and his voice was back to normal.
'But it didn't work out,' he declared.

That was clearly the end of conversation on that topic.

It was with some relief that Robert drove Grace back home later that afternoon. The atmosphere had been getting a little sombre. He also dropped off Joby at his cottage at the end of the farm lane.

Boxing Day followed a similar pattern, except that neither Grace nor Joby was there and Ivy had produced the most delicious bubble-and-squeak to go with the cold turkey.

In the sitting room afterwards the chat was much lighter. Sandra regaled them with some hilarious anecdotes from her experiences at the stables and frequent laughter made the evening altogether sunnier.

Later that night it began to snow.

It snowed heavily, on and off, over the next four or five days, every fresh fall adding to the problems already being experienced for transport and communications throughout the country.

It had stopped snowing on New Year's Eve. By next morning, the first day of 1963, a bright sun in a cloudless blue sky shone on a white blanketed Britain.

The Trenchards had invested in snow clearing equipment and, with snow ploughs fixed to the front of the tractors, kept the farm lane open.

It wasn't long before they got the expected call from the county council.

In common with a number of local farmers they had an agreement to assist the highway authority during severe winter weather by keeping some of the minor public roads passable.

Their help was needed now.

There was very little new snow but during the next few weeks the whole region was gripped by an intense freeze-up. Temperatures barely struggled up to freezing point during the day and each night brought the mercury plunging to record sub-zero readings.

Brisk winds drifted the fallen snow back into the lanes and the Trenchard brothers were out most days keeping the byways open.

Villagers cursed the lack of buses, the problems of getting to and from work. Some vehicles did manage to travel over the hard-packed snow on the road surfaces of the major roads, especially the ones fitted with chains on the rear wheels.

It was a time for the children.

Even when the new year term began, no school buses were running and, to cap it all, the heating system at Binfield School collapsed completely under the strain.

School was well and truly "out" and it would be a week at least before the pupils could be recalled.

They made the most of it.

There were children sliding on the ice of frozen ponds and, where there was no available water, they made slides on the nearest patch of frosty ground. When school did eventually resume they would create more slides on the concrete surface of the school's netball court.

And toboggans appeared everywhere.

The Trenchard's field nearest the village, appropriately known by local youngsters as "The Mound", had always been considered the prime spot for sledging.

The winter revellers now arrived by the score, using the snow to build ever more adventurous jumps and ridges on the hillside for their toboggans to negotiate.

The toboggans themselves were a wonder to behold.

Just one or two kids had shop-bought models but mostly they were home made.

Here and there a more sturdy one knocked up by an obliging parent but mainly pieces of wood nailed roughly together. There was one young lad using a large tin tray from home. Another had a length of corrugated iron, bent up at the front. Yet another was using the broken-off back and legs of an old dining room chair!

All this gadgetry was in use from dawn to dusk, being pulled up the slope on lengths of twine to come careering down again with anything up to four youngsters on board, hanging on grimly, their shrieks echoing over the silent countryside.

Broken toboggans received slope-side running repairs and were soon in use again.

Knees and hands red raw with the wet and cold, failed to dampen the enthusiasm of the sledgers. They went home sore and aching each night and were back for more straight after breakfast next day.

On the first morning that school reopened Benjamin was driving his tractor, snow plough fitted to the front, steadily along School Lane. Just a quick tidying up job before lessons started.

There was still half an hour to go before the children were due to arrive but he very soon caught up with a figure plodding along the side of the snow-packed road.

The figure stepped aside to let him pass.

As he came up level he saw that it was the new school teacher.

She turned to face the tractor, missed her footing and stumbled, half falling into the snow piled high at the edge of the road where the verge should have been.

The new teacher was wearing a thick coat, woollen hat, large multi-coloured scarf wound several times around her neck and a pair of ridiculously short rubber boots, hardly more than galoshes.

She managed a weak smile at Benjamin as she tried to pick herself up from the pile of snow at the roadside.

He at once hauled on the handbrake, threw the tractor out of gear and jumped down, striding over to bend and help her up.

'Are you all right?'

'Yes. I think so. A bit damp that's all.'

'You're the new school teacher aren't you? Can I give you a lift to school?'

'Well…'

'Come on, jump up. Have you there in no time.' He helped her climb up onto the tractor then took the driving seat and with his passenger hanging on behind him drove the two hundred yards to the school.

He switched off the engine, jumped to the ground and helped her dismount.

They stood beside the tractor just outside the school gate.

'I can't thank you enough. By the way, I'm not all that new. I've been teaching in Binfield since last September. I'm Jean Blythe.'

She held out a hand and he shook it.

'Sorry…I mean, I'm Benjamin Trenchard. I mean sorry I forced you into the snow like that.'

'Not your fault at all. I usually cycle to school but today I thought two feet would be safer than two wheels. Seems I was wrong.'

There was a moment's silence.

'Do you do this for a living? I mean, what happens when it doesn't snow?'

'Good Lord, no. I'm a farmer. We only help out the county council when the weather gets really bad. No, Longdown Farm takes up all my time normally.'

Her eyes lit up a little.

'Look I have to go. Setting up for the children. They're back today. Perhaps we'll meet again?'

It was a question rather than a statement.

'Perhaps we may.'

They said goodbye and she turned, tramped through the snow up to the school door, gave a wave and disappeared inside.

That evening in the farm sitting room Benjamin sat reading a newspaper when Robert came in.

The younger brother slumped into an armchair and picked up a farming magazine. For once he wasn't "out on the town" or at least, not until later.

Benjamin was the first to speak.

'Have you met the new school teacher?'

'No. But I've heard she's surprisingly average.'

It would have been remarkable if Robert had known nothing at all about a new, eligible female in the village.

'Well I suppose she is, really.'

Robert sat up, his interest aroused.

'You've met her then?'

'Yes. Saw her this morning while I was clearing School Lane.'

Benjamin went on to describe his encounter with Miss Blythe.

'And?'

'And what?'

'What happened? What's she like?'

'Nothing happened.'

'What's she like then?'

'Well, average height, dark hair, wears glasses, average figure. From what I could see, that is. Quiet. Well…you're right. She's…well. Average.'

'Any chance of any developments? I mean, you and her?'

'No. Of course not. It was just a chance meeting. She seems nice enough. Nothing to write home about. I'll probably never speak to her again.'

But Benjamin was wrong.

One evening towards the end of January she rang the farm.

Benjamin, who was in the farm office at the time, answered the phone.

'Benjamin? It's Jean. Jean Blythe.'

'Oh…hullo…how are you?'

'Look, I didn't get the chance to thank you properly for being my knight in shining armour. I looked up your number in the phone book. I hope you didn't mind?'

'No. No of course not.'

'The thing is…I wonder. Would you like to be my guest? I've got two tickets for the music recital next week. At the Guildhall in Witherstoke. I didn't know who to invite. It's nothing too highbrow….'

The words came flooding out as though they had been well rehearsed (which they had) and as if the speaker wanted to get the whole thing done as soon as possible (which was also true).

'I'm sorry. I wanted to thank you properly. You must think I've got an awful cheek ringing you like this.'

'Not at all.'

Benjamin thought for a moment.

Jean Blythe wasn't bad company. Intelligent. Not bad looking.

'What day are we talking about?'

'Thursday. Next Thursday evening. Seven thirty.' She paused. 'It's a string quartet, a solo pianist and a soprano and tenor. I'm not sure what your tastes in music are?'

It sounded a little bit up market for Benjamin but he was not averse to a little light classical music.

He made one of those instant decisions which you always hope you're not going to regret.

'Yes. All right. That's very kind of you. Shall I pick you up? What about a quarter to seven?'

'Wonderful! I shall look forward to it.'

There seemed to be little more to say, so after exchanging information about her address they rang off.

Robert, who had been expecting a call himself, was hovering in the hallway outside the office when Benjamin came out.

'What was all that about?'

'It was Jean Blythe. You know, the new school teacher. Seems she feels she owes me a favour after our meeting the other week. She's invited me to go to a music recital with her.'

The explanation came out easily and casually, as if it was no big deal to be going out with Jean Blythe which, as far as he was concerned, it wasn't.

'I thought you said there was nothing in it?'

'There isn't. The lady is just grateful for a lift to school and she's treating me to an evening out. That's all there is to it.'

'Huhoo. You want to watch these quiet ones. Get their claws into you before you know it they do.'

And Robert chuckled, his eyes twinkling.

'Don't be so daft,' was Benjamin's only retort.

Thursday came.

Half past six found Benjamin on his way to collect Miss Blythe who lodged with an elderly widow in a substantial detached house at the far end of the lane from the school.

Jean Blythe had been ready for half an hour or more.

Although perfectly at ease with the children in class, she was still, at times, quite painfully shy with strangers and it had taken all her courage to telephone Benjamin Trenchard.

Now here she was, about to go out for the evening with one of the district's most eligible young men.

She could scarcely believe her own boldness.

Jean Blythe was aware that, at twenty-eight, she might have been considered by some in these modern 'Sixties, to be all but "on the shelf".

Benjamin rang the front door bell of the ivy-covered house and had only seconds to wait. Jean Blythe answered the ring and was ready to go.

They exchanged brief and rather shy 'hullos' and he escorted her to the waiting car.

At first their journey was in silence.

'No more snow…' 'How's the new term…' they both began simultaneously, then each stopped just as abruptly.

'Sorry…you….' 'No, what were you saying?'

They both laughed and somehow the atmosphere warmed. Soon they were chatting almost like old friends.

They arrived at the hall in Witherstoke and parked the car. The night was dry and not too cold as they walked the short distance to the entrance.

Inside they handed in their coats at the cloakroom, found their allotted seats and settled down.

Benjamin glanced around. There was a good attendance but apart from one or two faces that he seemed to have seen before, he saw nobody he knew well.

It was a good evening.

Benjamin was not on naming terms with all he heard but found most of the melodies familiar.

Pieces from Handel, Vivaldi and Mozart. Debussy's "Clair de Lune". These were interspaced with performances from the vocalists who included numbers from "Oklahoma" and "South Pacific" in their repertoire. They also performed a selection from the new 'modern' musical film "West Side Story".

During the short interval Benjamin and Jean had a drink and chatted politely about the programme.

Afterwards, with the time past ten o'clock, Benjamin suggested another drink at a Witherstoke hotel but Jean said she thought they should be getting back.

On the journey home they chatted for a while but were mostly silent.

At the house Benjamin went round and opened the door for his passenger then walked with her up to the front porch.

It was an awkward time.

Benjamin, quite truthfully, said how much he had enjoyed the evening. Jean was shy and simply replied 'Oh…good.'

Then she turned her key in the lock.

'Well…goodnight.'

'Goodnight,' returned Benjamin.

As he went to shake her hand she suddenly stretched up and planted a kiss on his cheek.

'I've enjoyed tonight as well, Benjamin,' she said. And then, as if overtaken by another bout of bravery, added: 'Perhaps we could do something like this again soon?'

'Why not?' Benjamin heard himself say.

The door closed and he was walking alone back down the path to the car.

Over the next three weeks they went out together twice more. Once to the cinema, at Jean Blythe's suggestion, to see a rather obscure film and once for drinks with another couple, former college friends of hers, who were visiting the area.

By the second week in February Jean Blythe was telephoning Benjamin two or three times a week.

And Benjamin was beginning to feel a little uncomfortable.

It was something he couldn't quite put his finger on.

Their evenings together were enjoyable enough, intelligent conversation, a few laughs, although they always ended the same way with a peck on the cheek at the front door of her lodgings.

But on the way home from their last meeting she had raised the subject of families.

Not mothers and uncles and brothers and cousins. But children.

Quite out of the blue she had asked: 'Do you want a family, Benjamin? Children of your own, I mean?'

His brain went numb. It was a subject he had really not thought that much about.

'Well...I suppose eventually. Yes. Everyone wants a family. I suppose.'

'Me too,' she had replied. 'But I do really believe in saving the physical side of a relationship until the right moment. For creating a proper family within a stable marriage. Don't you?'

'Well...yes...'

He was at a loss for anything else to say.

'I'm so glad we agree,' she had said.

And the subject of the possibility of a physical relationship outside of marriage became a closed book.

It was at their next meeting, when she led their conversation around to asking what were his views on formal white weddings and whether wives should or should not work that mild uneasiness began to creep in.

And when the telephone calls to the farm began to come ever more frequently the moment finally arrived when Benjamin's brain hit the panic button.

An easy-going and relatively casual friendship with a not unattractive member of the opposite sex was one thing.

Being railroaded down the aisle was something entirely different.

Next morning in the milking parlour he confided in Robert.

His brother's reaction was not exactly unexpected.

After he had finished laughing, or rather while he was still trying to stop laughing, Robert gasped out: 'I told you the quiet ones will always try to get their hooks into you. Poor old Benny. You've really got yourself landed.'

'The thing is, what do I do now?' Benjamin wanted to know. 'You must have been in this sort of situation enough times.'

'Tell her you're not the marrying kind. Weddings are not on the agenda,' said Robert. 'Make it clear. Tell her straight. She'll try the old sympathy-tug-at-your-conscience approach. Burst into tears, perhaps rant and rave a bit. Call you a heartless cad and a rotter, but it's the only way.'

Benjamin had hoped there was a less painful alternative. He hated confrontation of any kind but deep inside he knew that Robert was right.

'But how do I DO it? I mean. Without all the upset?'

'You can't,' was Robert's blunt reply.

There seemed no way round the problem. Benjamin instinctively knew that simply trying to cool down the friendship was not going to work.

He could feel the mother of all bust-ups coming along.

As usual with family problems, Robert, who worked virtually all day every day with Joby, had passed on the essence of this conversation to the old man, and the solution, when it came, was both quick and unexpected.

That is, it came from an unexpected quarter.

It was one late afternoon during the following week. Benjamin was out, collecting Auntie Grace from the railway station in Witherstoke after a visit to her daughter, Robert was in the implement shed, clearing up after a little repair job, Ivy was away at the village Post Office and Sandra, of course, was at the stables.

Joby was alone in the farmhouse kitchen, where he had gone to hang up the key to the tool locker on its customary hook when the phone rang.

It was clear to Joby that nobody else was about so he went through to the hallway and picked up the phone. He'd never used the instrument before.

Joby's tentative ''ullo' was answered by Jean Blythe's 'Oh, Benjamin…?' but then Joby quickly broke in.

'No, no. T'ain't Mr Trenchard. It's Joby.'

There was slight pause.

'I do beg your pardon. Is Mr Trenchard there? It's Jean. Jean Blythe.'

'Oh, 'ullo Miss Blythe. No, he ain't here at the moment.'

There was another pause and then he added: ''E's out with Grace.'

There was a much longer pause.

'Grace?'

'Yes, Grace Cope. They're old friends. Ain't 'e never mentioned Grace?'

Joby knew he was treading on very dangerous ground but he was guessing that Auntie Grace had never entered into their conversations and he was right.

'No. No, he hasn't. Are they....?'

'Well,' went on Joby, now getting into his stride. ''E and Grace have known each other for yers an' yers. They've always 'ad a sort of…well…understanding…about their cernection. G'd Lord, 'ave I said somethin' I shouldn't oughter 'ad?'

So far Joby had not exactly told any out and out lie. He hadn't told the whole truth but he hadn't lied.

There was an even longer pause from Jean Blythe.

It was Joby who broke the silence.

'Can I take a message then?'

'No…uh. No…no message.'

And she hung up.

Two days later Benjamin received a rather curt little letter breaking off what Jean Blythe described as 'our unofficial engagement.'

It mentioned, among other things, his deceit at failing to tell her about Grace and praising Joby for having the good sense to spare her further humiliation.

Benjamin cornered Joby in the yard.

'What's all this about?' he demanded, waving the letter in the old man's face.

'Wha's what about Mr Trenchard?'

Benjamin read him relevant parts of the letter.

Joby explained how Jean Blythe had rung while he was out, picking up Auntie Grace. How nobody else was around to answer the phone and, more or less how the conversation had gone.

'She must 'ave misunderstood me,' he said, a huge smile on his face.

'If you've been telling a pack of lies…'

'I swears to God I ain't told nobody no lies,' cut in Joby. There was still a wide grin on his face. 'It worked though, didn't it?' he added with a chuckle.

'Why didn't you tell me before?'

'Well, she said 'as 'ow there weren't no message.'

Benjamin stormed off.

Well, he appeared to storm off.

In reality he was mightily relieved at the outcome of the incident.

The hole he had inadvertently dug for himself had been neatly filled in and tidied up by Joby. The association with Jean Blythe was well and truly over, as emphasised by the final sentence of her note: "Please do not try to contact me again."

Benjamin should have been happy. In many ways he was. But the spectre of yet another failed relationship played heavily on his mind.

It was in this frame of mind that, one Saturday evening in early March, he was sitting in his room, reading, or at least flicking through, a farming magazine and contemplating his future.

The house was empty, or so he supposed.

At least Robert was out on one of his 'hot dates' and Sandra had mentioned earlier that she was going straight from work for an evening out with the other employees at the stables.

Benjamin had helped himself several times from his personal whisky bottle over the past hour and, though by no means drunk, was feeling decidedly relaxed. The downside was that he was becoming more and more melancholy.

His mind went back over the past few months. To the dreadful Erica at the party last year. To Molly from the pub. To Kate, the nymphomaniac reporter. To Deborah, who cost so much for so little. And to the thankful escape from Jean Blythe.

His depression deepened.

Benjamin sat on the edge of his bed and buried his head in his hands. Without realising it, he suddenly found himself crying.

At first the sobs were silent, then, as all his frustration began to pour from him, so did his tears.

His shoulders heaved and emotion took control, his sobbing growing louder every second.

Then there was a gentle tap on the bedroom door.

Ivy's voice came softly.

'Benjamin? Is everything all right. Benjamin?'

He had no time to reply as the latch lifted, the door edged ajar and Ivy's worried face appeared in the opening.

'Benjamin. What on earth's the matter?'

He was startled. And very embarrassed. His already red face turned a deeper shade of crimson.

'Ivy…I thought. It's nothing. Really. It's…it's just…'

She opened the door, walked straight in and sat on the bed beside Benjamin.

Ivy, with a quiet evening in, had been having a long, relaxing hot bath. Hence Benjamin's belief, because of the silence, that the house was empty.

She had climbed out of the bath, dried herself, put on a thick white towelling bathrobe and, hair still pinned up loosely as she'd arranged it to keep it out of the water, came out of the bathroom to return to her own room along the passage. That was when she'd heard the sound of Benjamin sobbing.

Ivy put her arm around Benjamin's shoulder, her other hand held her bathrobe front together.

'Whatever's the trouble? I've never seen you like this. Can I help?'

Nobody had ever seen Benjamin like this. All his frustrations and disappointments had been bottled up for years. He'd never confided in a soul. Now Ivy became a surrogate mother, mother confessor and counsellor all rolled into one.

Without really meaning to, Benjamin told his sorry tale.

At first he blurted out his woes. Then, the more he said the easier it became, assisted in some measure by the relaxing influence of the alcohol he had consumed.

All the while Ivy listened intently, cradling his dark head in her arms, nodding occasionally, patting his shoulder and murmuring words of consolation and encouragement.

At last Benjamin was through and he almost collapsed with exhaustion and relief, his face nestled against Ivy's generous bosom.

Then she began to speak, softly, with that delightful country burr.

'You've really had a bad time Benjamin. But believe me everything will turn out fine in the end.'

Ivy herself was well versed in taking the disappointments and heartaches that life had to offer.

'It seems that some people have to suffer, and get knocked about a bit, before things go right. And it's funny, you know, those people who get things too easy don't fully appreciate the good times.'

A thick lock of her chestnut hair fell across Benjamin's face and she carefully brushed it aside.

'I believe the more pain you have to bear, the better the rewards. 'Take that old oak tree outside the front door. Last autumn it was covered with thousands of acorns, did you notice? Where are they now? There should be at least hundreds of little oak trees growing by now.'

Benjamin's brow furrowed into a frown of non comprehension.

'But there aren't, are there?' Ivy continued.

'And why?'

She continued without waiting for a reply.

'Because most of them fell straight down onto the grass. They had it easy. But they got eaten by the chickens, squirrels, everything else that eats acorns. Those that did grow got cut down by the mower.

'But the ones that bounced on the branches on the way down and got thrown over under the hedge, then got trampled on by the cows or somebody's boot, they are the ones that are growing now. They might not have had a good start but that's where the tiny saplings are growing now, right under the hedge.'

Benjamin looked up at her. It seemed a bit complex but she was basically correct. He nodded and smiled. She bent her head and kissed him lightly on the lips.

He responded. His head was now resting against her almost uncovered breast. She smelt soapy and clean. More of her thick silky hair fell over his face.

They kissed again, still gently but with a little more intensity.

What happened next was neither planned nor foreseen by either of them.

They were already sitting on the bed.

Then they were lying on the bed in each others' arms.

Neither of them would later remember when the towelling robe or Benjamin's clothing were discarded or when their mutual yearning for physical and mental consolation turned into love making.

What both would remember was that each had had a deep need fulfilled. And it seemed then, and always would, to have been a perfectly natural and beautiful experience.

Afterwards they lay snuggled together beneath the bed covers. Ivy's long thick hair, with hardly a strand of grey yet to be seen, had shaken out and was spread across the pillow. Her eyes were open, but misty and content.

Benjamin lay in silence, his eyes closed.

After a quarter of an hour he fell into a deep sleep.

Ivy carefully raised herself and, without disturbing him, slid out of the bed. She retrieved her bathrobe, slipped it on, switched off the bedside lamp and left, quietly closing the bedroom door behind her.

Benjamin slept like the proverbial log.

He woke feeling better than he had done for months. Then recollection began to dawn. At first he firmly believed that the whole episode had been a dream.

He washed and dressed. It was Sunday morning and, as usual, Ivy would be preparing a fried breakfast.

Downstairs, Robert was sitting at the kitchen table, knife and fork poised, about to start.

Sandra, naturally, had already left for the stables after snatching a slice of toast.

As Benjamin walked in, Ivy was leaning against the sink, chatting with Robert, a mug of tea in her hand.

Everything looked normal but Benjamin had the overpowering feeling that all of them, indeed the whole of Binfield must by now have been discussing last night's events.

'Ivy…I…'

She cut in.

'One egg or two, Benjamin?'

'Oh. Two please…I…'

'Tea or coffee?'

'Coffee…I…'

'Come on then. Sit yourself down. Won't be long. What are you two up to today?'

Breakfast passed as all Sunday breakfasts do.

No word about last night was uttered. No inferences. No meaningful looks or knowing smiles.

It was as if nothing had ever happened.

Almost three months had passed since Reggie Broadman had been in the area. He'd had enough to cope with at home with family and friends during the Christmas break and then business in his home patch had started to pick up.

There was also the worrying little whisper on the grapevine a few weeks earlier that a certain farmer's daughter had discovered the distinct possibility that she could be in an embarrassing condition.

Still, he reckoned, that was her problem.

He had steered completely clear of a chance meeting in that part of the locality but the Witherstoke area was, in a number of ways, too rewarding to abandon entirely and anyway, as he rightly calculated, neither Hazel nor her father had connected him with the mysterious "Clive".

Now he was looking for business again. Any business that would turn in profit or pleasure, preferably in that order, but he was not too fussy. Ideally there should be a bit of both.

There was still the promising little potential for some ready cash to be made out of the careful "redistribution" of agricultural fuel oil. Ever since the Suez Crisis produced a shortage there had been a healthy black market among those willing to pay for illegally obtained petrol.

It would need a very delicate approach. After all, it wouldn't do to have the Inland Revenue getting too interested in his activities. But then "delicate" was one of Reggie's specialities.

And he prepared to put the next part of his plan into action.

For some time Reggie had been planning to get a new motor. Well, not a new one, that was still a bit out of his financial reach, but something more up market from his aging Vauxhall.

At an ever-so-slightly seedy second hand car sales site, in a side street just down the road from Witherstoke station, Reggie had seen the very thing.

A two-year-old Ford Zephyr Six, complete with chrome trim, spotlights, sun visor and white wall tyres.

The bonuses were obvious.

Doing a decent trade-in—and he was top notch in that department—would not only result in his obtaining a vehicle more befitting his self-supposed standing in society, but would bring him into direct contact with a not exactly whiter than white car dealer, with clear possibilities of a tie-up in the intended fuel scam.

In addition, there was a rather tasty looking black-haired female who appeared to work part-time in the dealer's office. Another possibility to be considered!

So, late the following afternoon, Reggie was driving away from Witherstoke in a flashy new car.

He was well satisfied.

The dark-haired beauty in the sales office had turned out to be the dealer's very bored and frustrated wife who was fed up with her husband spending most of his time, including evenings and weekends, a telephone glued to his ear, "doing deals".

She had jumped at the chance of a bit of innocent fun and had agreed to meet him the next night "just for a drink".

It would have to be well out of town. But what a chance to "christen" the new motor!

Chapter nine

THROUGHOUT the next two or three weeks Benjamin waited anxiously for the dreadful revelation, that awful moment of truth, to arrive.

It didn't.

Life at Longdown Farm went on as normal and after a while he began to feel more comfortable.

It was clear that neither Robert nor Sandra suspected a thing and it seemed that Ivy had no intention of telling them.

As March became April there were other things to occupy their attention.

One of the highlights of the early Spring calendar locally was the point-to-point races organised by the local hunt and held in a part of the parkland of Ashley Hall.

Traditionally it was held on Easter Monday Bank Holiday and regularly attracted virtually the entire rural population from many miles around, as well as several thousand residents from the town of Witherstoke who streamed out into the countryside by bus, car, bicycle, and even on foot, to enjoy a day at the races.

The Trenchards had never been particularly avid followers of the Mid-Wessex Hunt but had always retained the keen interest of a farming family in all field sports. This year there was an added interest for the Longdown household.

Sandra was booked to ride one of the entries in the Ladies' Open Race.

Through her job at the riding stables she had been asked to exercise an energetic young hunter owned by one of the farmers over whose land the hunt met, although she had rarely ridden to hounds.

The farmer, who was happy to attend the meets, and thereby qualify his horse for the point-to-point, had decided he was now too old to take part in the rough and tumble of race riding and had asked Sandra if she would like to take the ride in the Ladies' Open.

She eagerly accepted.

The day of the races arrived.

There had been a fair amount of rain over the previous week but Bank Holiday Monday dawned bright and clear and looked set for a fine spring day. A warm breeze was drying the ground and the going for the racing would be perfect.

The first race was at 2pm but the parkland course began to fill from mid-morning with vehicles taking up much of the centre of the great oval racetrack and more piling into the overflow car parks at one end of the course.

By midday the picnics were in full swing.

There were farm and country workers with their families, many of whom had walked to the races. They sprawled out on any convenient area of grass, tucking into cheese and pickle sandwiches and swigging bottles of beer, their children screaming with delight over lemonade and packets of crisps.

In the more expensive car parks around the finishing post, the boots of Bentleys and the backs of Land Rovers were flung open to disgorge proper picnic tables, gingham table cloths, wicker hampers, china tableware, silver cutlery, cold game and raised pork pies, whole hams, Stilton cheeses and, of course, bottles of Champagne.

As the alcohol took effect, voices grew louder and pleasantries were exchanged in ever increasing decibels.

Meanwhile thousands continued to crowd into the public area inside the course. The beer tent was doing a roaring trade—as were the ice cream sellers and the hotdog stands.

The atmosphere of the whole park was like that of an enormous fairground.

With half an hour still to go before the opening race, crowds were already thronging around the dozen or so bookmakers who had set up their stalls close to the makeshift, rope-circled parade ring where the first of the eight entrants in the opener were being walked round.

Even more were pressing three and four deep against the ropes of the paddock, eager to assess the potential of the runners.

Knowing faces studied every move of the animals.

Less knowing ears tried to pick up snatches of whispered conversation between the "experts".

Know-nothings looked for the number card tied on the stable lad's arm to see if it was a lucky one.

As the horses were being mounted and starting to make their way out of the parade ring, Joby Fulbright had made his choice.

Muttering "Royal Chief, Royal Chief" to himself, he elbowed his way through the milling punters around the bookies' stands and looked up at the board immediately in front of him. "Alf Barnes" said the name on the board.

The favourite was little better than evens. Just 11-10. Royal Chief was joint second favourite at 3-1.

Joby pulled a face of total disgust.

'Bloody daylight robbery,' he complained.

Alf Barnes, standing on a box beside the board, was a big, red faced, even redder nosed, character.

'D'yuh want a bet or not,' he demanded.

'Not at your prices,' returned Joby. 'Gis fours on Royal Chief and I might change me mind.'

'How much you betting?'

'A tanner.'

Alf Barnes threw back his head and bellowed a laugh. Then he looked back down at Joby, a smile still on his face.

Nobody else seemed to be in a hurry to bet.

'Give us it 'ere,' he suddenly said. And to his book keeper behind the stand called: 'Two bob to a tanner, number 147.'

He took Joby's sixpenny piece and chucked it into the huge leather satchel at his side, almost in the same motion handing him a small white ticket with the number 147 printed on it.

Joby elbowed his way back out of the crowd, his look of disgust replaced by an expression of joy.

'Under starter's orders…They're off!' came the tinny voice over the loud speaker system and the day's racing had begun.

Royal Chief was well in contention through two circuits of the course and surged into the lead as the field rounded the bottom turn and came up the final straight with two jumps to take. He soon had all but the favourite struggling in his wake.

Over the last. Just a couple of hundred yards to go.

Then the favourite rallied. As the winning post approached, Royal Chief's lead was being whittled away. He seemed to be running on the spot.

Only yards to go and the favourite was almost upsides. They flashed across the winning line together.

With no photo-finish facilities it was up to the judge to decide the outcome.

It was some minutes before the metallic voice on the tannoy announced the result.

'First, past the post, number six, Royal Chief...' the rest of the announcement was lost in the combined roars of relief and shouts of disbelief. '...the distances a short head and ten lengths.'

Joby was first in the queue for Alf Barnes.

His upturned leathery face was wreathed in a gap-toothed grin.

'Told yuh that favourite weren't no use. 'Bout as much good as a chocolate teapot!'

Alf Barnes looked down at Joby.

'You'll be the ruination of me,' he laughed.

At that moment the announcer's voice came wavering again on the afternoon air. 'Weighed in.'

Joby handed up his ticket.

'147!' called out Alf Barnes.

''alf a dollar,' returned his bookman.

Alf Barnes pressed a shining half crown into Joby's hand.

Joby spat on it and slipped it into his trouser pocket. Not a bad return for sixpence. And he pushed his way out of the crush to have a look at the runners in the next race.

Benjamin had driven Ivy to the race course in almost total silence. Sandra had gone on much earlier in the horse box with her intended ride and Robert was playing host to another of his many dates.

It was the first time Benjamin and Ivy had been alone together since, well, since that fateful night.

The atmosphere in the car on the way to the races was tense.

'You're very quiet, Benjamin,' Ivy ventured at last as they approached the entrance to the race course.

'Yes…I was….'

In truth, Benjamin was at a total loss for anything to say.

'Do you mind if I say something?' asked Ivy.

'No. No of course not.'

'I know you've been stewing inside over the past few weeks. I just want to say that you are a very thoughtful, gentle person. You've nothing at all to worry about. Not in any respect. Or to blame yourself for. Let's agree that the matter is closed.'

She reached over and patted the back of his hand.

Benjamin heaved a sigh of relief.
'Thank you, Ivy…I…'

'Shh…Not a word. It's closed.'

And it was.

'Now. Let's get on with the races shall we?'

He smiled. She smiled back. Then they both laughed and all traces of the earlier tension disappeared.

Benjamin parked the car in the central "expensive" area and they made their way on foot through the gathering crowds towards where all the action was taking place.

After his earlier success on the first race, things were not going so well for Joby.

Two more races had brought him no further winners and a shilling of his half crown had already made its way back into Alf Barnes's leather satchel.

No need for any of the Longdown contingent to study form for the fourth race. This was the ever popular Ladies' Open and the natural bet would have to be Sandra riding Charlie's Darling.

The riders, fourteen of them, mounted up and made their way out of the paddock and around to the starting post.

Sandra, riding her first ever race, looked serious as they went down to the start but her attention was fully occupied with keeping her horse under control.

Charlie, a six-year-old chestnut with a big white blaze, was really on his toes, tossing his head and taking a keen interest in everything that was going on. He certainly looked a picture but, as an unknown quantity, the bookies were offering odds of ten to one.

Benjamin came up to the bookies in time to smile as he watched Joby once more try his trick on Alf Barnes. Alf, however, was having none of it and refused to give better than tens. This time a whole shilling went on.

Then Robert and his escort, a lanky redhead in boots, Barbour and wide-brimmed hat, hove into view and the five of them made their way together to a point where they could see the "off" and most of the course, including the winning post, as well.

Benjamin had placed a five shillings each way bet for Ivy. He himself, in his only real bet of the afternoon, had invested five pounds "on the nose".

'All or nothing,' he had laughed.

The tinny voice came through the loudspeakers.

'Under starter's orders…They're off.'

They got away to a pretty even break and the runners were held to a respectable gallop as, in a tight bunch, they made their way down to the first.

People lining the inside of the course, craning over the single restraining rope for a closer view, took a collective, involuntary step backwards as the group thundered by just a few feet away, hooves thudding and clods flying.

Sandra had "buried" Charlie, who at the start was pulling a bit much for his own good, somewhere in the middle of the field of runners.

That steadied him and he bowled happily along with the rest of the field.

They all took the first at a sensible pace and Charlie, ears pricked, who had never galloped in so much company at such close quarters before, seemed to be enjoying himself.

The field, with the exception of one horse which was obviously having some kind of a problem and began to fall back, continued throughout the first circuit in fairly close order.
As they started into the second circuit the favourite upped the pace appreciably and moved into a two lengths lead.

The others responded but at the next fence two runners came crashing down under the increasing pressure.

Sandra had Charlie in about fifth spot by this time and it was clear he was travelling easily and jumping like a stag.

The pace quickened again as they went into the final circuit and by now the field was being well and truly strung out.

The favourite still led by four lengths from the second horse which was beginning to come under pressure. Charlie was still bowling along just half a length further back, Sandra, her face set, sitting still as a statue.

Round the bottom turn they raced. Three fences to jump and Sandra pushed Charlie up into second place, still three lengths down on the favourite which was also going easily and seemed to have only to jump the fences to have his race won.

Up the final hill and into the second last Charlie made up another length and began to move ever closer.

Between the last two the favourite's rider snatched a glance round at the opposition and surprise clearly showed in her face to find Sandra and Charlie so close.

She got to work on her horse and drove him hard at the last.

He took it well.

But Charlie, matching him almost stride for stride, was in the air with him and only half a length down. Their hind hooves hissed through the top of the birch fence as one continuous sound.

Now the favourite's jockey could hear the only other horse in contention and could see him from the corner of her eye.

The roar of the crowd, rising to a crescendo, was urging their chosen favourite to greater exertions and with the winning post just two hundred yards away his rider roused him with hands, legs and whip.

Sandra gave Charlie two smart slaps, which startled him, then pushed him out hands and heels towards the line.

He surged ahead and sailed past the post nearly a full length to the good.

Most of the crowd was stunned to silence at the unexpected defeat of the favourite.

But one small section of onlookers went wild with delight.

Old Joby was almost beside himself with glee.

Benjamin and Ivy, Robert and the redhead, who had all been screaming encouragement as Sandra and Charlie came scorching up the run-in, now flung their arms around each other and danced about madly.

Joby, his face split by an even wider grin than before, headed off immediately for the bookies.

The other four hurried over to the unsaddling area of the parade ring to applaud as the victorious duo was led into the winner's enclosure.

Sandra, back slumped and breathing heavily, was exhausted but her face, though spattered with mud, was a picture of happiness as she acknowledged the cheers and congratulations of a delighted band of friends and connections.

The owner, hat in hand, led his horse in, his face scarlet from a combination of vocal exertion and pleasure.

Joby, meanwhile, was once again first in the queue in front of Alf Barnes's stand when the magic words "weighed in" were announced.

And it was a decidedly less jocular Alf Barnes who handed him his returns.

A ten shilling note and a shilling piece.

Ivy's winnings came to a very welcome three pounds, twelve shillings and sixpence.

Robert and his friend added nearly another ten pounds to the total. Benjamin picked up an extremely healthy £55.

The rest of the meeting, another two races, was virtually forgotten by the contingent from Longdown. Even old Joby declined to trouble the bookies again. So flushed was he with his success that the next hour was taken up with telling and retelling the story to friends and acquaintances. In fact, anyone who would listen.

Later, they all met up again for celebrations in The Drovers Arms where the happy owner was lavish with praise for the way Sandra had ridden his horse and with drinks for the assembled party.

Sandra herself was absent. She had gone back to the stables with Charlie's Darling to make sure he was properly tucked up for the night and to potter about with the other duties of the yard.

After a couple of hours the party broke up and they went their separate ways. Benjamin and Ivy went back to the farm where Benjamin had some paperwork to catch up on, while Robert and his companion went into town for a late restaurant meal.

Joby stayed on at the pub, glowing with the satisfaction of his day's activities and with the five or six drinks he had downed—none of which he had had to pay for.
But he was eventually brought down to earth by 'Badger' Brock, the huge farm worker of cricketing fame, who, although well-known for his gentle disposition, was not noted for his tact.

He had listened to Joby's umpteenth and even further embellished account of the day at the races and as the old fellow finished his tale once again, commented: 'Don't tell Fred Appleton. He won't believe you.'

At the mention of the hated gamekeeper's name, Joby's smiling face darkened.

'Wha'ja mean?' he demanded.

'Fred was in 'ere last night, goin' on about you and sayin' 'ow you wouldn't know the truth if it stood up and smacked you in the mouth,' returned Brock, a genuinely innocent smile on his enormous face.

'Oh. And what else did the shit-stirrin,' useless old bugger 'ave to say then?' Joby wanted to know. ''E's not usually got the nerve t' show 'is face in 'ere. 'E knows 'e's about as welcome in The Drovers as a sore arse to a trick cyclist!'

'Said as 'ow he was goin' to get you back if it's the last thing he did,' said Brock. 'Said you told a pack 'o lies to the court last year and that you're nuthin' but a thievin,' lyin' poacher.'

The bar went suddenly quiet and Brock, looking round, realised he may have gone a bit too far with his information. 'Mind you, he'd had a few drinks,' he added, a little sheepishly.

'I'll give the bugger somethin' to drink about,' shouted Joby. ''E can't go around shoutin' 'is mouth off about me and get away with it. I'll bloody soon sort 'im out!'

And with that he stomped out, leaving his glass unfinished on the bar.

Joby was furious.

Stoked up with a little more alcohol than he was accustomed to, mixed drinks at that, he was just about ready for a final showdown with Fred Appleton.

He started off down the road towards the gamekeeper's cottage, which stood on its own at the far end of the village.

Then he paused.

The likelihood was that Fred was out on a Bank Holiday evening and his long trek would be in vain. But he would almost certainly be in tomorrow morning.

Joby turned around and went home instead. He was still seething but managed to get a good night's sleep, aided, in no small part, by the drink.

Next morning his fury had abated, to be replaced by a determined resolution to have it out with Fred Appleton.

After early milking he asked Robert for a couple of hours off and by mid-morning was making his way on foot, through the village, passing the pub on the way.

Fred Appleton's estate owned cottage stood back from the lane. It had a large front garden, mostly laid to grass and flowers, and an even bigger back garden where Fred had his vegetable patch and dog runs.

A feature of the cottage was the enormous walnut tree which stood just inside the front gate, overhanging both the lane outside and the gate and path to the front door.

Children from the village regularly raided the tree when the walnuts were ripe and it was a matter of pride to Fred that he managed to keep most of the harvest safe from these predators. Some were sent up to the big house each Christmas, some were consumed by Fred and his wife, and in a good year, more than a few were sold to augment Fred's beer money.

Joby paused at the gate. There was no sign of Fred in the front garden.

He undid the latch and strode purposefully up the path to the front door which he treated to a prolonged hammering with his fist.

He paused.

There was no reply.

Joby repeated the clobbering.

No response.

Joby peered in at the front window. Then he walked cautiously round the path at the side of the cottage to the back garden. It was empty. Of Fred Appleton and his wife there was no sign.

'The bugger's out again,' muttered Joby under his breath.

Disappointed at his intended showdown plans being thwarted, he strolled back round to the front of the cottage and up the path towards the gate.

It was then he noticed the lorry.

It was on the grass verge right beside the gate and must have pulled up while he was investigating Fred's back garden.

The driver's window was wound down and a large, scruffy individual, with several days growth of beard on his face, was leaning out. Beside him sat an equally scruffy lad of about fourteen.

Joby walked up to the gate.

'Don't very much like the look o' that,' called out the man, nodding towards Fred Appleton's walnut tree.

Joby turned and surveyed the scene.

The flatbed lorry had a few lengths of wood lying on it and some nondescript equipment, partly covered by an old tarpaulin. The driver, clearly of itinerant dealer extraction, was another of the numerous self-styled "forestry experts" or "tree surgeons" who travelled the countryside offering to lop "dangerous" trees for a few quid.

'What's wrong with it?' Joby demanded.

'Well,' said the man, warming to his theme and jumping down out of the lorry. 'Look at that bough there. That one hangin' over the road. That's a danger to the public. Could come down an' injure somebody—or kill 'em!'

'So, what am I s'posed to do about that?' asked Joby.

'I wouldn't want to be the owner if that 'appened,' returned the man. 'Land you up in court. Damages an' compensation an' the like. Tell you what. I'll take it down for you. Nice and tidy. Only cost a coupla quid.'

The faintest flicker of realisation crossed Joby's face, quickly followed by an equally faint mischievous twinkle of the eye.

The man had obviously assumed, seeing Joby come from the back of the house, that he was the owner.

''Ow long would it take?' asked Joby.

''Bout ten, fifteen minutes at the most,' returned the man, whose young accomplice, sensing the possibility of a cash transaction, had joined him at the gate.

'Um...,' dithered Joby.

'Tell you what,' said the man quickly, the scent of easy money heavy in his nostrils, 'I could take the whole tree down for a tenner. Clear up the problem once and for all. Do a nice clean job.

'Tidy up. Take away the lot. Wha'ja say? That's a bargain. OK, I'll do it for eight quid, I can't say fairer than that, can I?'

Joby looked at the man again and then back up at the tree.

'It does seem a fair price,' he said. 'Are you sure it's dangerous?'

'Certain of it. Could come down any time,' said the man. He had already worked out how much he would get for the valuable timber and he was raring to go. 'Tell you what. Seven quid. Last offer.'

'Well…,' said Joby. 'You must do what you think best.'

'Right,' said the man and, turning to the boy, 'Let's get started.'

Joby came out of the gate and walked across the lane to the far verge to get a better view as the two got started.

They unloaded ropes and chainsaws from under the tarpaulin on the lorry and within minutes the sound of the motors chattered merrily away on the morning air.

The boy was up the tree like a monkey, sawing off boughs which came crashing down on the lane and into Fred's flower beds.

Joby, watching from the opposite verge, looked up and down the road. Of Fred there was still no sign.

After nearly an hour of hectic activity there was just the main trunk of the now-denuded walnut tree to come down.

The man and his young helper, using ropes to guide it, tried to get the trunk to fall parallel to the front boundary but were only partially successful. As it came down it demolished a long section of Fred's neatly trimmed privet hedge.

'Whoops!' exclaimed the man. 'Sorry about that. It'll grow back in no time,' he assured Joby with a grin.

Joby smiled from across the road.

It was at that precise moment Fred Appleton appeared, riding his bike from the direction leading away from the village.

As he approached he realised something was seriously wrong.

His beloved walnut tree had disappeared.

There were branches, twigs and debris all over the road outside the cottage. Even more littered his front garden flowerbeds. The trunk of the tree was lying in the remains of his front hedge.

He got off his bike.

His face was grey, his eyes were staring and his mouth was working up and down but no sound was coming out.

He seemed not to notice Joby standing on the far side of the road.

Eventually he exploded.

'WHAT THE BLOODY 'ELL'S GOIN' ON 'ERE?'

The man and his boy looked up.

'What's the problem mate?' the man wanted to know.

'WHO GAVE YOU BLOODY PERMISSION TO TAKE MY BLOODY TREE DOWN?' bellowed Fred.

'Your tree?' asked the man, obviously bewildered.

'YES. MY BLOODY TREE…' Fred Appleton's shout tailed off. He was too furious to say anything else.

The man turned and pointed to Joby, still standing on the other side of the road.

'This chap says it's HIS tree,' he yelled.

'Oh no I didn't,' replied Joby calmly.

'But you said I should cut it down for safety's sake,' hollered the man.

'I ain't said no such thing,' returned Joby, still cool as a cucumber. 'I didn't tell you it was my tree 'cos you never asked. Seems to me I recall you doing all the talking. If you want to go an' cut somebody's tree down that's up to you.'

'But we agreed a price!' thundered the man.

'No. You said as 'ow much you would charge the owner for takin' it down an' I said as 'ow it wus a fair price. I d'ain't asked you t'cut it down 'cos it ain't my tree.'

Fred Appleton finally got his power of speech back.

'Well, what the bloody 'ell are you goin' to do about it?' he demanded.

The man stared aghast at the stricken walnut tree, now lying in several dozen pieces all over the road and Fred's front garden.

'Look. You gimmee a fiver and I'll see it's all tidied up and carted away. All smart. No mess. You won't even know it's gone.'

'WHAT?' bellowed Fred. 'Look, sunny Jim, Squire will have somethin' to say about this. So will the police.'

The man tried again. At the mention of the law he was starting to get worried.

'OK, how about if I give you a fiver an' we'll say no more about it. Look.'

He took out a roll of banknotes thick enough to choke a camel and peeled one off.

'Cash in hand. Can't say fairer than that. After all, that chap said…'

He turned towards Joby but Joby wasn't there.

In fact he was already a hundred yards away, strolling casually back towards the village. This was worth a noggin in The Drovers he thought to himself, as the noise of the continuing row between Fred and the travelling tree surgeon faded in the distance behind him.

And the story of Fred Appleton's walnut tree was the main topic of conversation in the public bar for many a day.

It was early May and Reggie Broadman was on the lookout for some action.

The dodgy fuel oil market had run out of steam earlier than he had expected, very nearly leaving him out of pocket, a disastrous state of affairs.

The black-haired beauty from the car sales office had proved very interesting, and stimulating, for a week or so but had suddenly got very serious. She started talking about leaving her husband and asking Reggie awkward questions about where he stood on their potential future together.

It was clearly time to move on. So he had moved on.

This morning he was in the saloon bar of the pub in a small village near Witherstoke, a village he had never visited before.

He was hoping to break some new ground in more ways than one. Sitting in the corner with a pint of bitter, Reggie was contemplating his next scheme—or rather trying to think up his next scheme.

At the same time he was considering making a move for the buxom, curly-haired daughter of the landlord. As she served his drink she had treated him to a very disarming smile and had returned his initial compliment with an even wider smile, complete with good, even teeth—and dimples.

There seemed to be definite potential there.

His thoughts were interrupted, however, by the arrival in the bar of two well-dressed men, not exactly city gents—one exhibited a broken nose, the other a scar on his cheek—but obviously successful businessmen of some sort. Their accents indicated that they hailed from Greater London.

Until now Reggie had had the room to himself. Now the two settled on stools at the bar, turned, and one gave him a slight, silent nod of acknowledgement. He nodded in reply.

The landlord himself came to serve them and appeared to know them, at least by sight.

'Morning gentlemen. What'll you have?'

'Two large Scotches please,' returned one. 'And water.'

The drinks were duly dispensed and paid for and the landlord placed a jug of water on the bar in front of them.

'Haven't seen you about for a few months, not since last season,' said the landlord. 'Will you be taking the shooting at Wallows Farm again this year?'

'That's just the trouble.' It was the other who spoke this time. 'The new owner's decided to take the shooting in hand at pretty short notice and left us floundering. We thought a trip down today might turn up a few possibilities. Don't suppose you've heard of any game rights lease available?'

The landlord thought for a moment.

'No. Sorry gents. Can't say as I have. I'll ask around for you if you like. Leave me your phone number and I'll see what turns up.'

At that point he called out: 'Just coming. I'll be right with you.' And scurried off to serve some new customers in the public bar.

Reggie had heard every word.

His brain, usually pretty agile anyway, was working overtime.

They didn't know him, neither did the landlord. No reason why they should.

He, however, knew what they wanted. And he knew the countryside well enough hereabouts to know that there was some good shooting land in the locality. None, as far as he was aware, was available for rent, but they didn't know that either so what did it matter?

An ingenious, preposterous and highly illegal plan was beginning to take shape in his mind. But one that would net him a really good return.

As soon as the landlord was out of earshot he rose and approached the two men at the bar. He put on his best respectable voice—which was very respectable indeed.

'Look, I'm sorry gentlemen, I didn't mean to eavesdrop but I couldn't help overhearing your conversation. I hope you'll forgive my presumption but I think I might be able to help you.'

The two turned to face him, anticipation clearly lighting up their faces.

'I do beg your pardon. My name is Ronnie Francombe. I run a shooting agency and I've just been landed the job of letting the gaming rights on a farm near here.

'Seems the owner died recently and the family want to hang on to the land but aren't interested in the shooting. Bit short notice for the coming season, I know, but I may be able to get it at a decent price.'

'That sounds terrific. What's the acreage?'

'What acreage were you looking for?'

'Well, last season we were shooting over about 450. Mixed wood and arable. We could have done with a little more.'

'This ought to suit you fine. It's just over 600. No birds being put down this year of course but terrific potential for the future. Plenty of neighbouring shoots putting down hundreds of birds anyway. First season should go for a song, perhaps £150, with options for at least five years I should think.'

The two men looked delighted.

'Do you think you can pull it off?'

'I can give it a darned good try.'

'There'll be a pony in it for yourself if you do,' added one.

Reggie looked around. This was by far his most ambitious project yet.

'Let's go out to the car park,' said Reggie casually. He touched his nose and winked. 'You know. Can't be too careful.' He glanced along the bar towards the public bar from which came a dull hubbub of voices. 'Walls have ears.'

The trio downed the rest of their drinks and went outside.

In the car park they finished their chat.

Reggie made an appointment to meet them again the following week at a convenient spot in the nearby countryside to show them the boundaries of the new "shoot".

'Can't meet at the farm itself. Family is still upset by their bereavement,' he had explained.

It would be a tricky thing but with no-one knowing his face or his name and with the likelihood that he would never see any of them again, the risk, he reckoned, was worth taking.

Meanwhile, inside the pub, the landlord and his daughter were both back in the saloon bar, surprised that all three men had made such an abrupt exit. They were still standing outside, deep in conversation.

'Who's that chap talking to the two shooting gents from Wallows?' Alf Blissett asked.

'No idea dad,' said Molly. 'Never seen him before. I thought he said his name was Frankham or something.'

Chapter ten

THE story of Fred Appleton's walnut tree went the rounds for weeks.

The tale was told and retold, to gales of laughter, in pubs throughout the area and a few paragraphs even found their way into the columns of the *Witherstoke Gazette* under the headline "Fred Goes Nuts Over Walnut Tree".

Of course the estate manager had something to say about the affair.

After all, the cottage, and the tree, belonged to the Squire, not Fred Appleton, so it was Fred who got it in the neck for allowing the situation to occur, a ticking off that pleased him not at all.

Meanwhile Joby kept his head down. He realised his little joke could still easily misfire badly at any time and that he had probably gone too far.

But, somewhat to his own surprise, no approach was made to him.

It seemed that Fred Appleton wasn't going to let on to the authorities that Joby had bested him once again. Anyway, if what Joby had said was anywhere near the truth, proving any wrong doing would be pretty nigh impossible.

The police made a few inquiries and tried to find the unnamed traveller who had perpetrated the deed. But as no-one had thought to take the registration number of the lorry, the man had simply disappeared and it was highly unlikely he'd be showing his face in that neck of the woods again in the very near future!

As spring began to turn into summer the gamekeeper's duties kept him busy almost twenty-four hours a day with the hatching, rearing and feeding of hundreds of young pheasants. Any thoughts of revenge on Joby would have to go on hold for a few months at least.

Wild flowers and cottage gardens were together transforming the countryside into a riotous combination of colour and fragrances.

Work at Longdown Farm continued apace and the next major event on the local social calendar was fast approaching.

The Midsummer Ball.

One evening in early June, Benjamin, Robert and Ivy were chatting around the scrubbed table in the farmhouse kitchen, a familiar diversion after the main meal of the day.

The past terrible events seemed almost a lifetime away for the two young men and they were now engrossed in a discussion about the forthcoming ball.

'Who will you be taking on Saturday?' Ivy addressed the question to the younger of the two.

'That's just the problem,' returned Robert. 'I still can't make up my mind. Might just go on my own and see if I can pick up a bit of spare!' he laughed. 'No. Seriously. It'll probably be Tina, you know …Christine, the redhead.'

Ivy turned to the older brother. 'And what about you, Benjamin? Who will be the lucky lady on your arm?'

'Oh. I don't know if I'll bother. Well, I've got nobody in mind.'

'I could fix you up with a nice bit of tasty if…' Robert began.

A glowering look from his brother convinced him that his assistance was not welcome and he left the sentence unfinished.

'I know a young lady who wants to go and who's hoping to find someone to take her,' volunteered Ivy.

The two men turned towards her.

'And who might that be?' demanded Robert.

'Sandra.'

'What, your Sandra?' asked Benjamin.

Ivy nodded.

'But she's only a gir... I mean she's only...well, she's not very old is she?' Benjamin managed to stutter.

To both Benjamin and Robert, who rarely saw much of Ivy's daughter, and even then only in old clothes or riding gear, Sandra was little more than a schoolgirl.

'She's nineteen, Benjamin.' There was quite an edge to Ivy's voice.

The two men were silent but when Ivy wasn't looking, Robert threw Benjamin one of those half smiling, half grimacing, "you've been put in your place" looks.

Sandra might be nineteen but to both of them she was still the scruffy tomboy who lived with her mother in the other end of the farmhouse.

Even Sandra's recent success in the racing field hadn't done much to enhance the brothers' views of her charms.

'Ivy,' said Benjamin.

She turned to face him.

Why he did it he had no idea but he heard himself say: 'I'll take her.'

Robert glanced at him quickly but Benjamin seemed to be in a state of shock by what he had done.

Later, when Ivy had gone off to her room, Robert turned on his elder brother.

'What on earth did you go and do that for? If you really wanted an escort I could have sorted something out easily.'

Benjamin just sat there, a forlorn look in his eyes. 'I don't know,' was all he could say.

At that moment there was the sound of a bike scraping the brickwork outside the back door and a few seconds later Sandra walked into the kitchen.

She took off her riding boots and turned to the two brothers. Neither said a word.

She was dressed in her worn sloppy sweater, stained and matted with horsehair, hay and other obscure stable material, and old, faded jodhpurs. Her hair was pushed up under a greasy looking cloth cap, from which a few untidy straggles drooped down.

'Hi!' she offered cheerily.

'Oh, hi.' 'Hello' They replied in unison.

The two brothers stared at her in silence.

Sandra looked quizzically at one searching but unspeaking face to the other.

'Anything the matter?' she asked quietly.

'No.' 'Nothing,' came the chorussed reply and both, now slightly embarrassed, brothers turned their heads away.

Sandra shrugged. Then she was gone, off to her room and to have a bath they supposed.

Robert started to laugh. Just a quiet little laugh that wouldn't be heard by Ivy or her daughter.

Still grinning, he said in a stage whisper: 'You're going to get yourself had up for cradle snatching.'

Benjamin picked up the folded newspaper from the kitchen table and threw it at him.

Robert got to his feet and dodged round to the far side of the table.

'Never mind,' he chortled. 'She'll probably scrub up quite nicely.'

And he was gone, out of the kitchen door before his brother had a chance to collar him.

Benjamin made to follow but changed his mind and went up to his own room.

Over the next few days there remained no contact between Benjamin and Sandra. Information, and there wasn't much of that, went back and forth between the two via Ivy who arranged for them to leave the house at half past seven on the night of the ball.

Saturday arrived, bright and clear, with the promise of a fine summer evening to follow.

The Binfield Midsummer Ball, held by invitation of Sir Oliver and Lady Evelyn Pumphrey-Haig at Ashley Hall, was traditionally the grandest affair of the local social scene.

In the magnificent setting of the Georgian mansion house with its elegant ballroom, the event invariably—when the weather allowed—spread out to include the immediate grounds, immaculate lawns and neatly trimmed flower beds.

On a warm summer's evening, such as the one in prospect, the scene was set for a wonderfully relaxed and enjoyable occasion.

Benjamin, however, was far from relaxed and noticeably short of humour. As the day wore on he had still not seen nor spoken to his intended date.

He prepared for the ball in his typicall meticulous manner and by a quarter past seven he was finished, down near the foot of the stairs, on edge, ready to go, glancing at his watch and pacing up and down the hall carpet.

A few minutes later he was joined by Robert who, although having still to pick up his own escort, wasn't going to miss seeing the reaction between his brother and the housekeeper's daughter.

The ticking of the grandfather clock in the hall seemed to echo more and more loudly as the pendulum swung to and fro and the minute hand moved inexorably towards the perpendicular.

The clock gave an eight-part Westminster chime to denote the half hour.

Benjamin paused in his pacing and both brothers stood at the foot of the staircase, faces raised, the elder showing in his eyes distinct signs of unease, the younger displaying more of an air of wicked anticipation.

Right on time, Sandra appeared on the landing and slowly made her descent.

Her long blonde hair, carefully shampooed and shining with vitality, fell away from a central parting. It was swept low around the sides, and piled up at the back, held by a single tortoiseshell comb grip, with a tiny pony tail, complete with curl, dangling delicately at the nape of her slender neck.

Her face, bearing no more than a hint of makeup, shone as she smiled, her even white teeth completing a picture of perfect natural beauty.

She wore a close fitting, calf length dress of the palest blue, cut low in the front with not-too-narrow shoulder straps.

It showed off to the best possible effect her firm young breasts, with just enough of a suggestion of cleavage to be exciting without being the least brazen. The slightly shimmering material hugged a tiny waist and nicely rounded hips.

Her slim, square shoulders were in perfect proportion to the rest of her exquisite figure while her trim ankles, complimented by navy court shoes with two-inch heels, gave the promise of long and slender legs.

Her total jewellery consisted of a pair of tiny drop earrings in silver and a matching single strand silver necklace.

She looked absolutely stunning.

And, not surprisingly, both Benjamin and Robert were absolutely stunned.

Two pairs of eyes gazed in admiration. Two jaws dropped in astonishment. Two men were temporarily mesmerised into silence as she paused two steps above them.

'Sandra...!' It was Benjamin who spoke first.

Robert could manage only a hoarse, half-whispered 'Christ!'

Ivy appeared at the top of the stairs with Sandra's only accessories, a pretty little navy evening bag and a matching stole.

She came down to join them, her face aglow with delight at the impression Sandra had created.

'Well? What do you think? How does she look?'

Benjamin groped for a reply. 'I just didn't...I had no...well...she looks great!'

Robert was still too staggered to say anything. He just stared, mouth open, at the rather grubby caterpillar which suddenly had been transformed into this beautiful butterfly.

They said their goodbyes to Ivy and walked in silence to their cars.

Robert was first to drive away, still astounded by the scene he had just witnessed, on his way to collect his date for the evening.

Benjamin opened the passenger door of his car for Sandra to get in, then walked round and climbed into the driving seat.

The drive to the Hall took only ten minutes or so and at first there remained utter silence between them.

Then, as they approached the lodge gate entrance to the estate, that silence was broken.

'I hope you don't think….'

'What have you been…'

They both began simultaneously.

Then they both stopped. Then they both laughed. The ice was broken.

'Look. Let's start again.'

During the slow journey up the half mile gravelled driveway they began to talk. Not just small talk but meaningful conversation.

Benjamin found to his amazement that his typical hesitancy in speaking with a member of the opposite sex had completely disappeared when communicating with the charming and beautiful young woman beside him.

Sandra seemed, quite naturally, to put him at his ease. He felt relaxed in a way he hadn't relaxed in years. By the time they arrived at the portico of the main entrance to Ashley Hall they were chatting like old friends and had exchanged probably more conversation in five minutes than in the whole of the previous year.

The magic for Benjamin continued throughout the evening.

They danced, they chatted, they paused for drinks and again for the buffet.

Their talk took in many subjects and they were both surprised at the wide range of interests which they shared; the countryside primarily and its many aspects, books, films, some music and even food.

Sandra at least appeared to be genuinely interested in the intricacies of farming, although, naturally, her main interest remained equestrian in nature.

They danced again. They danced several times. In fact they spent the whole evening in each other's company and seemed to be completely unaware of the many admiring glances and nods of approval that, as a couple, they were receiving. Robert, not least among their admirers, threw many a satisfied and appreciative smile their way.

Benjamin could hardly take his eyes off Sandra's face.

In close-up dancing clinches they seemed almost to merge, their bodies pressing tightly together. For the first time Benjamin noticed the grey/green colour of her eyes, the way her nose tilted ever-so-slightly at the end, the tiny upward creases at the corners of her mouth, the sheen of her hair.

Long before midnight Benjamin Trenchard had fallen in love.

Just at the moment he was standing alone, leaning against one of the banqueting hall's marble pillars, drink in hand but hardly touched, trying to work out what had hit him. Sandra was making a visit to the ladies' room and it was the first time they had been apart all evening.

He watched the other dancers without really seeing them. He had never felt so happy in his life. It was as if he was caught up in some unfamiliar parallel universe, some fabulous dream.

'Ben? Ben Trenchard?'

The somehow vaguely familiar voice startled him back to reality.

He turned, to be confronted by a young man of about his own age, smartly dressed and looking just a little like some famous film star.

A surge of partial recollection, quickly followed by a feeling of distinct unease swept over him.

'It's Reggie. Reggie Broadman. Don't you remember? Springshott College 1953-54.'

'Yes...yes of course.' Total recognition had jolted into Benjamin's brain.

Reginald Broadman had been an almost constant cause of problems throughout their two years at agricultural college. His attitude to study had been a source of exasperation among the college staff and his activities, both on and off the campus, a distraction to those students who took their learning seriously.

Benjamin hadn't liked him then. Although he'd not seen him since those college days he had no reason to suppose he had changed for the better.

'I thought it was you. Noticed you several times this evening. What are you up to these days?' Reggie wanted to know. 'And who's the lady with you? Not married, surely?'

'No, we're just, well...' The rest of the sentence was lost as the two men were suddenly joined by the returning Sandra.

Benjamin smiled at her and in spite of his personal feelings his good manners immediately took over the situation.

'Ah, Sandra, this is Reginald Broadman. We were at Springshott together some years ago. Reginald, this is Sandra Green. She's, well, she's a friend of the family.'

'So pleased to meet you. I was hoping I might get the chance of an introduction all night,' he gushed. 'Perhaps we could have a dance. You don't mind, do you Ben?'

And without waiting for a reply he took Sandra in his arms and waltzed away with her into the melee of dancers.

Over his shoulder Sandra gave Benjamin a kind of helpless raised-eyebrows smile as they disappeared into the throng.

Benjamin was furious.

Everything had been going so well, so perfectly. Then this contemptible creep from the past had crawled out from under a stone and appeared to be doing his best to ruin the entire evening.

Benjamin tried to pick them out among the other dancers but got only the occasional long distance glimpses of them across the hall.

Having finished that dance on the far side of the room, to which position Reggie had skilfully manoeuvred his partner, he gave Sandra no chance to refuse the next and it was fully ten or fifteen minutes before they returned to where Benjamin was waiting.

Reggie had wasted no time.

He had ascertained that Sandra was nineteen, unattached and had no formal commitment of any kind to Benjamin. He had found out about her career at the stable yard, her hobbies, such as she had time for, her likes and dislikes in music, food and entertainment and, most importantly, that she had a free evening the following week.

His continual flattery—along with the exaggerated claims about his own career—had certainly impressed Sandra.

He had not, of course, mentioned his latest little project which had netted him a cool but fraudulent £25. Once more he had rightly judged that the two shooting enthusiasts from The Smoke would hardly be attending a local mid-summer social event so the chances of meeting them again in this vicinity were remote. And nobody else in the village, apart from Benjamin Trenchard, knew him anyway.

On the way home from the ball Sandra was full of excitement about the evening, especially her brief meeting with Reggie Broadman.

Benjamin, by contrast, was subdued.

When they arrived at the farm Ivy was waiting up and wanting to know the full details.

They sat together drinking coffee in the kitchen while Sandra relived the whole evening, including her Reggie Broadman interlude.

Robert joined them some time later but by then the story was told and Sandra and her mother were preparing to go to bed.

After they had retired Robert sat at the kitchen table with his elder brother.

'Well? How did it go? I was right about Sandra scrubbing up well. I'm sorry I said that now. She looked absolutely terrific. How did you get on? You certainly seemed to be enjoying yourselves every time I saw you.'

'Everything was going fine.' Benjamin paused.

'Then that nasty little shit Reggie Broadman turned up and managed to screw up the entire evening.' He hissed the words out with obvious venom.

Robert was taken aback and wanted to know more.

Benjamin explained about Reggie at college and how he had reappeared and elbowed his way into Sandra's attentions.

'I didn't like him at college. I like him even less now. Didn't even know he was in the area.'

For two days Benjamin's mind was in turmoil. He wanted desperately to ask Sandra out again but decided it might be better to wait a while. In any case he saw practically nothing of her for the whole of that time.

The bombshell came on Wednesday when Ivy casually announced over breakfast that Sandra was going out on Friday night with the "nice young Reggie Broadman chap" that she met at the summer ball.

Benjamin was aghast.

'Did she say so?' He managed to stutter. 'When did he ask her?'

'Seems he rang her at the stables. He rang several times in fact. She put him off a couple of times but he was pretty insistent,' said Ivy. 'I think Sandra was disappointed that somebody else didn't ask her out.'

And she gave Benjamin a meaningful sideways look.

'But the man's a complete rat,' exploded Benjamin. 'He was always trouble at college. In trouble and causing trouble and he's…'

Benjamin cut himself short. He realised he was sounding very "sour grapes" and was certainly doing his own campaign no good at all.

'He's been the perfect gentleman as far as Sandra's concerned,' returned Ivy. 'Made sure she wasn't going with anyone else before he invited her out. Perhaps he's changed since you knew him.'

'I don't think so,' was all Benjamin could say. And, frowning, he rose and stalked out of the kitchen.

Robert turned to Ivy. 'Tell me about this Reggie Broadman,' he said.

And Ivy told him all that she had learned from her daughter.

That Reggie was one of the top men at the big agricultural suppliers. That he was destined for even bigger things. That he seemed to have a ready supply of money. That his intentions towards Sandra appeared to be perfectly honourable.

'I see,' said Robert and he rose from the breakfast table. He went out with a thoughtful look on his face.

Over the next two days Benjamin fretted and fumed in turn. He wanted badly to confront Sandra and warn her about the new man in her life but knew that his interference would sound like out and out jealousy. He was totally at a loss as to his next move and eaten up by the thought of Sandra falling for that Broadman cad.

He saw nothing of Sandra and very little of Robert.

Meanwhile, Robert had confided in Joby, who apparently had heard a few odd things about the mysterious Reggie Broadman on the local pub bush-telegraph grapevine. Together and separately they had made further inquiries and between them had made half a case against the man. But only half a case, not enough for a confrontation.

By the time Friday arrived Benjamin was in a state of nervous tension.

The day passed slowly for him. Evening arrived and he had eaten nothing since breakfast time. He sat in silence with Robert and Ivy in the kitchen as though awaiting the executioner's call.

Sandra had returned early from the stables, had gone to her room and was obviously getting ready to go out on her date with Reggie.

Just after seven o'clock came the sound of the flashy Zephyr pulling up outside, followed soon after by a knock at the front door.

Ivy rose and went to answer it.

The two brothers heard the exchanges on the doorstep.

'Hullo, you must be Reggie. Sandra's told me a lot about you.'

'And you're...no, surely not her mother. You must be a sister.' Reggie was playing his flattery cards to the full.

'Do come in. I'm sure it's all right for you to wait in the sitting room. Sandra won't be a minute.' And then the call up the stairs. 'Sandra! Someone for you!'

Ivy led Reggie into the extensive farm house sitting room. Robert rose and went in after them. Benjamin remained seated in the kitchen. He had no desire at all to come face to face with Reggie Broadman again, especially under these circumstances and in his own house.'

He could just about hear the conversation.

'Hi. Reggie Broadman? I'm Robert Trenchard, Benjamin's younger brother. Seems you're taking our Sandra out tonight, lucky devil.'

'Yes. We met at the ball last weekend, I happened to be in the neighbourhood and decided to drop in. Good for business you know. Lucky meeting really, for me I mean.'

'You're right there. I understand you're with Smith and Whitley. One of their top men, I hear.'

'Well, could be higher. Hoping to do better in future.'

'We don't see a lot of their people hereabouts. What brings you so far from head office?'

Reggie was warming to his theme. 'I saw the opportunity to expand our trading potential and took it upon myself to open up a new sales area. It's developing quite nicely. Perhaps I can do some business at Longdown in the not too distant future?'

'We'll have to see about that. I believe we're well sorted at the moment.'
Robert paused.

At that moment Joby, who appeared to have been absent from the farm for most of the day, arrived at the open back door, walked straight in without an invitation and, after a glance at Benjamin, strode through in silence to the sitting room which he entered unannounced.

Robert and Ivy gazed at him in surprise, astonished by this totally out-of-character performance.

Reggie turned to face Joby, then to Robert and Ivy in turn as if seeking an explanation for this interruption.

Joby wasted no time in pleasantries. Striding up to within two feet of the visitor he looked up into the taller man's face and demanded: 'How's yer wife and baby, Mr Broadman?

'Or is it Banham?

'Or is it Frankham?

'Or even somethin' else?'

Reggie Broadman's body stiffened visually and the colour drained from his face.

'What...what do you mean?'

That was all he could manage. All his usual swagger, self-assurance and composure had drained in an instant.

Robert had been busy these last two days. He'd contacted the company on the pretext of being interested in buying some farm machinery and had found out some interesting facts about their 'top salesman.'

Joby, it seems, had today been even busier and discovered many more secrets about the man.

He had, of course, like everyone else in the village, heard about the local shooting rights scam and had had a word with Molly at The Drovers Arms. Her description of the mysterious "Mr Frankham" seemed oddly familiar to a number of people.

Visits to some of his many other contacts in the area, including Witherstoke, brought even more interesting stories to light.

At this point Robert, whose eyes had lighted up at Joby's onslaught, joined in.

'Seems you've been developing the area in more ways than one, Reggie, doesn't it? Some of your business, I'm sure, would come as quite a surprise to your employers.

'Not to mention the police. Or the Inland Revenue. And quite a number of other people would be interested in having the chance to talk to you again, wouldn't they? Certain pretty tough gentlemen from London for instance?'

Reggie had been washed, wrung out and hung up to dry.

Ivy had been standing there, open mouthed, listening to this exchange and now Benjamin appeared in the sitting room doorway, a look of utter astonishment on his face.

Reggie tried one last bluster.

'Look…if you think you can threaten me with…'

Robert cut him short.

'Oh come on Broadman. You've been rumbled. You're finished here. My advice to you is to get out and make what amends you can while you have the time. And talking of time, you haven't got much because in exactly ten minutes I'm ringing the police. If I were you I wouldn't show my face again in this area. Ever.'

Without a word Reggie Broadman strode to the door. Benjamin had almost to jump aside to let him through.

The slamming of the front door was quickly followed by the sound of the powerful Ford's engine revving and the screech of tyres as Mr Broadman drove out of Longdown Farm and out of the lives of all its residents.

As the car disappeared down the track Sandra appeared at the bottom of the stairs. If anything she looked even more attractive in casual going-out gear than in her formal outfit of last weekend.

There was a look of complete puzzlement on her face.

From her room she had heard something of the raised voices from downstairs and had come to investigate but she had no idea what the commotion was all about.

'Where's Reggie?' were her only words.

Ivy came forward and put a half protecting arm about her shoulder.

'He had an urgent appointment dear. I'll tell you all about it.'

With that she led Sandra back upstairs.

Meanwhile Benjamin turned to Robert and Joby.

'How the devil did you know about all that? About the shoot and all?'

'We didn't,' replied Robert. 'But through various friends we'd heard about a few things that had been happening around the district recently, things you probably wouldn't be aware of. And Joby's been tying up some loose ends this afternoon.'

He gave Benjamin a broad smile and an even broader wink. 'A few more calls to the right people soon started making the sums add up.'

Benjamin's own smile had returned.

'You absolute beauties,' he cried and flung his arms round the two in a spontaneous double bear-hug.

'Hang on, hang on,' said Robert, as he disentangled himself from Benjamin's grateful embrace. 'I've got things to do—like telephone Pc Wheeler. No reason why putting CID onto Reggie's little games shouldn't put a feather in the cap of our local bobby is there?'

Robert went off to make the promised phone call.

Joby just stood there, his usual gap-toothed grin wider than ever.

'Cudn't let that cheatin' bugger ruin our Sandra's life cud we? I knows wot iss like t'lose somethin' precious.'
Then mindful that he may have said too much already, he sauntered out.

From what he had heard in the last ten minutes, Benjamin reckoned that, whatever happened, Reggie Broadman would be getting no more than he deserved. From his own former experiences of the man he wouldn't have been at all surprised to learn that he was involved in other shady activities, more than any of them had ever imagined.

He was back in the kitchen when Sandra came downstairs. Ivy had told her the whole story, no holds barred.

She stood in the kitchen doorway looking pale and shaken.

'You all right?' he asked.

'Benjamin. I feel such a fool. To think a man like that could pull the wool over my eyes so completely…I…'

He came over to her and put a comforting arm around her. She looked up at him, her eyes misty. He bent and planted the lightest of kisses on the top of her head.

'He's had almost a lifetime's practice. Dozens of people have fallen for his stories, mainly because he believes them himself.'

He turned and held her by the shoulders at arms' length.

'Now! What are you doing this evening? All dressed up and nowhere to go! It's still early. Fancy a night on the town with me?'

The gorgeous smile he had come to admire so much returned to light up her face.

'Yes please!'

She went to the foot of the stairs and called: 'Mum! I'm going out after all! With Benjamin!'

Upstairs in her room Ivy smiled to herself and called back: 'Fine!' And under her breath she added 'And about time too!'

The couple left and Robert came out of the study where he'd been on the phone to Pc Wheeler's police house. Official inquiries into Reggie Broadman's recent activities in the area were already getting under way.

Ivy came back down the stairs.

'What's all the shouting about?' Robert wanted to know.

'Just Sandra. Letting me know that she and Benjamin are going out for the evening.'

'Brilliant!' exclaimed Robert.

As they drove down the track towards the village, passing Joby walking back to his cottage and who responded with a vigorous wave to the toot-toot-toot on the car horn, Benjamin hadn't the vaguest idea what Sandra would expect from a night out.

Then his hunger kicked in.

'Look. Have you eaten?' he asked.

'No. I was supposed to be going to some swish restaurant but there's been an obvious change of plan. I'm starving!'

And she laughed.

'So am I!' exclaimed Benjamin. 'Fancy a Chinese?'

'Will the sun rise tomorrow?'

And she laughed again.

Although it was Friday evening they managed to get a table at Witherstoke's only Chinese restaurant, The Silver Capital, a relatively new addition to the town's facilities.

They enjoyed a long and leisurely meal, drank a bottle of wine between them, finishing off with tiny bowls of green leaf tea.

Throughout they chatted ceaselessly. Reggie Broadman was already well and truly forgotten.

Afterwards they strolled hand in hand along the river bank path, taking the long route back to the car park.

It was a fine June night, still not dark, and they sat for a while on a bench watching the nearly-full moon rising over the river away to their left.

His arm was about her shoulders. She nestled her head into his chest, her hair, loose tonight, cascading down and smelling delicious. The place was deserted.

Benjamin cupped the left side of her face in his free right hand, his fingers gently touching her soft scalp and working delicately between the locks of her silken hair.

He gently but firmly turned her head up towards his own. Their eyes met and locked for a long moment. Then they kissed, tenderly and passionately.

They drove home more or less in silence, Sandra clutching Benjamin's arm and leaning her head against his shoulder.

Back at the farm Ivy was sitting in the kitchen with a satisfied smile on her face.

Pc Wheeler had been on the phone, wanting to speak again to Robert who, of course, had been out. The conversation between policeman and housekeeper had turned more and more personal, culminating in another invitation from the constable to Ivy. She had accepted.

As Benjamin and Sandra came into the kitchen, hand in hand, it was obvious that their evening, too, had been successful and Ivy's smile became broader still.

Throughout the rest of the summer, romance blossomed at Longdown Farm.

In early September, just as the harvest finished, Benjamin and Sandra announced their engagement.

By October the wedding date had been fixed for early the next year and arrangements were started for the winter wedding at St Swithin's church.

Robert, of course, would be best man, Ivy was to be maid of honour and Joby, swelling with pride, was quick to tell everyone who would listen that he had been invited to be Chief Usher. After all, it was largely his timely interference which had finally smoothed the path of true love.

Weather permitting, or even if not permitting, Benjamin and Sandra would be driving from the church in a horse drawn carriage, arranged by the proprietors of the riding stables.

One evening in mid-October, Sandra and Ivy were alone in the house and, unusually for them, snuggled into the comfy armchairs of the sitting room.

They were discussing details both for Christmas and the forthcoming nuptial celebrations.

'Happy dear?' asked Ivy.

'Couldn't be happier, mum. How about you?'

'Everything's perfect—and I'm rather expecting Percy to make a move any day now.'

'Mum, that's terrific. Has he said…?'

'I just KNOW,' returned her mother.

Then she added: 'How about Benjamin. How's he shaping up?'

'Oh mum, he's just the most thoughtful, caring and loving man in the world.' Then, with a mischievous smile she added. 'Mind you, Robert's pretty dishy too!'

'No, dear,' returned Ivy, quietly. 'I think you've got the right one.'

Her assessment was based firmly on experience. After all, she *had* taken the opportunity to try them both, hadn't she?
And Ivy smiled a knowing little smile to herself.

Outside a chilly wind stirred the leaves on the massive oak, leaves that had lost their summer gloss and were turning to autumn brown.

A single acorn, one of the last left on the tree, slipped from its little anchoring cup and tumbled down.

It glanced against several branches in its descent, finally bouncing off one of the lower boughs.

The impact flung the acorn sideways, spinning it end over end, to land roughly among the dead grass and leaves in the bottom of the hedge.

Chapter eleven

IT was a wonderful ceremony. A white wedding in every sense. Another new year, 1964, and a mid-January Saturday when the sky was blue and the air icy-cold.

The sun, never very high in the sky at this time of year, cast pale rays and long shadows that allowed the frost to linger all day under every hedge and in the shelter of woods and buildings.

Benjamin Trenchard arrived early at St Swithin's Church with Robert, his younger brother, the best man.

As they sat together in the front pew on the right of the nave, the groom stole a nervous glance over his left shoulder every few seconds towards the west door of Binfield's little church and at the tightly packed congregation.

Joby, almost unrecognisable in an immaculate, new brown suit, was chief usher.

For a full half hour before the proceedings were scheduled to begin, he was hard at work. With loud demands of 'Bride or Groom?', even though he knew most of them on sight, he ushered dozens of guests into their allotted seats, whether they wanted to be ushered or not.

Sandra arrived a few minutes late, as tradition expects, travelling in a long, black limousine with Ivy, her mother, and accompanied by her employer, the riding stable owner who, in the absence of any close male relative, was to perform the duty of giving the bride away.

As she stepped from the shimmering vehicle, wearing a full length white wedding gown with veil and carrying a tiny posy of flowers, she looked sensational.

Ivy, as befitted the family name, was dressed in palest green and hurried into the church ahead of the bride, before the opening bars of the wedding march began, giving a reassuring nod to Benjamin as she took her seat opposite him on the left of the nave.

Then the organ roared into the rousing "Here comes the Bride" of Mendelsson's Wedding March and, as one, the congregation clambered to its collective feet as Sandra and her escort stepped into the church. Her face was aglow with happiness as she acknowledged the many nods and smiles of admiration and approval from those who turned to watch her calm and confident progress down the aisle.

At an almost imperceptible hand signal from the Rev Simon Pindle, Benjamin and Robert rose and moved to their left as the bride joined them in front of the Vicar.

The ceremony went off without a hitch, with the Rev Pindle assisted by his young curate directing the ceremony flawlessly.

Then, after the signing of the register and the official photographic session outside the west door, the couple prepared to leave for the reception at the cricket pavilion which doubled as Binfield's village hall.

They travelled in a spectacularly turned out open horse-drawn carriage, well rugged up against the chill of the late afternoon, and with Sandra now also wrapped in a white fur stole. Meanwhile the church bells echoed out across the village on the frosty air.

As the guests arrived at the hall, the newly-weds stood, smiling, just inside the door to receive them and the congratulations came thick and fast.

The wedding breakfast, speeches and all, (including an hilarious leg-pull from Best Man Robert) had just been successfully completed when Joby, making his unsteady way up to the top table, began loudly proposing yet another unofficial toast to the bride and groom.

With a good few too many unaccustomed glasses of Champagne inside him, Joby, while wheeling round to address the assembly, overdid his pirouette, his legs twisted into an impossible tangle and he went down, grabbing the white table cloth in the process and causing the three-tier wedding cake to wobble alarmingly.

Robert leapt from his seat to steady the structure as Joby's smiling face reappeared from below the edge of the table.

'Sorry guv'nor,' grinned Joby. 'Dunno what came over me.'

But no harm was done and the episode was treated by the assembled guests as added entertainment. Joby, of course, would afterwards claim it was simply the excitement of the occasion that had caused him to slip and lose his footing.

Later Benjamin and Sandra left the still revelling guests to make their honeymoon getaway, a ten day visit to Italy, including a visit to the island of Capri.

Later still the Rev Simon Pindle, another who had indulged in perhaps a little too much of the celebratory bubbly, was making his unsteady way back to the Vicarage, alone and in the dark.

The young curate, realising the task of taking the next day's Sunday morning service would probably fall on him, had left an hour before and retired to his room at the Vicarage to prepare his sermon.

And the Vicar had declined the offer of a lift from Robert.

'Gracious, it's only a couple of hundred yards,' he had nonchalantly replied. 'I don't think much can happen in that distance can it?'

But the road was icy and Mr Pindle's steps were none too steady. He was beginning to think he should not have refused Robert's offer of a ride home when, just as he turned into the double gates of the Vicarage, his feet went from under him and he went down, base over apex, to land on the rock-hard ground with an ominous sounding crack.

Nearly two weeks had passed.

'Did you hear about the Vicar?'

The question was addressed to Alf Blissett, landlord of The Drovers Arms and came from one of his regulars. If anyone knew the whole story, Alf Blissett would.

'About his broken leg? I thought everyone knew by now,' returned the host. 'Nasty business. Broken in three places. They say he had a bit too much of the…' and Alf Blissett used the international sign for imbibing, a hand, clutching an invisible glass, held in front of the face with a slight oscillatory movement of the wrist.

'What's happened about the services at St Swithin's then?' the inquirer wanted to know.

'Well,' replied Alf. 'New curate's done pretty well so far, along with a bit of help from the Rector of St Mary's over at Maplewell but they do say Reverend Pindle's going to be in hospital for ages yet and even then he won't be fit for months. Seems he might even be retiring—which means, I suppose, we'll be getting a new Vicar soon.'

Binfield didn't have long to wait.

The Rev Michael Stott, until very recently the curate of St Swithin's, was fairly rapidly and somewhat surprisingly appointed to the position of Vicar. He was physically so like his predecessor he could have been closely related. But he wasn't.

A somewhat striking figure and a handsome man, tall and thin, and with a rather prominent nose and dark eyes, at a distance he might even have been mistaken for Mr Pindle.

But physical appearance was where all similarity ended.

For one thing he was nearly forty years younger and for Michael Stott a parish of his own, at the age of twenty-eight his first proper, permanent appointment, was pretty good going and he was going to make sure he made a success of it.

Within a very few weeks he had upset a number of locals, including virtually the entire parochial church council, with his forceful manner and somewhere-left-of-centre politics.

Almost immediately he had announced, on learning of the fragile state of the church restoration fund, that not only the members of the regular congregation but the entire population of the village should be "persuaded" to pay a monthly "tariff" to help pay for repairs and redecoration.

'It was not so very long ago that all parishioners had, by law, to pay their tithes to the church,' he told astonished members at his first PCC meeting. 'People are much better off today. I don't suggest anything like the ten per cent of income, as it used to be,' he added with a wry smile. 'But a regular cash contribution, however small, would be a great help. Just think how much money is totally wasted by people every week on smoking and drinking.'

Major Malcolm Danders, long time member of the parochial church council and, coincidentally, the true-blue Tory chairman of the parish council, spluttered into his military moustache.

'Well Vicar,' he began. He was already going red in the face. 'I can't see how you can expect to convince very many churchgoers, let alone the rest of the villagers at large, to give up a proportion of their earnings on a…on any…to pay…uh…uhuh…'

Words failed him.

Major Danders was a retired army officer of the old school with a military pension and a substantial private income and was clearly totally opposed to any suggestion that might involve the redistribution of his or the community's wealth and which might threaten a reduction in his own enjoyment of pipe tobacco or the weekly bottle or two of Whyte and Mackay.

'Come now, Major,' returned the new Vicar. 'Let's not be defeatist. It's merely a suggestion at this stage but I'm sure, with the right will, we could find ways of bringing such a scheme to fruition.'

By the time leaked reports of the proposal had reached the public bar of The Drovers Arms the story had, of course, been embellished and enlarged upon almost to the point of panic proportions.

'Going to take half of everyone's wages, he is!'

'He ain't taking half of mine, I can tell you!'

'He'll get it stopped from your pay packet.'

'How'll he do that? He's got no right.'

'Well, he's got the employers in his pocket ain't he?'

'I tell you. He'll get nothing from me!'

'We'll see. You mark my words.'

'What's he want all this cash for anyway?'

'Dunno. New vicarage I 'spect. New church hall. New church for all I know!'

And so the gossip continued until the parishioners of Binfield were virtually in a state of open rebellion against their new young Vicar before ninety per cent of them had even set eyes on him.

Joby passed on the news to Robert one morning soon after, as they did the milking.

'Goin' to 'ave everybody's wages paid into church funds, 'e is. Then 'e's reckonin' on lettin' us all 'ave a little bit back every week as pocket money,' Joby confided. 'Houtrageous! Never 'eard o' such a thing.'

Robert looked up from where he was fixing the rubber suction teats onto the udders of a black and white cow. There was a mischievous twinkle in his eye.

'That's right, Joby. Been on to us already about you. He's worked out that you should be able to get by easily on ten bob a week.'

'Ten bob!' Joby exploded. 'Wassee know about a bloke's private hexpenses then? Houtrageous I tell yer!'

At that moment Robert looked up and spotted his brother who had come into the milking parlour and, standing just inside the door with a smile on his face, had heard most of the exchange. Robert gave him a broad wink and both brothers burst out laughing.

'Wasso bloomin' funny?' Joby wanted to know.

'Where ever did you get that story from?' asked Benjamin. 'The new Vicar won't take your money. He won't take anybody's money. I spoke to him yesterday, he's quite a decent sort, bit enthusiastic perhaps but he'll soon get the rough edges knocked off him. He's going to *ask* people to make *voluntary* contributions every month to try to get the church back into a decent state of repair. That's all.'

'Y'mean we don't HAVE to pay no money?'

'Not if you don't want to.'

'Well, why din't somebody bloody well say so then?'

The brothers smiled again.

'We ought to be listening more carefully to what he's trying to say—and doing our best to make him welcome in the village instead of spreading wild rumours,' offered Benjamin.

'From what I 'ear, since 'e got 'ere 'e's about as welcome as a wasp at a Sunday School picnic,' returned Joby.

The other two laughed again, this time with him rather than at him.

It was with this new information firmly established in his brain that Joby, making his way to The Drovers Arms on Saturday morning, happened upon the new incumbent.

He was cycling in the opposite direction, his long black cassock billowing about him, a sight that was becoming more and more familiar in the village.

''Ere. Vicar. You're jus' the man I wants t'see,' Joby called out, standing in the middle of the road with both arms wide and forcing the cleric to come to an abrupt halt.

Joby lost no time in voicing his opinion and, almost before the cycle had stopped, he launched into a lengthy tirade about village inhabitants and their finances, and who had what, and who could afford what, and how some could afford plenty, and how some could cough up a lot more than others, and how some could manage very little, and how he couldn't afford anything at all, and how new Vicars shouldn't be going around upsetting folks.

'I ain't sayin' it ain't a bloomin' good idea, gettin' the church up to scratch an' all, but you needs t'be a bit more sneaky, like,' he concluded and he paused to draw a long breath.

'I see,' returned the Rev Michael Stott, who had been left speechless by this full frontal verbal assault. 'You think I should take a more subtle approach then?'

'What?'

'You think I'd do better if I...if,' he looked at Joby and smiled. 'If I was a little more...furtive?'

'The very thing, Vicar. Furtive.' Joby rolled the word around his mouth again and liked the sound and the feel of it. 'Furtive. I couldn't 'a' put it better meself. You'd be surprised what you can do when you're furtive,' and he gave the Vicar a sly wink while tapping the side of his nose with a forefinger.

'I'm sure I would,' replied the cleric. And he cycled off with a very thoughtful look on his face.

Over the following few days The Reverend Michael Stott thought long and hard about what Joby had said. He had to admit to himself that his idea for a kind of "tithe" on every villager for the restoration fund had not met with very much enthusiasm.

In fact it had met with no enthusiasm whatsoever.

By the end of the week an exciting new plan was taking shape in his mind.

Perhaps old Joby was right. Why not use a bit of stealth? Why not be a bit "furtive"? Instead of just blatantly demanding money, why not offer to give away some cash instead? Now there's an idea. After all, it was 1964.

'Hmm,' he mused as he sat in his office at the Vicarage one evening. 'It might just work.' He took up paper and pencil and began to do some basic financial arithmetic.

Mr Stott reckoned that with some hard sell tactics, cajoling, blackmail, flattery, pleading and persuasion he should be able to get three or four hundred people in the village to part with just a shilling a month.

And every month the names of all the contributors would go into a hat. The lucky winner would receive a fiver—leaving anything up to fifteen pounds to go straight into the restoration fund. As long as the payout was a relatively small proportion of the total money collected it should be successful.

The more he thought about it, the more he liked the idea.

At theological college they had always been told that they should always try to involve the whole of the community in any scheme to improve the parish—and here was a splendid opportunity to do just that!

He knew the bishop would concur and also be impressed at his plan to generate a regular income for church funds. Indeed, the bishop might easily put his name forward as a young and progressive sort of candidate for the church's 'fast track' for promotion!

And all because of a chance meeting and a chat with old Joby Fulbright.

Mike Stott was not much for believing in Divine Intervention but…perhaps this could be the start of something really big. The scheme could be taken up by others. Go nation-wide. Even go global!

It couldn't help but make a tidy profit. And it would cost almost nothing to administer!

"Spend a shilling—win a fiver". What an enticement. There could be the added inducement of a double payout at Christmas. It couldn't fail.

Could it?

He tried to think of all the drawbacks but there seemed to be none. Fifteen pounds a month for the fund was not exactly a fortune but in time it would make a substantial contribution to the cost of urgent work on the church roof.

Before Easter had arrived the Binfield Church Lottery had been launched and was proving a great success. Wonderful what furtive can do!

It was about that time that Jane Grayling arrived in the village.

Jane was the new district nurse, taking over from the aged and recently retired Nurse Spiller, a stick-like spinster who, for generations it seemed, had ministered to the immediate medical and nursing needs of the locality and had been an awesome figure in the area.

On visiting a potential patient, Nurse Spiller's inevitable opening question, regardless of the severity of any pain and discomfort being suffered, would be: 'How on earth did you manage to do THAT then?'

She would then proceed with her usual complete and forceful inquisition into the exact cause of the current accident, injury, pain, itch, ache or malady, followed by a severe lecturing about the foolishness of using knives, hammers, lawnmowers and ladders, the stupidity of smoking, drinking intoxicating liquor, lying in the damp grass, of failing to eat porridge for breakfast, or of not wearing a hat, and the iniquities of the present government— whoever they might be.

The hapless victim would then either receive two aspirin tablets or have an Elastoplast applied to the affected area—on rare occasions, both—and told not to be so silly again.

Indeed, it was a brave man or woman, or someone in serious need of immediate medical attention, who called on the services of Nurse Spiller.

Villagers treated the news of her successor with understandable suspicion. Until they saw the replacement.

Nurse Grayling was twenty-four, extremely attractive, with neat figure (accentuated, it seemed, by her equally neat uniform), very pretty blonde hair, usually scraped back into a short pony tail, a delicious smile and a very shapely turn of ankle, emphasised by dark stockings which also enhanced the display of leg, occasionally glimpsed, as she cycled the district on her rounds. And she was single.

It wasn't long before the residents of Binfield and its environs were calling on Nurse Grayling for attention to all manner of ills, real and imagined. Especially the men.

It was, however, a genuine reason that brought Robert Trenchard into contact with the new nurse.

He had been working on a piece of machinery at Longdown which needed some slight adjustment and, when all else failed, had resorted to the time honoured cure-all for agricultural equipment problems, a large iron lever and a heavy hammer.

Somehow, as these things do, something slipped and he succeeded in crushing the little finger on his left hand between the metal bar and an equally uncompromising part of the machinery.

Result: a nasty cut and a badly bruised pinkie.

'Oh, sod!'

Robert was working on his own in the implement shed but still let out an expletive that could be heard over a wide area of the county. As blood began to run down his wrist he chucked both hammer and lever to the ground with a clang, reached round with his right hand and took a handkerchief out of his left trouser pocket.

Wrapping the hankie tightly around the injured finger he walked over to the farmhouse, still cursing under his breath, and met Benjamin, who had heard the ruckus from inside the farm office and had come to the kitchen door.

'What's up?' Benjamin asked.

'Bashed my bloody finger on that bastard machine,' Robert hissed with considerable feeling.

'Let's take a look,' returned his brother turning and leading the way inside and over to the large kitchen sink where he turned on the cold tap. 'Stick it under there.'

Robert gingerly unwound the handkerchief to reveal a sadly damaged and still bleeding finger which he held under the running tap, wincing with pain as the cold water hit the open wound.

They both had a look.

'It's not too bad. A clean cut and no dirt. Your finger will be black and blue in the morning though,' said Benjamin. 'It might need a stitch or two. I'll tape it up and then we'll get you down to the Cottage Hospital in Witherstoke.'

He reached for the farm's first aid box, which was always kept on a shelf just inside the kitchen door, and rummaged inside for some lint and adhesive medical tape.

'No need to go all the way into Witherstoke,' said Robert. 'The new district nurse has arrived in Binfield. She's moved in to the Brownlows' place down in Church Close. It'll give her a bit of practice.'

He grimaced some more as Benjamin placed a good wodge of lint on the finger, wrapped it round tightly with a length of bandage and finished off by fixing it firmly with a piece of the sticky tape.

'That's better. Don't worry. I can drive down there. You get on with the bookwork.'
And with that he was on his way.

Robert drew up outside the large bungalow in Church Close, owned by Mr and Mrs Brownlow, an elderly couple, and two rooms of which were now serving as digs and surgery for the new district nurse. He was gratified to see her bicycle leaning against the front wall. At least she was in.

He went up the path, rang the bell at the side door and stepped back. Within seconds a shadowy figure appeared behind the frosted glass and the door was opened.
Robert gazed.

Before him stood a strikingly enchanting blonde vision, her hair for once was not tied back and fell in short waves about her face. Her nose was perfectly straight, her blue eyes seemed to sparkle and she was wearing the most disarming smile. In her smart blue uniform and dark stockings she certainly was a stunning sight.

'Yes? Can I help?' Then, seeing Robert's bound finger, added: 'Oh dear, what have we done there?'

Robert remained both motionless and speechless, mesmerised by the delightful scene before him.

It was several more seconds before Nurse Grayling broke the spell with: 'Well then. You'd better come in.'

She led the way along a short passage and into what was originally a small back bedroom and which now served as a treatment room, signalling Robert towards an upright chair with black padded arms.

Robert sat down and looked up at her. He had still not spoken.

She bent over him. 'Let's see what we've got here then,' she said, taking his wrist in one hand and carefully unwinding the blood stained dressing. 'Hmm. That's nasty. Throbs a bit I expect, doesn't it? How did you manage that?'

'Trapped it between a crow bar and the…' Robert was about to use a very descriptive adjective but managed to stop himself, 'the baling machine axle,' he concluded.

The mere hint of a smile returned to the corners of Nurse Grayling's lips.

'What were we doing playing about with farm machinery?' she asked.

'I wasn't playing about,' returned Robert with a touch of sharpness in his voice. 'I'm a farmer. Repairing farm machinery is one of the things I do.'

'You'll have to be a bit more careful next time then, won't you,' she responded, looking straight down into his eyes. They were, after all, very handsome blue eyes in a very handsome weather-brown face.

She smiled again and Robert couldn't but help smiling back.

Nurse Grayling gently bathed the injured finger in a small bowl of warm antiseptic solution.

'I must say it's nice and clean. But I think it would be best to have a couple of stitches in that cut. You could go to the Cottage Hospital in town or, if you trust me, I could do it myself here.'

'I trust you,' Robert heard himself say.

Robert winced as the little suture needle went in and the edges of the cut were pulled together.

Then the nurse bandaged the injury, strapped the damaged little finger to its neighbour and finished off by placing a waterproof stall over the two digits, making it fast by tying the strap around his wrist.

'There we are. Finished. If it keeps throbbing or aching take a couple of pain-killers. Have you got any?'

Robert nodded.

'You'll need to come back in ten days or so to have the stitches taken out. Meanwhile, I'd better take down some of your details.'

Five minutes later "Robert Trenchard, farmer, of Longdown Farm, Binfield near Witherstoke" was a statistic in Nurse Grayling's medical records book.

He was also feeling much better.

The redhead who had been a major feature in his life in recent months had moved, with her career, to the other end of the country and there had seemed little point in trying to continue the relationship at such long distance. So they had parted, still the best of friends.

And Robert was without a woman in his life, for him, an unusual situation in which to find himself.

Enter Jane Grayling. An extremely attractive and intelligent female who, as far as he could tell, was also unattached. Robert wasted no time.

'Is there a Mr Grayling…or anyone else involved in that kind of role?' Robert was standing up now and looking directly into the nurse's blue eyes.

'Why?' Nurse Grayling was facing him and looking directly back into his own, equally blue, eyes.

'It's just that…well, you're new to the village and may not have many friends in the area. I know the place well, have done since childhood, and thought perhaps I might be able to…to show you around a bit.'

'We'll see, shall we?' There was the faintest of smiles on her lips and the faintest of twinkles in her eye.

'And IS there a Mr Grayling?'

The nurse smiled again and gave a slight shake of her head but Robert was unable to discern whether it was an answer in the negative or an expression of her amusement at his presumption.

'Don't forget. Keep it clean and dry. Ten days or so for the stitches. Give me a ring for an appointment. Here's my card.' And she handed Robert a small oblong of white, led him down the passage to the side entrance, let him out, and firmly closed the door behind him.

Robert was, to say the least, a little nonplussed.

Ever since his late 'teens he had been used to being in control of communication and interaction with the opposite sex. His many conquests over the years had been accomplished with seemingly natural ease. He was always in the driving seat, so to speak, and that's how he liked it.

He now stood outside the door of Jane Grayling's home, gazing down at the card in his hand, and with the distinct feeling that he had somehow come off a pretty poor second best in this latest encounter.

And his finger had starting throbbing painfully again.

'Hullo there.'

Robert, standing deep in thought at the gate of the bungalow, was suddenly aware of a tallish figure in black, wearing a white back-to-front collar, who had appeared, suddenly and silently, and was now dismounting from an ancient bicycle.

It was the new Vicar.

'Can you tell me if Nurse Grayling is in?' The priest parked his bike against the low privet hedge, put one foot on a pedal to remove the cycle clip from his right trouser leg and looked up at Robert. 'I'm sorry, I'm Michael Stott, new Vicar. I don't think we've met.' He held out a hand.

'Well. Yes. I've just this minute left her.' They shook hands. 'Trenchard. Robert Trenchard. Longdown Farm.

'Ah yes, I do believe I've met your brother…uh…Benjamin isn't it? Haven't seen either of you at church as yet. Still…' he didn't give Robert chance to make excuses '…I'm sure you'll both be along sooner or later.

'Look. Nice to have met you. I must dash and catch the nurse before she disappears on her rounds again.' And he was walking away along the path towards the side door that Robert had recently discovered was so inviting.

Robert drove back to the farm in something of a daze and with an inexplicable feeling of resentment coupled with jealousy at the appearance of the new Vicar.

Meanwhile, although the reason for his visit to the surgery was entirely different, a scenario was being played out between the village priest and the district nurse, in many ways similar to that between the nurse and the farmer.

They had, of course, seen each other once or twice from a distance while about their respective parish duties but had not yet been formally introduced.

There was the same ring on the side door bell. The same shadowy figure a few seconds later behind the frosted glass. The door opened and the reaction of the Vicar to the appearance of Nurse Grayling was almost identical to that of Robert Trenchard.

For a moment the Rev Michael Stott stood speechless and there was the same, slightly amused, smile on the lips of the vision before him.

However he regained his composure rather quicker than the previous caller. 'Nurse Grayling? I'm…I'd…I must confess you're not exactly what I'd expected. Michael Stott. New Vicar. Might I have a word?'

At her invitation Mr Stott followed Nurse Grayling along the passageway and into the same treatment room and soon found himself sitting in the same black padded-armed chair.

'Now, Vicar. How can I help? You don't appear to be ill, or injured in any way.'

The young priest's eyes took in the scene before him. Nurse Grayling was half leaning against and half sitting on the edge of the desk on the other side of the small surgery. He was as impressed as Robert Trenchard had been.

But for the moment he had to concentrate on other things.

'You've heard about the village lottery?' he began. It was more a question than a statement.

Before she could reply he had continued.
'The idea is to raise money for, initially at any rate, repairs to the church roof. It's been pretty successful so far but we need to push it a bit more and I thought that…'

'You thought that I might be interested in being a regular subscriber.' She finished the sentence for him.

'No. No, not at all.' The Vicar blushed visibly. 'Although I should be delighted of course if you did decide to make a monthly contribution. No, it's just that quite a lot of people come into your little surgery and a small notice advertising the draw could bring in a few extra customers.'

He waited for her reply.

'They've put one up at The Drovers Arms,' he offered.

'Is that some kind of inducement, or a recommendation for me to put up an advertisement in the surgery?' she asked. Once again that certain twinkle was in her eyes and the ghost of a smile played on her lips at the Vicar's obvious embarrassment.
'No. No, of course not.'

He was clearly flustered. What was it about this disarmingly attractive young woman that seemed to keep him wrong-footed at every turn? 'It's just that I thought you might be able to help in a good cause for the village and…and…'

His explanation tailed off weakly.

The Nurse's facial expression became much more sympathetic until she was virtually beaming, her even white teeth and wide lips adding enormously to the allure.

'I'm sorry, I was just joking,' she said. 'Yes, I'll put up a little notice. Do you have a copy with you?'

Mr Stott fumbled beneath his gown and eventually produced a somewhat crumpled piece of paper which he handed to Jane Grayling. She smoothed it on the top of the desk and laid it to one side.

'Was there anything else?'

Michael Stott had no further business around the parish that couldn't wait awhile and would have welcomed the chance to get to know the new village Nurse a little better, but found himself saying: 'No. Uh, thank you. That was all…I…Thank you again, you've been most kind.'

Outside it was a confused young priest who climbed onto his bike and cycled away.

In the space of less than half an hour, two of Binfield's most eligible bachelors had fallen under the spell of the enigmatic Nurse Grayling.

Meanwhile Robert was back at Longdown Farm.

A lot had happened during the two years since the tragedy that took his parents' lives. Benjamin's marriage to their housekeeper's daughter. The appearance in court of Joby on a trumped-up charge of poaching. The demise of conman Reggie Broadman whose downfall was precipitated by the Holmes and Watson detective work of Robert and Joby. And, of course, the destruction of gamekeeper Fred Appleton's walnut tree through an unfortunate "misunderstanding" between Joby and a travelling so-called tree surgeon.

But, as always on a farm, there was forever work in hand and Robert was now engaged in helping Joby with the afternoon milking of Longdown's dairy herd.

Then there was the possibility of a late frost this evening—which could mean that the farm's several hundred acres of newly sprouting wheat and barley would need rolling tomorrow.

Benjamin came into the milking parlour when they were half-way through the milking.

'How's everything going? How's the hand?' he called out.

'Fine, on both counts,' returned Robert from somewhere behind a black and white cow. 'But tomorrow we could be pushed, especially if I'm on rolling in the morning. Joby's going to need a hand with the milking.'

'Just what I've been thinking. I'm going to have to try to postpone some of this damned paperwork. It just takes up so much time…'

'Look,' Robert, bucket in hand, had now appeared from behind the black and white cow, 'isn't it about time we thought about getting some permanent help? Now that you're tied up with the office so much? It's got to come to it sooner or later, especially for harvest.

A youngster would be fine. He doesn't have to be a potential brain surgeon.'

'You must have been reading my mind,' said Benjamin. 'Let's talk some more over supper tonight.'

As a result of their evening's deliberations, and the appearance of an entry in the small ads of *The Witherstoke Gazette*, a few weeks later a tall and skinny 15-year-old made his appearance in the role of the new trainee farm worker at Longdown.

Paul Plummer, known to all who knew him as "Pongo", had left school early to take up his position. Neither his teacher nor his parents considered that an extra few weeks of schooling would make very much difference to his future prospects and, after all, a job was a job.

For his part he embraced his duties with great enthusiasm and naivety, hanging on to every word uttered by Joby, his self-appointed mentor, even instructions for the simplest of tasks. He may have been quite a few degrees short of being the hottest spark in the fire but he was monumentally keen.

And Joby's oft-repeated criticism: 'No, no, not like THAT! Gawd, boy! Yer like a cow with a musket!' was invariably met with a broad, ear-to-ear grin, as if Pongo considered any comment from Joby to be a compliment of the highest order.

This was his first job in the grown-up world and working on a farm had been his sole ambition since childhood. He was jolly well going to make a success of it.

Before long he was to be seen following the old man like a well-trained dog, both on and off the farm, learning not only the rudiments of farming but also the intricacies of some of the much less publicised activities with which Joby had, during his sixty-odd years, become associated.

By the time the May blossom began to appear on the hawthorn hedges, Pongo was a well-established addition to the little Longdown Farm community.

In spite of the frequent admonitions from Joby, which were just as frequently shaken off like water from a duck's back, the old fellow secretly enjoyed the lad's company and in a short time was treating the newcomer almost as the son he had never had.

It was after months of careful tuition from Joby that Pongo, engaging on his very first solo 'extra-curricular' expedition, fell foul of the Squire's gamekeeper, Fred Appleton.

As a lad Joby had frequently indulged in egg-nesting, searching for wild birds' eggs for a collection, as many country boys were wont to do. He had also been the accredited local expert in the gathering of the eggs of gamebirds, water fowl, pigeons and the like for the breakfast table.

He was now passing on that expertise to Pongo.

Chapter twelve

AT LAST it was April.

After a March Easter that was the coldest for 30 years, with temperatures only struggling up to a few degrees above freezing for the whole weekend, the signs of Spring finally began to arrive.

The Beatles were breaking all music chart records following their highly successful February tour of the US and the Rolling Stones were well into their stride, and set to follow the example of their Liverpool chums and rivals.

And April is the month when wild birds become totally engrossed in building nests and laying eggs, including, for those people who might have a particular interest, gamebirds.

The time of year when the eggs of pheasants, partridges and wild duck, as well as those of moorhens, wood pigeons and plovers, all of which make excellent eating, were likely to find their way on to a countryman's menu.

In mid-month Pongo was out on his own on Saturday afternoon after pigeon and moorhen eggs.

In the ten years since the 1954 Bird Protection Act was introduced, when it became illegal to take the eggs of most wild birds, the country hobby of building up a collection, a pursuit enjoyed by generations of youngsters, had virtually come to a halt.

But a few species, notably wood pigeons, which were considered as pests, were excluded. The law regarding some others was sometimes a little confusing. And anyway, who was worried about moorhens losing an egg or two. Their culinary value was excellent.

The taking of pheasant, partridge and wild duck eggs was a much more serious offence, with court appearances and severe penalties for those caught doing it, although many country folks took the view, understandably, as these eggs are so delicious, that it was perfectly acceptable to take them—as long as you didn't get caught.

Pongo started down by the river, where, armed with an eight feet long ash pole with an old teaspoon lashed to the end, he had managed to liberate the clutches from two moorhens' nests, anchored in reeds too far from the bank to reach without wading, just as Joby had instructed him.

'Why don't we use a bigger spoon on the pole?' Pongo had wanted to know. 'Wouldn't it be easier?'

'It'd be easier to get the eggs out o' the nest and into a bigger spoon,' admitted Joby. 'But bringin' it back to the bank on the end of a long pole it would wobble. Jus' can't stop it. Wobble, wobble. Egg falls out of spoon. Egg goes plop into the river. Last you see of *that* egg! A moorhen's egg fits nice an' snug in a teaspoon. Won't wobble out,' he confided.

Pongo already had seven of the bantam-sized, purple blotched and streaked eggs divided between the two pockets of his big loose jacket ('Never put all yer eggs in one pocket,' Joby had told him.) and was making his way home along the hedgerow that separated Longdown's fields from the estate property keepered by Fred Appleton.

By chance it was the very boundary hedge where Joby had had his run-in with the gamekeeper over ferreting for rabbits months earlier.

Pongo spotted the pigeon's nest, a simple flat platform of twigs, no more than six or seven feet from the ground in the branches of a hawthorn tree. He could also make out the outline of two eggs through the flimsy structure of the nest.

Only problem was the tree could only be reached from the other side of the fence and would have to be approached from Squire's land.

Still, thought Pongo, glancing up and down the hedge, no-one about. Only take two or three minutes to get over the fence, climb onto the top strand of barbed wire from where he could reach the prize. Hop down. Back over the fence to the 'safety' of the Longdown field. Bob's your uncle. Job done. Two minutes top whack.

All went according to plan for the first 90 seconds.

Dropping down off the fence, the two eggs held safely in his mouth, as Joby had taught him, Pongo jumped almost out of his skin as he felt the sudden weight of a heavy hand on his shoulder.

'And wot we got 'ere then?' Fred Appleton demanded.

Yes, it was the dreaded gamekeeper who had been watching the egg collector from behind that same tree whither he had pounced on Joby all those months ago. He had bided his time until Pongo was in a position to be caught red-handed on estate owned land.

Pongo hastily popped the two pigeon's eggs out of his mouth and into his hand.

'I…I…I'm just collecting a few p…pigeons' eggs,' spluttered poor Pongo, visibly quaking with fear. 'Nothin' wrong in that is there?'

And he held his hand out for Fred to see.

'No, 'course not. Nothing wrong at all,' return the gamekeeper. 'Just so long as you don't have any of my pheasants' eggs in yer pockets.'

'I ain't seen no pheasants' eggs,' replied the quivering youth truthfully, but mindful of the half dozen or so moorhens' eggs nestling in his jacket.

'That's all right then, ennit. I'll just check though to make sure.'

And with one swift movement Fred's two bony hands firmly and expertly slapped the pockets of Pongo's jacket, startling the wearer, so that he dropped the two pigeon's eggs on the ground. Both broke.

A huge grin came over Fred's face with the realisation that whatever eggs Pongo had had, as he was fairly certain was the case, they were now nothing more than a gooey, sticky mess lining the inside of the lad's pockets.

'No, nothing there,' Fred's grin grew even wider. 'Lucky for you!

'Pity you dropped them though,' he chuckled, indicated the remains of the white shelled eggs on the ground. ' They were good ones too.'

Fred hadn't wanted the complication of taking the youngster to court over a few eggs, but he did want to teach him a lesson he wouldn't forget in a hurry.

'Off you go then. On yer way,' he ordered the miserable boy.

Shoulders slumped and head downcast Pongo, watched by the still grinning Fred, shuffled off towards the gate at the end of the field. As soon as he was out of sight he plunged both hands into his jacket pockets to see if there were any survivors.

There weren't.

And both hands came out covered in sticky egg-slime which, even after numerous wipings in the grass, remained uncomfortably tacky until he got home and washed them.

Is was not until Monday morning at milking that Pongo was able to relate to Joby the full story of his disastrous brush with the hated Fred Appleton.

Joby was furious.

"'E's got no right,' he almost hissed through clenched teeth. 'No right at all. Pickin' on people goin' about their lawful business,' totally ignoring the basic fact that Pongo had been on Squire's land. "'E bloody thinks he's God or summat. Don't you worry son. We'll find a way to get back at 'im.'

And Joby did no more than get on with the milking. Quiet, he may have been but thoughts were already whirling around inside his fertile brain.

The village at large, however, had other things to occupy its composite mind.

News quickly spread about the death of Gertrude Lailey, a lifelong and well-loved resident of Binfield.

Mrs Lailey, widow of retired but late farmer Tom Lailey, had been something of the village benefactress for fifteen years or more. Her home, just off the main street, was a large detached house in nearly five acres of land, only a small portion of which was maintained, with help from a part-time handyman, as a formal garden.

The rest was more or less allowed to develop on its own, although a few sheep were occasionally penned there to keep the grass and some of the other vegetation under reasonable control.

There were some patches of blackberry bushes, which produced wonderful fruit in October, a little ditch that sometimes ran wet and sometimes ran dry, and ten or a dozen decent sized trees that were ideal for climbing.

Its official title was Lailey's Meadow, though to several generations of village children it had always been known as "Lallyfield".

Binfield had its own cricket ground with a pavilion, which also doubled as the village hall, but no children's playground. For years the youngsters of the village had used Lallyfield as their unofficial recreation area, along with, it must be said, the full approval of the benevolent Gertrude Lailey.

She had even had a couple of swings set up on the branches of two of the larger trees and a tiny rough wooden bridge of old railway sleepers constructed over the ditch.

During the summer holidays there were always little groups of children laughing and playing, the sounds of their enjoyment carrying along the village street.

'What's goin' t' 'appen with Lallyfield now Mrs Lailey's gone then?'

The question was posed, to no-one in particular, by one of regulars in the bar of The Drovers Arms where, as was normal with any topic of local interest, much of the public debate went on.

'Dunno you,' came the reply.

'Be sold for buildin' development I 'spect,' was the opinion of one of the gathered forum. 'Can't expect a valuable bit 'o land like that, right in the middle of the village, to be a kids' playground for ever.'

And from that casual remark was born the rumour, as rumours often are born, that the land was under threat from building speculators.

But wild rumours can so often be frighteningly near the truth.

Soon after came the revelation that the entire property had been purchased by an estate agent from Witherstoke.

Peter Hillory was something of a self-made man. He'd started out as a junior negotiator with one of the town's largest estate agents and, through sheer hard work and dedication, it must be said, worked his way up to be their top salesman. Mr Hillory certainly had the gift of the gab and through several shrewd negotiations and acquisitions had built up quite a reputation as someone who could make things happen in the world of local development.

He had recently left the old firm to set up in business on his own account and acquiring the estate of the late Gertrude Lailey was his first major business deal.

'Now we know what's goin' to 'appen to Lallyfield,' was the knowledgeable statement at The Drovers.

'Whad'y' reckon then?'

'S' obvious ennit? Five acres o' prime buildin' land. At least four or five houses to the acre. Little up-market, private estate for townies who want to live in the country. Twenty, twenty-five houses. That land's worth a small fortune. And not so small at that! Wish I 'ad a bit of it.'

There was a silence as this latest information was absorbed.

'But I 'eard as 'ow this 'illary bloke wanted to do the place up and live in it 'isself.'

'Oh yeah, 'e might do. But 'e's not goin' to want a five acre garden is 'e you? Still be plenty o' room left over fer a dozen or more new 'ouses.'

And a further silence set in.

A team of painters and decorators had already been busy on the old Lailey house for a week or more and it wasn't long before the new owner moved in.

Peter Hillory was in his mid-forties. His babyish face suggested that he was ten years younger—although the rest of his body indicated quite the reverse.

He could possibly be described as handsome, nearly six feet tall with a pleasant round face, with just one too many chins, fair hair, now thinning and often-smiling grey eyes.

But nearly 15 years of living alone in a bachelor flat and too many self-catered meals of the wrong type 'on the run' while chasing his next deal had done him no favours. He was overweight by at least two stones.

He had had a few fleeting attachments with members of the fairer sex but his work always came first. Actually it came second and third as well.

Last minute cancelled dinner dates and theatre trips (some, sadly, with no notification at all to the affected partner and all created through his insatiable appetite for yet another property sale) are not exactly designed to encourage a potential long-term relationship. His liaisons had all been decidedly short term.

Now, with a larger home to keep in order it soon became clear to Mr Hillory that he badly needed some domestic help and a small ad in the 'sits vac' column of the *Gazette* brought applications from a number of likely candidates.

And among them was one from Ivy Green.

For some months now, since her daughter Sandra's wedding to Benjamin, at Longdown Farm, where she had been the paid live-in cook and housekeeper, she had argued with the young couple that it was time she was moving on.

'But mum,' Sandra had declared. 'You know there's always a place for you here and, well, we'd miss you.'

'She's right,' Benjamin added. 'I know Sandra's not spending so much time at the stables now but...'

'No. There's no room in any home for two mistresses,' interrupted. Ivy, whose role had so recently altered. 'Housekeeper, yes, but you don't need a live-in mother-in-law!'

And she laughed.

'Anyway you'll be thinking of starting a family of your own soon, I've no doubt,' she added with a twinkle in her eye. 'And a wife should be the head of her own household. Time for me to step back.'

Her casual attachment with village bobby Percy Wheeler had gone cold over a month ago when Percy was promoted to sergeant, with a posting to the County Police Headquarters.

He had wanted Ivy to move with him but she felt that their relationship was not so close that she was willing to uproot and move nearly 50 miles away into an entirely new, and urban, environment.

When she saw the ad in the local paper she had decided to apply. It seemed the perfect career move, perfectly timed.

With her experience of running a large house and a glowing reference from Benjamin she was, not surprisingly, offered the position and agreed to take it. Soon after, she moved into the newly named "Lailey House" (the place had never had an official name before) as cook/housekeeper.

Within a short time Peter Hillory realised the value of his still pleasing-looking employee. The house was kept in perfect order and her skills in the kitchen soon found him positively looking forward to proper, home cooked, regular meals. With much more healthy fare he was even surprised to find that he was actually beginning to shed a few excess pounds.

But the rumours about Lallyfield grew in intensity and it was the Rev Michael Stott who decided to take on the task of firing the opening shots in what looked likely to turn into an epic village confrontation.

Calling unannounced at the house one evening, 'for a little chat,' he was invited into the expansive, newly decorated drawing room and was offered a seat.

He settled into one of the big tapestry-designed armchairs, face to face with Peter Hillory sitting opposite in its twin.

Leaning forward he wasted no time on formalities and came straight to the point.

'You do realise, Mr Hillory, that for many years now the children of Binfield have used Lailey's Meadow, at the express invitation of the owner of course, as an unofficial playing field?' he began. 'And now we hear that you're intending to rob them of this facility by building houses on the land.'

The new proprietor was totally taken aback.

What he had imagined was a goodwill visit by the local priest, with perhaps the hint of a small donation to church funds, had unexpectedly turned into a direct assault on his intentions for the site.

'Well I...er...well I...haven't any finalised plans at the moment. Haven't yet thought it through completely,' he replied, starting to regain some of the composure he had lost at the outset of this onslaught. Peter Hillory, with his vast experience in business dealings, was an expert at thinking 'on the spot.'

Mr Stott opened up with his second barrel.

'And if Lallyfield disappears under tons of bricks and mortar, the youngsters of the village will have nowhere safe to play, except that tiny corner up on the cricket field—which is not really big enough, is a bit too tucked away, and quite unsuitable as a play area.'

'Well now,' returned the estate agent. 'First of all there are no plans at all to do anything with the meadow.' He was warming to his theme. 'As I told you, I've had no time to think about it.

'Secondly, when I do decide what I want to do with my own land I'll submit the relevant planning applications through the official channels. If you're so concerned about a children's play area, it seems to me there is an awful lot of land around the church which is doing little more than producing an excess of long grass, nettles and weeds. Perhaps some of that space might be more usefully employed?'

And he smiled a satisfied half-smile.

It was the Vicar's turn to find himself on the defensive. He had to admit to himself that he had discovered nothing factual about the future of the playground, neither had he wrung any sort of a promise from the new owner that Lallyfield would not be forfeited to development.

It was a somewhat chastened but thoughtful cleric who made his lonely way back to the vicarage.

First round to Peter Hillory.

By pure coincidence it was later that same evening, as Joby pedalled his way home from The Drovers after his customary two pints, that 'the plan' was conceived. For weeks the old rascal had been racking his brains for a way to get back at Fred Appleton for his treatment of Pongo. The idea, when it came, was unexpected—and beautifully simple.

It began when Joby's front bike lamp began to dim, the battery losing power, so that by the time he reached his cottage it was a mere glimmer, though fortunately it was not a dark night.

As soon as he got in and lit the gas light in the little sitting room he got out his diary and started turning the pages.

'Got it!' he murmured to himself. 'Monday 11 May. Nearly three weeks time. No moon. Gets dark about half past eight. Bit earlier if it's cloudy. Perfect!'

Fred Appleton was a creature of habit. He didn't realise it and would have denied the very suggestion. After all, gamekeepers need to keep the rest of the community guessing for fear of creating opportunities for certain folk to indulge in a little, shall we say, 'opportunism' among his precious pheasants.

Like most 'keepers he tended to keep his own company. He seldom drank with the rest of the male population of the parish in The Drovers Arms. No point in letting the whole world know where he'd be on any given night of the week.

He preferred to cycle the five and a half miles to the King's Head in the neighbouring village of Netherham every week for a few quiet pints and a game of dominoes. And it only took him twenty minutes.

And, as you might expect, Joby Fulbright knew perfectly well where his old adversary would be, come rain or shine, every Monday, Wednesday and Friday evening!

He went back outside and grinned as he unclipped the front bike lamp from its bracket. He grinned again as he came back inside and made sure the lamp, now very faint, was switched on. His grin was even wider as he placed it in the middle of the kitchen table.

Then he went to bed.

Next morning the light was as dead as a dodo. He opened the top of the lamp and took out the now-spent double cylindrical battery and placed it on the table.

Hadn't liked that battery very much anyway. Bought two at a cheap price from a shop in Witherstoke. Didn't seem to last as long as the ones he usually bought from George Goodall down at the village garage. He fitted the new spare battery into the empty lamp, switched it on and off to make sure it was working all right, then went outside to refit it to the bike.

The useless battery stood on the kitchen table for another two and half weeks.

Meanwhile, April slipped out and May slipped in.

It was a good start to the month.

West Ham United, captained by Bobby Moore, won the FA Cup, beating Preston North End 3-2 in the final at Wembley.

The following weekend the Monaco Grand Prix Formula One race was won by Britain's Graham Hill driving the British built BRM. The other BRM, driven by American Ritchie Ginther, was second.

And two more Britons, Peter Arundel and Jim Clark, both driving Lotus Climax machines, were placed third and fourth.

Frank Barlow won £5,000 on Premium Bonds, sold his DIY shop in Coronation Street and moved to a new home in Cheshire, meanwhile Cilla Black was climbing the charts into the top three with her new release *'You're My World.'*

Monday the eleventh dawned bright and clear but with the forecast of increasing cloud with the chance of rain later.

'Perfect!' chuckled Joby.

He was busy all day at the farm, morning milking, some general repair work and machinery servicing under Robert's guidance, all of whose instructions he passed on, word for word, to Pongo. Then it was afternoon milking and still he had uttered not a word to his protégé about 'the plan.'

'Fancy a game o' darts at The Drovers s'evenin'? Pongo asked him.

Joby looked up from where his head had been resting against the belly of a cow as he fixed the four suction-operated milking teats to the animal's udders.

He looked at Pongo, treating him to an exaggerated wink.

'Can't make t'night. Got a bit o' business which will take up most of the evenin. Might make it a bit later on though for a swift 'alf.'

And he said no more.

Right on schedule Fred Appleton wheeled his bike out of his front gate, turned right and pedalled off out of the village. It was 8 o'clock, still light, although gathering clouds made for a long, gloomy twilight.

The road to Netherham was just a winding country lane, with only three or four farm buildings, set well back off the highway, throughout its entire length. Fields and woods bordered the route and traffic of any kind was just about non-existent.

Fred's lanky but wiry frame forced the cycle along at a fair pace and he arrived at the King's Head twenty minutes later, leaned his bike against the side wall, just out of sight behind the lean-to outside urinal. No point advertising the fact that he was inside. He took off his cycle clips, walked round to the front of the pub and, after a quick look up and down the road, opened the door and went inside.

It was perhaps fifteen minutes later that Joby carefully propped his own machine in the hedge fifty yards away from the King's Head, turned off the lights, and silently crept the short distant to the inn.

It was almost dark.

The lights were on in the public bar but the curtains were already drawn From inside came the muffled sounds of conversation and laughter. Round the side of the building, in the dim light thrown from the tiny high window in the wall of the gents' toilet block, Joby located Fred's bike.

It took less than thirty seconds to remove the top of the front lamp, take out the battery and put it carefully in his right hand jacket pocket. From the other pocket he produced the dud battery he had been keeping for the last couple of weeks and slid it into the lamp, clipping the top cover back in place.

In less than a minute he was back on his own bike and pedalling out of the village. Soon after nine o'clock he walked into The Drovers Arms at Binfield.

'You managed to make it then?' It was Pongo.

Although he had not yet reached the legal drinking age, Alf Blissett reckoned that anyone who was old enough to work was old enough to drink. In fact the lad invariably drank Coca -Cola— unless someone slipped him half a shandy.

'Yeh. All finished with me business,' returned Joby. 'We still on for that game 'o darts then?'

And for the next hour there were plenty of witnesses who would swear that Joby had been playing darts in The Drovers all evening.

He got home from the pub soon after ten, sat in the kitchen and gave another chuckle.

Outside the night sky had darkened totally as the cloud cover increased and the wind had got up a bit. It was black as pitch out there.

'What a pity it ain't rainin,' Joby mumbled to himself. 'Still, can't 'ave everythin!'

At just about that same moment it was 'turning out' time at the King's Head in Netherham and Fred Appleton stepped out of the public bar doorway into the half light of the pub forecourt, stooped to put on his cycle clips and made his way round to the side of the building where his bike was parked.

Fred pushed the bike out to the front of the pub, bent and turned on his red rear light, then turned the knob on the top of the front lamp. Nothing. He turned the switch off and on several times.

Still nothing.

He looked into the front of the lamp. There was the tiniest red glimmer coming from the filament of the bulb.

'Bloody battery's dead!' exploded Fred. 'It was perfectly all right earlier on,' he muttered to himself.

The two or three other late customers were already disappearing up the road and there came the sound of locks and bolts being engaged as the landlord locked up for the night.

'Ah well, just have to ride home without lights. Shouldn't be too bad.'

And it wasn't too bad.

At first.

For the first fifty yards the outside light from the pub illuminated the way. Then there was the glow from the lighted windows of cottages along the main street of the village which made it just about possible to make out the roadway. They became fewer and farther between until at last, after a quarter of a mile, he reached open countryside—and a solid wall of blackness.

No moon, no stars, no glimmer from cottage windows—and no distant glow in the sky from any nearby town. The countryside at night in these circumstances can be very, very dark indeed.

Fred thought he knew the way pretty well but even though he slowed his pedals to a crawl it was like riding with both eyes tightly closed and it wasn't long before a slight bend caught him out. He mounted the grassy verge and finished up on his back in the ditch, luckily for him, a dry ditch.

'Bugger!'

Scrambling back onto the road he had some difficulty in re-orientating himself. It was as black as being blindfold in a coal cellar.

He even tried removing the rear light in the hope that he could use its faint red beam to at least lighten his way a little but as it was bolted to the frame and he had no tools with him, even if he could have seen what he was doing, he had to abandon the idea.

Trying to push his bike backwards, so that the rear light faced forwards, was even less successful.

The awful realisation hit him that he would have to walk all the way, pushing his bike, and slowly at that. The twenty minute outward journey would be nearer an hour and a half going back. It was already half past ten. He wouldn't be home until well after midnight. Unless some vehicle happened along. Which he knew it wouldn't.

And then it started to rain.

It was a very wet, very cold and very annoyed Fred Appleton who eventually got home at a quarter to one.

Later that morning the still irate gamekeeper was at the village garage.

'My bloody bike lamp battery,' he raved at an open-mouthed George. 'Bloody dead. Only bought it the week 'fore last. What y' goin' t' do about it?'

George, well used to dealing with customers for whom something was always not quite right, regained a little of his composure.

'Well let's take a look shall we?' And he removed the top of the lamp, took out the battery and gave it a long, hard look.

'Sorry Fred. Can't help you with this one.'

'Why the hell not? It's less than a fortnight old.'

George held the errant battery out for Fred to see.

'Don't matter how old it is. This is a Varta battery. I only sell Eveready. It didn't come from me. Looks like you've been got at.'

'What…?'

The truth suddenly dawned on him that last night's misadventure was no misadventure at all. Rather, the truth smacked him in the face with the force of a pick handle. Someone had swapped his battery.

He was certain, of course, that he knew exactly who was responsible. But he also realised, with a dreadful sinking feeling, that he had not a snowball's chance in hell of proving it.

'That damned Joby Fulbright,' he spat out through clenched teeth as he cycled off up the road.

George watched him go, a smile playing about his face. He, too, was pretty well sure he knew who the culprit would have been.

About the same time Nurse Jane Grayling was busy in her little surgery. Her patient was a young lad who seemed to have scrapes and bruises on most parts of his body. Including a black eye.

'What's your name young man?'

'Billy.'

'Billy who?'

'Billy Painter.'

Billy Painter was sitting in a chair and Nurse Grayling was stooping before him, carefully cleaning up a nasty weeping graze on one leg. The opposite elbow had a gash just below the elbow and there was dried blood on his short trousers. Both arms were bruised.

'Any more war wounds?'

'Me back 'urts.'

'Let's see it then.'

Billy peeled off his tee-shirt to reveal a very sore looking weal running almost diagonally across just below the shoulders.

'Where did you get all these injuries, Billy?'

'Fell off me bike.'

'And the black eye?'

'Walked into a door.'

'What about your mum and dad. What did they say? Did your mum send you here?'

'No.'

'You're not telling me the whole truth, are you Billy?' demanded the nurse.

Billy was silent and it was clear she was going to get no more information out of him.

She patched him up with Elastoplast and carefully smoothed some antiseptic cream onto the wound on his back.

After noting his name, age and address in her report book she sent him on his way. Then, her normally calm forehead furrowed into a frown as she reached for the telephone.

The young looking constable who had been allocated to take on the duties of village bobby, following the promotional move of Percy Wheeler some months earlier, was seated at his desk in the small office section of the police house.

Around him on the walls were an array of small notices warning about the dangers of rabies, foot and mouth disease and the folly of leaving houses unlocked or windows open, as well as a table of lighting-up times.

There was an 'in' tray and an 'out' tray on the table before him. Both were empty. He was gazing somewhere into the middle distance, contemplating whether he should do another trip round the parish on his bike, when the jangling bell of the big black telephone almost made him jump. It didn't ring that often.

Quickly composing himself he lifted the receiver.

'Binfield Police House.'

His voice was clear and authoritative.

It was the new District Nurse.

'Yes?'

'Is it urgent?'

'Well if it's that important you'd best call round to see me.'

'I'm available now.'

'Come straight round then.'

'Yes, now.'

'Fine, I'll see you in about ten minutes.'

He thoughtfully replaced the receiver in its cradle and leaned back in his chair. So, the new District Nurse had something 'important and somewhat alarming' to say to him. And she didn't want to discuss it on the phone. Things could be warming up.

It was actually less than five minutes later that he heard the scrape of Nurse Grayling's bike against the wall outside. He waited until the bell rang before rising from his chair and going to the door.

Before him stood the new District Nurse. It was their first face-to-face meeting although they had passed in the street several times in the last few weeks.

'Come in.'

He closed the door behind her, then led the way through from the hall into the little office, motioned for her to sit in the chair in front of the desk, pushed the office door shut and took his own seat facing her.

'Now. How can I help you?'

Jane Grayling took stock of the young man who represented the law in Binfield and quite liked what she saw.

He was, not surprisingly for a policeman, quite tall, just over six feet. His thick black hair was tidily groomed, shortish, with a left-hand parting. The face was narrow with traces of 'five o'clock shadow' although it was barely midday. And his eyes were startlingly blue. Pc Alan Arlett was also lean and athletic looking.

He met her inquiring gaze steadily. And if the District Nurse imagined her own appearance would have the usual effect of totally disarming a new male acquaintance she was to be sadly disappointed. There was not the slightest flicker of appreciation on Pc Arlett's features.

'Well, it's a bit difficult.'

She dropped her eyes for a few seconds, then looked up again. He was still viewing her face with the same intensity.

'As I intimated over the phone I had a patient in today and, well, to judge from his injuries I'd say the cause he gave seems highly suspicious.'

'Who was this patient?'

The question was more of a demand.

'I don't know if I've the legal right to identify the person concerned.'

'So how do you suppose I may be able to help in any way over the injuries of some unknown person?'

'What I can say is that this patient is a juvenile. And I suspect he's been either badly bullied or…'

'Or what?'

'Well…abused…I mean by an adult…or parents even.'

She paused, shocked by the allegations she had made. But made they had to be.

'So. We've established that you have a young boy—what age?'

'Just twelve.'

'A 12-year-old lad who has some suspicious looking injuries. Local?'

'Yes. Netherham Lane.'

She then detailed the various wounds and contusions she had dressed not an hour before.

'What do you want me to do about it?'
Pc Arlett had put the ball firmly back in Nurse Grayling's court. She, in turn, was unsure of exactly what it was she expected him to do. She was totally flustered.

'I…I don't really know. I thought that…that you might have a word or something… or some advice. Or…perhaps…'

Her voice trailed away into an embarrassed silence.

The policeman stood up.

'Sorry I can't help any further,' he said. 'If I knew who we were talking about…but well, there it is.'

Jane Grayling took a deep breath. 'I can see that it's difficult,' she started.

'It's downright impossible,' the constable cut in.

Another silence as she remained seated while he stood at the side of the desk, as if waiting for her to leave.

'Well, I can't see that it can do any harm,' she began. 'Look, his name's Painter, Billy Painter.'

There, the deed was done and she gave a deep sigh of relief at having unburdened herself.

'Billy Painter.' Pc Arlett repeated the name thoughtfully. 'I see. Well you needn't worry about things any more. I've got an appointment to see Master Painter, and his parents, on a certain matter this evening. I think we may find out where he got his cuts and bruises.'

'Oh, what's happened then?'

Nurse Grayling wanted to know.

'I'm sorry. I'm unable to disclose police business,' came the blunt reply.

'But surely you can let me know some of the details. After all, it was me who…'

'Miss Grayling. This is part of an ongoing police investigation.'

His manner now was curt.

'The details you speak of may, or may not, be made public at the appropriate time. And now, if you don't mind, I'm rather busy.'

Jane Grayling was red-faced as she cycled away from the police house in a very confused state. Not only had she decidedly not impressed a young man at their first encounter but he had also managed to put her well and truly in her place. She felt not unlike a chastised schoolgirl.

And she was very indignant.

Chapter thirteen

IT was early evening and Pc Arlett was sitting in one of the two armchairs in the small front room of the Painter family's terraced cottage home in Netherham Lane, just off the village main street.

Facing him on the sofa were Mr and Mrs Painter. Standing between them was their young son.

The policeman leaned forward in his seat, his policeman's helmet crooked in his left arm.

'Now then William.' His voice was firm and there was a grave look on his face. 'I want a few words with you and I want you to tell me the truth. Is that understood?'

Billy's eyes were on the floor as he nervously answered. 'Yes.'

'You know Springfield Farm, just up the lane from here, Mr Hurst's farm?'

'Yes?'

There was a questioning tone in his reply but Billy's gaze was still on the carpet a few feet in front of him.

'Were you up there late yesterday afternoon, with some other boys?'

'No...well...I might have walked by. I was...'

'And where did you get those bumps and bruises?'

Billy's manner brightened up considerably.

'I fell off me bike.'

'That's just what he told us,' interjected his mother.

'Is that what you and the others decided to say?'

'Yes. Well no. We didn't do anything. We…'

'Did you go into the calf shed Billy? The truth now because one of Mr Hurst's workers saw someone who looks like you—and wearing the same coloured pullover you've got on now—running out of the farm yard. And he thought he recognised two of the other lads as well.'

Billy's game was up and he knew it, but still he tried to stall.

'We *might* have gone in the calf shed,' he replied guardedly. 'Accidentally,' he added.

His mother broke in again.

'*Billy*,' she snapped. 'Did you or did you not go into Mr Hurst's calf shed yesterday?'

'Well. Yes.'

His mother let out a lungful of breath in an exasperated sigh. Her voice was still sharp. 'Now just tell Mr Arlett what he wants to know. What were you doing there?'

Billy looked up at the policeman for the first time.
'It's like this. We didn't mean any harm. We wus comin, through the farm yard on the way back from the rookery where we went to see if we could find any young rooks to keep as pets…'

'Did you find any?' cut in the constable.

'No. But we saw the calves in a sort of open fronted shed and Brian, Brian Bell, bet Jimmy Woods all his marbles that he couldn't ride one, like they do in the rodeo on the cowboy films.'

He paused for breath and looked round at his parents, then back to the man in uniform sitting before him.

'Then what?' said the officer. 'Come on now son, may as well get it all out and be done with it.' His tone had changed to a more understanding note and the merest suggestion of a smile had lightened his fierce face.

'Well, Jimmy climbed over the wooden fence along the front of the shed and all the calves ran away from him. They trotted round the shed and he ran after them. When he caught up he grabbed one round the neck and sorted of vaulted up onto its back. It went racing round and after about half a turn Jimmy fell off and we all laughed.'

Billy was getting into his stride now.

'Then I had a go and stayed on for nearly a whole circuit but the calf bucked me off and I banged me elbow on the back wall. Then Brian had a go and only stayed on for about three seconds.'

Billy laughed out loud.

'Dave had a go...'

'Dave who?' interrupted the policeman.

'Dave Smith. But he didn't do no better. Those calves bucked and kicked, especially the bigger ones. Jimmy tried again and beat my record. We decided to have a competition to see who could stay on the longest. I fell off against the fence and hurt me back and while I was lyin' on the ground one of the calves jumped right over me and kicked me in the face. Didn't mean to. It was jus' an accident.'

'Is that where you got the black eye?' It was Billy's father who took over the questioning.

'Yeh, it was,' returned Billy sheepishly.

'So you didn't fall off your bike at all then?'

'No.'

'What about the others? Did they get hurt?'

'We all did. We all fell off lots of times. Only I got hurt most,' Billy announced proudly.

'Then what?' demanded the man in blue.

'Well when we'd been at it for about half an hour a farm worker came from further up the yard and he could see what was happening. He shouted at us and we all ran off.'

'Billy,' the officer's mood had changed back to serious. 'When the stockman came to check on those calves he found they were all exhausted and in a terrible state of stress. That means they were very upset. It's taken them all day today to recover. They could have been badly injured. You boys could have been badly injured.'

Pc Arlett stood up and was on his best 'stern talking to' form.

'I'm going to talk to your three friends and give them this same warning. I don't want to hear that any of you have been up at Mr Hurst's farm—or any other farm for that matter—disturbing the livestock. These farmers have got a living to make, same as the rest of us.

'If I do, there'll be trouble. BIG trouble. Your mum and dad don't want me coming in here, arresting you, putting you in handcuffs and taking you off to jail in a big black van do they? You promise me you won't do anything like this again. Right?'

Billy, the wind well and truly taken from his sails after the excitement of his epic adventure tale was again looking dejectedly at the floor.

'Right,' he answered tamely.

Pc Arlett looked over the lad's bowed head straight into his father's face. And gave him a broad wink.

The boy's mother, who had also seen that twinkle in the policeman's eye, gave a slight nod. 'I think he's learned his lesson all right,' she said.

'I'll let myself out,' announced the village bobby. And with that he was gone.

Some time later, after similar visits to other households in the village and with all the would-be young rodeo riders well and truly chastised, Pc Arlett made a detour to call in on the new district nurse.

His ring on the bell was again answered by the shadowy figure behind the frosted glass door pane and Jane Grayling materialised in the now-lighted aperture.

'Yes. Can I help you?'

She was not wearing her uniform, it being well into the evening and her official duty time over, but in casual sweater and jeans she looked, if anything, even more attractive than before.

As soon as she saw him her manner changed and a slight frown creased her face.

'Oh, it's you.'

Although she knew not why, the recollection of his curt manner at their earlier encounter was still niggling at the back of her mind. 'Won't you come in?'

He removed his helmet and followed her through to the little treatment room. She sat behind the desk and motioned him to take a seat in the big black treatment chair. She now held the position of control.

'Now, what brings you round out of hours. I assume you've nothing ailing you?'

'No. Nothing like that.'

A faint smile had lightened his face, a smile that she noted had turned a somewhat stern face into a distinctly handsome one.

'It's just that I wanted to apologise for what must have seemed my pretty abrupt behaviour when you came to see me today.'

It was Jane's turn to smile. Here was a turn-up. And one that was greatly appreciated.

'You see,' continued the constable, 'That young lad was part of a fairly serious police inquiry and I have to be particularly careful with what information I'm legally allowed to disclose.

'The thing is, it's all cleared up now. Billy and his friends have been warned about their conduct and I'm sure they won't be doing it again.'

He paused and she looked at him quizzically.

His face was creased by a broad grin.

'Little blighters were using Farmer Hurst's calves to play rodeo bucking bronco riders. Didn't really do the animals much harm, gave them a bit of exercise, but you saw what it did to the boys, could have been much more serious. Case closed now.'

Jane's own face reflected the policeman's broad grin. And then they both began to laugh. Whatever tension had existed between them that morning was now well and truly dispelled.

It was the Friday of that same week when just a few lines appearing in the 'do these plans affect you' column of the

Witherstoke Gazette had the potential to create a reaction akin to World War Three in Binfield.

Confirmation came the next day in the form of a white, plastic-covered notice fixed to a wooden stake on the road boundary of Lallyfield.

'Application to the Witherstoke Rural District Council Planning Department for the development of 4.2 acres of land at Lailey's Meadow, Binfield...'

The notice went on to outline the plan, submitted by Mr Peter Hillory, 'to provide a private entrance and driveway from the road at the northern boundary of the field to serve the existing property known as Lailey House...'

But the real meat of the notice came a little further down.

'To clear the remainder of the land and construct 16 semi-detached houses with garages served by a new access at the centre of the premises from the existing road.'

So there it was. The bombshell the regulars in The Drovers had predicted. The Lallyfield playground was to be replaced by a building site.

The news went round the village like wildfire, with, of course, various embellishments on the way, although the more ludicrous ones were quickly dismissed by reference to the official development application notice.

And in The Drovers the regulars got down to serious discussion of the plan.

'Well. That's it then. Told you there'd be a bloody great 'ousing estate there.'

'An' that 'illory bloke seemed a pleasant enough chap when 'e moved in.'

Joby was sitting at a table by the window, a half empty ale glass in front of him.

'Bout as pleasant as a fart in a 'phone box,' was his only comment.

The debate went on.

'Jus' 'cos he's put a plan in, it don't mean to say 'e'll get permission.'

'Course it do! Them sort always gets what they wants! Back 'anders to the council an' all that!'

'Council can't be off it, spare bit o' land in the middle of the village. Just askin' t' be built on.'

'What about all the kids that play there? Where they goin' t' go?'

'Kids don't count, not where there's a lot o' money t' be made!'

'Somebody wants t' do somethin' about that man!'

' 'e ain't doin' nothin' illegal. After all, it's 'is own property.'

'Still, it's a bloody shame the kids'll lose their playground!'

'Bet the new Vicar will 'ave somethin' to say though!'

And the room fell silent.

The Rev Michael Stott did have something to say. The evening after the notice appeared in the newspaper he again visited the estate agent's home where he was received with decidedly cool politeness.

Remembering the verbal defeat he suffered at his previous encounter he was on a different tack.

'Mr Hillory. I appreciate you are the owner of the land and that you're simply making the best use of your asset as you see it...' he paused…'but can you imagine the loss this will be to the village if the playing field is built on?'

'Well now Reverend,' returned his host. 'Firstly the land is *not* designated as a playing field and never was. And can *you* imagine the happiness my scheme will bring to sixteen families desperately looking for new homes—especially the children of those families?'

It was clear the man was not for turning and after a few more polite exchanges the colloquy came to an end.

The Vicar made his way home, head down, brow furrowed, deep in thought.

But his concerns over the future of Lallyfield were about to take second place to a more pressing problem, one that was to make local, and eventually national, headlines.

The Binfield Bogeyman.

As he reached the Vicarage he was met in the gathering gloom of this mild, late Spring evening by two elderly women who were just coming out of his gate. In spite of the fading light he recognised them immediately as spinster sisters Felicity Pemberton and her younger sibling Maud, who lived in Rose Cottage, just down the lane, the other side of the church.

They were a regular part of his Sunday congregation, which was not so large as to pose any difficulty in remembering each member by name, even in the relatively short time he had been in the parish.

'Ladies!' he exclaimed enthusiastically. 'What brings you out tonight? How can I help you?'

'Please. May we talk to you?.'

Felicity, usually so brusque and self-assured, as befitted the long time (now retired) headmistress of the village junior school, sounded uneasy to the point of agitation.

'Of course. Come in, come on in.' He unlocked the front door. 'Let me put the lights on.'

As the hall light lit up the doorstep he glanced round to see the anxious look on Felicity's pale face.

'Are you all right? You seem upset. Come through to the drawing room both of you. Can I get you a cup of tea or something?'

The pair declined and meekly followed him through to the spacious Victorian sitting room where, after switching on two standard lamps, he motioned for them to sit down.

He sat in a huge armchair, they sat facing him on the edge of the seat of an equally spacious sofa.

The Rev. Michael Stott leaned forward himself.

'Now then ladies. What appears to be the trouble?'

Haltingly, Felicity opened the proceedings.

'Well, it's difficult to know where to start…'

'Why don't we start at the beginning?' suggested the young man.

Felicity stared at the floor. Normally she was in total control of any exchange—often to the point of being overbearing, Someone, or something, had quite clearly got her rattled.

'Well…I…'

'We've got a ghost,' declared Maud.

The Vicar's attention was transferred swiftly to the younger woman.

'A ghost? What do you mean? Well, what I mean is, how do you know? Whatever leads you to suspect such a thing?'
The Vicar was rightly astonished.

'We've got a ghost,' insisted Maud firmly. 'And we want to know how to get rid of it.'

By nature, Maud had always been the quiet, retiring one of the two sisters. She had endured a lifetime of more or less keeping house for her parents, caring for and nursing them as they grew older while Felicity followed her teaching career, and then, when the old couple finally expired, carrying out the same duties under the domination of her older, more successful sister.

'Well…what happened was…it was like this…'

Felicity began falteringly but was almost immediately, and uncharacteristically, interrupted by her younger sister.

'Things go missing, things…get moved, all on their own, there are noises. We believe it must be a ghost. We want something done about it.'

'Well I…'
It was the Vicar's turn to be hesitant.

He quickly regained his composure, however, and continued. 'What exactly went missing, what moved, did you see anything move? And when did all this begin?' he wanted to know.

'About two weeks ago,' Maud replied. 'That's it. It was a week ago last Wednesday. I was making the tea as usual about four o'clock but couldn't find the sugar bowl. I asked Felicity if she had seen it, well, it's usually on the worktop in the kitchen, next to the tea caddy, and she said "no". Then she said: "don't be so silly", here Maud gave her sister a disdainful glance, "sugar bowls don't just disappear".'

'I said "well this one has". I looked all over the kitchen but couldn't find it. We had to take two spoonfuls of sugar out of the packet in the cupboard.' Maud paused and with a little more than a hint of drama added: 'Felicity found the sugar bowl later, standing in the empty fireplace in the front room.'

The parish priest looked from one sister to the other. Felicity's face pale and drawn, Maud's features noticeably lighter with the excitement of telling her story.

'I'm sure there's a perfectly rational explanation for this…erh…occurrence' he said. 'Uh perhaps…'

'Then there was the case for Felicity's spectacles,'

Maud broke in.

'That disappeared two days later. We never did find it. Good job her glasses weren't inside. The following night we were woken up by a banging sound coming from the bathroom between our two bedrooms.'

Maud glanced at her elder sister who appeared to be on the verge of tears, then turned back to the Vicar.

'Yesterday the money went missing from the tin on the dresser shelf in the kitchen, the tin we put change in from time to time to pay the milkman who calls for it every…'

'But couldn't it have been taken by the milkman himself if he knows where it's kept?' the cleric interposed.

'No.' Maud was adamant. 'Last night the tin was empty. This morning all the money was back inside—except that there was a shilling and twopence more than there was before. How do you explain that?'

'Well, I can't. Not without looking more closely at all the circumstances,' Mr Stott paused, looking from one sister to the other. His mind was racing. Here was a turn-up. He had, naturally, heard about cases like this and there had been some brief elementary advice touched on during his time studying for the priesthood but he had never expected to be faced with such a case.

'Look, I'll take some advice from a higher authority on this and come round to see you in the next few days. Meanwhile go on home. Try not to worry and try to get some sleep. I'm sure we'll be able to sort this thing out. I'll walk down the road with you.'

The three of them got up and left the house, walking slowly down the lane in the ever-deepening darkness, the Vicar keeping up a light-hearted stream of calming and encouraging chatter.

On his way back he was deep in thought.

By the time he reached the front porch of the Vicarage he had more or less decided upon a plan of action.

He would seek the advice of the bishop.

The bishop would like that and in any case could put him in touch with the small, and in many ways mysterious, though unofficial, team of clerics who specialised in dealing with such things. He knew they existed but had never dreamed he would ever need to call on their expertise.

As soon as he was through the door he went through to his study and sat down to compose a long explanatory letter to the bishop.

But even before Mr Stott had received a reply to his communication, the secret, somehow, was out.

First it was the local newspaper whose Friday edition, on one of its inside pages, carried a somewhat restrained story of the alleged haunting.

This was followed two days later by a "red masthead" national Sunday publication's version, with big headlines on page three announcing the advent of the *'Binfield Bogeyman,'* the eagerly anticipated arrival of the *'Church Ghostbusters'* and with a large picture of Maud standing at the front door of the cottage with Felicity peering nervously over her shoulder.

After all, two elderly spinsters being terrorised in their own home by some wicked spirit was, as any newspaper editor worth his salt would confirm, a darned good yarn.

Maud, especially, appeared to be relishing the unaccustomed attention the sisters were receiving and the whole situation naturally became the sole topic of discussion, night after night, among the locals in The Drovers Arms.

'Wha'ja reckon to this 'ere pottigost thing at the Pembertons' cottage?'

'Them two ole biddies? Imagination most likely.'

'I dunno. That's a bloomin' ancient ole place. No sayin' what could've 'appened there 'undreds o' yers ago!'

'E's right y'know. May 'ave bin all manner o' murders an' goin's on for all we knows.'

'Well I ain't never 'eard nuthin' about no murders nor nuthin,' an' our family's bin 'ere for generations.'

'Just becos you ain't 'eard nuthin' don't mean nuthin' ain't 'appened.'

'We would've 'eard sumthin,' I'm damned sure.'

And so it went on.

Meanwhile the mysterious manifestations continued, with some ghostly disturbance or another occurring on an almost daily basis.

There was the alarming message, scrawled in crayon on the dressing table mirror in Felicity's bedroom, which warned *'your time is up'*.

The appearance of half a wall brick in a saucepan in the front porch.

The contents of the wicker laundry hamper which they found one morning scattered around the floor in the sitting room.

The whistling kettle on the gas stove in the kitchen which woke them both up well after midnight although they had both been in bed and asleep for over two hours.

And there was the mantel clock in the cottage dining room, which over the course of a week or so, was discovered to be facing the wall on four or five occasions.

Each incident was faithfully reported in the Witherstoke weekly and evening newspapers, with more visits from both local and national press reporters and photographers.

The story had gone fully national but as yet there was still no sign of an ecclesiastical involvement.

Then came the bizarre lupin incident. The sisters woke one morning to find that eight spikes had been cut from the cottage garden flower bed under the kitchen window and laid out in a frightening floral display on the back lawn, spelling out the chilling word *'KILL'* in vivid lupin colours.

Once again the Press was out in force with notebooks and cameras, traipsing all over the garden to record the event.

Later, Felicity told Maud to call in Joby, as they sometimes did, to tidy up the garden and perhaps mow the grass.

That Saturday afternoon Joby arrived at Rose Cottage and was met by Maud, who asked him to be as quiet as possible as her elder sister, on whom the latest incident had provoked a mild attack of nervous shock, was resting in bed. He decided to give the mower a miss for today and set about tidying and weeding in the flower beds.

While he was crouched under the kitchen window, trying to put some order back into the sadly depleted lupin patch, he heard a faint tapping sound from inside. Standing up he was just able to peer through the lower part of the window, over the high outside sill.

Maud was standing at the worktop on the far side of the kitchen, her back half turned to the window. She glanced momentarily towards the open kitchen door which led to the hallway—and the stairs—then continued with what she had been doing.

She was holding the tea caddy in her left hand and was pouring something into it by gently tapping a red carton against the rim.

Salt.

Joby moved quietly away from the window and walked slowly across to the garden shed. Inside he leaned his elbows on the potting shelf, chin propped up in his cupped hands, reflecting on what he had just seen, and considered all his options.

Joby fully realised that he was now in possession of some very interesting and very secret information, the kind of information which could be both useful and profitable.

Should he report what he had seen?

But report to whom? The Police? The Vicar? Miss Felicity? Should he let the newspapers in on his secret? And maybe get a bit of national publicity himself?

Then he had a better idea. A much better idea.

Joby was still deep in thought as he left the shed, walked across to the back door and gave three gentle knocks.

Maud was quickly opening the door.

'Oh it's you Joby. All finished? How much do we owe you?' She spoke in a half whisper.

'Well, I didn't do the grass 'cos I didn't want t' disturb Miss Felicity, so it'll only be five bob,' Joby replied in the same semi-muted manner.

'Right. I'll go and fetch it for you.'

Moments later she was back with two half crowns in her hand which she dropped carefully into Joby's outstretched palm.

The old man slipped them safely into his trouser pocket.

Then he said: 'Miss Maud. Can I 'ave quiet word?'

The question took her a little by surprise but she immediately regained her composure and beckoned him in. He followed her through to the little utility room just inside the back door.

She turned to face him and, after putting a finger to her lips, continued the conversation in the same hushed tone. 'We'll have to be quiet, Felicity's still resting upstairs.

'Now, how can I help you?'

'It's more a question of how I can help *you*, Miss Maud.'

She was puzzled. 'How do you mean?'

'Well, I think that all this nonsense has got to stop.'

Maud was visibly taken aback. She turned a decidedly lighter shade of pale and it was some seconds before she could speak.

'Why, whatever do you mean?'

'What I means, Miss Maud, is all this mumbo-jumbo ghost rubbish. It's time it ended.'

She appeared to shrink a little and took a step backwards. Then she quickly straightened herself up to her full height and a look of defiance hardened her features.

'I really don't think…I really don't know what you're talking about.' Her voice and her demeanour had become suddenly challenging.

Joby stood his ground and looked her straight in the eyes.

'Come on Miss Maud. I know what's bin 'appenin' 'ere an' I think I know why. If I wos to tell a few people wot I seen through the kitchen window jus' now, people like the Vicar, or the newspapers, or your sister for instance, they'd be very, very interested indeed. An' I'm sure they'd 'ave plenty t' say on the matter. We wudn't want that now, wud we?'

Maud shrank back and buried her face in her hands. Then she began, ever so quietly, to sob.

Through the clasped hands and with many an intake of breath, her small voice began to tell her tale of her woe.

'You can't possibly know what it's like,' she whimpered. 'All my life I've wanted…I've wanted to be someone and do things…I've wanted to go to places I've never seen…places I shall never see now…life has passed me by.'

She paused to dab her tear-stained face and blow her nose in a handkerchief taken from her blouse sleeve.

'Always being told what to do…told to do this, told to do that…fetch this carry that…never doing what I want to do…always doing what I've been told to do…what other people want me to do…never any consideration for what I want.'

She paused and dried her eyes once more. She was a little calmer now, as though the many years that it had taken her to get this burden off her chest were at last behind her and she could now look forward to a more peaceful existence.

Joby placed a sympathetic hand on her shoulder.

'We don't 'ave t' let this go any further y' know.'

His voice was quieter too, and altogether gentler.

'If you promise me there'll be no more o' these silly pranks agen' at Rose Cottage, not ever, mind, I can promise you that nobuddy will never hear nuthin from me.'

He placed both hands on her slight shoulders and looked straight into her reddened eyes.
'Ave we got a deal then?'

She gazed back at him, a mixed look of thankfulness and relief on her face.

'Oh yes.'

'Promise? Cross yer 'eart an' 'ope to die?'

'I promise…and…thank you Joby.'

''Now we'll say no more about it.'

And with that he gave her a broad, friendly wink, let his hands fall from her shoulders, turned and walked slowly out of the cottage,. Joby collected his bike from where it was leaning against the garden shed and was gone.

Upstairs Felicity stirred, turned over, and fell back into a much-needed slumber.

That evening, it being Saturday, there was a larger crowd than usual in the public bar of The Drovers Arms and Joby had already taken up his customary position in the window seat.
Everyone in the village had, by now, seen, or had heard reports of, the latest happenings at Rose Cottage so, inevitably, the foremost topic of conversation was the "Binfield Bogeyman". And many and varied were the theories being expounded.

'Kettle whistlin' in the middle of the night! One o 'em put it on over a low gas an' fergot it!'

'Clock that turns round on its own? Well you gotta turn it round to wind it up ain't you!'

'Yeh but what about the flowers? That couldn't 'appen on its own.'

''That's true y' know. Someone—or somethin'—must've 'ad a hand in that.'

'And who'd be daft enough to risk getting' caught tryin' t' put the wind up two 'armless ole birds like that?'

'No buts about it. Some things may be just chance. But there's a lot more in it than that.'

'Anyway, what're the police doin' then?'

'T' ain't a police matter. I 'eard the Vicar was tryin' to arrange somethin.'

'Can't see what good the church can do. Can't see what anybody can do.'

'Well, d' y' reckon it's jus' gunna go on forever then?'

'Bet I could put a stop to it.'

There was a sudden hush and all eyes swivelled to Joby sitting quietly, pint in hand, and who, as yet, had not joined in the discussion.

'Wha' j' mean. YOU could put a stop to it?'
'You got some super-natural powers or summat?'

And there were guffaws around the bar.

'That's a laugh! A pint says you can't.'

Joby smiled and looked around the room.

'Anybody else want to bet I can't stop it?'

He was almost drowned out by a chorus of takers who all wanted to bet a pint on his failure. It seemed like a sure-fire winner.

'OK then. I'll take you all on.'

Amid a great deal of banter and laughter, arrangements were made for Harry the barman to record the names of everyone who wanted to be in on the wager and also to agree on the terms of the bet.

Harry, too, was laughing and said the house would also stand him a pint if he succeeded.

'Joby,' he said. 'You an' your mouth. This lot is goin' to cost you a small fortune!'

It was agreed that if no further ghostly incidents occurred within the next full fortnight, Joby would be deemed to have won his boast. If he lost he was to provide the drinks over the subsequent two weeks.

In the unlikely event of him winning, he would have the same two weeks to down his winning pints.

Harry posted no less than 11 names on a slate behind the bar—a number that was to increase to 15 over the following two evenings as word got round about Joby's boastful promise.

Bearing in mind the fact that over the previous six weeks some weird event or another had been announced on an almost daily basis, when nothing was reported from Rose Cottage after three days the list stopped getting any longer and an uneasy air of expectation could be detected in The Drovers public bar.

After a week of no more other-worldly activity the tension was mounting. Joby, in his usual position and, outwardly at least, acting perfectly normally was saying nothing.

Sunday morning came. No news. Monday, Tuesday and Wednesday. Nothing. Thursday came and went. Blank again.

By Friday evening the atmosphere in The Drovers was almost unbearable. Most of the usual topics of conversation seemed to have been put on hold and the only consideration was, would there be, or would there not be, another manifestation. All talk appeared to have been reduced to a whisper.

Early next evening the public bar at The Drovers began to fill up unusually early. As well as all those involved, dozens more who had heard about the historic wager on the village grapevine crammed in, eager to witness the outcome. Landlord Harry was enjoying one of his most profitable nights ever.

Joby strolled in around 8pm and there was a prompt shuffling of bottoms as room was made for him in his customary place by the window. Harry even presented him with an immediate pint on the house.

It had been decided that the appropriate time for the matter to be decided should be 9pm—the time the wager had been struck two weeks earlier.

By half past eight, when the big old clock on the wall struck a single tinny note, conversation had once again dropped to no more than a whisper and many were the time checks made against wrist watches and fobs.

By ten minutes to nine even the whispering had ceased and the crowded bar room fell silent. Faces turned from Joby to the clock on the wall, back to Joby, back to the clock, then, with just a few minutes to go, all eyes focussed on the closed door to the street, as if the watchers were expecting it to burst open with a last-second messenger bringing exciting news of some new "happening" at Rose Cottage.

But no messenger came.

The door remained firmly shut and, as the old wall clock began its apologetic little nine-chime count a mighty roar of cheering rang out that could probably have been heard in Witherstoke.

Needless to say, most of the noise came from customers, at the moment in the majority, who had nothing to gain or lose from the result, a simple outpouring of jubilation that the old man had won himself a fortnight's free beer.

There were even a few of those people who insisted in 'getting one in' for the now smugly smiling Joby.

'Will you have a celebration drink with me, Joby?'

'Rude not to!'

And it was a decidedly unsteady Joby Fulbright who eventually made it home and into bed at Longdown Farm Cottage.

Towards midday the following morning, it being Sunday, Joby, looking just a little ruffled by the previous evening's activities, was pedalling his way steadily to The Drovers to partake in just a little of the "hair of the dog" in the hope of a slight relief from some mysterious ailment.

Never a big drinker, the extra pints consumed last evening had resulted in his awaking to the distinct sensation of a little man inside his skull using a club hammer to try to escape.

In something of a daze he very nearly cycled straight past Ivy Green walking in the opposite direction on her way to visit her daughter, Sandra Trenchard, at Longdown Farm.

It was only Ivy's cheery 'Morning Joby,' that jerked him out of his reverie.

He quickly pulled up and dismounted to stand, leaning heavily on his machine as Ivy came across the lane towards him.

'I hear there was great celebration in the pub last night,' exclaimed Ivy with a smile. 'Tell me Joby, how did you do it?'

'There are things that some people jus' wudn't b'lieve even if you told 'em,' returned the old man. 'Best not to say anythin' at all.'

And he placed his right forefinger against the side of his nose in a gesture of intended secrecy.

'By the way, Ivy,' added Joby, changing tack completely, 'Can't you do anythin' 'bout that boss o' yourn. I 'ear 'e's plannin' t'build 'ouses all over the kids' playground.

'Ain't there somethin' you can say to 'im? Ain't there some way t'make 'im change 'is mind?'

'It's nothing to do with me. He's the owner. He's the boss. I'm just the housekeeper.'

Then Ivy's smile quite suddenly grew even wider.

'Mind you, there is a little something I might have in mind. But there are things that some people wouldn't believe, even if you told them. Better to say nothing at all!'

And she placed her right forefinger along the side of her nose and gave Joby a broad wink.

''Bye Joby. And thanks for the idea!'
And she walked jauntily on down the road, leaving Joby leaning against his bike, flat cap in one hand, scratching his head with the other.

Once again Joby found himself in possession of what sounded like some very interesting information, except that, this time, he had no idea what that information was.

Still, he thought to himself, all will become clear eventually. He turned to catch a last glimpse of Ivy, now fast disappearing down the lane.

Then he shrugged his shoulders and shook his head in puzzlement. He replaced his headgear, clambered back into the saddle and pedalled on towards the pub. After all, there were still a number of free pints to be imbibed before his allotted time expired.

As she walked away, Ivy grinned to herself. And her face continued to display that enigmatic little smile as her mind ran over what Joby had had to say about the children's playground at Lallyfield.

She had, indeed, thought about the problem before but Joby's words had sown the tiny seed of an idea in her head. And, as we have seen, from little acorns mighty oaks do grow.

Chapter fourteen

'**FLAMING** June' arrived in Binfield as more of a damp squib and continued as such, on and off, for the rest of month, unsettled weather and cooler than usual temperatures being the main features.

The release of the *'Hard Day's Night'* album by The Beatles raised the spirits of the younger generation but the life imprisonment sentence on Nelson Mandela in South Africa appalled thousands of supporters of the anti-apartheid movement.

Life in the village got back to normal after the excitement of its recent national news exposure and, as Joby had so rightly predicted, no more paranormal events manifested themselves at the Pemberton sisters' cottage.

The three-way rivalry between the Vicar, the village bobby and farmer Robert Trenchard for the attentions of Jane Grayling, the new young district nurse, intensified to some extent but with each of the potential suitors seemingly remaining about level on points.

And although none of the trio would have admitted to any form of competition at all, many in the village realised what was quietly afoot and began to take an interest in the situation.

Not least, naturally enough, in the public bar of The Drovers Arms.

'Who d'you reckon she'll choose then?'

'Vicar's got t'be favourite. What with 'im bein' educated an' that. And she'd 'ave a nice big vicarage t'move into.'

'What? You reckon 'er as a vicar's wife then? Garden parties and Mothers' Union an' the like?'

'No chance. Policeman's got the inside track there. 'E's young an' ambitious. Few years time there'll be promotions to sergeant an' p'rhaps inspector. Good job, good money an' a decent pension to come.'

'Yeh but can you see 'er as a bobby's wife?'

'Ha-ha! Just about as much as a vicar's wife!'

'What about young Bob Trenchard? 'E'd be a good catch y'know.'

'Woss 'is prospects though? Once Benjamin starts a family 'e could be out in the cold.'

'Course he won't. He'll always 'ave a share in the farm.'

'Ho-ho! And she a farmer's wife?'

'Just like the Vicar's wife if you ask me, all jam makin' and Women's Institute!'

'Whoever gets the nod's goin' t'be lucky. She's quite a looker!'

The debate on this intriguing topic would become a regular item on the agenda in the pub for months to come.

Meanwhile, with so-called summer well under way, the village cricket team was doing its darnedest to keep up with the fixtures schedule, numbers of matches having to be abandoned or shortened due to the unsummery weather.

None of which did much for the reputations of the three protagonists in the District Nurse Attraction Saga.

All three were members of the village team but had very little chance to demonstrate their prowess publicly—or more importantly to Jane Grayling—by feats of derring-do on the cricket field.

Robert had, for some years been a leading light in the team and a very useful all-rounder to boot. New members, Alan Arlett and

Mike Stott, were also shaping up well, when given the chance, the policeman as a pretty formidable batsman and the vicar a very useful spin bowler.

On the two days' full play the team had recently enjoyed, they came out just about even, with the policeman turning in two excellent batting performances, the vicar taking a total of seven wickets in the two games and the farmer clocking up one good run-scoring appearance, one wicket and three fine slip catches.

Still, it all made for some lively discussions in the local hostelry.

Meanwhile, just down the road from The Drovers, at Lailey House something else was quietly happening, something that no-one else in the village had noticed at all.

Owner and estate agent Peter Hillory, the one responsible for the village furore over the development of Lallyfield, had, for the last few months, enjoyed the cooking, the care and, dare to mention it, the companionship of Ivy, his new housekeeper.

He had become a much less aggressive character, less tense, more laid back—and two stones lighter through Ivy's prudent but delicious dietary manipulation—a remarkable change in a man who, hitherto, had lived solely for business success.

Equally extraordinary was the fact that, during those same months of change, the business he had formerly laboured constantly to improve by pugnacious effort began to bloom significantly under the influence of his new, more approachable persona.

Indeed, to such an extent that in the very recent past he had pulled off some extremely attractive land and property deals, involving large development companies, which had resulted in some astonishing increases in his personal fortune.

It was under these circumstances that he and Ivy had, shall we say, become rather closer than normal for employer and employee. Not that anything improper was involved, just that they had been drawn together as friends, enjoying each others' company, conversation and sense of humour.

Not surprising, given that they were of similar age and situation—unattached. There had even been a couple of times during the last fortnight when they had gone out together for a drink at a quiet inn some miles away, as well as one occasion, a few weeks earlier, when they had partnered each other in a visit to the cinema in Witherstoke to see the recently released Zulu, the new British-made Michael Caine blockbuster. Feelings were afoot!

Meanwhile July had arrived—and with it, summer.

For the next two months the country would enjoy a spell of warm dry weather, allowing the village cricket team, with its three participating rivals for the attentions of the District Nurse, to get into its stride. And the aforesaid three, into theirs.

More importantly for the general economy, the harvest was at last able to get under way in near-perfect conditions although the Tory government, now more than 12 years in office, was rapidly losing the plot as shattering disclosures and associated court cases and publicity associated with, and following on from, the Profumo Affair the previous year, were dragged into the public domain.

Briefly, at a time when the 'Cold War' with the eastern bloc was at its height, John Profumo, the British Secretary of State for War, was found to have taken a mistress, one Christine Keeler, who, it was alleged, was simultaneously, very physically engaged with a suspected Soviet spy.

Quite embarrassing for the government, one might say.

But things were to get worse.

Much worse.
Profumo, it transpired, had lied about his relationship with Keeler when questioned in The House and further high-profile court

appearances involving Christine Keeler and her associates, including a big-time drug dealer, as well as a suicide, which was widely suspected to be a contract killing, added to Conservative Prime Minister Harold Macmillan's distress. He resigned soon after, citing ill-health, and the reins of government were taken over by Foreign Secretary Sir Alec Douglas-Home.

All this with a General Election looming in the autumn. Prospects for the government looked decidedly bleak.

However, back in the harvest fields at Longdown Farm things looked very much brighter. The improvement in the dismal weather of June promised a straightforward harvest with good yields. By the end of August all was safely gathered in and the farming community had a collective smile on its face, much wider than could have been anticipated a few weeks earlier.

As Joby and his underling Pongo cleaned and greased the massive combine harvester, preparing to stow it away for another year in the farm's implement shed, the old fellow paused in his oily-rag wiping activities to gaze at this amazing piece of gleaming machinery.

'I dunno what the world's comin' to,' he finally announced with a sigh. ''Tweren't no more nor ten years since we wus usin' the ole binder fer 'arvest.'

'Wossat then?' Pongo wanted to know.

'You dunno 'ow lucky you are,' exclaimed Joby, wiping his nose with the rag in his hand, then, realising what he had done, vigorously scrubbing at his face with his shirt sleeve to remove an oily black smear.

'Ten years ago, p'rhaps only nine, we had to get the 'arvest in using the reaper and binder,' he explained.

'I remembers seein' them,' interjected Pongo.

'Well,' continued the old man, 'Once we'd a'finished cuttin,' the corn, the sheaves left on the stubble by the binder 'ad to be shocked up in rows to dry out prop'ly. Then a week or so later they 'ad to be carted, that's lifted and carried by tractor and wagon back to the rick yard at the farm. Then we 'ad to build the ricks—and rough thatch 'em to keep the weather out—then wait fer the threshin' machine contractor, months sometimes, before the threshin' wus done and the grain wus stored.

'Real 'ard sweat that lot wus. You young 'uns don't know you're born! Look at it now, this 'ere machine does the lot, all in one go!'

He paused to note the look of astonishment and admiration on Pongo's face.

'Don't know you're born,' he repeated.

With August at an end, the next big event in the Binfield calendar would be the annual Grand Village Flower Show, held towards the end of September on the cricket field, once the match programme was ended. It was an occasion much enjoyed by the entire village.

Although nominally a flower show, fierce competition was the order of the day throughout the horticultural spectrum from flowers and the entire range of fruit and vegetables, to home made wine, honey, baking and needlecraft. There were special classes for everyone, including children, who were encouraged to enter the painting and wild flower arrangement competitions.

The most unlikely prize was a cash reward of five shillings for the child under sixteen who collected the highest number of white butterfly wings. This was specifically designed to try to reduce the numbers of Cabbage White Butterflies, both large and small varieties, whose caterpillars regularly decimated the brassicas in Binfield's gardens and allotments each summer.

Small groups of boys would form butterfly wing collection syndicates in an effort to win the five bob on offer and some began swatting well in advance of the show by predating the unfortunate Brimstones that emerged during early Spring.

By September various groups had each collected two or three glass jam jars of butterfly wings but whether this made much difference to the survival rate of local cabbages and sprouts is not known.

Also anonymous was the person responsible for actually checking and counting the number of wings claimed on the label of each jar, the tally being scrawled alongside the name of the syndicate member who had been chosen to represent the group.

Meanwhile rivalry for the hundreds of other prizes on offer at the show rose to almost fever pitch as the day of the show approached.

Nowhere was it keener than in the vegetable sections where four or five individuals habitually fought it out for the most class wins—and receipt of the impressive silver Perpetual Challenge Trophy for the most successful.

During the past five years Joby Fulbright's name had appeared on the cup three times, Fred Appleton's twice.

So it was with a little more determination than usual, considering what had passed between the two over the past twelve months, that the pair prepared to battle it out head to head once more.

Joby's farm cottage garden, in contrast to the interior of the building, looked a picture.

Neat, weed-free rows of peas and beans, potatoes, carrots, beetroot, greens and a host of other vegetables, were a pleasure to the eye. In his compact greenhouse, cucumbers and tomatoes were nearing showtime perfection.

At the other end of the village, Fred Appleton's garden appeared no less a delight. This year's show would be a difficult one for the judges.

The big day was just a week away when a dramatic turn of events occurred.

Early on Sunday morning Fred, making his usual daily inspection, discovered that some of his plants, particularly most of the runner beans, showed definite signs of wilting. Later the same day the situation had worsened.

By next morning it was clear that a large proportion of his vegetable crop was suffering badly. Not only was the foliage drooping and yellowing, the peas and bean pods showed symptoms of the same malaise. It was clear that none of them would pass muster to grace the competitors' tables at the flower show during the following weekend.

Fred called in the police.

'What the hell happened here?'

The question came from Pc Arlett, as he stood, helmet in the crook of one arm, scratching his head with the other hand, surveying the scene of devastation in Fred's vegetable garden.

'S'bloody obvious ain't it?' returned an equally devastated Fred. 'Some bastard's sprayed my garden with bloody weed killer.'

'Why would anyone do a thing like that?' the constable wanted to know. 'Do you know of anyone who has a grudge against you?'

'Only one,' lied Fred, knowing full well that there were at least half a dozen men in the neighbourhood who would be delighted to get the chance to do him a bad turn,

'That bastard Joby Fulbright. He's out to stop me winning top trophy in the Flower Show on Saturday.'

'Have you any proof it was him? Did you see him do it?'

'Course it was 'im! Who else could it be? That sneaky bloody little weasel Fulbright's responsible an' I'm gonna make 'im pay. I want 'im arrested an' charged.

'I'll get the bugger this time if it's the last thing I do!'

Fred was furious.

'Calm down Mr. Appleton,' urged the policeman, placing his helmet back on his head and taking a notebook from his tunic breast pocket. 'I'll take down some facts and I'll have a quiet word with Mr. Fulbright but without some concrete evidence, or unless he admits it, I don't see much chance of making an arrest.'

''Course 'e won't admit it, lyin' little shit!' Fred's face was contorted with rage. 'But 'e's done it and 'e's gonna suffer. Wait 'til I get my 'ands on 'im!'

'Wait a minute now Mr. Appleton. You've no direct proof of the identity of the offender and I strongly advise you to leave this investigation with the proper authority, that's the police. Don't try taking the law into your own hands or you could be in a lot of trouble yourself.'

But this advice served only to stir up the gamekeeper's ire even more as with a parting: 'Don't worry Mr Appleton, I'll look into it,' Pc. Arlett replaced the notebook in his pocket and walked off slowly towards the front gate, leaving the aggrieved Fred Appleton spluttering with indignation.

After leaving Fred's cottage with its ravaged garden, the policeman's first port of call was to speak to Harry, the licensee of The Drovers, before calling at Joby's place where the village bobby found the old man sitting in the kitchen with the back door standing wide open.

Joby looked up as Pc. Arlett tapped on the open door.

'Come in constable,' called Joby, apparently visibly surprised at seeing the officer in the doorway. 'What can I do for you?'

The man in blue took a few steps into the kitchen and stood with his feet apart facing Joby.

'Well Mr Fulbright….'

'Uh-ho, sounds serious if it's "Mr. Fulbright",' interrupted Joby.

The policeman's notebook and pencil were already poised.

'It's like this Mr. Fulbright. I should like to know where you were between about 8.30 and 9 o'clock last Saturday night.'

'Why? What's the….?' the old man started to reply but he was interrupted by the investigating officer.

'Just say where you were and what you were doing and we may be able to clear this up in a few minutes.'

Joby pondered a while.

'Sat'day night? Well… I would'a bin in The Drovers, 'avin' a pint or two as I always does of a Sat'day night.'

'But I understand you didn't arrive at the pub until later than usual that night. Some time just after nine I hear.'

'No, come t' think on it. I dropped off in me armchair that evenin.' We've 'ad a very tirin' few weeks on 'arvest. I wus 'ard pushed t' get t' pub and get me two pints in! Why? What's the problem?'

'Were you at Fred Appleton's cottage last Saturday night?'

The question couldn't exactly be more direct.

'Fred Appleton's place? Why should I be there? Anyways, Fred's always out of a Sat'day evenin,' over at the King's Head in Netherham.'

The bobby's eyebrows arched.

'Oh, so you were aware that Mr. Appleton would be out all that evening?'

'Everybody in the village knows when 'e's out an' where 'e goes. T'ain't no secret, 'cept that Fred thinks it is!'

'By the way, Mr Fulbright, what's the matter with your face? Your eyes seem red and you've a sniffy nose.'

'Summer cold. Dust from the combinder.'

'It wouldn't be blow-back from a weed killer spray now, would it?'

'What?'

'That's all for now, Mr Fulbright, but I have to tell you I shall probably need to speak to you again.'

'What is all this? What the devil's goin' on?' Joby did sound genuinely mystified.

But the policeman quietly put his notebook away again and took his leave with a curt nod.

The Drovers public bar that night was full of it. Fred Appleton's ranting had certainly got around. Just about everybody had heard about the weed killer spraying raid on the gamekeeper's garden, just a week before the annual Flower Show, and Joby was well and truly in the frame as the perpetrator.

'You crafty old sod Joby.'

'Didn't know you 'ad it in you!'

'Bit extreme wusn't it?'

''Ow you gonna get out o' this one?'

'Could be a nasty fine.'

'Even prison!'

'Look,' said Joby. 'If someone's dun in Fred's vegetable garden it's nuthin' t' do with me. I ain't bin near 'is place.'

'No. Of course not!'

'We understand!'

'Who could think such a thing!'

'Nice one, though, Joby!'

Joby knew it was no use arguing. He shrugged his shoulders and sat in silence.

Friday's local newspaper carried the story on its front page with a picture of Fred standing in his now even more badly damaged garden and carrying the headline
:
'FRED FURIOUS AS SHOW
ENTRIES ARE NOBBLED'

And there were hints that an, as yet, unnamed rival show competitor was suspected as the villain.

Joby was in a lot of trouble.

But as the village policeman had insisted, rumours and suspicions are not enough and as no further proof was forthcoming the Law was helpless to take the matter further.

Show day duly arrived and all the competitors were up early, preparing their various exhibits for the scrutiny of the judges. Joby, with more entries than anyone, was up with the lark, carefully digging, picking, washing and choosing his best examples for display.

Throughout the morning there were comings and goings galore in the marquee as the exhibitors fussed and fiddled, preparing their entries for the big occasion and while most were working silently, a few took the opportunity for banter and derision, remarking on the poor quality of their opponents' efforts.

As Joby carefully arranged his maincrop potatoes on a small, round white plate, a rival looked over his shoulder and commented: 'I see your spuds ain't very big this year, Joby.'

'Ah,' returned Joby drily. 'Tha's 'cos I grows 'em to fit my mouth, not yourn!'

All entries had to be in to the big show tent, properly laid out and numbered, by mid-morning so that the adjudicating panel had plenty of time to consider and make their many decisions before the public was allowed to inspect the exhibitions, and the results, at 2.30pm.

Considering the total absence of anything from Fred Appleton's garden, it turned out as no surprise that Joby had very nearly swept the board in the vegetable classes—and was thereby named as the winner of the grand silver trophy for most points for the fourth time in six years.

Even so there were still quite a few whisperings and mutterings in some quarters questioning the fairness of the competition in view of the fact that 'someone' had nobbled the gamekeeper's chances.

That didn't prevent Joby from having a celebratory pint or three in the show's beer tent during the afternoon and with no produce to take home—every exhibit was auctioned at the end of the afternoon to raise more funds towards the show's running costs—that evening the old man cycled down to The Drovers to continue his merry-making.

It wasn't until closing time that Joby, unsteadily exiting the public bar, discovered that his bike, along with the machines of three other Drover's regulars, had been linked together by having a chain threaded through the wheels and secured with a small padlock.

Of a key there was, of course, no sign.

'Wot the bloody 'ell's bin goin' on 'ere then?' Joby wanted to know, standing, hat in hand and scratching his head, gazing at the quartet of united bicycles.

Not unexpectedly the owners of the other three machines were just as miffed and turned on Joby.

'See what's 'appened. This is Fred Appleton's doin' this is.'

'Said you shouldn't 'v done 'is garden.'

'You went too far an' it's obvious. Fred's out to get 'is own back.'

It was nearly half an hour before, thanks to landlord Harry rummaging in the toolbox in his shed for a hacksaw, the four were eventually freed and were able to make their separate ways home.

But the mystery deepened further when, the next day, it came to light that Fred Appleton had spent the previous evening, from soon after opening time until, well, late, drowning his sorrows in the King's Head at Netherham.

Not only that, he had at least a dozen witnesses who could confirm it, including the pub landlord who drove him home as he was too far gone to ride his bike.

Fred Appleton was undeniably innocent!

That same Sunday morning came another surprise.

The handful of Binfield parishioners arriving for early Holy Communion at St Swithin's Church were faced by a neatly printed announcement pinned to the south door:

'CHURCH CLOSED UNTIL
FURTHER NOTICE.
URGENT ROOF REPAIRS'

By five minutes to eight a little group of would-be worshippers was gathered half-way down the gravel path leading to the village's main street, discussing this unexpected turn of events.

'No-one told US about this.'

'You'd have thought the vicar would've let us know.'

'Haven't seen anything in the parish magazine, or the local paper.'

'Must have been sudden like.'

'Well, I think it's a disgrace.'

'Us regular church-goers too.'

As the church clock struck eight, the hour at which the service was scheduled to start, the Rev Michael Stott, who, as usual, had entered the church via the north door leading into the vestry, strode into the chancel, his surplice and stole billowing behind him.

Glancing down the nave he pulled up short as he beheld the rows of empty pews.
'What the…!'

He seldom had more than 15 or 20 attending the 8.00 am communion but had never before experienced a total absence of devotees.

Clearly shaken and deeply puzzled, he hurried down the central aisle of the nave, turned left to the south door, the one normally used by parishioners, turned the ornate iron ring handle and pulled the heavy door open wide.

Stepping outside, he immediately spotted the little huddle of his flock members 20 yards away down the gravel pathway.

'Hello!' he called, the surprise obvious in his voice. 'What's the problem?'

There was a babbled chorus of response from which he managed to distinguish the words 'notice,' 'closed' and 'door.' And several souls were pointing at the church door behind him. It wasn't until that moment that he became aware of the piece of paper fastened to it.

Turning and taking the two paces back to the church entrance, he paused, one foot on the worn grey stone step and leaned forward to read the text.

'What…? How did…? Whoever put this here? And when?'

Visibly angered, he ripped the offending sheet of paper from the door.

Turning to his little congregation, who had now straggled their way back and were standing around the south door, the Vicar's next words were through clenched teeth.

'Look friends,' he growled. 'I don't know who is responsible for this…this…prank but I can assure you, it's just not true.
'I also don't know why someone should think this might be amusing. I am decidedly not amused! The communion service will begin as soon as you have taken your seats.'

With that he strode back into the church, followed by the little gaggle of parishioners. Communion at St Swithins was 15 minutes late that morning but no real harm was done and in normal times the incident would have been forgotten within a day or two.

But these, it seems, were not normal times.

Two days later, on the Tuesday morning, early travellers making their way to work in Witherstoke by car found the only direct road to the town blocked by a 'Road Closed' sign just outside the village and a 'Diversion' arrow pointing up a narrow side lane.

Motorists who followed the instructions soon found that, in fact, the diversion led nowhere.

Cyclists, more numerous and not looking forward to a longer bike ride to work, were quick to discover that beyond the 'Road Closed' sign the way was perfectly clear.

Once again it became apparent that someone had deliberately set out to mislead the people of Binfield—but this time the police became involved as a phone call brought Pc Arlett to the scene. A swift message to the main police station confirmed that no road works or road closures were scheduled on Witherstoke Road that day—or, for that matter, the foreseeable future.

Following the weed-killer raid, the bike chaining incident, the church closure notice and now this, it was obvious that some mischievous soul was at work. Not surprisingly the local press got hold of the story and, with a little journalistic licence, the 'Phantom Prankster' was created!

And more was to follow.

Over the next few weeks 'For Sale' notices appeared overnight on the windows of The Drovers Arms and the village shop, the door of the cricket pavilion, two of the bus shelters in the main village street and the front gate of the rather smart detached house owned by the chairman of the parish council—who had also had all four tyres of his car, parked in the driveway, let down and the valves removed.

In addition a 'Free Fuel!' sign had been posted on the lone petrol pump at the garage in the main street while, the same night, all the lights had suddenly failed at the tiny parish rooms a short way down the road, where a meeting of the Women's Institute was in full swing. The meeting had to be abandoned and it was later discovered that the main electricity cable had been cut through.

The Phantom Prankster, it seems, really had it in for just about everyone.

Speculation in the public bar of The Drovers was, of course, rife.

Suggestions about who could be responsible were many and varied. And, naturally, everyone wanted to know 'What the hell are the police doing about it?'

Pc Arlett was doing his best. He had made several reports to his sergeant in Witherstoke explaining that the exploits of Binfield's Phantom Prankster were causing considerable disquiet in the village.

The sergeant's response was considerably less than helpful.

'What d'you expect me to do about it? Send out squad cars to tour the village every night in the hope of catching someone at it? It's too minor a case for CID to get involved in. It's your patch son. Get on and do the best you can. But don't go clocking up any overtime on it!'

The village bobby was on his own. And so determined was he to crack the case that he found himself putting in considerable hours of his own, unpaid, time.

He revisited Fred Appleton's garden and, after a search, recovered an empty weed killer spray can from under the hedge in the field next to the keeper's cottage.

Harry at The Drovers handed over the chain and padlock which he had removed from the bikes outside the pub. He closely inspected two of the offending 'For Sale' notices that had been salvaged from waste bins, as well as the sheet off the church door, talked to the electrician who had repaired the parish room electricity supply and even had a word with George at the garage to see if he could shed any light on the car tyres incident.

At home in the police house office he pored over his little collection of clues and went through the details of the jottings in his notebook yet again. Somewhere there must be a connection.

Both the empty spray can and the little padlock had tiny price tickets on them. But they only gave the cost and no hint as to where the purchases had been made.

Next day the policeman happened to meet Joby in Binfield's main street.

'Mornin' officer,' was the old man's greeting. 'You worked out oo's bin buggerin' u all about yet?'

They both dismounted from their bikes.

'Not yet Joby but I'm working on it. I've got a few ideas.'

He was just about to remount his machine when he had second thoughts and turned back to the farm worker.

'Tell me Joby,' he said in a quiet and confidential sort of voice. 'Where would you go to buy the sort of padlock and chain used on the bikes outside the pub?'

Joby, his complete innocence in the whole prankster affair now established, performed his usual act when faced by a difficult question. He took off his cap and scratched his head.

'Well, George at the garage might have it, village shop wouldn't. Otherwise it'd be the 'ardware and ironmongers in Witherstoke.'

The officer had a thoughtful look on his face.

'Thanks Joby. That's a possible lead. And who would be the sort of person who would get up to this kind of behaviour d'you reckon?'

'Dunno,' returned Joby. Then added thoughtfully: 'Cept it's got to be somebody with a big chip on 'is shoulder. Can't think it'd be a local. More like an outsider—or someone new in the village.'

'Thanks again Joby. You've been very helpful.' And with that and a slight nod he remounted and pedalled off, leaving Joby gazing after him.

''E's got summat up 'is sleeve,' muttered the old fellow under his breath.

The following day found Pc Arlett, on his day off, a small haversack over one shoulder, standing outside the door of 'Scott's Hardware' in a side street just off one of Witherstoke's main shopping thoroughfares.

He pushed down the handle of the glass panelled door and, swinging it open, stepped inside, accompanied by the 'jangle-jangle-jangle' of the small brass bell which was activated by the action of the opening door.

The interior was virtually as it had been 50 years earlier. A wide wooden counter ran down one side, backed by row upon row of small, deep drawers extending from floor to ceiling, all clearly labelled and containing every imaginable size, length and type of nail, screw, tack and staple, each one available to buy individually or by weight.

The rest of the store was taken up with shelves stacked with pots of paint, tins of oil and grease, jars and packets of everything from rose fertilizer to rat poison.

Elsewhere on walls hung such items as coils of wire, cord and rope, available by the yard, racks of hand tools, rabbit snares, mole traps, rolls of netting, and, in one corner, a selection of power tools, drills and the like, with their arrays of accessories, polishers and grinders.

It resembled an Aladdin's Cave of DIY equipment and an unidentifiable, workshop-like aroma hung over the entire establishment.

A cursory look around confirmed to Pc Arlett that Scotts did, indeed, stock cans of weedkiller spray and chain of the type that now rested in the bottom of his shoulder bag.

'Can I help you sir? Anything special or are you just looking?'

As far as the middle-aged male sales assistant in the khaki warehouse coat was concerned, Alan Arlett, out of uniform, was just another confused and overwhelmed customer.

'Yes, can you help me? Do you stock small padlocks, like this one?'

At this point he produced the 'Drovers Incident' padlock from his bag.

The shopman took it, gave it a quick inspection and replied immediately.

'We certainly do. Over in the display cabinet against the wall. In fact, this is one of ours, it's still got the price tag on it.'

'How can you tell it's one of yours just by the price tag?'

'You see that thin blue edge on the label? Those are the ones we're using at the moment. I'm 99 per cent certain that this is one that I stuck on to a new batch of padlocks we had in only a week or two ago. Don't think you'd find a similar tag, or a similar padlock for that matter, in Witherstoke.'

'That's very interesting,' returned his customer. 'Perhaps you can help me with one or two other things.'

'My pleasure,' returned the salesman, who didn't seem a bit interested in knowing why this potential client wanted to know.

'I see you stock this brand of weedkiller,' the policeman went on, producing the empty can from his bag.

'Certainly do,' said the assistant. 'And that's one of ours as well.' He indicated the little white and blue label on the tin.

'What about marker pens, black marker pens?'

'Just over here. All sizes. From fine-tipped ones to these big commercial waterproof sticks.'

Pc Arlett picked one up and inspected it. Easy to see how anyone could produce an impressive 'For Sale' notice—or even a 'Road Closed' sign with one of these!

'Tell me, do you sell a lot of these?' he asked, indicating the large cylindrical marker in his hand.

'Not very many,' came the reply. 'Mostly to other shopkeepers for making up special bargain or sales signs I should say.'

'And,' here came the $64,000 question, 'what about the chains, and the padlocks, and the weedkiller? Get much call for those? Anyone bought any of these in the last couple of weeks?

'Well, yes. Funny you should say. I'm on duty almost every lunch time about now, usually on my own, and there was this bloke. He came in three or four times.'

The storeman's face wrinkled up and he half closed his eyes, raising one hand to rub his chin.

'He did buy some weed killer, and a chain and padlock, and one of those big marker pens.'

'Did you know him?'

'No but I recognised him as the same bloke each time he came in. Seemed an odd combination of items to me. Oh, and one time he bought a pair of side cutters.'

'Sidecutters?'

'Yes, you know those things that look like pliers, specially made for cutting through wire and cable and suchlike.' With that he moved over to the hand tool display and pointed out what he was describing.

'Would you know him again if you saw him?'

'Well, yes. Look, what's all this about?'

'Just a little bit of private undercover investigation,' replied the policeman, and gave the salesman a knowing wink.

'Mr Scott, the shop owner, was here one day when he came in. His family have been here for generations and he seems to know everything about everybody. I mentioned that this same man had been in several times recently and he said he thought he was one of the candidates for election to parish council out in one of the villages. Mr Scott knows about such things. Can't remember which village is was. Didn't get in though.'

A smile creased the policeman's face.

'Wouldn't have been Binfield by any chance would it?'

'Oh, come to think of it, how strange, I think it might have been.'

'I'd like to thank you for your assistance today.' The inquisitor shook the shopman's hand. 'You've been very helpful.'

Then he was gone, the shop door bell clanging as he went.

The assistant stood in the still empty shop, a decidedly puzzled look upon his face.

'My pleasure, I'm sure,' he said, half to himself, as the bell-ringing subsided and the street door closed.

Back at the police house PC Arlett shuffled through one of his box files until he found what he was looking for, a printed sheet from the returning officer at the Rural District Council listing the names and addresses, as well as the pictures, of the fourteen candidates for membership of Binfield Parish Council at the local elections back in May.

There were ten seats to be filled and the system was that the ten receiving the most votes would automatically be elected. The others would be deemed to be "not elected".

Next he went through his box file once more to dig out a copy of the result of the May election. There it clearly identified, in order of the number of votes cast, the ten successful candidates. More importantly it named the four who didn't get in.

And the likelihood was that the Phantom Prankster would turn out to be one of these. The net was closing.

A telephone call to the chairman of the council got him an appointment to speak to the man who, himself, had been one of the victims of the joker.

That evening the young policeman was seated in Mr Roger Beddingham's drawing room, notebook and pencil in hand, eager to get his interview under way.

After explaining the investigations he had made over the past few days he asked if the chairman was aware of any reason why any of the four unsuccessful candidates would hold a grudge against the council, indeed, against the village in general.

'It's not quite as straightforward as that,' replied the parish's leading politician.

'Not long after the election, one of the members, old Major Danders, he's served on the PC as chairman for years, had to give up for health reasons. Since then he's been in and out of hospital several times with heart problems. I was elected chairman to replace him.'

'But how does that complicate things?' the policeman wanted to know.

'Well, it doesn't really complicate things. You see, what happens in a case like this, when a councillor retires mid-term, the other councillors are empowered to co-opt another member without the need for an election,.to make up the numbers again.'

'And have you…uh…co-opted…another member?'

'Yes we have. Normally what happens is that we would contact the person who polled the highest number of votes without being elected in the previous election—that was back in May—and invite him or her to fill the vacancy.'

'And is that what you did this time?'

'Actually, no, it wasn't. The choice is entirely at the discretion of the serving members and, after considerable discussion, we agreed that the next person on the list, who has only lived in the village for a little over a year, was not necessarily the best choice and opted for the following candidate—there were only three or four election votes' difference—a woman who's been a resident here for over 20 years, children at the village school and the like, well we decided she would make a more suitable councillor.'

'So what you're saying is that you, in effect, chose to pass over this man in favour of a woman?'

'Ahem, well, yes, I suppose we did. But I repeat that the choice is entirely at the discretion of serving councillors and that's what the serving councillors decided.'

'Which means that this man,' the constable pointed to the person whose picture appeared at the top of the 'unsuccessful' list, 'was the one passed over?'

'That's correct.'

'Which means he might well feel aggrieved and hold a grudge?'

'Hadn't thought of it like that but, well, I suppose he could.'

Pc Arlett left the parish chairman's house with a satisfied smile on his face. Next day he visited the man who had become the prime suspect as Binfield's 'Phantom Prankster' and from him obtained a full and at times tearful confession to all the misdemeanours that had occurred in the village over the past few weeks.

A full report of his investigation was handed in to the main police station in Witherstoke where his sergeant gave him a 'well done son' acknowledgement, before passing it on to the Superintendent.

Next day the village bobby was summoned into the Super's office and told to sit down.

'First of all, constable, I'd like to congratulate you on a really thorough investigation. Good, solid police work, methodically carried out, some of it in your own time. I do like to see keenness. I'll make sure this commendation goes onto your record.'

The Superintendent leaned forward over his desk. 'But there's something else. I've passed this on to the office of the Director of Public Prosecutions who've looked further into the case and contacted their medical experts. They wouldn't normally become involved in what are considered to be minor cases.

'But it seems this man has suffered a major breakdown. The DPP feels that a written warning about his future behaviour is the right procedure in this case. That a prosecution in court would serve no really useful purpose and could make his medical condition much worse.

'I know it must be an enormous disappointment to you that no charges are to be brought, which of course would also add to your personal record standing but we have to think of the wider issues here.

'What are your thoughts on this?'

Pc Arlett thought for a second or two.

'I see that a court case with inevitable publicity would do no-one any good, least of all me, or the police force,' he replied. 'I'm just perfectly happy that a very aggravating situation has been brought to a satisfactory close and that the residents of my patch can relax into a normal life again.'

'Good man,' concluded the Super. 'That's all.'

Chapter fifteen

A FEW days later Joby was to be found on the bridge half a mile from his cottage, where the road to the village spans the river.

It was a pleasant, sunny evening, late September but as yet with no sign of approaching autumn. The old man had propped his bike against a nearby field gate and was leaning nonchalantly over the parapet, to all appearances gazing idly at the water.

But appearances can be deceptive.

In fact he was watching, intently, the motions of a small dead twig some 20 yards away which bobbed and swung in the ripples and swirls of the current as it made its slow progress down the stream.

The casual onlooker may well not have realised, or attached any significance to the fact, that, even on this fine evening, Joby was wearing his old dark overcoat. They could certainly not have guessed that, attached to that small twig, was two feet of fishing line connected to a hook, baited with a large worm from the old rascal's garden.

From the twig, a long length of nylon monofilament ran back upstream, under the archway of the bridge above which Joby was standing, came up the brickwork on the upstream side of the bridge, on the opposite side of the road, and was slowly paying out from a six-inch hazel baton on which was wound about another fifty yards of line.

The wooden line-holder had an eyed screw in one end. The eye of this screw was hanging on a metal hook fixed just below a protruding course of decorative brickwork that ran the length of the bridge, just below the parapet and totally out of sight from the road above.

Several years before, the crafty old poacher had spent a considerable number of secret moments screwing the hook into the brickwork so that, with his primitive fishing gear, he was able to catch a trout or two for his supper table. And no-one was any the wiser.

To be fair he only partook of this particular activity three or four times a year. The wonderful thing about trout, as Joby had discovered long ago, was you usually caught a good one by this method as the flow of river took the bait into the very places where the biggest fish were likely to lie. When the "boss" fish was removed the next biggest one would move into its place—waiting for the next juicy worm or piece of bread to drift by!

Joby's secret pastime had been put to the test several times over the years as friends and acquaintances passed by and stopped for a chat, without ever realising what was going on.

And it was just about to be tested once again as a figure in blue appeared on a bicycle and was quickly recognised as Pc Alan Arlett.

Joby acted as if he'd not even noticed the approaching policeman and carried on with his idle gaze down the river, elbows propped up on the bridge's half-rounded brick parapet.

'Joby! Just the man I want to see.'

For his part the old man appeared startled, and looked up quickly as though he'd just been woken from a dream.

The young bobby dismounted from his bike and pushed it over to where Joby was now leaning with his back against the bridge. Propping his machine up on the low wall the constable turned to Joby.

'Yes, I just wanted to tell you that the information you gave me last week was a great help in my investigations. The matter has all been cleared up now and we've seen the last of the "Phantom Prankster" I'm sure.' And he gave a little laugh.

'Ah, good,' returned the secret fisherman, turning casually and looking downstream, inwardly anxious that a sudden bite followed by a lot of splashing would give the game away.

'What are you up to anyway Joby? Thought you would have been in The Drovers by now.'

'Tha's where I'm off. Such a nice ev'nin,' though, I jus' stopped to admire the view.'

'Didn't know you were much of a person for admiring views.'

'Ah, there's lotsa things folks don't know 'bout me.' Joby replied with a chuckle.

'Well, best be on my way. Thanks again for the information. Enjoy the view.' With that the policeman remounted his bike and pedalled off, much to the relief of Joby Fulbright.

It was hardly ten minutes after this, during which time Joby hooked and hauled up a nice trout of just over a pound, that a second, decidedly unwelcome individual happened along.

This time it was Fred Appleton, Joby's long-time adversary and one who would be even more delighted to make trouble about his unorthodox angling method. Although the Squire employed a part-time river bailiff to look after the estate's fishing interests, it was Fred Appleton, as head gamekeeper, who was nominally in control.

'What's goin' on 'ere then Fulbright?'

The newcomer wanted to know. He had stopped his bike and was standing in the road, one leg each side of the crossbar.

Joby turned to face his old enemy and treated him to a contemptuous stare.

'I dunno, bloke can't stop for a peaceful look at the river without some nosey parker turnin' up and askin' questions. 'N any case, t'ain't no concern o' your'n what I'm doin.

'I'm on a public road in a public place mindin' me own business. An' you might do well to mind your own business too, Appleton.'

The final syllables contained as much venom as had Fred Appleton's original question.

'Spose you'll be wantin' me to turn out me pockets next? 'Cept, o' course, you ain't got no right to ask me. Never mind. I'll show you any way.'

Joby dived his right hand into the right hand pocket of his overcoat.

'Look, in this one I got me ole baccy tin.'

He replaced it and put the other hand into the left pocket, bringing out a small, paper wrapped package.

'And in this one I got wot's left of me cheese sammidge left over from tea. Satisfied?'

Fred Appleton had to admit to himself, albeit grudgingly, that there seemed to be nothing about Joby's person that aroused suspicion of any wrongful or illegal activity.

After a quick look over the bridge and a fleeting glance around the nearby road surface for any other tell-tale signs he gave a grunted 'Uhuh,' remounted his bike and pedalled away.

What Fred didn't realise was that the 'old baccy tin' contained, not tobacco, but half a dozen big worms in a packing of damp moss. And the 'cheese sandwich' was used solely for baiting his fish hook with a lump of bread if the trout grew tired of worms.

Joby heaved another sigh of relief and treated himself to a broad smile of satisfaction.

He had shown Fred Appleton what he had in his overcoat pockets. Except, of course, that there was another deeper pocket inside the coat in which nestled a newly caught—or rather poached—trout.

Joby had acquired a couple of the new-fangled polythene shopping bags in which some big stores were now packing customers' purchases and he found these absolutely ideal for containing all manner of wet, muddy, bloody or fragile items which he somehow managed to accumulate during his forays in the countryside.

Within a few minutes of the 'keeper's departure there was another splashing downstream and by hurrying over to the other side of the bridge, Joby was able to haul in another plump trout.

'That'll do me nicely,' he muttered to himself as it joined its twin in the polythene bag. Rewinding his fishing gear he stowed that in the same inside overcoat pocket, went over to retrieve his bike and was soon riding up the hill towards The Drovers Arms.

His catch could safely lie there until he reached home again, later that evening.

There was big news breaking in Binfield.

The excitement of a number of recent happenings was quickly forgotten as a new story burst upon the unsuspecting village scene. This time it was a tale of pleasure and surprise.

Only a very few people were in on the secret until the local weekly newspaper announced in its 'hatches, matches and dispatches' columns (newspaper speak for 'births, deaths and marriages') the engagement of Mr Peter Hillory to Mrs Ivy Green.
Yes, the relationship of the local estate agent with his live-in cook and housekeeper had progressed from initial friendship, to companionship, and had finally blossomed into romance.

No-one was really that astonished, merely bemused that it had managed to occur right under their noses without an inkling of what was happening. And of course the public bar at The Drovers was abuzz with speculation as soon as the news got around— which it did in double quick time.

'Reckon they'll move out o' the village then, once they're wed?'

'Nah, why should they? Got that nice big 'ouse and I shouldn't think there are likely to be kids on the way.'

'Tha's true enough. They're both gettin' on a bit to be startin' a young family.'

'Well, Ivy's done 'erself a bit o' good all right. She's now well set up with a bit o' cash behind her.'

'Mebbe so, but 'e could 'ave done a whole lot worse an' all. I know she ain't no spring chicken but she's still a fine lookin' woman.'

'Damn fine cook an' 'ousekeeper too!'

'Spose they're a nicely matched pair then.'

Joby, sitting in his usual seat in the corner by the window didn't join in the discussion but he did have a very thoughtful look on his face.

Ivy's daughter Sandra and her husband Benjamin Trenchard had rejoiced at the news, when they had been let into the secret a week or so earlier at which point they had received a preview of the diamond engagement ring.

When Joby happened into Ivy as she came out of the village shop two days later he was full of praise and also wanted to see the ring.

'Seems congrat'lations are in order,' he said.

Joby and Ivy had always got on well together since she went up to Longdown Farm to run the house for the brothers following the earlier tragic death of their parents.

'When's the weddin?'

'Not yet awhile. Not 'til next year anyway. So many things to do, so many things to arrange.'

'I 'spec Mr Hillory will be wantin' to get you a nice weddin' present then?'

'I expect he will. In fact I have a little something in mind. An idea that you gave me Joby, some time ago.' And she gave a quiet little laugh, accompanied by what could only be described as half a wink.

Joby looked at her in amazement.

'You mean he's.......'

'I'm saying nothing more Joby. We'll all just have to wait and see won't we?'

With that she turned and strode off, leaving him gazing after her retreating figure in admiration. He had a good idea of what she was talking about. Something of which certainly no-one else in the village had the slightest notion.

As he mounted his bike the old man's face had once more taken on that look of secretive thoughtfulness.

That evening in The Drovers the nightly discussion, quite naturally, once again turned to the subject of Ivy's engagement to her employer.

'So you don't reckon they'll be movin' then?'

'No need, is there? He'll be wantin' t' be close at 'and to oversee that damned 'ouse buildin' lark.'

'If it ever goes ahead.'

Heads turned to Joby who had so far stayed out of the discussion. Now he was casting considerable doubt on the whole project.

'Wha' j' mean? Course it'll go ahead.'

'Course it will! Bloke like that's not gonna let I dunno how many thousands o' pounds slip through 'is fingers!'

'Not 'ardly. Shoulda thought that was obvious.'

'Still, I shouldn't bank on it. Certainly wouldn't bet on it,' returned Joby.

'I would!'

'So would I.'

There was a pause.

'Well now, as you gennlemen are so fond of a bit o' local bettin,' wot I say is that I've got an even pint that sez it won't never take place. Any takers?'

There was laughter all round as several of the public bar regulars rapidly added their names to a list that landlord Alf Bassett quickly organised on a slate behind the bar.

As for Alf, this time he declined to accept the challenge.
'I know your record too well to risk a pint with you,' he smiled.

'Why? D'you imagine 'e's gonna abandon the scheme then?'

'Jus' got this little feelin,' tha's all.'

'Well it won't be fer a while yet anyway, will it?'

'No, but it'll come, jus' you wait an' see.'

'Sure it will. An' it won't be too long.'

'Them 'ouses will go up, sure as eggs is eggs.''

'Bet it'll be all done an' dusted within the year.'

'I bet it won't,' said Joby.

And the wager was struck. They were all going to have to wait twelve months before the outcome was decided but it looked like prolonging a debating subject of great interest in the public bar of The Drovers for the foreseeable future.

In the event nobody had to wait that long.

The following week's weekend copy of the Witherstoke Gazette carried a large feature on one of the early news pages headlined "Houses Plan Ditched."

And, under a large picture of a smiling Ivy and Peter, standing in the middle of the Lallyfield building project site, ran the story:

A scheme to turn a derelict field at Binfield into a housing estate has been ditched by owner Peter Hillory. The field, known locally as Lallyfield, has been used for years as an unofficial playground by children of the village and its proposed development caused considerable controversy between residents and Mr Hillory Now, following the announcement of his forthcoming marriage, the estate agent owner has exclusively told the Gazette that he is donating the land to the parish. Development will still go ahead but it will be development of the site as a permanent children's play area.

He has disclosed that he will personally foot the bill and that the whole idea is at the suggestion of his fiancee, Ivy Green, to whom he is dedicating the credit for the scheme as a special wedding present.

Meanwhile villagers are expected to be delighted by the decision. Binfield rector, the Rev Michael Stott, said: 'This is wonderful news. The whole village will be overjoyed at the prospect. We all owe a huge debt of gratitude to Mr Hillory and his fiancee for their generosity...'

The story went on to describe the types of play equipment and 'adventure' facilities it was planned to provide.

Many details, it said, were still to be worked out but the extent of the provision would be 'considerable' and Mr Hillory had pledged to finance the upkeep of the area for the first five years before handing over responsibility to the parish council.

So, in the shortest possible time scale Peter Hillory had, in the eyes of Binfield, been transformed from sinner to saint.

And Joby's already formidable reputation for having some kind of mysterious second sight into the future was further enhanced, while the man himself enjoyed several more evenings of free entertainment at the expense of the regulars in the public bar of The Drovers Arms.

It was also about this time that the builders moved in to Joby's cottage.

After years of failing to persuade him to allow improvements, he had finally, and unexpectedly, caved in to a suggestion from Benjamin Trenchard that his home should be provided with a proper bathroom, new kitchen and a central heating system, based on what came to be described by Joby as 'one o' they nu-fangled wood burner thingies.'

The reasons for Joby's sudden capitulation were two-fold.

Firstly, Benjamin had been more than a little economical with the truth when he had hinted to his employee that 'the public health people' had been in touch to say that all tenanted properties had to be improved to new minimum standards on pain of prosecution for owners who did not comply.

And then there was Joby himself who, with his advancing years frequently reminding him that he was not getting any younger, had gradually come round to the thought that a cosy inside loo might be infinitely more preferable than a trek down the garden in the dead of winter. A warm bedroom also began to take on a more seductive proposition.

He had responded to Benjamin's approach with: 'A'right then, if it's gotta be done it's gotta be done. Don't wanna get you into any trouble boss.'

Benjamin had offered Joby the use of a spare bedroom at the farm for the few weeks the work was expected to take but the old fellow had politely declined, preferring to stay in the cottage while the builders worked round him.

'In any case, I'll be out mosta the time and they'll be done fer the day by the time I gets 'ome from work.'

So local builder Tony Cookson arrived with two men and began the preparations for the big improvement job.

On their very first morning drama and excitement unfolded when Tony, while crouched in the front room fireplace to inspect the inside of the chimney in readiness for fitting a metal flue liner, discovered some loose bricks just up at arm's length in the side of the interior wall.

'This'll need making good,' he told Benjamin, who had arrived to oversee the commencement of the project.

'Whatever it needs, do it,' the farmer had replied. 'It's high time something was done to this old building. Don't think it's seen any major work since grandfather bought it as a worker's cottage way back in, when, probably 1900.'

Tony wiggled out one of the loose bricks, then another.

There was a small cavity behind them and next time his hand appeared it held a small oblong tin box with a close fitting metal lid, covered in dust.

'What's this then? 'Twas jammed in the wall behind those loose bricks.'

He handed it to Benjamin who blew off the brick dust then placed it on Joby's kitchen table. They both bent over the object. It was not very large, just three or four inches square and the same height, and seemed to resemble a very old-fashioned metal tea caddy.

Benjamin took a firm grip on the lid and wrenched it open.

'Good God!'

'Bloody hell!'

The cries exploded almost as one as the two men realised what the box contained.
Bright yellow coins, lots of them.

The pair fell silent, apart from gasps of surprise, as Benjamin carefully tipped them into a little pile onto the kitchen table. There were a couple of dozen or more. They were gold sovereigns and half sovereigns.

Benjamin was the first to speak.

'Good Lord!' Then he began to chuckle. 'Joby's up at the farm milking at the moment. Will he get a surprise when he finds out he's been sitting just a few feet away from this little lot every evening for the last forty-odd years!'

Surprise was something of an understatement when Joby arrived home an hour or so later.

Benjamin was still there and although some discussion had taken place about exactly what work was to be done, how and in what order, the main interest was in the little tin box of treasure, still sitting on the kitchen table.

Total speechlessness was more of an appropriate description of the long-time tenant.
Joby gazed, open-mouthed, at the coins. Then he gazed again. When, after some moments of spluttering, his power of speech returned he managed to gasp:

'Up the chimney? But I 'as a fire there ev'ry night when it's cold. Sits there in me ole chair before I goes t'bed!'

He paused.

'Who do these all belong to then?'

Benjamin and Mr Cookson exchanged glances.

'That's a very good point. Who DO they belong to?' Benjamin replied. 'I suppose we'll have to get that all decided legal and proper. I'll contact the main police station in Witherstoke and get some advice.'

This was duly done and the police reported the find to the District Coroner who in turn ordered an inquest.

Part of a coroner's duty, apart from ascertaining the causes of apparently inexplicable or suspicious deaths, was the little-known responsibility for conducting an inquiry into the ownership of all substantial quantities of valuables and money discovered in his area of jurisdiction.

This took the form of a public hearing, presided over by the coroner, and decided upon by a jury of eight local residents. It was known as a Treasure Trove Inquest and usually attracted very considerable interest, not only from the general public but also from the Press.

It was several weeks before the hearing was arranged during which time a good deal of investigation had to take place. Firstly to establish whether or not there was anyone living who might lay claim to the hoard.

Not surprisingly it transpired there was not.

Then the find had to be evaluated and this was done by a famous London coin dealer who concluded, in his report, that: *The total number of coins in the discovered hoard is 87, comprising 59 gold sovereigns and 28 gold half sovereigns, all dating from the first quarter of the 19th century.*

For the most part they are unremarkable, being of relatively common mintage and consequently of normal worth, taking into consideration the current value of gold. However a number of them, notably the 1819 specimens for example, are more uncommon, indeed some are quite rare and would be of considerable interest to coin collectors. These would, of course, be substantially more valuable.

Taking account of all our researches we therefore assess the total value of the collection as approximately £1,800.

So there it was.

The little tin box that had been found hidden in the chimney of Joby's farm cottage was worth something like a small fortune.

It was now up to a Treasure Trove Inquest to decide on its fate. And the regulars in The Drovers had a field day.

"'Oo gets it then?'

'Well I 'spose Joby's got some claim to it. After all, 'e's the tenant.'

'Yeh but the Trenchards are the owners.'

''Twas Tony Cookson as found it..'

'Betcha the government will want to get its 'ands on it!'

'Ha-ha. That's fer sure!'

The day of the inquest arrived and in Witherstoke Courthouse the main players were assembled. The coroner, Mr Julius Rumbold, took his accustomed place on the bench and looked around. Down below was the jury box where eight Witherstoke residents had been chosen to deliver the verdict.

There were a number of witnesses, including Benjamin Trenchard and Tony Cookson, seated in the front row, ready to give their evidence, the Press table was filled, as was the main part of the courtroom. In fact it was packed with the interested and the curious of the district.

Mr Rumbold began by explaining how unusual these proceedings were, supported by the fact that he himself, with nearly 30 years experience as District Coroner, had presided at only one such previous inquiry. And that was many years ago.

The coroner then explained that the duty of the inquest was to decide exactly who had found the treasure, exactly where and when it was found, on whose property the find had been made and whether or not it legally constituted a Treasure Trove.

'In which case,' he added, 'it would in earlier times have become the property of the Crown.'

A murmuring groan of disappointment rippled around the courtroom and the coroner was obliged to bang once with his gavel to restore silence.

'However,' he continued, 'in more recent times it has been the practice of the Lords Commissioners of the Treasury to transfer this right to the British Museum. If they decide to keep all or part of the find they then reward the finder, or the owner of the property on which it was found, with the full value of the items retained.

'Any such item not retained is handed back to the finder or property owner to be disposed of as they think fit. If the finder is not the same person as the property owner it is a matter for them to decide between themselves how that value should be divided.'

The earlier groans of disappointment were replaced by a ripple of quiet chatter mingled with sighs of relief when it became apparent that the hoard would then, after all, benefit someone locally.

This time the coroner allowed the murmuring to continue a while until, within a few seconds, the courtroom once more lapsed into silence.

The hearing got under way, The witnesses were called in turn and gave their individual accounts of the discovery in Joby's cottage kitchen chimney. Then the valuation report was read out, bringing gasps of surprise from the assembly.

Soon the coroner began his summing up.

'This appears to me to be a very straightforward situation. What the jury must decide is who found that box of coins and in what circumstances. That, I believe, has been clearly defined by witnesses this morning.

'Then they must decide on whether those coins were lost, stolen or scattered with no intention of being recovered. Or whether they were deliberately hidden by someone who had every intention of recovering them at a later date.

'If the former, then they must be handed back to the finder. If the latter then they must be declared Treasure Trove and offered to the Crown.'

The jury was allowed to retire to discuss their verdict. They trooped back into the courtroom in a little under 15 minutes.

Not surprisingly the verdict was that the tin box and its contents had been found by Mr Tony Cookson at the property, and in the company, of Mr Benjamin Trenchard. And that it did, indeed, constitute Treasure Trove.

The room was abuzz. The Press representatives jostled to question the builder and the farmer.

'How was the money to be shared?'

'What were their first thoughts on opening the tin box?'

'What was it like finding out that the little tin was worth so much money?'

'What were they going to do with the money?'

'New car?'

'Luxury holidays?'

The two men were overwhelmed with demands and suggestions. But apart from their initial reactions about the actual find they had to admit that no decision had yet been made about who would get what or what it would be spent on.

Later, over a quiet lunch in the Red Lion, they at last had a chance to talk about it. After a relatively short discussion they agreed on a formula suggested by Benjamin Trenchard.

Tony Cookson should have one third,

Benjamin Trenchard should have one third.

And the other one third should go to Joby Fulbright.

Job done!

Joby was easily the most astonished at the development of the situation. The generosity of his employer in declaring that he should receive a third of the find's value meant he would be better off, once the coins were disposed of, by £600.

Allowing that his present wages were £9 10 shillings a week, plus a few bob a week overtime during the harvest season, plus a few more small sums for the odd rabbit he sold during the winter (not to mention the receipts from the occasional gamebird he managed to 'acquire') and a bit of casual gardening money, it constituted well over his total earnings for a full year. That was an awful lot of pints at The Drovers!

Benjamin Trenchard was perfectly happy with the fact that his share would almost certainly more than pay for the extensions, renovations and alterations to the cottage and still leave a few score pounds for some little extras at the farmhouse.

Builder Tony Cookson was beside himself with delight. For more than a year his ancient van had been playing up more than somewhat and he was already resigned to having to find the finance for a replacement. This substantial windfall was more than enough to buy a brand new van and pay for a really nice holiday into the bargain.

It took quite a few weeks for the hoard to be sold to the same London coin dealer who had made the original assessment of its value, especially as around a dozen of the coins had to be offered for sale at a special auction where they were eagerly snapped up by a number of serious collectors.

The upshot of all this activity was that towards the end of November Joby found himself, for the first time in his life, the holder of a Post Office Savings Account—with a credit balance of £614 7s 6d.

It was one evening soon after, while sitting at the kitchen table in the newly-refurbished cottage, with the open shiny-covered PO account book in his hands, that Joby made a startling decision.

Gazing at the neatly printed figures on that first, pale blue page, and coming to the realisation that he was suddenly relatively well off, familiar memories once again flooded into the old man's mind of a time long past. Memories he had lived with but had been able to do nothing about for well over 40 years.

'I'll go,' he suddenly announced loudly to no-one but himself.

Of course it was absurd but he had made up his mind to try to find Delphine, the long lost love of his youth, or at least discover what had become of her.

He gave no inkling of his intentions to a soul but he did get permission from Benjamin to take a two-week break from work specifically 'to do sumthin' I should've done years ago.'

On a visit to Witherstoke he went into the town's newly-opened travel agent's office and asked about the cost of going to France and how he could achieve it. Then there was the question of accommodation once he was there. The language problem. And just exactly what he was going to do once back on French soil. Where should he start his search? He had no idea whatever of what had happened to Delphine or where she might be.

That Saturday afternoon Joby was sitting in his bright new kitchen, shoes and socks cast aside on the floor and both feet immersed in a large bowl of warm water. There were a number of, to him, rather baffling travel brochures scattered over the pine kitchen table.

'That should be enough now Joby.'

The voice was that of Jane Grayling, the district nurse, who had called in to give the old man's feet a "going over". The pair had got on well together ever since the nurse's arrival in the village and she had promised she would call in one weekend to inspect his feet for corns and callouses, "give them a tidy up" and cut his toenails.

For which Joby, lately finding it difficult to bend over that far, was genuinely grateful.

He lifted his feet out of the water and placed them on the towel spread over a little four-legged stool that stood beside the bowl. Nurse Grayling sat forward in another kitchen chair facing him and began to dry his toes.

'Nurse…' Joby began hesitantly.

'Yes Joby, what is it?

'Well, you've bin about a bit, I mean travelled around some. P'raps you c'n help me plan a little trip abroad of me own. You see, I ain't bin abroad before.' He paused for a moment. 'Well, not for very many years anyway,' he added.

'Tell me what it's all about and I'll see what I can do to advise,' replied the nurse. 'Mind you, I haven't done a great deal of foreign travel myself.'

'It's like this…' Joby began, trying hard to pick his words carefully. 'A good many years ago, a long time ago, during the First War, I…'

The rest of the sentence was interrupted by the robust sound of the front door knocker echoing through to the kitchen.

'Now who the 'eck can that be?' exclaimed Joby, who rarely got more than one visitor to the cottage in the same day. And without waiting for Nurse Grayling's offer to answer the call, as she was about to do, he shouted: 'Come roun' the back!'

After what seemed a long wait there was a gentler knocking on the big back door and this time the nurse was already on her feet and undoing the black iron latch.

The door swung wide open and an unexpected view met their gaze.

Standing on the back step were two strangers, a tall, dark-haired young man in his mid-twenties and a petite, dark auburn-haired woman aged around 50 or perhaps a little younger.

Both were well-dressed, he in a grey suit with tie, she in a fashionable coat.

Joby was still seated in the chair, his bare feet on the stool. There was a kind of a surprised silence as the four people looked at each other. Then the young man spoke.

'Please excuse me. Uh…Mr Jonathan Fulbright?'

'Yes, that's me.'

He swung his feet off the stool and padded his way, barefoot, to the door where he faced the curious couple outside.

The young man spoke again.

'My name is Laurent, Étienne Laurent.' His voice had a tiny bit more than the trace of a foreign accent. 'And,' turning to indicate the woman at his side, 'this is my mother, Madame, errh, Mrs Aimée Laurent. We have been looking for you.'

'Lookin' fer me?'

The woman spoke.

'Oui. Je voulais vous montrer cette vieille photo.'

Joby was visibly startled at this foreign newcomer gabbling at him in what he rightly guessed was French. Meanwhile the woman took from her handbag a faded and creased picture which she handed to him.

It was of a young man in army uniform posing stiffly, standing with one hand on a three feet tall pillar at his side. Obviously a very old studio photograph. He turned it over. In faded pen-written handwriting on the back could be made out the words *"Pte Jonathan Fulbright"*.

Joby gasped.

He clearly recognised that it was him. He even recalled having the photograph taken nearly 50 years before. A whole group of his friends had been with him and they had all decided to have their snaps done while awaiting embarkation for France.

He stared in amazement at the woman before him. There was something about the slight tilt of her nose, her dark eyes and the curl of her deep chestnut hair that brought vivid memories racing back into his confused brain. But it just couldn't be. It just didn't work out.

She spoke again.

'Il y a quelques années, j'ai trouvée cette photo dans les affaires de ma mère. Elle s'appelait Delphine Fournier. Je pense que vous la connaissiez lorsqu'elle était infirmière dans un hôpital militaire durant la première guerre mondiale.'

Joby goggled at her in total disbelief. He had understood nothing of what she had said. Except for that magic name, Delphine. He turned in bewilderment to her son.
'What?...How is...? I don't...' his voice trailed off.

Étienne Laurent translated.
'My mother found the picture in my grandmother's house about 20 years ago. My grandmother was a nurse in the Great War. We believe you knew her. Her name was Delphine Fournier.'

'Ma mère m'a parlé de vous de nombreuses fois quand j'étais petite sans jamais mentionner votre nom. Elle ne s'est jamais mariée. Elle avait toujours déclaré qu'elle n'avait eu qu'un seul amour dans sa vie.'

Aimée Laurent spoke quietly and Joby watched her face intently, not comprehending a single word.

He turned a questioning face once again to Étienne.

'She says her mother spoke of you many times, although not by name, as the only love of her life. Delphine never married.'

'Nous n'avons jamais vraiment pris le temps de faire des recherches pour vous retrouver. Mais cette anneé nous nous sommes attelés à la tâche…et voila!'

Joby's gaze went once more from Aimée to Étienne who obliged.

'We have not had sufficient time until now to try to find the father of my mother but we have at last succeeded. And here we are!'

Joby's jaw dropped with the eventual realisation of what had happened, what all this meant. Nurse Grayling stood just inside the kitchen door equally astonished with all that had occurred in the last five minutes.

'But where is Delphine? What happened? 'Ow did…?' Joby's confused brain and jumbled thoughts spilled out a mess of words and questions. He turned to Aimée.

'That means you are…' and turning to Étienne: 'And you are…My God. I can't believe it!'

'Oui. Je suis bien votre fille et mon fils que voici est votre petit-fils!'

Joby's face swivelled once more from one to the other.

'Yes this is your daughter and I am your grandson!'

The two held out their hands as though for a handshake. Joby, tears streaming down his face, threw out his arms and grasped them both in a huge embrace.

For more than half a century Joby had existed believing that he was alone in the world, apart from the distant memories of a burning love and a lifetime obsession. Now, suddenly, it seemed he had been presented with a ready-made family——his own flesh and blood.

His surprise and his utter ecstasy were beyond description.

For a full minute or two the three of them hugged and laughed and cried together until, breaking free, Joby exclaimed:

'For God's sake come in, come in. I want to know everything. Sit down, sit down.'

And soon they were all sitting round the kitchen table, faces aglow with a mixture of smiles and tears of joy.

Meanwhile Nurse Grayling stood by, a big grin on her face and just the trace of a tear trickling down her cheek. She too was invited to sit down and join the reunion.

Aimée was the first to speak.

'Alors, laissez-moi tout vous raconter depuis le début.'

Her son quickly interrupted.

*'Non Maman ! Laisse-**moi** tout raconter sinon on y sera encore là demain!'*

Joby didn't comprehend but it appeared that Étienne wanted to give the details and the young man's mood became quite serious as he began the story.

'Sadly my grandmother, Delphine, died in 1944, by which time my mother, Aimée, was already married herself and I was six years old.'

Aimée broke in.

'Morte? Tuée tu veux dire! Tuée par les Bosch!'

'Oui, Maman, tuée. Laisse-moi continuer.'

Étienne continued: 'Delphine was killed, murdered by the Nazis, but I'll come to that in a while.'

Joby's face was a shocked white mask.

'Murdered? But where? How did it happen?'

'Let me tell you the whole story.

'After being parted from you in 1916 my grandmother, Delphine, continued for several months as a nurse but then had to leave to have her baby. Her daughter Aimée, my mother, was born the following year. Her family were very displeased so she went south and made her home in Limoges, in central France.'

Chapter sixteen

THE four of them sat around the kitchen table as Étienne recounted all that he knew of the family history. Aimée was patient and motionless as her son held forth in near-perfect English. The expressions on the faces of both Joby and Jane changed with each emotion as the full story unfolded—from sadness to surprise, to pity, indignation and, eventually, anger.

After Aimée was born, said Étienne, Delphine went back to work as a nurse at the local hospital in Limoges, assisted in child minding by the kindly widow who owned her rented flat and with financial help from her own parents, with whom she gradually became reconciled, and who were keen to be a part of their only grandchild's life.

Aimée, who bore a striking resemblance to her mother, grew up and went to school in Limoges, later training to be a secretary. She left home to further her career, securing the post of personal secretary to M. Jean Laurent the elderly senior partner in a law firm in Angers, in the Loire valley where she met, and eventually married, the boss's son Jean-Paul, a junior partner who was to take over the company on the death of his father.

'I was the result of that marriage,' smiled Étienne.

'Born in Angers in 1938.'

Continuing the story, he told how his grandmother, Delphine, had remained in Limoges where she had made a number of lasting friendships, including that of a young school teacher of her own age who travelled by tram each day the 12 miles or so to school in a village north of the town.

'The Second World War broke out the year after I was born and France once again found itself on the wrong end of German aggression,' went on Étienne. 'Limoges is in what was "Vichy

France", the unoccupied zone, so life went on very much as before, except for strict rationing and severe restrictions on travel and communication.

'Then in June 1944 news started to come in that the Allies had landed in Normandy and everyone started looking forward to the end of the war and a liberated France.'

It was only a few days after the start of the Allied invasion, on Saturday, 10 June that Delphine Fournier made the fateful decision to visit her long-time school teacher friend who was teaching that day (as they did on Saturday mornings in France) at the village school in Oradour sur-Glane.

On that bright and sunny summer day she caught the mid-morning tram, arriving at the village just before lunchtime when her friend was due to finish her duties. They had planned to spend a relaxing afternoon together in the village before returning to Limoges on the evening tram.

The peace of the village was shattered at exactly 2pm.

'Several hundred German soldiers, members of a Waffen-SS Panzer Division, suddenly arrived in the village and started rounding up the inhabitants.'

Étienne paused and took a deep breath.

'They said they wanted to check everyone's identity papers, in reality they were looking for members of the French Resistance movement who had been very active in the area once the invasion news was broken. A number of attacks had been made on German military groups, one senior German officer was kidnapped and executed, and dozens of Frenchmen and women had been killed in reprisal.

'The women and children were locked in the village church and the men and boys were divided into smaller groups and confined in various garages and barns. Delphine and her friend found themselves crowded with the other women and youngsters in the church.

'A large incendiary device was placed in the church and the explosion, which killed many of those inside, was the signal for the groups of men and boys to be machine-gunned,' continued Étienne.

'When the bomb and smoke failed to kill all those trapped in the church the German soldiers threw dozens of hand grenades in through the windows, raked the interior with machine guns and set fire to the building. All but one woman perished in the blast, the hail of bullets and the flames.

'Of the men, just a few escaped. More than 640 innocent men, women and children, all civilians, were slaughtered for no apparent reason. My grandmother, Delphine, died in this atrocity. After all the killing, the village was destroyed by fires, deliberately started by the Germans who had already ransacked the houses, stealing everything of value.

'The tragedy was compounded further by later revelations which indicated that the German intention was to make a reprisal attack on a different village which had actively supported the Maquis. There are a number of villages named Oradour in the Limousin.'

Joby's head slumped onto his chest, there was no sobbing but tears streamed down his face. Jane, too was visibly shaken and leaned over to place a comforting arm around his shoulder. Aimée duplicated the move from his other side.

There was a long silence.

'But… We 'eard nothin' about this over 'ere.' The old man's voice was quiet and low. 'An,' after the war. Wusn't there an inquiry or, well, a war crime trial or somethin'?'

'Eleven years ago, in 1953, there was a trial of sorts in Bordeaux, a military tribunal,' replied the young Frenchman. 'Of the 200

German soldiers who took part in the massacre only a handful had been detained and most of them were conscripts from Alsace, a French region annexed into Germany in 1940 and handed back to France after the war.

'Complex legal arguments over their status made the hearing very long and very complicated. In the end one German was sentenced to death, later reduced to a prison sentence, the others were jailed for varying terms. Everyone involved is now free again.'

'Isn't there nothin' left to see?' Joby asked.

'Indeed there is,' returned Etienne. 'After the war the President of France, General Charles de Gaulle, ordered that the entire site be preserved in the state left by the Germans. The ruins are standing still as a national memorial to all the people who died there. There is also a memorial garden.'

'I want to go there and see it,' declared Joby. 'I want to go there and see where Delphine died.'

Not surprisingly the astonishing story of Joby's new-found family went round the village like wildfire and even warranted a full page feature, with pictures, in the local rag.

Both Joby and Nurse Jane, who because of her presence at the reunion, quickly came to be looked upon almost as one of the new family, were questioned endlessly about the remarkable development.

The young Frenchman and his mother, who were staying at the Red Lion Hotel in Witherstoke, acquired a kind of celebrity status in Binfield, which they visited a number of times in the next few weeks, especially so at the Drover's Arms.

And, of course, the regulars in the public bar had a field day every evening as they discussed the merits and otherwise of the situation.

'An' Joby? What'll 'e do now then?'

'Dunno, 'e won't need t' carry on workin,' that's fer sure. That young froggy bloke an' 'is mum are well 'eeled by all accounts. The company belongs t' them since 'er 'usband died. The boy was only small then but 'e's top dog now.'

'Didn't know 'is dad wus dead!'

'Oh ah. 'pears he wus stayin' in Caen on business when the Allies bombed and shelled the place to get the Jerries out. He was one of 'undreds who got killed.'

'Seems to me war's a bloody silly thing when ord'nry folks gets killed.'

'Never a truer word!'

'Ow come young Etty-whatever-'is-name-is speaks such good English then?

'Seems 'e 'ad a lot of 'is education in England after the war, then studied for 'is law degree in Paris.'

But what with the travel details, passport and various other arrangements it was to be some time before Joby got his wish to go back to France, particularly now that he insisted that he be accompanied by his new friend Jane Grayling.

They were met at the ferry by Étienne and Aimée who had arranged accommodation for the trip and were to drive them south, down the long road route to Limoges.

And two days later, on a grey and chilly November morning, the four of them paused briefly at the gated entrance to the once picturesque village of Oradour-sur-Glane before walking slowly through, past the 'SILENCE' and 'REMEMBER' signs and on up into the main street, once a bustling thoroughfare, now a strangely empty street lined by the ruined shells of shops and houses.

In whispered tones Étienne pointed out the tiny plaques on each of the buildings, naming the people who had lived there and who had died in the massacre, each inscription ending with the words *'Murdered by the Bosch.'*

They saw the doctor's car, rusted and decrepit, standing in the street exactly where it had been parked on that fateful day 20 years earlier, The rooms inside wrecked and blackened cottages still showed the remains of what had been inside, a burned-out sewing machine, a bed frame, a bicycle, cooking pans, bottles.

Later, they stood in a silent huddle in the stone-flagged nave of the parish Catholic church where all the children and women, save one, had perished. More than 450 innocent women and children, one of them Delphine Fournier.

Joby stood gazing at the smashed east window above where the altar had once been the focus of village life each Sunday. Tears were streaming down his face and there was a scrambled mass of thoughts and emotions streaming through his confused mind.

The brief but sublime joy of being with Delphine, his longing for her over the last 50 years, his great feeling of guilt that in all that time he had done nothing to retrieve that love, the loneliness of his life apart, the thought of her loneliness and hardship as she struggled to raise their daughter alone, and, worst of all her terrible suffering at the end, the explosions, the screams, the fire, the bullets…

He hunched his shoulders, dropped his head, covered his face with the palms of his hands and wept aloud.

He was joined in a nestling, snuggling, sobbing huddle by his daughter, grandson and Nurse Jane. The five or six other silent visitors in the church looked quickly at this little group, and lowered their heads in sympathy.

Back in England once more Joby finally felt as though a great, heavy veil had been lifted.

His beloved Dephine was now lost and gone forever but all the love, joy and contentment he had once enjoyed with her, all the ache and emotion which he had suffered since and which had dissipated wastefully away, were now just as powerfully focussed on his new family, his daughter and grandson.

At an age approaching 72 a brand new life is now opening up to him. He is indeed retired—apart from the odd helping-out with the milking—and Benjamin allows him to live in the newly refurbished cottage free of rent in his retirement.

He still enjoys his frequent visits to The Drovers, his gardening, his umpiring at the annual cricket match and the occasional morning in winter ferreting or organising the beaters at the farm's traditional shoot. Although he has eased off on a few of his less legal activities. For instance the metal hook hidden below the parapet of the river bridge is still there, although now rusty and unused and he seems at last to have ended his feud with Fred Appleton, the local gamekeeper.

The rest of his time is filled with his new found kin. There are frequent trips to the family home in France's Loire valley and regular visits to England by Aimée and Étienne. Joby is even learning French and Aimée is improving her English.

Benjamin and Sandra have added to the family by producing a son and heir to the Trenchard farm at Longdown, while younger brother Robert has moved out of the house to take over the running of a farm which the brothers lease from the neighbouring estate, the two farms being developed as a single larger unit.

The village bobby, Pc Alan Arlett, after his initiative in solving the village's 'Phantom Prankster' mystery, has been transferred to plainclothes duties in the Witherstoke CID as a Detective Constable.

The Rev Michael Stott, Vicar of Binfield, continues his successful ministry of the village congregation, has joined in community activities further by being elected to the parish council and is tipped as a future 'upwardly mobile' member of the Anglican Church.

Estate agent Peter Hillory, the benefactor who had ceded the Lallyfield playground to the village, made several spectacular development land deals in the area, making him a very wealthy man. He and his new wife Ivy spend a good deal of time in their recently acquired holiday home in the Channel Islands, a good move as far as tax is concerned.

The Drover's Arms public bar's old chestnut debate about who would win the hand of the District Nurse was also brought to a conclusion when the local paper printed a notice of the engagement between Miss Jane Grayling and M. Étienne Laurent.

Further afield, the Conservative Party under Sir Alec Douglas-Home did indeed, as predicted, suffer defeat in the October election with Harold Wilson's Labour Party gaining control with a majority of just four seats. It proved to be virtually unworkable and in a snap election 18 months later Labour was returned with a healthier majority of 96 seats.

And life in Binfield goes on as before.

By the same author: **Country Capers.** An autobiography.

Made in the USA
Charleston, SC
28 October 2014